L. P. Hartley

L. P. Hartley (1895–1972) was a British writer, described by Lord David Cecil as 'One of the most distinguished of modern novelists; and one of the most original'. His best-known work is *The Go-Between*, which was made into a 1970 film. Other written works include: *The Boat, My Fellow Devils, A Perfect Woman* and *Eustace and Hilda*, for which he was awarded the 1947 James Tait Black Memorial Prize.

He was awarded the CBE in 1956.

D0618881

Also by L. P. Hartley

L. P. Hartley

The Betrayal

JOHN MURRAY

First published in Great Britain in 1966 by Hamish Hamilton Ltd

This paperback edition first published in 2013 by
John Murray (Publishers)
An Hachette UK Company

1

© The Trustees of the Estate of Annie Norah Hartley, 1966

The moral right of the Author of the Work has been asserted in
accordance with the Copyright, Designs and Patents Act 1988.

All rights reserved. Apart from any use permitted under UK copyright
law no part of this publication may be reproduced, stored in a retrieval
system, or transmitted, in any form or by any means without the prior
written permission of the publisher, nor be otherwise circulated in any form
of binding or cover other than that in which it is published and without
a similar condition being imposed on the subsequent purchaser.

All characters in this publication are fictitious and any resemblance
to real persons, living or dead, is purely coincidental.

A CIP catalogue record for this title is available from the British Library

ISBN 978-1-84854-864-0
E-book ISBN 978-1-84854-865-7

Typeset in Sabon by Hewer Text UK Ltd, Edinburgh

Printed and bound by Clays Ltd, St Ives plc

John Murray policy is to use papers that are natural, renewable and
recyclable products and made from wood grown in sustainable forests.
The logging and manufacturing processes are expected to conform
to the environmental regulations of the country of origin.

John Murray (Publishers)
338 Euston Road
London NW1 3BH

www.johnmurray.co.uk

To Phyllis
my friend of many years

'Tis not onely the mischief of diseases, and the villany of poysons, that make an end of us; we vainly accuse the fury of Guns, and the new inventions of death; it is in the power of every hand to destroy us, and we are beholding unto every one we meet, he doth not kill us.

Religio Medici

'Oh, Richard,' said Denys, 'someone rang up when you were out, but wouldn't leave a name.'

Richard dropped into a chair. He was tired, and his doctor had told him never to stand when he could sit.

'How tiresome of them,' he said. 'Perhaps it was a burglar, trying to find out if anyone was in the flat.'

'If so, it wasn't the burglar himself,' said Denys. 'It was a woman's voice.'

'She may have been his stooge,' said Richard. 'What sort of voice was it?'

'Oh, quite a cultivated voice – the voice of someone you might know.'

'And she left no message?'

'No, I said you were out, and I didn't know when you would be back. I know you don't want to be bothered with the telephone.'

'All the same,' began Richard, and stopped, because he didn't want to seem to be criticizing his friend and secretary. 'I wonder who she was. Did she say anything else?'

'She asked me how you were.'

'And you said, better?'

'I should have liked to,' Denys said. 'But how could I? I said you were much as usual.'

'Funnily enough, I do feel better,' Richard said. 'I believe I've felt better ever since that evening when—'

'When you made the Great Confession? When you came clean?' said Denys, smiling. He got up and examined the chimney-piece. 'I was just making sure those tablets were there. Yes, here they are.'

'Good,' said Richard. 'How wonderful it would be not to need them. Since that night, I've sometimes felt as though I didn't – but the metaphorical heart hasn't anything to do with the physical heart, has it?'

'I wouldn't know,' said Denys. 'You must ask your doctor.'

At that moment the telephone bell rang. Richard got up.

'I'll take it, Denys.'

'Do you think you ought to?'

'Oh yes, it might be the lady who rang me up before.'

A moment later he put his hand over the mouthpiece.

'It's someone for you, Denys. Would you like to take the call in my room?'

'I don't see why,' said Denys. 'Who is it?'

'She didn't say.'

'Oh, it was a woman? I've always told my friends not to ring me up here, because I know that it disturbs you. I'll go into your room.'

'Nothing to worry about, I hope?' asked Richard when Denys came back.

'No, why do you ask?'

'I thought you looked a bit worried.'

'I worry about you sometimes,' said Denys, 'but not

about myself, or not much. Should we have a drink? It's getting on for drink-time.'

Richard looked at the little ormolu clock on the chimney-piece. It was surmounted by a gilt Cupid, toying with his bow.

'It's nearly twelve o'clock,' he said. 'Perhaps we might. Be barman for us, Denys.'

Denys got up, and with slow but practised gestures went through the necessary rites. Richard watched him. 'Where should I be without Denys?' he thought.

But of course Denys had to go out sometimes, just as Richard had, he couldn't be a watch-dog all the time, he had to have his days off. Richard thought of him as a friend, not as an employee, but an employee he was, in the eyes of the world, and had an employee's privileges, as well as duties. Sometimes Richard asked him what he did in his spare time, sometimes not; it depended on whether he was in the mood to think curiosity a good thing or a bad thing. Lack of interest must be a bad thing, where someone you were fond of was concerned; it was unnatural too. Yet how easily interest sharpened into inquisitiveness, and even into suspicion! On the whole Richard was grateful to people who asked him questions about himself. He hadn't much to hide, except that one thing, the secret he had confided to Denys. But supposing that in the blissful days of his love-affair with Lucy, or in the dreadful days after her death, someone had had an inkling and had questioned him! Charlie Wittold might have; Charlie, but for whose information on sex matters

– but for whose obsession with sex matters – there might have been no serpent in the garden. Richard believed he owed such happiness as he had enjoyed in life to the fact that no one had suspected, still less, accused him, for if they had, he would have given himself away, and he could never have survived the shame of a public exposure. He couldn't now, for that matter, when, as the doctor told him, he had so little time left for feeling ashamed in. How lucky he had been to find at last a confidant!

Whether his disclosure had shocked Denys he didn't know. He had worked himself up so much, first by re-living the events and then by relating them, that he had hardly noticed their effect on Denys. Denys wouldn't have shown what he felt in any case; that baby-face was also a poker-face, and, besides, he wouldn't have wanted to seem too critical of an employer even if Richard had confessed to committing a murder – as in fact he had, for if he hadn't actually killed Lucy, he was to blame for her death. But for him, she might still be alive. The degree of his culpability didn't much matter. Denys *must* have been shocked; horrified, Richard hoped; for if his own intensity of feeling hadn't evoked a like intensity of feeling, his relief would have been proportionately less. The remedy had to be as drastic as the disease, or almost, for it to work. And it *had* worked, or why did he feel better? Not really better, of course; the heart had its diseases that an easier conscience couldn't cure: the doctor's verdict still stood, as Denys had reminded him.

Waiting for Denys to come back, Richard wondered how he, Richard, would have felt had their situations been reversed and he had received a similar confidence from Denys. Would he have shrunk from Denys in horror? Would he have said, 'Your engagement is terminated – leave next week'? Denys had come without a proper reference because he had never done a job of this sort before – and the reference he had was rather negative and non-committal. Supposing it had said, 'Mr. Aspin is sober, honest and trustworthy, but we are obliged to say that he did once commit a murder,' would Richard have engaged him? And if Denys had asked for a reference from him (employers were not under the same obligation, fortunately, to produce credentials) and someone had said, 'Mr. Mardick is honest, sober, and trustworthy, and to the best of our knowledge solvent, *but* he has committed a murder,' would Denys have accepted the post? Richard doubted it.

Denys – Denys Aspin. The Aspin was in a way the key to their relationship which had grown stronger and closer as the years passed. Denys had told him a good deal about his life, of course, and there was no murder in it, or any crime at all; it had been a pillar-to-post existence, cramped, after his schooldays, by lack of funds. At twenty-eight Denys had been as glad of a comfortable home and an assured income as Richard had been to give him one. It had proved an ideal arrangement, but it wouldn't have been so ideal but for the Aspin element. That they were, he and Denys, employer and employee, might have been an obstacle to friendship; but the Aspin aspect somehow equalized their relationship. There might be money on Richard's side, but there was birth and breeding on Denys's – the blood of the ancient Border family which had outlasted the ruins of their

Norman castle ran in his veins. He had the right to use their motto, which they shared with other families: 'Tyme Tryeth Troth,' whereas Richard had no motto to fall back on. Richard was not specially a snob; but he had a romantic feeling that amounted to reverence for such vestiges of the past as had survived the Great Divide of 1939. When Denys fixed on him that long reflective stare he liked to think of it as an Aspin trait – and that the height, and long fingers, and deliberate movements, too, had come down through a long line of Aspin ancestors.

It was half-past ten, too early for Denys to be back from whatever he was doing, but not too early for Richard to start hoping for his arrival. He might go to bed, but he wouldn't go to sleep until he knew that Denys was home; it brought him a sense of security that was more efficacious than a sleeping pill. Denys knew this and rarely prolonged his absences beyond midnight. How happy Denys had made him. Most of his friends had been older than he was – he seemed to have gravitated towards older people; and when they died, taking a part of his life's experience with them, he hadn't had the emotional energy to replace them. How much easier it was to let such emotional outgoings as he had left – a thin enough trickle – centre on Denys, who was paid to accept them uncritically – than venture out into a new world of friendships. And ever since he had told Denys his secret, the bond between them had been strengthened immeasurably. Let other suns decline, so long as this one shone!

At peace with himself, at peace with posterity who, thanks to Denys' memoir, would not have a totally false idea of him – at peace, almost, with God, Richard awaited Denys's return.

The memoir would be a compromise with Truth, but it would be a gesture to Justice which posterity could interpret as it liked. *Toute vérité n'est pas bonne à dire;* some truths were better unspoken; nor, except in the law-court, was it essential to tell the truth, the whole truth, and nothing but the truth. A vague suggestion that, as his father used to say, there was a smell of rum somewhere, would be enough; no need to indicate exactly where it was. And it was just possible that there were others to consider besides posterity and himself. Others who might be hurt or scandalized by too much truth-telling. Not his father and mother, they had lived to a great age, pleased by his success though regretting (at least his mother regretted) that he was not married; but they were dead many years ago. And Lucy's father, their contemporary, must long ago have joined his wife – and Lucy. And the lady who had passed as Mrs. Soames and Lucy's mother – she too must be dead. *Their* attempt to deceive posterity hadn't succeeded; their relationship had been brutally shown up at the Coroner's Court by the governess who blew the gaff. Richard had never heard what happened to them afterwards, hadn't wanted to hear; for they, too, were his victims. But were they, altogether? Were they not also victims of their own unwisdom, their selfishness where Lucy was concerned? Were they not to blame for keeping her to themselves and never letting her go out? Were they not to blame for refusing her request – the request which must have cost her so much to make – to be allowed to see him,

Richard? For if they could have met openly and not clandestinely, as even in those days boys and girls were allowed to meet, those sweet encounters in the Brickfield, with their disastrous consequences, might never have taken place. Instead, a long, innocent, conventional courtship, meetings at St. Botolph's and the Hollies, rambling jaunts together, without the fatal seal of secrecy on them, might have culminated in marriage, as Mr. and Mrs. Soames, so called, realized when it was too late. Too late they had a vision of where Lucy's true happiness might lie, too late, but so compelling that they had offered, so Richard's mother told him, to help to pay his fees at a public school. His father refused; but it was their idea that he should go there, to be made a worthy husband for Lucy. But by then it was too late, just as it was too late to acquaint Lucy with the facts of life, which today every schoolgirl knows and sometimes acts upon, long before she has reached sweet seventeen.

Mr. Soames and his wife's sister were behind the times, in more ways than one.

Was there anyone else to consider, in defence of the doctrine of the economy of truth? Yes, there was. Richard's cousins, in and around Rookland, and their children, for Aunt Florrie's descendants had increased and multiplied. Though he seldom saw them he was their blood-relation. How would they like this scandal exploding in their midst when he was dead and gone?

And lastly, Aunt Carrie, the only survivor of his mother's brothers and sisters. The darling of her family, the Holy Family, as Uncle Austin used to call it, idolized, almost deified by his mother: how could he expose her to such a blow? She might not outlive him, for she must be nearly eighty; but if she did! He had been her favourite once, or so he thought; but many people, outside the family circle as well as inside it, thought they had been her favourites. She was still out in Australia, where she had been granted to the full the life of self-sacrifice she always seemed to crave, for not many years after she and Uncle James arrived there, he had a nervous breakdown from which he never recovered. He went on with his work, he was well enough for that, but a cloud settled on his mind which never lifted, religious melancholia it was, and she, who had never been particularly religious, daily searched the Scriptures for texts that would relieve him. For a long time she and Richard corresponded, she followed his career with interest, she congratulated him on his success. But she had to keep up with everyone; small wonder if, after a time, her pen flagged and some of the urgency and intimacy died out of her letters. She had her life there, too, and friends who prized her: it was inconceivable that she should not have. She dwelt lovingly on their peculiarities and foibles and tried to make them real to Richard; but she must have known that as news (and what other news had she?) they couldn't be of much interest to someone years younger than herself, who would never see them, and to whom they were only names. And Australia was so far away, a letter was almost dead after the six weeks it took to reach him. And even after the air-mail had speeded letters up, hers had begun to come more sparingly, and when they did come were not always quite coherent. Her legend had survived in Richard's imagination, not she herself: but that legend was strong enough to make him dread more than anything else the thought of hurting her.

It was her marriage to Uncle James that had put the idea of marriage with Lucy into his head. If only it had occurred to him earlier, how much might have been saved!

Sometimes he wondered whether Aunt Carrie, through some slip on his part or second-sight on hers, had divined the fact that he was seeing Lucy. He remembered his last conversation with her, and how she warned him not to let his whole affection centre on one person; she was referring, as she told him, to her own case, her absorbing love for the man who died in her arms; but she might have had some premonition of what was happening, or going to happen, to him. He hadn't thought so then; then he had taken her warning as a sign that she was not in love with Uncle James. Whether, later, she fell in love with him Richard doubted; that she loved him was certain, and loved him increasingly as his mental state grew worse. There had been no children; child-bearing was as inconceivable in connection with Aunt Carrie as it would be with a phoenix. How close she had always been to him in one way, and in another, how remote! For months at Rookland they were living under the same roof and yet, but for one or two conversations, she might have been as far away as she now was, in Australia. But the climate of her mind had enfolded him as it had his mother, and it was when he was spiritually most in touch with her that the thought of Lucy became most unbearable.

Thank goodness, Aunt Carrie would never know.

And it was this consideration, more than any other, that was ministering to his peace of mind, when the telephone bell rang.

'Can I speak to Mr. Mardick?'

'Yes, this is Richard Mardick.'

'Oh, Mr. Mardick, I rang you up some time ago, but I was told you were out.'

'I am so sorry. Did you leave your name?'

'Yes, I think I did, I'm almost sure I did. Lucilla Distington. You wouldn't remember it, but I met you at a cocktail party, and you were kind enough to say you would come and have a meal with me sometime.'

'I should love to,' said Richard, but he couldn't remember her from Adam – or from Eve. How mortifying that this sort of thing was always happening to him now.

'I hope it wasn't too late to ring you up,' she apologized in a pleasant, rather low voice, that oddly enough seemed to ring a bell, although her name didn't. 'I thought I might catch you before you went to bed. I'm such an admirer of your work – that is my excuse.'

'I'm so glad,' said Richard automatically. 'But I'm on the retired list now.'

'Oh no, you mustn't say that. Well, I was wondering if luncheon some day next week might be possible.'

'I'm sure it would be,' Richard said. 'I have very few engagements.'

'Should we say Wednesday then, about one, at 105 Onslow Square?'

'That would be perfect.'

'I shall look forward so much to seeing you,' she said. 'Good night.'

Richard went back to his chair in a confused state of mind. He hadn't wanted to accept the invitation, he didn't want to accept any invitation. He was much happier here, snug in his flat, dreaming away his time with Denys. A luncheon-party! Sometimes he still went to them, but only with people he knew, and people who knew about his state of health.

He didn't want to make any more friends or even acquaintances; the process of withdrawal must go on. He was happier when reconciled to his fate than when fighting it, or trying to ignore it. And his physical infirmity still embarrassed him. If he went out he felt he ought to explain: 'You mustn't mind if I pass out before lunch is over.' Most troubles mattered less if you kept them to yourself, and illness was certainly one. A few were better shared, but only by one person.

Still Denys didn't come and presently Richard's mood of pleased acceptance gave way to anxiety. Denys knew that Richard fretted if he stayed out late; he worried lest Denys should have forgotten to take his latch-key, or been run over: a dozen things might have happened to him. And yet how could Richard expect a young man, with plenty of friends, to be in before midnight, as if he was living in a College? It was neurotic to get into this fuss. Like a sensible person, Richard went to bed; but unlike a sensible person he didn't go to sleep; he kept an ear cocked for the click of the door. And when it came, how overwhelming his relief. Trying to scold Denys without seeming to, he said: 'You are a monster! You said the lady who rang up when I was out didn't leave her name.'

'Well, did she?'

'She said she did – Lucilla Distington, it was.'

Denys, who had the irresponsible and optimistic look of someone who has enjoyed his evening out, said airily: 'Yes, I remember now. But I didn't think you would want to be bothered with her. You've often told me you didn't want strangers impinging on your life.'

'That's true, only you might give me the choice where to draw the line.'

'That's just what I was trying to save you from,' said Denys, putting on Richard's dressing-gown and walking to and fro as if it was fancy dress. 'I know how you hate decisions. This Mrs. Distington—'

'She didn't say she was Mrs.'

'I should give her a miss.'

Richard laughed half-heartedly.

'And I hope you did. Madam I cannot, mistress I would not call you. But what did happen?'

'Well, I've got to lunch with her,' said Richard, moving his head restlessly on the pillow. 'If you had warned me, I could have thought up an excuse.'

'Because her name's Lucilla?'

'No, it's a pretty name, but next time—'

'Next time I'll let you stew in your own juice,' said Denys threateningly. He took off the dressing-gown and threw it on a chair. 'There! I wash my hands of you. I won't try to protect you any longer from a designing female, Miss or Mrs.'

Richard laughed happily, and five minutes later was asleep.

2

Miss Lucilla Distington (for unmarried she proved to be) was tall and distinguished-looking, as befitted her name. She had high cheek-bones, black hair with threads of white in it, and what Richard thought of as a Spanish complexion. She wore rather long earrings, two pearls on each, with pear-shaped rubies depending from them; she looked like someone who has always had money, and her flat, with its beautiful French furniture, seemed to bear this out. At first sight she struck Richard as a little formidable, a thing which he rather resented, for he had known women with better claims to self-importance than she appeared to have. But later he decided she was shy; the diffident, unpractised way in which she offered the pre-luncheon drinks was evidence of this. Many women and men did it automatically, as though born to be Hebes or Ganymedes; they went to the drink-tray, and appeared to know instinctively what everybody wanted, or could want, and poured it out. She hesitated, scanning each face inquiringly as if she might be asked for something she hadn't got. There were only three guests to consider, Richard and a married couple whom he knew slightly. They had the exploratory conversation of people who don't know each other well and use a topic to find out about each other. It was the sort of conversation Richard enjoyed, for he liked to approach newcomers through the facts that interested them, rather than through the chit-chat of conventional social usage, which was often more disguising than revealing.

Miss Distington seemed to be drawn to him, by some sort of interest for which he couldn't account: an elective affinity, perhaps, for though he was known among his own set, he was anything but headline news, and it flattered and touched him that she, a stranger, many years his junior (she couldn't have been much more than forty-five) should go out of her way to be pleasant to an elderly man, already under sentence of death – she didn't know that, only a few of his friends did, but in certain moods he thought that everyone must know.

A few of his friends! They were very few and becoming fewer, their ranks thinned by death. Since he had taken on Denys as his secretary, he hadn't seemed to need them. Was it laziness, and he didn't want to make the effort that a free and equal friendship calls for? Denys was his employee, paid to listen to him, to his soliloquies and anecdotes (hadn't he recently listened to a very long one?), paid not to argue and have opinions of his own – though in fact Denys had plenty. And they, his few remaining friends, didn't seem to have much need of him, either. At any rate they came less and less to his flat. Perhaps they were losing interest in someone who wasn't long for this world, someone 'on whom death had set his broad arrow' (how he loved Sir Thomas Browne!) And yet it wasn't like them – it wasn't even human, still less humane – to avoid a man just because he was dying. One of them had said to him jokingly: 'Your secretary – Aspin, Denys, whatever you call him – isn't very welcoming on the telephone!' Could it be that Denys was jealous, and didn't like him having his friends around? Richard rather wished that it were so, but he didn't think it was; his friends were always nice to Denys. It might be that Denys, in common with some other people, had an unfortunate telephone manner, abrupt and disconcerting. Richard had always heard him cooing as gently as any sucking-dove, but perhaps when he was by himself he felt the need for self-assertion. He must 'speak to' Denys about it, sometime . . . sometime.

Denys had certainly been remiss, whether as a secretary or a friend, in forgetting or pretending to forget Lucilla Distington's name. This mustn't happen again. It was a name he liked, as he liked its owner. How nice she had been to him, treating him with just that shade of deference that made him feel he was still someone, whereas he had been feeling anyone – or no one. During luncheon she had turned to him constantly, and asked him questions meant to draw him out – to make him feel he was on his own ground and in some way King of it. Vanity, vanity of course: but he didn't think she was playing on his vanity; she just wanted him to feel as well and as happy as circumstances allowed him to be; she couldn't know, of course, how adverse those circumstances were.

He and the other two guests shared a taxi on the way home, and inevitably they talked about her. The others didn't know much, but they knew more than he did. She had come to London several years ago, having hitherto lived in the country with her parents. When they died, leaving her well off, she came to London, vaguely in search of the wider horizons she had missed in her country retreat – missed to the point of not getting married, heiress though she was. She was too much her mother's daughter, that was the explanation; her mother was a good deal younger than her father, and had outlived him by ten years. Lucilla had kept her power of affection and her love of life, as women do so much more readily than men; but in London she did not at first find an outlet for them, perhaps it was too late in the day to discover a satisfying pattern of London life – a quest in any case easier for a man than for a woman. And perhaps as a result of living so much with her parents she couldn't easily adjust herself to the rapid give and take of party talk; she got left behind, and when she did speak it was as though she was trying to catch up and put her word in.

So her friends said, but Richard hadn't noticed it; to him she talked eagerly and freely, as if to someone she had known for a long time, and he, too, seemed to know the bent of her mind and the kind of thing she would be likely to say.

He wanted to ask her back but he was chary of beginning a new friendship which might involve new social commitments; if she was already too old, too square for the social round, he was much more so. Besides, he didn't quite know how Denys would take it. Denys was eminently presentable; how could an Aspin not be? But he was a little on the defensive with strangers, and would sometimes conversationally trip them up or lay small verbal traps for them. In private, alone with Denys, Richard enjoyed these verbal skirmishes, but not in company, where they had the wrong effect. He didn't want to see Denys through critical or hostile eyes; he depended on him too much to run such risks. Denys was essential to his welfare: Lucilla Distington was not. And yet!—

He decided to invite her to luncheon, and with her a woman friend of old standing who found Denys's sometimes unruly tongue amusing.

'Oh, God,' said Denys, when Richard broached his project, 'you don't really mean to have Lucilla here?'

It irritated Richard that he should use her Christian name.

'Well, yes, I think I must,' he said, 'and you know you like Diana Alkaly.'

'She's not a bad old thing,' said Denys, 'compared with some of them. But couldn't you count me out? Please do, Richard; I could so easily have a date that day.'

'You've had so many dates just lately,' said Richard, with all the severity he could command, 'your friends must need a rest. Besides, I rely on you to do the cooking.'

'Oh, Richard, wouldn't Mrs. Cuddesdon oblige?' Mrs. Cuddesdon was the daily help.

'But you cook much better than she does, and besides, we want your company.'

'How can you have my company if I'm cooking?'

'You talk as if you would be actually in the oven.'

'Well, the kitchen is just like one. . . . Anyhow you shouldn't be having visitors; Dr. Herbright said you ought to keep quiet.'

'He said a little social life did no harm so long as I don't get excited.'

'Lucilla will excite you,' Denys said. 'That's why you invited her.'

Richard asked himself if this was true, and decided that it wasn't. But it was gratifying that Denys showed slight signs of jealousy.

'I find her company most soothing,' he replied. 'It's just what the doctor ordered.'

'More soothing than mine?'

'My dear Denys, I shouldn't dream of comparing you.'

'She's well off, isn't she?'

'Yes, I believe so.'

'What would she think,' asked Denys, 'if she knew what a dark horse you were?'

Richard smiled, but the smile soon faded.

'I don't know — I suppose she would be horrified, brought up the way she was. She's much more old-fashioned, I should guess, than most women of her generation. In my youth, Denys, our sort of people didn't lead irregular lives. The upper crust, to which your family belonged, may have done — I don't know.'

'Thank you,' Denys said.

'I'm not criticizing them,' said Richard. 'I dare say that in some ways they were more right than we were. We didn't give the flesh its due. Or perhaps we did — I've never known what my relations really thought — the Holy Family, you know. I know how they behaved, but their thoughts may have been less rigid than their practice. Perhaps it's just that today the lid has been taken off a saucepan that was always simmering.'

'You shouldn't use these kitchen metaphors,' said Denys. 'If you knew more about cooking you'd know that most saucepans don't have lids. But I see that your subconscious is bent on my cooking this meal. You're a tyrant really – you will have your own way. I think I ought to warn Lucilla.'

When she came into the flat, it was with the diffident, slightly abashed air that Richard found so difficult to account for. He could only meet it by apology – apology for the flat, for the meal they were going to have, for bringing her out on false pretences. It seemed necessary to reinstate her in her own opinion. He wasn't sure that his other guest would co-operate – for women are not always anxious to put other women at their ease, and there was no obvious reason to be tender to Miss Distington. But Mrs. Alkaly, perhaps because she was so sure of her own ground in the world, and of Richard's regard, couldn't have behaved better. She was especially charming to Denys, complimenting him on his cooking, and his ability to be in two places at once.

'What a wonder-worker you are!'

'I am glad that someone gives me credit for it,' Denys said.

'I should like to add my tribute,' said Lucilla shyly. 'I wish we could have the whole meal over again.'

'You mustn't say that to Richard,' Denys said. 'You've no idea how greedy he is.'

'Are you greedy, Richard?' asked Mrs. Alkaly. 'I haven't noticed it, but you have every reason to be, here.'

'My appetite depends on the company I'm in,' said Richard, feeling that Denys had been praised enough. 'When Denys and I are alone together—'

'When we are alone together,' interrupted Denys, 'he tells the most interminable stories and sometimes forgets to eat.'

'*Do* you, Richard?' asked Mrs. Alkaly, incredulous. 'I've known him a long time, Miss Distington, but I've never known him tell a story that lasted more than a minute.'

'Oh, but he can be very long-winded,' Denys said, 'when he gets on to the subject of his murky past.'

'His murky past?' repeated Mrs. Alkaly, brightening at the words. 'That must have been a very long time ago – forgive me, Richard, I wasn't thinking in terms of age, but only of your short and blameless life.'

'It has reached the allotted span, you know,' said Richard, as lightly as he could.

Mrs. Alkaly, who did know, suppressed a sigh.

'We must believe you, I suppose,' she said, 'in spite of all appearance to the contrary.' She felt that none of this should have been said, and it was owing to her clumsiness that it had been. 'I think you like to boast of your age,' she went on, 'because you look so young.' Her eye caught Miss Distington's across the oval table. 'You don't believe him, do you? He's trying to make fun of us. But, Richard, we long to hear about your murky past.' She felt she was on safer ground now. 'Won't you tell us some of its darkest incidents? We shan't believe you, of course. It would be just another way of showing off.'

Richard tried to hide his confusion. 'I do sometimes ramble on, I'm afraid,' he said, 'and Denys gets the benefit of it. Now be a good fellow, Denys, and bring us our coffee.'

Sometimes he had to give Denys orders.

But when the guests had gone his mood changed and he felt he had been hard on Denys, not so much with his tongue as in his thoughts. For Denys's position was no easy one, by turns a companion and an employee, and all the time an Aspin of Aspin Castle, whose forebears wouldn't have deigned to know his forebears, if he had any to speak of in medieval times. It wasn't surprising if Denys sometimes wanted to assert himself and throw his weight about, little of it as there was attached to his tall frame. As an Aspin Denys was one thing, as a secretary he was another, as a cook he was a third – a Trinity in Unity, a strange lop-sided figure in which the parts, socially, were anything but equal. How could he be expected to achieve a consistent way of feeling, or behaving, which would synthesize all three?

It sometimes, but not always, happens, that one feels fonder of a friend for having done him an injustice, and a new wave of affection came over Richard for Denys, who had done so much for him and who meant far more to him than any Distington or Alkaly, or anyone else in the diminishing circle of his friends – a circle that he had already half made up his mind to drift away from when Lucilla Distington turned up to make him feel that he was still a person – which he wasn't, for a person is someone with a future, however precarious, whereas he had none, the doctors said so.

He waited until Denys had finished washing up (the sounds of which always made Richard feel guilty) and then said:

'I hope you enjoyed your lunch as much as we did.'

'Oh yes,' said Denys, 'when I had time to think about it. I wasn't sure I liked your new friend though.'

'Lucilla Distington?'

'Well, yes. The other is an old friend, isn't she?'

'Oh yes, a very old friend.'

'You must be careful with Lucilla, Richard. I think she has designs on you.'

'Oh, Denys, me, with one foot in the grave?'

'She doesn't know that, does she?'

Richard thought for a second or two.

'Sometimes I think that everyone must know. No, I expect she doesn't – but even so, do I look like a prospective bridegroom?'

'I can say without flattery that you look younger than your years – all this resting has rejuvenated you.'

'Thank you,' said Richard, turning round to steal a glance at his reflection in the looking-glass which mirrored the tree-tops in the square outside. Seen like that in shadow with the green light behind him, he didn't look so old. But Denys's idea was preposterous and besides it blurred the image of a possible friendship in which marriage would have been a discordant element.

'Oh no,' he said. 'You're quite mistaken, Denys. If she had wanted to get married she would have got married long ago – what was there to stop her? She had money and looks too, though I daresay she's better-looking now than she used to be. No, perhaps she felt an affinity and followed it up, just as I did, when I met you.'

'That's what I'm afraid of,' said Denys, 'these affinities. You ought to have just one affinity – me.'

'Don't worry, that's all I have,' said Richard. 'And talking of affinities, wasn't it amusing that she had known some Aspins in Devonshire?'

'Oh, had she?' said Denys. 'I wasn't paying much attention at that moment. I was busy changing the plates. Some Aspins in Devonshire, did you say? I believe there are Aspins in Devonshire, though of course it's a long way from Northumberland. What sort of people were they – crooks?'

'Oh no,' said Richard. 'They were country neighbours. She was going to tell them that she'd met you.'

'I hope she won't,' said Denys. 'There's nothing people like less than being confronted by some distant relative they've never heard of. I had a hunch she might be that sort of person – a retriever bringing back all sorts of things that nobody wants. You wait till she presents you with some distant branch of your family tree. I'm sure she is a trouble-maker, Richard. Take my advice, and cross her off your visiting-list. If you ask her again, I shall refuse to cook for her. It's brains or brawn for lunch, I shall say; you can take your choice.'

'I hoped you'd like her,' Richard said. 'You'd like her food, I'm sure. It's up to your own standard. No brains or brawn or anything like that.'

'There's nothing wrong with my brains,' said Denys, 'cooked or uncooked. If it's brawn you want, you must look elsewhere.'

He stretched himself languidly, occupying the room and Richard's consciousness with his physical presence. I'd better not ask her again, thought Richard; but if she asks me I'll go to her. Entertaining is so much easier for women.

Denys knew that Mrs. Cuddesdon didn't like him. He said she was jealous of Richard's affection for him. 'She's more than half in love with you,' he said. Since Lucy's death Richard had preferred to believe, and come to believe, that no one could possibly be in love with him (he hoped and thought that Denys loved him, but that was another matter), and how could anyone love a septuagenarian, with at least one foot in the grave? Yet he had noticed that when Mrs. Cuddesdon brought him his early morning tea her hand would sometimes brush lightly against his toes (not turned up, thank goodness), and when she helped him into his bed-jacket, she did so with marked solicitude. If she really had a tender feeling for him, it was very silly of her, and he didn't like her any the better for it: she was nearly as old as he was, old enough to know better.

3

When Denys asked for a rise, Richard was taken aback.

'Of course, my dear fellow,' he said. 'I ought to have thought of it before.'

'Don't think me ungrateful,' Denys said, 'but sometimes one wants some ready money. This evening for instance—'

'You're short?'

Denys nodded, and Richard, fumbling with his pocket-book, pulled out a five-pound note.

'You couldn't make it ten?'

Richard rummaged again.

'Well, I can make it nine.'

'Bless you,' said Denys. 'When I go out I have to drink your health – I am sure you would wish me to. And my prayers for you, whenever I go to church, they cost me something.'

'I'm sure they do,' said Richard.

'And while I'm writing the memoir I shall need extra sustenance of various kinds.'

'Why, are you writing it now?' asked Richard.

'I thought I'd begin it now, while the . . . the facts are still fresh in my mind. Besides, I shall probably have to consult you about various things – points of style, and so on.'

'That's quite a good idea,' said Richard.

'And I shouldn't want to put in anything you would rather I left out.'

'Well no,' Richard said. 'But you've got the general idea, haven't you? An uneventful life, with a hypochondriac background of illness and semi-illness and imaginary illness – such as a good many people had in those days, handicapping but not crippling. And then something else – an unfortunate experience in youth. Something that cast a shadow, a running shadow.'

'Does the shadow still run?' Denys asked.

'Yes, but I've left it behind.'

'You don't think it could ever catch up with you again?'

'Oh no, not now,' said Richard, decidedly. 'Once you have let the cat out of the bag, it doesn't go back.'

'Somebody might put it back,' said Denys.

'I doubt if they could, besides the cat wouldn't want to go back.'

'What about the seven devils who came back after one had been cast out?'

Richard looked worried, then his face cleared.

'I think the cases are different,' he said. 'The seven devils found the place swept and garnished, but as far as we know, unoccupied. Now there wouldn't be room because it's occupied.'

'By whom?' asked Denys.

'By you, of course.'

'Not by Miss Distington?'

Richard laughed.

'How you keep harping on her. I might almost think

you were jealous. Naturally, I should be flattered if you were.'

'Well, aren't you going to dine with her tonight?'

'Yes, I am, she's *simpatica*, I like her, and the time passes agreeably. But—'

'But what?'

'Need you ask, Denys? And anyhow, you often go out in the evening. You've been out a lot just lately.'

'I have to keep my end up,' Denys said. 'I have to stand on my own feet. I'm sure you would rather I wasn't always on yours.'

'I might say the same to you.'

'But it wouldn't be true of me. I am always delighted to see you prostrate.'

'Yes, I'm afraid you are a bully,' said Richard with a sigh.

'Wait till I really bully you,' said Denys, with a faint tone of menace.

'Do I know you well enough,' said Miss Distington, 'to ask you to call me by my Christian name?'

'Yes, Lucilla, you do,' said Richard, and wondered if his tone wasn't too paternal. After all, he was old enough to be her father. When other men adopted a fatherly air with younger women he didn't like it. But it was hard to make the manner fit the relationship, and first one had to make sure what the relationship was. 'And please call me by mine,' he said, more distantly.

'Indeed I will, it's a name I like,' she said. 'Does no one ever call you Dick?'

'Well, a few of my friends do, but in inverted commas,

you know. My mother never wanted me to be called Dick. Perhaps she thought I might get "dirty" tacked on to it.'

'Oh no. I don't imagine she had ever heard of such a person,' said Lucilla, slightly shocked. 'Were you named after anyone?'

'No, I don't think so. Were you, Lucilla?'

'I believe I was, after someone who was dead.'

'But you don't know who?'

'No. She was a great friend of my parents, but they never told me who she was. In those days people were much more reticent than they are now – now they tell you everything, don't you find?'

'Do you think that is a good thing or a bad thing?' Richard asked.

'I don't know. I'm all for a private life, and I think that feelings suffer if they are aired too much – they evaporate somehow, or get rubbed away, like coins that have been too much used. But of course it does cramp conversation if you can't gossip, and if there are tracts of forbidden territory you must keep clear of. One of my difficulties, not knowing many people, is lest I should say something I ought not to, through ignorance, you know, about their ex-wives or husbands.'

Richard liked her seriousness.

'I don't think you're in danger of doing that,' he said, with a good deal of warmth.

'Oh, I don't know. I never quite know how far to go, or in what direction. Social life is a habit, isn't it? which I haven't properly acquired. At home we didn't see many people. Did you, in your early days?'

'I was a good deal bounded by relations,' Richard said. 'The outside world wasn't quite real to me – it was like something one reads of in a novel. I thought of it as alluring and disreputable. For a good many years my life was very local and provincial – at Medehamstead and in the Fen country around.'

'We always lived in Devon,' said Lucilla, 'ever since I can remember. Where my parents lived before that I don't know. It's odd, isn't it, that they didn't tell me. My father had money of his own – he could afford to live where he liked. His father was a brewer, and he still had some connexion with the family business, but he had no occupation. I think he would have been happier if he had, and found it easier to make friends. Your occupation must have brought you a great many friends.'

'It did,' said Richard, 'but most of them are dead. For some reason I never found it easy to make friends with people younger than myself.'

He thought he saw a shadow cross Lucilla's face.

'But you like your secretary, don't you?' she asked. 'He seemed a very nice man. We had some friends in Devon called Aspin – as I told you. It was an old family which used to own a castle in Northumberland. Colonel Aspin was very keen on genealogy – he was always working on his family tree and finding new branches or cutting off old ones. He would be thrilled to know I have met someone with the same name. Your Mr. Aspin might be a relation. Do you mind if I tell Colonel Aspin? It would give the old boy so much pleasure.'

'Of course you can,' said Richard. 'Denys would be

interested, too. He doesn't talk much about the Aspins, but I know he's proud of being one. So you still keep up with your friends in Devon?'

'Oh yes, I write to them,' Lucilla said. 'But when my mother died I felt I wanted to change my way of life completely – the place, the people, everything. I was born in 1908 – that tells you how old I am – I shall be forty-nine next Thursday – rather old to be starting afresh.'

'Oh no,' said Richard. 'Not at all too old – just twenty years younger than I am. Couldn't we celebrate it – your birthday, I mean? Or perhaps you are giving a party?'

'I was thinking of having a few friends,' Lucilla said, 'but without telling them why, you know, or at any rate till afterwards, or they might think they ought to give me presents. I should be only too pleased if you would join us. Could you?'

Richard said he would be delighted.

'But on condition that you don't give me a present,' said Lucilla, and Richard unwillingly agreed.

Why, he wondered as he walked home – for Lucilla's flat in Onslow Square was so near his that there was no need to take a taxi. Why did he feel disappointed because she hadn't wanted him to give her a present?

The only person now that he felt like giving presents to was Denys. He had given Denys a great many presents – clothes, books (though Denys wasn't a great reader), a wrist-watch, a cigarette-case, trinkets of one sort and another – and, of course, money: Denys seemed to get through a good deal of money which was, of course, quite understandable at his age: he needed all sorts of indoor recreations and indoor recreations were expensive. If he hadn't given him a car it was only because Denys had the use of his. He liked to think of Denys enjoying himself and if he couldn't enjoy himself without money – well, that was how young people were in these days.

What a boon the Brickworks had been. He owed his material prosperity to it, as much as he owed his spiritual poverty to the Brickfield. The clay of the Brickfield had been an age-old synonym for mortality; the clay our bodies are made of, and to which they must return. But the clay of the Brickworks was life-enhancing. Without it he couldn't have given anyone presents – Denys or . . . or . . . Lucilla. She wouldn't accept a birthday present, but she might accept another, later on.

Why did he want to give her one, when she had everything she needed? In his time he had given plenty of presents, but the cases had been few in which he felt he was giving something of himself. Why did he have this feeling about her, a friend of his old age, and of such short standing? Presents, of course, meant many different things, both to the giver and the receiver. There was the parting present, that marked the end of a relationship. Such a present might be a reward for faithful service, a golden handshake accompanied by smiles to match: donor and donee looked each other in the eye, remembering past times which had brought satisfaction, or pleasure or profit to them both. The camera has flashed and there they stand, two middle-aged or elderly men, perhaps, bending towards each other with the object – a clock or whatever it might be – mid-way between them, seeming to belong so equally to both that were it not for the caption one could hardly tell who was giving and who receiving. Often it is a clock, for a clock is not a dead thing, it recollects the past, it has been ticking through the past, it is ticking now and looks forward to times ahead. A clock lives in the present but it lives in the past and in the future too. It is the ideal present, for it has the freedom of Time's three dimensions. Present . . . present . . . did the two words come from the same root?

Should he give Lucilla a clock?

In her case it would be a forward-looking present, suggesting that they had a future together. But they hadn't, of course; and wasn't it a form of deception to intimate that they had? No matter if it was; he couldn't flatter himself that she would mind when the clock became a memento instead of a time-keeper, ticking away their living hours.

It needn't involve either of them in anything. It didn't mean that she would feel obliged to give him a present in return, or that he would have to give her further presents. Nor did it mean that Denys would have one present the less. Dear Denys, he must have come to look on presents as his due. Denys never asked for them, but Richard continued to pour them out, when he could think of anything that Denys wanted, as if— There were so many types of present, signifying as many attitudes on the part of the giver, and all happy-making, all a release of the ego from the thraldom of itself. Yet there were presents one didn't always want to give: wedding

34

presents, Christmas presents, birthday presents: they were dictated by compulsion. Compulsion from within, not from without. 'I *ought* to give so-and-so a present', not 'I *must* give him or her a present', for no one, not even the most barefaced or most brazen, had ever *insisted* on being given a present. People had a lot of cheek, but in all ranks of society the convention against *asking* for a present was very strong, almost unbreakable. Who had ever known a porter, or a waiter, *ask* for a tip? They might look black if they didn't get one, but they never asked for one, or hardly ever. It had been assumed, throughout the ages, that present-giving was a voluntary act, an act of grace, an inalienable privilege. Richard had known presents refused – in effect Lucilla had just refused his – he had known tips refused: but demanded, no. Governments came nearest to it. In times past kings asked for a loan, a forced loan, nowadays the State took anything it could get but didn't pretend its exactions were a present. Whoever heard of a State supported by voluntary contributions? In the old days hospitals were, and generous people still subscribed to them. But not to the State; the State had restricted and debased the currency of giving, the activity which shows the individual at his best. Had anyone ever made a donation to the income tax? Yes, in a way they had: the Chancellor of the Exchequer sometimes acknowledged this or that sum – generally a small one— for Conscience Money. But such sums weren't really voluntary: they were sops to conscience: conscience which, with its myriad voices, was always blackmailing one.

Blackmail, what an unpleasant word. Richard had begun to thread the network of small streets, lively and charming by day, a little furtive and sinister by night, which separated Brompton Road from the Square, or oblong, of tree-lined houses in which he lived. In this dark night, pitch-black but for the scanty street-lamps, the thought of blackmail was a visitor that came more readily than it went. For here, at last, was the compulsory present: the present that wasn't the natural offspring of a generous heart, fertilized by sweet influences from without, but a monstrous never-ending brood, engendered on the victim by some act or acts of imprudence connected, it might be, with love.

Richard quickened his steps but he couldn't shake the thought off; it seemed to envelop and possess him, and subdue his imagination to its gloomy hue almost as obsessively as if it had been a dream, and it was only when he turned the corner into his square that the familiarity of his surroundings asserted itself and gave him a feeling of security. *This* was real – so was the hall, so was the lift, which rumbling and creaking bore him upwards; and so was, or would be, the company of Denys, which seemed with every moment more desirable.

But Denys wasn't there. He had said he wasn't going out, but he must have changed his mind. Of course he was at liberty to do so, Richard wasn't his gaoler, and he liked to think, or liked to like to think, that Denys had a life of his own outside the comfortable but restricted precincts of Relton Place. How could Richard hope to absorb the energies, whatsoever they might be, of a young man of twenty-eight? It wasn't reasonable, it wasn't even desirable. Richard, approaching seventy, with nothing to look forward to, might centre his affections upon Denys; but Denys needed friends of his own age, and all the more because he was a single man and should have some variety in his life.

He will come in soon, Richard told himself, while he lay awake listening for the click of the outer door, such a stupid occupation when he might just as well have gone to sleep – he will come in soon. Mingling with his automatic anxiety was a slight feeling of resentment that an evening which had passed so pleasantly should finish so discouragingly. But Denys didn't come and the next thing Richard heard was the click of the latch which announced the arrival of the daily woman. Or was it Denys? He wouldn't know till later.

4

Denys appeared at breakfast showing, Richard thought, signs of wear. His complexion was so delicate and transparent that the least change in his health affected it; the bluish whites of his blue eyes were normally so clear that a vein of red in them was visible from the other side of the room. It's nothing to do with me, Richard reminded himself, how Denys spends his time off; all the same he had to make an effort to refrain from some comment on Deny's dilapidated appearance.

'Did you have a good evening?' he asked, after they had faced each other for a minute or two over the eggs and bacon.

'Not too bad,' said Denys. 'I got in a bit late, though. You know how it is, they wouldn't let me go away. But I was worrying all the time about how *you* were faring, with Miss . . . Miss . . .'

'Distington.'

'Oh yes,' said Denys lightly. 'With Miss Distington. How did that go?'

'All right,' said Richard, 'it was a pleasant evening. She has an excellent cook – don't look at me like that, Denys, she doesn't cook any better than you do, or as well.'

'I'm not a professional cook,' said Denys, 'I only do it

to oblige, so I don't compete. But tell me more about Miss Distington. Isn't she rather a dark horse, or mare, or whatever is the right expression for a dubious female?'

Richard felt and looked offended on Lucilla's behalf.

'Her hair is dark,' he said, 'and she has the sort of colouring that goes with it. The odd thing is, though, Denys, that I have a feeling I've seen her before.'

'You have seen her before,' Denys rejoined, 'a good many times, just lately.'

Richard was aware of this, but it came with added force from someone else's lips.

'I know,' he said, 'but I didn't mean that. Perhaps "seen" isn't the right word. I feel I've *heard* her before – her voice, you know.'

'Voices do run in families,' Denys said. 'I expect I've got an Aspin voice.'

'With a slight hiss in it,' said Richard, 'to emphasize the asp?' He was rather pleased with this, but Denys didn't smile, and Richard realized he had never before tried to make a joke at Denys's expense. Was it in revenge for Denys's crack at Lucilla?

'I can't remember what the family voice was like,' said Denys. 'It's so long since I heard it. I expect it had a Norman twang. I know I roll my r's, but I don't hiss, as you suggested.'

'That was only my fun,' said Richard, penitent.

Denys gave Richard one of his long brooding stares, which some people found disconcerting. Richard was so used to them he hardly noticed them. They weren't meant to be rude; they were a sign of mental withdrawal, of self-absorption so complete that sometimes Denys's mouth fell slightly open. Coming out of his brief trance he said:

'I'm not sure how much I like your fun . . . But I was thinking of Lucilla's voice. I didn't notice it particularly. Does she speak with a West Country accent – a burr? She's like a burr – the way she clings to you.'

'I suppose she might say that about me – two burrs together.'

'It looks rather like it. Distington is a place in Cumberland – I know, because it isn't far from my ancestral home. Has Lucilla a north-country accent?'

'I expect you would have noticed if she had,' said Richard.

'I really didn't notice her particularly. Perhaps she had a Fenland accent?'

Richard laughed, then looked more serious.

'That's a sort of bastard cockney, it goes right through the East Midlands to South Lincolnshire. No, what seemed to ring a bell wasn't an accent, it was an intonation, a tone, that might have been an echo from my youth, from Rookland, or anywhere. I might not have noticed it, only I found myself saying the kind of things I used to say once but haven't said for ages.'

'What sort of things?'

'Oh, I don't know – the half-automatic responses that one makes to people one knows well – that I make to you, Denys, when I speak without thinking. Talking to strangers, one has to adjust oneself to their way of talking and thinking. With her, I don't.'

Denys's long hand travelled slowly towards his glass, for drink-time had come.

'How lucky for her.'

'Well, perhaps it is. I'm no good at prepared speeches. Are you in tonight, Denys?'

'As a matter of fact, I have a date,' said Denys. 'I don't know why I seem to be so popular just now. One thing leads to another – or one person leads to another. You always wanted me to have friends, didn't you? You have so many friends yourself.'

'I used to have,' said Richard.

'You have a new one now. I'll leave you some soup and the cold chicken – will that be all right?'

'Of course,' said Richard.

'And I promise I won't be in late.'

But Denys hadn't come in when Richard finally dropped off, and his sleep was far from dreamless. He was back in Rookland, and the scene was a familiar one – familiar to his dreams, that is, because it was the graveyard of the Abbey. In life he had never revisited it, but in dreams he often had, to find out which of the two graves was Lucy's, and to lay a wreath on it. Sometimes he carried the wreath in his hand, but sometimes he forgot to take it and had to turn back, for without it his quest would only end in the torments of frustration. But whether he remembered to take the wreath or not, the object of his search still eluded him, for though the two headstones he expected to see were there, he couldn't tell which was Lucy's because it was too dark to read the inscriptions. It was always dark when he went, darker than on an ordinary night, so that he often stumbled over grave-stones before he reached his goal. It was dark on this night too, but there was a difference, for someone had got there before him, a shadowy figure that made the darkness solid: she might have been a nun but she was too tall for a nun, nuns were nearly always short. As he reached her she turned and he saw it was Lucilla.

'This is her grave, this one,' she said, pointing to it, 'lay your wreath there.' 'But how did you know it was her grave?' he asked. Instead of answering she said: 'But don't you recognize my voice?' And then he knew it was Lucy's voice – her voice from the grave, and an inexpressible feeling of sweetness and release came over him as he bent down to lay the wreath under the headstone. 'But you must take my hand,' she said, 'otherwise you might slip.' He smiled at this unnecessary precaution, but all the same he took her hand. It was ice-cold, and he thought, 'I should have managed better without her help,' and just at that moment he felt himself slipping, and he clutched her hand. But it wasn't strong enough to hold him. 'I mustn't drag her with me,' he thought, and let go. All the ecstasy of the moments before ebbed away, in the terror of sinking – not into earth but into water – water that pulled him down and quenched his being.

He awoke with a start and was out of bed before he knew it. The dreaded feeling of powerlessness came over him, yet he was still able to walk, walk as far as Denys's room, just round the corner. The light sprang on, but Denys's bed was empty: the clock beside it pointed to three o'clock. 'Oh, Denys!' – still boys will be boys. Forgetting to turn off the light he went back to his room and took the cardiac stimulant and a sleeping tablet too. Instead of lying down he sat on the edge of the bed; it wasn't what the doctor ordered but on his back he always felt more helpless. Gradually his being began to re-establish itself; he felt familiar with himself once more, and knew the attack was passing. Soon he was strong enough to lie down between the sheets, and sleep enfolded him.

The daily help brought him his tea. 'Mr. Aspin is asleep,' she said, 'so I didn't wake him.' 'Quite right,' said Richard. 'Let him have his sleep out. He's young and needs sleep.'

He breakfasted alone, and as soon as he had finished rang up Lucilla. The maid told him she was away; she had gone to Medehamstead, for the day, but would be back at dinner-time.

Medehamstead was the nearest main-line station to Rookland. Considered in connexion with his dream, it seemed an odd coincidence. But odder than the coincidence was the way the feeling of his dream went on vibrating in his consciousness; it didn't melt away at waking, as is the habit of dreams, but lingered, making him feel strange to himself. Towards the middle of the morning Denys came in, looking slightly the worse for wear but none the less elegant and distinguished. Richard wanted to talk to him about his dream and how it tied up with Lucilla. But something restrained him. Denys had not taken kindly to her and to discuss her with him would go against the grain, especially as Denys's present mood was less communicative than usual, almost morose in fact.

So he bottled up his feelings until such time as he should see Lucilla again.

He hadn't long to wait before Lucilla asked him to dinner. He accepted, as always with a slight sense of shame, for the meals she gave him were better, as well as more frequent, than those he gave to her. He didn't really mind feeling inferior, whatever the cause: it wasn't masochism, he told himself, it was humility, one of the greatest of the Christian virtues. He had, as we all have, a special, recognizable mood for approaching every friend. Lucilla conjured it up for him as surely as Denys did. But tonight something new entered into it that could only be described as the Rookland feeling. For years it had been eliminated from his consciousness, except in dreams; but it was with him, very strongly, as the flat-door opened into what might reasonably be called a hall, lined with the severe and dignified furniture that used to belong to halls. Where had he seen it before? – but wasn't the recognition, if such it was, something suggested to him by his dream?

Lucilla, on the other hand, hadn't changed at all; she seemed quite unaware of having met him, the night before, over a watery grave, and she clearly expected from him such responses as he had always given her. But he was restless and fidgety and couldn't concentrate: and at last he said:

'Did you have fun in Medehamstead?'

She seemed surprised, even startled. 'It wasn't exactly fun. How did you know I was there?'

'Your maid told me,' Richard said. 'I only ask,' he excused himself, 'because Medehamstead was my home for many years, and I wondered what took you there.'

At that she showed signs of agitation. Her earrings swung. She stretched her hand out for the toast, she re-assembled herself, as it were, before she answered.

'I go there sometimes, you know, on – on business. My parents had an interest, not in Medehamstead itself, but in a place near by. So sometimes I go, just to . . . just to . . . keep up the connexion, and because I feel they would have liked me to.'

'The district has so many memories for me,' said Richard. 'That was why I asked you.'

'I never lived there,' Lucilla said. 'My parents did, but I don't think they were very happy. They never talked about it, unless – unless they had to. It wasn't exactly a forbidden topic, but I suppose that many people have passages in their lives that they would rather forget.'

'Yes, indeed,' said Richard.

After this it was difficult to switch to another topic, but they managed to find one, and it was invested with a new intimacy, as though, unspoken, it had brought them closer together.

But how could you be close to someone, when you didn't know who they really were? Lucilla Distington! The name didn't ring a bell, and why should it? Medehamstead was a large place, three times the size it had been in his youth, and changed out of all recognition. In any case she wasn't a resident, only an occasional visitor. He, too, went there sometimes, as Lucilla had, on business; business with the Brickworks, on which his livelihood still depended. He didn't suppose Lucilla was a brickmaker; there were other industries in and around Medehamstead besides brick-making. Neither he nor she had mentioned Rookland, solitary in the Fens; why should he associate her with it? The intonation of a voice remembered from youth, an unexpected appearance in a dream which was one of the routine activities of the sub-conscious mind. What were they to go on?

Richard believed gratitude to be one of the supreme virtues; if he did not feel it spontaneously for a benefit conferred by some agency, divine or human, he practised it self-consciously for at least three minutes: assume a virtue though you have it not. Not to be grateful for a kindness seemed to him the absolute nadir of human feeling; anything, even murder, was more forgivable than ingratitude. He had been spontaneously grateful for the gift of Denys's friendship; it had seemed like the last bene-fit from Fate (and he had had many) that he was likely to receive. Thanks be for Denys; and if Denys didn't always come up to scratch, or act up to Richard's expectations, all the more reason to be grateful for the wonderful chance that had brought them together.

And Lucilla, how grateful he ought to be, and was, for her! She had come into his life when his life was practi-cally over. Even if she didn't know that his days were numbered it was none the less wonderful that she, a woman who could have taken her pick from a wide range of younger and more attractive men, had singled him out for special favour. Be grateful for Lucilla, be grateful to Lucilla – he had no need to remind himself of that. When he deliberately practised gratitude, as he did, for many blessings, including the prolongation of his days, he left Lucilla out.

But an object of gratitude, however heaven-sent, may also be a human being, and as such the recipient of other emotions besides gratitude. Love, perhaps. Love came into his relationship with Denys; he hadn't associated love with his feeling for Lucilla. But though still an object of gratitude she had become more and more a person to him, and as a person he wanted to know more about her, who she was, who her parents were, and many other things.

That was why, after his dream, and after dining with her, he set about making certain inquiries. He didn't altogether like doing it, nor did he really want to find out what he thought he might find out; he didn't like playing the detective and whenever he met her (as he now did regularly more than once a week) the thought that he was spying on her while he talked to her vaguely troubled him. But something stronger than his own will drew him on, and there was also, for someone who had shaken hands with life and never expected to come to grips with it again, the excitement of the chase. His quest took him into many places where he had never been before; Government offices, record offices; he waited, patiently or impatiently, while clerks searched through papers. He even took a long train journey, which he had never thought to do again, to distant Distington in Cumberland; and while there, in the intervals of prosecuting his search, he visited the ruins of Aspin Castle, perched on a U-bend of the River Aspin. They did not disappoint him, nor did the trees of Rockden, waving below.

He had asked Denys to go with him, for company and support, but rather half-heartedly, because he didn't want Denys to know what his business at Distington was. Never before had he kept anything back from Denys except the exact sum he meant to leave him – a middle-class counsel of prudence which he rather despised himself for. The same scruple prevented him from giving Denys the legacy outright; he could not possibly expect to live the statutory five years which would exempt the legacy from death duties, so he might just as well have given it him now, but secrecy about money was in his blood. Even his mother, the most generous of women, had had it; she would never tell him how much she had offered Aunt Carrie and Uncle James to leave Australia and return to England. They had refused it, why? Was it because Aunt Carrie couldn't face the hot-bed of affection awaiting her in her own country? Was it because she wouldn't again present herself as a failure, she who had raised so many hopes? Or was it for Uncle James's sake? A struggling neurasthenic schoolmaster, a nice enough fellow but also a failure, not a distinguished one as she was – she didn't want to subject him to the mortification of living humbly and penuriously cheek by jowl with the rest of the Holy Family, who had all got on so well in the world? Pride, pride – Richard didn't think that she, the emblem of unselfishness, could be guilty of it, but whatever the reason, she had refused his mother's offer.

Richard had told Denys about that, too. But he didn't tell him about the legacy, at least not its amount – for Denys knew that it was coming – and for quite another reason he hadn't told Denys about his researches into Lucilla's history. It was because Denys didn't like Lucilla, and whenever her name cropped up he made fun of her.

So Richard was relieved, as well as disappointed, when Denys didn't want to go with him to Distington. He had so many engagements in London – that was his excuse. He deprecated Richard's journey. 'Why on earth do you want to go there, of all places? I think the name "Distington" has bewitched you!' It wasn't far from the truth; and when Richard said half-heartedly: 'But if you came you'd see Aspin Castle, too!' Denys answered, 'No more ruins for me, thank you! I'm quite enough of a ruin myself!'

When Richard came back to London, one link in the chain was still missing: it would be supplied, the authorities assured him, in the course of a day or two. Suddenly he had an unaccountable reaction: a violent antipathy to all his sleuthing of the past few weeks. Why, oh why, had he not let well alone? Uncertainty was often better than certainty. You could enjoy a rose just as well without knowing its name or who had grown it. Crowding into his mind came myths and fairy stories of couples who had been happy together – blissfully, unbelievably happy – until one asked the other a question he or she had been forbidden to ask – as Elsa had been forbidden to ask Lohengrin. It was a symbol of the mystery of personality: one wanted to pluck the heart out of it, but one couldn't, and it was vain, and might be fatal, to try, because the mystery was the secret of the attraction, and once divulged, it ceased to attract. How many people, in his own experience, had become estranged by knowing each

49

other too well! Perhaps that was why Aunt Carrie had taken refuge with a man with whom she could preserve herself intact, emotionally and perhaps physically too, in a country which was strange to her and which might never grow familiar.

Would he have found Denys attractive without the background of Aspin Castle?

As day followed day Richard's unease increased, until he nearly wrote to the person at Distington, begging to keep to himself any information he might have gleaned. When the letter came he recognized it before he saw the post-mark, and knew what it said before he opened it. But he didn't open it at once, he sat with it in his hand, dreading the confirmation of his fears – fears which had once, inexplicably, been hopes. 'Denys,' he called out, 'Denys!' He wanted to make sure that Denys was at hand, for sometimes he was in bed and asleep when the post came. 'Denys!' There was an answering rumble from the bathroom, and Richard tore the letter open. He had hardly time to throw it on his writing-table before Denys emerged. 'Denys, I'm ill!' he cried. 'Just a moment,' Denys said. 'No, no, please help me.' Denys lent him his wet, slender arm and half lifted him on to his bed; the tablets, which were never quite where Denys thought they would be, were slow in coming. Propping himself on his elbow, for he hated to lie down, Richard swallowed one. 'This is the last time,' he thought and lay back on the pillow. Denys stood and watched him. 'Why can't he *do* something?' thought Richard irritably, for in the greatest crises, mental or physical, the surface irritations of the mind are apt to assert themselves. Then he realized he had done Denys an injustice, for what *could* he do? Telephone for the doctor, perhaps; but by the time the doctor arrived he would either be better or dead. His mother had believed, or appeared to believe, that any doctor could, in any circumstances, save one from dying; Richard inherited this belief from her, but of late years he had outgrown it. Doctors were fallible, like other people, but they were harder-worked than other people, and must not be summoned to bedsides where there was little they could do except exhibit a good bedside manner. Richard hated to be watched; and the moment he felt the tide turning, he said, 'Run away now, Denys. I'm all right. If I'm not, I'll call you.' Denys, with a relief that was just noticeable (and quite excusable, for why should the young and healthy be tied to the moribund?), went out, leaving Richard to count his heart-beats, as gradually they pumped life into him. After a timeless interval he tried his feet on the carpet and went back to the sitting-room where, on his writing-desk, lay the hurtful letter. Innocuous now, its venom spent, he folded it and put it in his pocket. 'Denys!' he cried quite gaily. 'Breakfast!' Denys was seldom out for breakfast.

5

Richard had caught himself out, not Lucilla, that was very clear. To her he was still the same as he had always been, with the same attraction for her – whatever it was – that he had always had. Her manner to him had not altered. Perhaps she thawed more quickly than she used to. With people she didn't know well, and even with him, she was apt to be a little stiff at first – it was a defensive mechanism dating from earlier days, and he understood now what had caused it. During the time of his detective work he had avoided her. It had seemed improper, almost indecent, to enjoy the hospitality of someone into whose antecedents he was delving. The word suggested a sexton with his spade. But actually the operation had not been interment, but an exhumation – touched off, if an exhumation can be, by his dream of Rookland Abbey.

When he looked across the table at Lucilla now, after the lapse in their relationship – ten days, a fortnight? – he could see behind her, in the candle-light, a shadowy figure by a tombstone. So absurd, for she was much more alive, and had a much greater expectation of life, than he. Talking to her he was talking to two people, the Lucilla he knew and the Lucilla he knew nothing about. It was hard to focus the two.

She was under no such disability. She wanted to know what had been happening to him, why he had been away, what in fact was 'up'.

'Your nice secretary,' she said, 'was most evasive. I was afraid you weren't *well*, but you are well, aren't you?'

She gave Richard a look that suggested that this was more than a routine inquiry, and it deepened his sense of guilt. Guilty he always felt, and never more than when someone showed concern for his well-being. Most of his friends knew about his state of health and had evolved a way of referring to it. The formula combined a general resignation to fate with compassion for his individual lot. But Lucilla, apparently, hadn't heard of it, and Richard who, especially in her company, wanted to appear a whole and healthy man, had been as unwilling to tell her as he would have been to show her, on some part of his person, a running sore.

'Oh, I'm all right,' he said, looking at the two Lucillas with an interest which might have been taken, or mistaken, for love. 'I wasn't very well a day or two ago. My heart's a bit dicky, you know,' (he had a sudden impulse to tell her this) 'but I'm all right now.' He gazed at her again so intently that she thought there must be something the matter with her appearance, and studied it in her little make-up mirror, as closely as he had. But she could see nothing wrong.

Richard, who himself hated being scrutinized, hastily turned away but this did not lessen her embarrassment, it increased it. 'Why is he behaving so oddly?' she asked herself, and it flashed into her mind for the first time that he might be in love with her.

Men had been attracted to her before, of course, and she to them; but neither she nor they were encouraged to see enough of each other for a tender feeling to ripen. Her parents were not only Victorian in outlook, they were ultra-Victorian; they had all but kept her behind bars, and striven, with the energy of two powerfully possessive natures, to centre her affections on themselves. With this in view they were in every other way exceedingly indulgent to her, and built up in her a love-gratitude attitude which was as resistant to alien pressures as it was vulnerable to theirs. Soon this became known in the neighbourhood and accepted with a smile and a shrug. The nineteen-twenties and thirties, reared on Freud, knew all about inordinate affections between parents and children. So, heiress though she was, and good-looking though shy, the young men began to leave Lucilla alone, and she, though every now and then she had been attracted to one or other of them, felt that parental claims were paramount.

Her parents did not leave their attitude quite unexplained. Someone near and dear to them had died, they told her, of love unworthily bestowed. They didn't tell her more than that when they asked her – or rather when her mother asked her – as a last request to do what she and her husband had done from time to time throughout the years, and put flowers on the grave of someone called Lucy Soames at Rookland Abbey.

So it was by intuition, not by experience, that she thought she recognized, in Richard's interested gaze, a look of love. She was mistaken, for Richard's interest didn't come immediately from that, it came from his over-mastering desire to reconcile, in his eye and mind and heart, the two Lucillas; but she wasn't altogether mistaken, for that desire came from an interest in her much more deep seated than he was aware of.

The meal was unlike their other meals together. It was uneasy and interrupted by long silences, and it had an unexpressed intensity of feeling which had before been absent.

Richard didn't expect to find Denys at home when he came in – he had been out so many evenings lately – and perhaps nights, too. But to Richard's surprise and pleasure he was there, making the thought of bed-time much less bleak.

'Have a drink, Denys,' Richard said. 'You've been such a good boy, you deserve it. And I might have one, too.'

Denys rose slowly and as slowly began to take the bottles out of their retreat beneath the sideboard.

'I may deserve it,' he remarked, 'but I don't think you do.'

'Why not?' Richard asked, noting that though the bottles had been put away there was an empty glass by Denys's chair.

'Because you've been out on the tiles already. With Miss Distington, I shouldn't wonder. Your bread-ticket.'

'As a matter of fact I was,' said Richard, slightly ruffled. 'But that needn't have prevented you from going out. It never has, before.'

'That's what you think,' Denys said. 'Before she flashed across your path you used to take me out. Now you don't, or not so much.'

Richard saw the truth of this.

'But you go out all the same,' he said. 'You're so much in demand, you hardly ever have an evening free.'

'I don't have many evenings *free*,' retorted Denys. 'That's just it. *I* have to pay my way. You, lucky fellow, don't.'

'Well, I have her here sometimes,' said Richard, nettled, and pouring into his glass more brandy than he meant to. 'I should ask her more often if I hadn't a feeling that you don't like her.'

Denys took a swig.

'I like her well enough,' he said, 'although she has never asked me to sample her cuisine. By the way, Richard, have you told her what you have found out about her?'

Richard put down his glass before it reached his lips.

'Found out about her, what do you mean?'

'What I say. Have you told her that you have found out that her father's real name was Soames?'

Richard gulped his brandy this time.

'How did *you* find out?' he asked, coughing.

'I saw the letter.'

'Which letter?'

'The letter from Distington.'

'You mean you read it? When?'

'When you were having that bad turn. You left it lying on your writing-desk, when you were taken queer.'

'And you read it?' repeated Richard.

'Yes, why not? I'm your secretary, and read your letters, that's what I'm for, in the intervals of cooking and dish-washing. If you didn't want me to read this one, you should have put it away.'

'I hadn't time. The . . . the attack came on so suddenly.'

'Well, you mustn't blame me. I wouldn't have read the thing if I'd thought you didn't want me to. But you used to have no secrets from me. You seem to have changed, somehow.'

Richard saw the force of this reproach.

'Of course you were at liberty to read it,' he said. 'I did tell you all about myself and Lucy, only she was dead, and I nearly am, and this was something that concerned the living, so I meant to keep it private.'

'Well, you'd better come clean about the whole thing.'

Richard thought there was no way out: besides, wasn't Denys his greatest friend?

'There isn't much to add to what you must have guessed,' he said. 'Lucy was born in 1889, while her mother and father were living at Distington. Her mother died in childbirth and, as so often happened then, and happens still, her sister stepped into her shoes. Mr. Soames was a man of very strong feelings, apparently, and didn't find it hard, in fact he found himself compelled, to transfer his affections from his dead wife to her sister. But by law they couldn't be married, and they took a farm, near Rookland, where they lived as man and wife. In those days places were further apart than they are now and it was easier to disappear and re-appear, even in England, without attracting attention. I've heard other cases of it.'

'So have I,' said Denys thoughtfully.

'Whether it was a good plan, from that point of view, to keep themselves to themselves in the way they did, I don't know. Rookland was a small place – the guide-books still call it "lost in the Fens", though it isn't, but by being so exclusive they did draw attention to themselves. As I told you – they almost created a legend. But it wasn't only, I'm sure, for fear of being found out that they lived that way. They didn't want communication with the outside world, they were hedged in by money, and they could afford to ignore it. Those were bad days for farmers, but even in Rookland, and at Fosdyke too, where we used to live, there were families with lots of money salted away, who never saw anyone socially except their relations, and not always them. My grandfather made money in the end, but he never lived a social life, in the way he would have now. So the Soameses were able to get away with their isolation until . . . until what you know, happened.'

'I see,' said Denys. 'It was you, really, who blew the gaff on them.'

Richard tried not to register a hit.

'After . . . after that,' he said, 'they seem to have left Rookland almost at once, perhaps before the headstone was put up to Lucy – I don't know. They managed things of that sort – lapidary arrangements for the dead – quicker in those days than they do now. I did once think of being buried near to Lucy, if there was room; after all I have a family link with Rookland. But now, as you know, I've decided to be cremated, so, as my executor, you won't have that trouble to contend with. No tombstones for me!'

'Oh!' said Denys, 'and I had so much looked forward to giving you a proper eighteenth-century epitaph, mentioning your virtues it is true, but dwelling on your vices, too.'

'Well, you'll have to forgo that pleasure. At any rate, the Soameses left Rookland, and settled in Devonshire and took the name of Distington and . . . and . . .'

'And what?' asked Denys, as Richard paused.

'And got married. You see, in 1907 the Deceased Wife's Sister Bill was passed. Lucilla was born in wedlock, ten months later.'

'A substitute for Lucy,' Denys commented. 'Why didn't they have another child before, since they were supposed to be married?'

'They may have been afraid of having their secret found out,' said Richard, 'and refrained for their own sakes and the child's. Birth control isn't a twentieth-century innovation. But I think the real reason was that Lucy was all in all to them. So long as they had her, they didn't want another child. When they lost her, he longed for another, just as when he lost his wife he wanted another. I don't think it showed lack of feeling, just the opposite.'

'He must have been quite old by then,' said Denys.

'Not much over forty. He looked old to me, of course. She, I fancy, was a good deal younger. But I didn't distinguish much between the ages of grown-up people, unless they were over seventy.'

'If you could have seen yourself as you are now, would you have thought of yourself as old?'

Richard glanced at the looking-glass, a thing he ordinarily shunned, except when shaving, as if it were Medusa. That face which someone had once called a perfect oval, was now lengthened by at least two double-chins. In the long ago it had attracted someone; could it, in the present, attract someone still? A concourse of feelings assaulted him, grief, shame, remorse; but among them (he could not disguise it from himself) was a tingling of hope.

'Where do we go from here?' asked Denys, as though reading his thoughts.

'Yes, where?' said Richard, automatically.

'It's easy for you, you just go on as you are doing, except for one or two heart-attacks.' Richard was a little hurt by this summary of his condition, but couldn't deny its truth. 'You have this brick-foundation,' Denys went on. 'But I, I haven't any, and I need money so much.'

'Do you? But I gave you some only a little while ago.'

'I know, and I appreciated it, but London is so expensive. You couldn't give me a little more, I suppose?'

Family caution about money rang a warning bell in Richard's mind.

'It wouldn't be very easy for me at the moment.'

'I was afraid you were going to say that,' said Denys, re-filling his glass, then he added, 'I wonder if I could raise a loan. Only I haven't any security except my own person, and I doubt if anyone would accept that. I could sell myself into slavery, if it wasn't illegal.'

'What should I do then?'

'Well, you're a bit of a slave-driver yourself.'

'Oh, Denys.'

'Yes, you are. I doubt if anyone has a slave but you. If I broke my chains and went away, you would still have Miss Distington.'

'That wouldn't be at all the same thing.'

'She's your bread-ticket, and she'd marry you tomorrow if you asked her.'

This was a possibility that had never occurred to Richard. It brought a host of thoughts and feelings, sweet, painful, contradictory, suggesting a future in the real world, where he had no future. Terribly upsetting, and yet—

'What makes you think so?'

'Well, doesn't it stick out a mile? She dotes on you, and so do you on her, if you only knew it.'

'Oh, nonsense, Denys.'

'It isn't nonsense. I wouldn't mind betting . . . only you disapprove of betting. She's so fond of you, she might lend me some money.'

Richard turned cold, and the room, so snug and familiar with its low ceiling and shaded lights, suddenly seemed inimical.

'You couldn't possibly ask her to, Denys.'

'I could, if I made it seem a favour she was doing you. All that Soames-Distington money. And if I told her—'

'Told her what?'

'Well, what you – what we – have found out about her, all those goings-on at Rookland, and the part you played – that you are, in effect, her step-brother-in-law, and the cause of her coming into the world – because she wouldn't have, Richard, if you hadn't murdered her half-sister – well, she might think the information worth a quid or two.'

Richard got up shakily, and walked about the room.

'You're not serious, are you, Denys?'

'Of course not, my dear Richard, it was only a sort of pipe-dream, brought on by money troubles. You don't have them, so you don't know what they are. Oh dear,' he sighed, 'there is no peace for the wicked.'

Richard thought, or tried to think, as quickly as he could. Did Denys really harbour this intention? He was given to fantasies, and one never knew how far to take him literally. No, it wasn't conceivable. But his heart was beating hard – not with the symptoms he most dreaded, for then it seemed to cease to beat – but in a way that threatened a bad night. He had suffered from insomnia as a child and had always dreaded it. He needn't try to explain: better not to.

'All right, Denys,' he said. 'Would a hundred do?'

'A hundred pounds would be more than welcome.'

6

Richard's friendship with Lucilla continued, but not quite on the old footing; something had gone out of it and something had come in. He was much more aware of this than she was – the loss of informality, the increase in intensity – but she sensed it too. They did not feel as relaxed with each other – they were groping towards something, or keeping something at bay. Lucilla interpreted this as a growing interest on Richard's part and hardly knew whether to welcome it or not. Her virginal life had become a habit to her: most of her energies went into keeping up appearances, her own especially. But they were appearances that denoted standards. Respect for standards was inherent in her, she was always trying to maintain them – social, cultural, personal – not hoping to get in front but afraid of lagging behind. Lucilla was hardly aware of being lonely, till Richard came into her life. Before her parents died, their health had failed them and their minds had failed them, so that they had left her in the spirit long before they left her in the flesh. Richard was a novelty and a challenge. 'What is going to happen?' she asked herself. She did not now have to remain unmarried, or uninvolved, for her parents' sake.

Richard's feeling for her was so complicated by the Lucy-Lucilla relationship, that he could not clarify it to himself. It was alternately a source of comfort and of guilt. In non-guilty moods he felt that Fate had sent her to him, to compensate him for what he had lost: the dreary years unfertilized by love. What was Denys? A substitute, who by the nature of his sex was not vulnerable in the way that Lucy had been. Physically he could do no harm to Denys. Morally and emotionally he might; but as for that, Denys was old enough to look after himself. There was a limit to responsibility!

He felt himself drifting towards Lucilla, and away from Denys, but it might not be as simple as that. For though he resented Denys's attitude to Lucilla, there were times when he enjoyed his company as much as ever, just as there were times when he felt in Lucilla's presence a conversation-crippling constraint. What would she think of him if she knew about him? If she didn't actually show him the door (he couldn't imagine her doing that) the door would be closed to him for ever. When he thought of how he would fare without her, he could almost feel the void expanding, pressing out of shape the emotional pattern that was to rule the remainder of his days. She must never know! Away from her, he felt bereft and lonely; with her he felt that he was sailing under false colours. The memory of the catastrophe at Rookland, which he had managed to thrust into the limbo of his consciousness, returned in all its horror; the wound bled afresh; some turn of phrase on Lucilla's lips that Lucy had once used was enough to start it, for as happens with many closely knit families she shared a language with her parents. He wondered why he had never noticed these likenesses before. Many a time he cursed himself for his disastrous, self-destroying curiosity about her, and yet he knew that once it had attacked him he was forced to give way to it, for it was stronger than he was.

So there were often gaps in their conversation which neither of them could fill, and it was during one of these that Lucilla, to break the silence, said:

'You remember, Richard, my telling you that there was a family called Aspin living in Devonshire, and old Colonel Aspin was a great genealogist – if that's the word – especially where his own family tree was concerned. He knew all its ramifications. Well, I told him I had met a Mr. Aspin here' (she never referred to Denys by his Christian name) 'and he was terribly excited and said he would look him up. There are still a few Aspins extant, but so far he hasn't been able to trace a Denys Aspin. Odd, isn't it?'

Richard agreed.

'But he's still on the trail,' Lucilla said. 'Poor old boy, he has nothing else to do – and he's promised to tell me if he finds out anything.'

'Denys will be interested,' said Richard. 'He has always told me he doesn't know what happened to his family.'

'That's quite possible,' Lucilla said. 'Devoted as we were – hardly ever apart for a single day, for as you know I never went to school – that's why I'm so badly educated – still there were things in their lives that I don't know about.'

'Oh yes, in everybody's lives there are,' said Richard as carelessly as he could. 'A little below the surface you'll find the most surprising things.'

Toute vérité n'est pas bonne à dire. . . . Yet secrecy is a bore, for the thing concealed has a danger area round it, a tender area, which the tongue must not touch or even the thoughts.

The conversation languished, and when it was time to go, Richard almost felt relieved.

Unpleasant things will happen even in London's most reputable districts. Someone – could it be the postman, could it be the laundry-man? – had taken to writing rude words on the sides of the lift. It must have been a man, for a boy couldn't have reached that high, and a woman wouldn't have done it, for according to report, women are much less dirty-minded and criminally inclined than men.

Richard was distressed that the lift, which served other flats besides his, should have some of the uses of a public lavatory; he was also ashamed of his own interest in the new development, which made lift-travel more exciting. Every morning the porter scrubbed out, as far as he could, the offending words; but during the day they, or others in the same vein, sometimes reappeared and Richard couldn't help looking for them. No doubt the culprit was a tradesman, or someone of that sort; but suspicion must fall on the tenants too, including himself. And what if some of these words, four-lettered or longer, should be aimed at him? It was all rather unpleasant and gave the snug, cosy flat a feeling of insecurity, as if something sinister from the outside world was trying to get in. Richard felt *smeared*, to use a current word.

But were women so much less criminally inclined than men? Only a few days ago Denys had told him that their daily help, Mrs. Cuddesdon, listened in to his conversations on the telephone – there was one in his bedroom, as well as in the sitting-room, so nothing could be easier than to tap it. Richard was surprised to hear this; he had always thought Mrs. Cuddesdon was quite honest, besides, why should she be interested in his affairs?

For some days after this revelation Richard felt in duty bound to try to catch her out, and on some flimsy pretext would break off a telephone conversation to dash into the sitting-room or the bedroom, as the case might be, hoping to find Mrs. Cuddesdon red-handed or red-eared. He rather despised himself for doing this, which went against his nature; still, one must protect oneself. However, he never caught her out, and began to think that Denys had imagined that she did it. It was his conversations with Lucilla that he specially wanted to safeguard – not that they had any secrets to confide, but the kind of things they said and the tone in which they said them weren't meant for the ears of a third person – in fact couldn't have been said if either Richard or Lucilla had suspected that they were being overheard.

Denys said you could tell if the telephone was being tapped by the click when the other receiver was lifted. Richard had never heard the click but he was a little deaf and when he telephoned all his faculties were concentrated on hearing what his interlocutor was saying.

Mrs. Cuddesdon came in the mornings from eight till ten or a little later: after that, as far as telephoning went, the coast was clear. Richard asked Denys to keep an eye on the telephone while Mrs. Cuddesdon was about, whether he was using the instrument in his sitting-room or in his bedroom. When speaking to Lucilla as a rule he used his bedroom, as being furthest out of earshot; he had always done this as a precaution against being overheard, even before Denys told him of Mrs. Cuddesdon's nefarious activities; and sometimes, if he was in the sitting-room when she rang up, he was guilty of the imprudence of leaving the receiver off, chattering to itself, while he used the one in his bedroom. After Denys's warning he discontinued this practice. He then believed that with Denys as watch-dog, his conversations would be safe from Mrs. Cuddesdon's inquisitiveness. He didn't dream of taxing her with it: he couldn't bring himself to accuse anyone of dishonesty.

Having taken these precautions he felt quite safe, and though he told Lucilla as much about his way of life as he thought might interest her, he did not tell her of the trouble with the telephone. It would only worry her and cramp her style – needlessly, since he had taken the necessary steps to insure privacy.

One morning she rang him up and presently broke into French, as she often did when she had something special to say. Richard's French was as rusty as his hearing, he couldn't always understand it, so he answered her in English. 'It's all right, Lucilla, let's talk in our native tongue.'

'Vous êtes bien sûr?' Lucilla said.

'Mais oui, bien sûr.'

'You are quite alone?'

'Oui, oui, tout solitaire, or however you put it.'

'Very well, I've heard something that might interest you from my friend Colonel Aspin in Devon about – you know who. It's quite surprising – but I'll tell you when we meet. Could you possibly dine with me tomorrow?'

Richard, with the usual twinge of guilt he felt at accepting Lucilla's invitations, said he would only be too pleased to. 'Very well then, eight o'clock.'

But when they met Lucilla didn't at once broach the subject of Denys and the Aspin family, and after a time it became clear to him that she was deliberately avoiding it. They talked of other subjects – books, theatres, and what have you; they couldn't talk easily, nowadays, without a subject. But not of Denys. Richard, who felt that Lucilla, who was paying the piper, should also call the tune, usually left the choice of subject to her; but when dinner was finished curiosity overcame him.

'You said something on the telephone about Denys,' he said, 'unless my French deceived me.'

'Oh yes, I did,' she said, and pushed the cigarette-box towards him. She knew he wasn't supposed to smoke; she didn't know why, but while he was with her she wanted him to feel perfectly free to do what he liked. Impelled by excitement, Richard took one.

'Yes, I did,' Lucilla repeated slowly. 'I thought it would interest and perhaps amuse you. But now I'm not so sure.

I'm not sure if I approve of digging about in people's private lives. It seems so mean, somehow. Everyone is entitled to their secrets. I should hate it if someone started trying to find out things about me, or anyone to do with me – and I daresay you would. Not that we have anything to hide.'

'Of course not,' Richard said, and smiled as well as he could. It took him a moment to recover from this thrust, but then curiosity got the better of guilt, the better of prudence and experience too, and he exclaimed with the uncontrolled excitement of a teen-ager:

'Lucilla, you *must* tell me! You've gone too far to draw back now! If you don't tell me, I shall think the most awful things about Denys. Tell me the worst, and put me out of my anxiety!'

Lucilla didn't answer at once, and then she said, 'Oh no, it isn't anything at all bad. It's just that . . . well, if he hasn't told you himself, I suppose he doesn't want you to know, and why should I butt in? I'm not so busy that I have to be a busybody. Besides, it mayn't be true, though it sounds as if it was. I know I come out of all this badly, Richard, and I'm old enough to have known better, but I'd rather not tell you unless you really want me to.'

Richard saw she was distressed. Having lived a detached and uneventful life, with little current to carry away a passing thought or emotion, she attached importance to what people more occupied than she might have thought of as trifles. Richard took this into account and respected her scruples; but all the same he wanted to know.

'Perhaps Denys has told me,' he said, 'he's told me quite a lot about himself, he's been with me three years, you know. I don't imagine he's a saint: present company excepted I've only known one saint, my Aunt Carrie, and I don't like to call her one, she would dislike it so much. I'm prepared to hear anything you tell me: I'm not so prepared not to hear something you don't tell me. What an array of negatives! – but you see what I mean.'

Lucilla saw and saw also that she had committed one of those mistakes which one must get out of as best one can. She was fond – increasingly fond of Richard, and felt she owed him something. She was not fond, she couldn't have explained why, of Denys, and didn't feel she owed him anything.

'Well,' she said, taking a long breath. 'You'll think I've made a mountain out of a molehill. As I said, it may have nothing to do with your Mr. Aspin at all, and in any case, what *does* it matter? But it appears there are some Aspins, distant cousins of Colonel Aspin, a childless couple who adopted a boy from an orphanage and gave him their name and a good education. But he turned out to be, well – rather wild, and after a time they lost sight of him. That's all – it isn't much – nothing to worry over. But you look worried, and I'm sorry now I told you. I knew I should be.'

Richard accepted the proffered coffee, though coffee, too, was against doctor's orders.

'Of course it doesn't matter,' he said, 'not in the least – and yet, in a way, it does. You see, Lucilla, I had built up this idea of Denys as the scion of a noble house, and somehow it equalized the position – the position of employer and employee, I mean. I had the money, but he had the rank, or whatever you like to call it, so as friends we met on equal terms. You can't have true friendship, can you, if it's based on patronage on one side, and self-interest on the other?'

Lucilla disagreed. 'In every friendship there's a predominant partner.'

'What, even in ours?'

'Well yes, and I needn't say who it is. When I am with you,' Lucilla told him, 'I feel at least ten feet high. Where do I get those extra inches, if not from you?'

Richard was gratified, puzzled, humbled. He couldn't answer for a moment. 'But that is how I feel with *you*!' he cried. 'In every direction you increase my stature – even my *girth*—' and he indicated rather sadly his middle-aged spread. 'You are the most marvellous inflationist!' She smiled a little wanly at this, and he went on, 'I speak as if I was a motor-tyre, and you a pump – but what I mean is, you give me such a good opinion of myself.'

'Well, you do that to me,' she said. 'You must have noticed that I have an inferiority complex – it doesn't only come from leading a sheltered life, but from being a sort of substitute – I haven't told you this before, but I don't see why I shouldn't – for my sister, my half-sister, to be exact. She died in tragic circumstances – she was drowned, or she drowned herself – I've never known which, and I don't think my parents did. She was so young, Richard, think of it, only sixteen, and she had to take her own life – or if she didn't, it was taken from her, which seems hardly less sad. Of course many people have had far worse things to bear, but it was before the two wars, when people hadn't learned to expect to lose those who were dearest to them – and my father and mother – my father specially – never really got over it. They couldn't have cherished me more than they did – I only had to be in a draught for them to run and shut the window – and it was years before I realized that this was at least as much for my dead sister's sake as mine. She was called Lucy and I was called Lucilla, after her, with just a shade of difference. Lucy is more lovable than Lucilla, don't you think?'

'Lucilla is a charming name,' said Richard. He glanced at the clock – it was half-past nine: another hour to go before he could decently take his leave.

'I don't know why I'm telling you all this,' Lucilla went on, 'I've never told anyone before. Perhaps it's a sort of expiation for having been horrid – indiscreet, at any rate – about your friend Mr. Aspin. I don't think I was ever jealous of Lucy – can one be jealous of someone who is dead? – and my parents never, never, *never* suggested that I didn't come up to her. But I felt I didn't. But even allowing for the myths that grow up, or used to, round children who have died, she must have been a charming creature, so sweet and gentle – rather like Wordsworth's Lucy. Perhaps she was named after her. My father didn't read poetry but I believe my aunt, her mother, did. Like Lucy, she dwelt among untrodden ways, in the Fens, you know, not beside a spring, but beside a dyke, but of course you know more about dykes than I do, having lived at Medehamstead.'

Richard glanced at the clock again. There seemed no way of heading Lucilla off.

'And there was no one to praise her and very few to love her, for I gather that my parents, while they were living near this place, Rookland, hardly went about at all. They loved Lucy most tenderly, but no one else did.'

'Of course not.' Richard hardly knew what he was saying.

'I have a photograph of her, would you like to see it?'

Richard felt he could stand no more of this. Warning symptoms started up in him. He rose shakily, and said:

'Yes, very much, Lucilla, but some other time, if you don't mind. I don't feel awfully well, to tell you the truth, and I think I'd better be getting back.'

Instantly Lucilla was all concern, and seemed as agitated as he was.

'Oh, Richard, why did you let me run on like that? I am so terribly sorry. Would you like to lie down here – or sleep here, I've got a room – or should I call you a taxi?'

'A taxi, please, Lucilla.'

'I'll ring for one now.' But the number of the taxi-rank was engaged.

'I'll try again in a minute or two,' she said, coming back. 'Are you sure there isn't anything I can do for you?'

Richard, who thought that this time he really must be dying, said: 'Give me a kiss.'

She bent over him, and it was not only Lucilla who kissed him, but Lucy too.

Then he knew that the attack was passing. Had the kiss restored him? Was it 'the kiss of life'? Had it supplied some vital principle that his being was in need of? He didn't know, but in a confused way he knew that he ought not to have asked her.

The taxi was coming now, she said. 'Are you all right? Are you sure you are all right?' He nodded, too happy, too relieved to speak. 'And you'll find Mr. Aspin there when you get home?'

'I'm sure he will be.' Utterance now restored, Richard added quite gaily:

'I shall tell him what you said about him – that he's an impostor, not a true-blue Aspin.'

'Oh no, you mustn't. Please, please, don't.'

Recovery had made him self-assertive and he wouldn't promise her.

She went down with him in the lift, and as the taxi-driver held the door open, they kissed again, quite naturally. How many kisses, Richard thought, must that taxi-man have seen.

As he entered the flat he was feeling quite proud of himself and his recuperative powers. Still cheating the undertaker! That would be something to tell Denys – not Denys Aspin, Denys who knew what? Did it really matter? Perhaps it did, but the thing was to see him, and talk to him, and tell him how he, Richard, had rounded another nasty corner.

The flat was dark and silent. Richard was used, if not hardened to, these disconcerting home-comings. Disappointed and deflated, he strayed into his bedroom, took off his overcoat, walked about, then went into his sitting-room, trying to take comfort from his familiar surroundings – the rugs and furniture and pictures which, though they could not speak, gave back to him something of what, consciously or not, he had put into them. 'Denys!' he called. It was a routine operation, and one that he knew would bring no answer. But perhaps Denys had already gone to bed? His bedroom door was shut. Richard knocked and opened the door, but got no further than the threshold. For the room was empty; empty not only of Denys but of all Denys's possessions. He had cleared out; he had left.

7

Richard did not see until the next day the note Denys had left on his bedside table. He did not find it himself, for after that one glimpse he could not bring himself to go into Denys's room. Mrs. Cuddesdon, the daily help, brought it to him with his early morning tea, the arrival of which he had been awaiting for at least three hours. He hoped that it would calm him after the agitations of the night, and to some extent it did. But he left the envelope unopened. Perhaps Denys will ring me up, he thought, and tell me what it says.

He spent the morning with his ears cocked for the call. As a rule he received several telephone calls during the morning; but latterly – since when he couldn't remember – they had fallen off. His friends didn't remember him as they used to. Why was that? Well, it was something that happened to elderly people – they dropped out, they ceased to count. Had Richard himself kept up with his friends – he had had a good many who were older than he was? Well, yes, he had. His conscience was clear on that point. But there was no reason why his younger friends should keep up with him.

How still and empty the flat seemed! Even the plane-tree outside his window, which had shed its leaves and much of its bark, hardly stirred. It was almost as motionless as the houses opposite – the white, cream, beige-coloured houses, which in summer it concealed. Their occupants could now see through it – see him too, perhaps, if he kept the electric light on. He turned it off, and sat in the twilight which was all the morning sun could offer in November.

It was three years since Denys came, three years since Richard had been really alone. He hadn't minded being alone, before he had this heart trouble; he could fend for himself, and if needs be take his meals out. He still could, he supposed; perhaps his present feeling of helplessness was just a result of depending too much on Denys.

'Be able to be alone,' Sir Thomas Browne had said. 'It will be useful to you in after life,' his mother might have added. He seemed to have unlearned this valuable lesson. But had he really been alone before Denys came? No, not really; people were always coming and going. They didn't come now, and if they didn't come, how could they go? Denys had gone, walked out, taken himself off.

This loneliness – how could he adjust himself to it? At the moment it didn't seem possible; he hadn't the resources in himself to invent a kind of otherness – an impersonal, disembodied otherness, with which he could communicate as with a friend. Religion would have helped him but he had not enough religion for the purpose; the projection of his needs into the Infinite would not bring an answer to his needs.

Denys's note lay on the chair beside him. He knew he ought to read it: there was nothing to be gained by putting off the evil day: to know the worst is far more salutary than to fear the worst. Reality is always a catharsis. But he couldn't stretch his hand out to touch the letter, any more than he could have touched a snake.

The telephone-bell rang. That will be Denys, he thought, and lifted the receiver. He had no inhibitions about doing that: it was a spontaneous, automatic action, not like opening a letter. But it wasn't Denys, it was Lucilla.

'I thought I'd ring you up,' she said, 'just to know how you were. I should have rung up earlier, only I thought you might be in bed, or asleep, or not want to be bothered. But you are better, I hope?'

'Oh yes, much better.'

'I'm so glad. You didn't look very well just at one moment, and I was furious with myself afterwards for having pestered you with all that family history, which couldn't possibly have interested you. There are silent bores and talkative bores – I'm usually one of the first kind. Boredom can be an illness – it can even be fatal – "and then a female sometimes talks you dead". For a moment I thought I had – you looked so ill, poor Richard. While I was babbling on, and your friend Mr. Aspin, too . . . Are you alone, by the way?'

'Very much alone,' said Richard, and he told Lucilla about Denys's disappearance.

Lucilla made horror-stricken sounds. At last she became articulate. 'Oh, what a shame! To have left you in the lurch like that! I hope it wasn't because of what I told you about . . . about the Aspin family?'

'Oh no,' said Richard, 'I didn't have a chance to talk to him – he was gone before I got back. I don't know *why* he left.' He stole a glance at the unopened envelope.

'How extraordinary,' said Lucilla. 'Does it mean you're *quite* alone?'

'Except for the daily woman, yes.'

'Can I do anything?' Lucilla asked. 'Shall I come in and cook your meals? I'm quite a good cook.'

'I know you are.' It was the first time Richard realized that in losing Denys he had also lost his cook. 'It's too kind of you to suggest it. But I can easily go out to eat. I always did, before Denys came.'

There was a pause in which Lucilla seemed to be wondering what to say next. What she said was:

'At any rate, do dine with me tonight if you are free.'

'Oh, Lucilla, but—'

'I don't wonder you hesitate, after last night. But I promise I won't monopolize the conversation. I promise not to bore you in that way, anyhow. I would ask you to bore me, in revenge, only I know you couldn't.'

'You didn't bore me, Lucilla. It was just that I didn't feel very well. I'm like that, sometimes.'

'Poor Richard, and you never told me. I really think you should have. You know me quite well enough by now. You ought to see a doctor.'

'I have seen several.'

'It's nothing serious, is it?'

Now it was Richard's turn to hesitate.

'Not really. You have to have something, when you get to be as old as I am. My mother always expected me to die – of some chest complaint, you know – just as she thought my father would. But he lived to a great age, and I daresay I shall. Longevity is hereditary, isn't it? My mother—' He stopped.

'Yes?' prompted Lucilla.

'Well, she lived to a good age too, but latterly, having always worried about my father's health and mine – she couldn't worry so much about Aunt Carrie's, because she was in Australia – she took to worrying about her own. She became a confirmed hypochondriac. She had great faith in doctors. At the end of her life she cost my father a fortune in specialists. If he didn't ask one to come down from London, she thought he didn't mind whether she lived or died, and sometimes said so. I realize now better than I did, and it's been, as she might have said herself, a lesson to me – a lesson, not to worry other people, or oneself about one's health – and not to believe that doctors can work miracles, because they can't. I've done very well to reach seventy, I think.'

'You mustn't talk in that defeatist way,' Lucilla said, 'you must live to be a hundred. I shall be very sorry if you don't.'

'Thank you, Lucilla.'

'A bientôt, then.'

Somehow this conversation, disingenuous as it was on his part, cheered Richard up. It wasn't so much the practical aspects of Denys's disappearance that affected him – he hadn't thought much about them until Lucilla reminded him of the cooking – it was the loneliness, the loss of companionship, the fire on the hearth gone out. Lucilla could never be as near to him as Denys had been, and yet, when he most needed someone, here she was, bringing into the dark, cold, empty chamber of his heart, light, warmth, and a presence, an occupant. He felt emotionally and physically renewed, so much so that he reached out his hand and opened Denys's letter.

Dear Richard, it said,

I am sorry to leave you like this, but I think it's for the best, because I'm rather shocked by the way you discuss my affairs with other people. I won't mention any names but you will know who I mean. It's true I know a lot about your affairs, but I don't go shouting them about, and I certainly shouldn't on the telephone. Nor do I listen in to your conversations, but someone else does, and she told me you had been taking my name in vain with you know who – your latest great friend in fact. Well, I don't like it, Richard, I don't think it's fair. I always thought I was your greatest friend and so I was, until this someone came along. So I have taken myself off. I have nowhere much to go to, being terribly hard up, but I'll let you know where I am and come and see you in a day or two. I really must find a job where I can earn more money than you have been paying me. If I ring you up it will be after 10.30, because I don't want a certain person to hear what we are talking about. Not that we have any secrets from each other, at least we never used to, though it seems from what I've been told that we may have now.

You will be hearing from me soon. Take care of yourself and God bless,

Denys.

To say that Richard read this letter with mixed feelings would be an understatement. He went cold and hot by turns. Indignation and shame followed each other in quick succession. The shame was for himself, the indignation for Mrs. Cuddesdon. How *could* she? How *dare* she? There must be a special place in Hell reserved for mischief-makers. No wonder Denys was angry; no wonder he had flounced out. Richard couldn't remember exactly what he and Lucilla had said on the telephone about the Aspin family; he believed it was non-committal, but in the mouth of a mischief-maker it might have been exaggerated to any extent – to an extent that justified both Denys's action and the tone of his letter, which, at a first reading, Richard hadn't liked. But his own conscience was far from clear, for if Denys had known what he and Lucilla had said to each other afterwards, he had every right to feel still more annoyed, outraged even. Whatever Mrs. Cuddesdon had told Denys, however richly she had embroidered it, it couldn't be as damaging to Denys as the truth would have been.

He had gossiped about Denys inexcusably. Perhaps one should never mention one's friends to other people. Richard knew those who didn't, and yet were interesting and lively conversationalists. But if all personalities were ruled out, how dull most talk would be!

Richard felt he had been grossly disloyal to Denys. The fact that Denys was not or might not be a true Aspin, made no difference, indeed, it only served to show up Richard's snobbishness, as if he had valued his friend for his name, not for himself. My secretary, Mr. Denys Aspin of Aspin Castle! I pay him, it is true, but he lends me the lustre of his ancient lineage, so we are quits. That had been his feeling, but how ignoble it was, and how out of date, for in these days no one thought about such things. Or did they?

As soon as Denys made a sign, Richard must apologize and implore him to come back. He must also tell some lie to explain to Denys what he was saying about him to Lucilla, or what she was saying about him to Richard when his name cropped up.

But how could he find out what story Mrs. Cuddesdon had trumped up? She didn't like Denys, Richard knew that from one or two hints she had dropped. When she arrived this morning and found him gone, and his place empty, she had made no comment, until Richard drew her attention to it. Then she said, with a slight smile, 'Oh, I expect we shall soon see him back again!' – rather as if she hoped they wouldn't. The old hypocrite! Perhaps her chief reason for repeating to Denys what she had overheard was to upset him and make him sling his hook; Denys was proud and touchy, even if he wasn't a real Aspin.

The more Richard thought about it, the higher his rage against Mrs. Cuddesdon mounted. As long as she was about, not only his conversations with Lucilla, but all his conversations were liable to be tapped. He would have no privacy at all.

Next morning he must tax her with it, have it out with her.

But when morning came, his mood changed. He still felt indignant with Mrs. Cuddeson, he still felt he ought to 'speak' to her, but he didn't like the prospect at all. He had always been on good terms with her until he was told that she listened in to the telephone: and even since then his demeanour towards her hadn't altered, or not much; it was a routine, a habit, the result of five years of friendly association, for Mrs. Cuddesdon had been with Richard at least two years before Denys had appeared on the scene. He had never in his life accused anyone of dishonesty, and couldn't bear the thought of doing so – especially when the person was Mrs. Cuddesdon. But at the time when he had a circle of friends (they had dropped off lately, but enough of that) he had heard several stories of apparently faithful retainers who, after long terms of service – much longer than Mrs. Cuddesdon's – had suddenly taken advantage of their employer's trust, and behaved far, far worse than she had. One must be realistic, however much it went against the grain, if only to keep up the standard of morality which (so people said) had fallen lamentably since the Second World War. Was he a good example of morality himself? Perhaps not, but that had nothing to do with it. Standards of morality were concerned with individuals, but applied to life they were impersonal, just as the law, which also was concerned with individuals, was impersonal. 'Dominion is founded upon Grace' – Richard remembered from his school-days what a heresy that was. 'Don't do as I do, do as I tell you to.'

These reflections made his impending interview with Mrs. Cuddesdon no easier, but confirmed him in the belief that it was necessary. Besides, he was very, very angry with her, or so he told himself.

He would have to get it over quickly, because she left at ten o'clock. At a quarter to ten he went into the kitchen, a small, narrow, confined apartment, and bearded her.

'Mrs. Cuddesdon,' he began, 'I want a word with you.' He disliked this opening so much that he nearly went away without saying what the word was, but the Moral Law must be upheld, and then, think of the trouble she had made for him and Denys. 'Mrs. Cuddesdon,' he forced himself to go on, 'I understand that you sometimes overhear conversations on the telephone that are not meant for you.' She stared at him, looking a totally different person from the Mrs. Cuddesdon he knew. Hating himself, he proceeded, 'I'm sure you realize that this can lead to trouble, and I hope you won't do it in future.' He stopped and searched his mind. 'That's all I have to say.'

'It isn't all *I* have to say,' said Mrs. Cuddesdon, with a promptness that took him quite aback. 'It isn't all I have to say, sir, by any means. I've been with you now five years, and I think that by this time you ought to know me better. And I'll tell you, sir, before I give in my notice, as I'm going to, that it isn't me as listens in to your telephone – I wouldn't demean myself – it's someone else.'

'Who?' asked Richard, staring at her.

'Can't you guess?'

Richard shook his head. 'Who else is there?'

Mrs. Cuddesdon closed her lips as if she would never open them again. But she did open them and said:

'That Mr. Aspin, of course.'

Before Richard had time to protest, she burst into tears.

'You're too easy, that's what it is,' she said. 'You don't know what he's like, you let him impose on you. Anybody else can see it, but you can't. That's all right by me,' she went on, 'but I'm not staying. I give in my notice from today, and I don't want my wages neither.'

'I should think not,' said Richard, with all the dignity he could muster.

'You may say that, but you won't find many as will work for you as faithfully as I've done. Yes,' she added darkly, 'and put up with as much as I've done. Others can see it, even if you can't. I've done my best for you, sir, honest I have. And you've been good to me, I don't deny that. But I'm fed up and I'm not coming back.'

Her tears started afresh.

'Very well, Mrs. Cuddesdon,' said Richard, repressively, 'if you want it like that. You realize you will put me to great inconvenience by leaving so suddenly. I shall be quite alone, with no one to look after me, and I'm not very well. I think you might have shown more consideration.'

Mrs. Cuddesdon's eyes blazed.

'Consideration, indeed! I should think I'd shown enough consideration, staying on here with this . . . this . . . well, I don't know what to call him. You won't find anyone to look after you as I have – and then, on top of it all, to be insulted.'

By now Mrs. Cuddesdon was quite beside herself, and Richard realized that it would be imprudent, as well as futile, to exacerbate her further.

'The only thing, then, is to say good-bye,' he said, more coldly than he meant to.

Through streaming eyes she looked at every object in the little kitchen, but not at him.

'Good-bye, sir,' she sobbed at last, 'and . . . and . . . take care of yourself.'

'There's no one else to take care of me,' he said.

He left her, her shoulders still heaving, and went into the sitting-room where he sat for some time with the morning paper in his hands, motionless and dazed. Presently he heard the catch of the outside door click softly, and knew that Mrs. Cuddesdon had been as good as her word.

8

But her prophecy was not fulfilled, for within three days one of the porters of the block of flats – converted houses they were really – in which Richard lived, had found him a replacement.

Mrs. Stonegappe was even smaller than her predecessor, and, unlike her, blunt of speech. She found, or professed to find, a lot of things wrong that Richard had not noticed or known about during Mrs. Cuddesdon's régime. Dirt everywhere, for instance; and pushed to the back of shelves and cupboards a variety of broken cups, saucers, plates and jugs, nearly always with the vital piece on which their re-integration depended, missing. One by one, inexorably, she held up these dismal fragments to Richard's view. As bad luck would have it, they were all objects that Richard had specially cherished – not particularly valuable but quite irreplaceable. Then he was shown, on surfaces which had always looked to him quite clean, layers of dust so thick that Keats might have written his name in them and been assured of immortality. And there were other, much worse things, including a black beetle which had been living at ease in the cupboard under the sink. 'If *they* had seen this,' said Mrs. Stonegappe darkly, extending her finger towards the crushed corpse, but without touching it, 'they might have asked you to leave. They don't like this kind of thing, you know, and you can't blame them.' Richard, who was easily frightened, had visions of himself being evicted from the flat with nowhere to go.

But in some ways he wasn't altogether sorry that Mrs. Stonegappe had found so much to criticize in her predecessor's work, for his conscience was far from clear about Mrs. Cuddesdon, and the abrupt and brutal ending to their long and happy association. Her giving notice took him by surprise, and he felt he had treated her badly. Yet what else should he have done? Apart from vindicating the Moral Law, he wanted to stop her listening in to his conversations on the telephone, and his other conversations too; from the hints she had thrown out he suspected she had overheard a good deal of what he and Denys said to each other. She was a dangerous woman. Her counter-accusation against Denys he discounted; it was just what she might be expected to say: no member of her class could bear to admit themselves in the wrong. Yes, he was well rid of her; she had deceived him all along.

More than ever did he feel that Denys had a genuine grievance: more and more anxiously did he watch the post and listen to the telephone for news that might herald Denys's return. Mrs. Cuddesdon he could replace, but Denys never.

Inevitably, in his loneliness, he turned more and more to Lucilla, and it was she, though Richard didn't realize it, who made Denys's absence somehow more tolerable than it would have been. For one thing she always said he would come back. She didn't really like Denys, of that Richard was pretty sure; but she was nice about him, and nicer now that he had gone. For that she held herself to blame, she said; how stupid of her, those few words on the telephone which had given Mrs. Cuddesdon her chance to make mischief! Denys was essential to Richard's happiness, she said; he himself must realize that, and come back to where his duty, and happiness, and advantage lay. Sooner or later, but probably sooner, he would turn up, like the Prodigal Son, and Richard must be sure to prepare for him the Fatted Calf. 'Remember he is so young,' she said, a little wistfully, 'and young people are rash. I never was, because of the way I was brought up, and from what you tell me, I gather you weren't either. But we are exceptions. It's natural for young people to fly off the handle, or whatever the phrase is. Really one ought to like them the better for it.' And when Richard told her how wounded he had been by Denys's behaviour 'going off like that without a word of warning, and my health isn't quite a hundred per cent, as he well knows, and then that rather casual note – because in one way and another I've done quite a lot for him – and then not letting me know where he is, or seeming to bother about me – it is rather much, don't you think? And then, as you know, I lost my daily help on his account – it wasn't his fault, I admit, but I had to do something about it – her listening in on the telephone, I mean—'

'You're sure she did listen in?' Lucilla said.

Richard remembered Mrs. Cuddesdon's counter-charge, but he suppressed it.

'Well, who else could have? By telling him, she paid off an old score, because she didn't like him, but it did leave me in a hole.'

'Until he comes back,' Lucilla said, 'please treat my flat as yours. There'll always be a meal here ready for you, and if—' She stopped.

'You have done far too much for me as it is,' said Richard. 'What could you do more?'

'I meant to say that if at any time you weren't feeling too well, you only have to ring me up and I'll come straight round. You wouldn't mind that, would you? I haven't had much experience of life, but I've had a lot of experience of' – she thought for the word – 'illness. Whatever my table-manners are like, I've quite a good bedside-manner.'

Richard laughed.

'I'm sure you have,' he said, 'and I shan't hesitate to call you in.'

He didn't have to call her in, however, because a few days later Denys came back. He had been away exactly a week.

He didn't write or ring up to announce his arrival: he just walked in.

It was half-past eleven in the morning, and Richard was having his elevenses. They were alcoholic, which was not what the doctor ordered, but since Denys's defection he had felt the need of something to carry him through the mornings. The doctor said he had a better chance if he tried to live; but with Denys gone, what was he keeping himself alive for, anyhow?

Denys was standing in the doorway.

'Good morning, Denys,' Richard said. 'This is a surprise.' As Denys's baby-face remained blank, he added, putting all the warmth he could into it, 'a very pleasant surprise.' And he got up and shook hands with the prodigal.

For a moment Denys was silent, then he said:

'I came back to see how you were getting on.'

'Oh,' said Richard, chilled by this. 'I'm getting on all right, thank you. But I hoped you had come back for good.'

'I wanted to talk to you about that,' said Denys, in a flat voice – a dead-pan voice Richard might have called it, had he known the phrase.

'Sit down,' said Richard, 'and make yourself comfortable. That's your chair, you know,' pointing to the one that Denys had occupied on and off for three years.

Denys let his long body slide into the chair and pulled out his gold cigarette-case.

'I hoped you had come back for good,' Richard repeated, as steadily as he could.

'Well, I have come back for good,' said Denys. 'I mean it was good of me to come back, don't you think so?'

Richard had to stifle an uprush of resentment. He was too glad to see Denys on any terms to risk quarrelling with him.

'Well, perhaps it was,' he conceded. 'Though I still don't quite understand why you left so suddenly.'

'You read my note, didn't you?' said Denys.

Richard said he had.

'Then you must know why I went away. I don't like

being spied on, and I don't like having my affairs discussed with other people.'

Richard was overcome with guilt, but tried to defend himself.

'My dear fellow,' he said, 'I don't know what Mrs. Cuddesdon may have told you, but I'm sure that whatever it was, it was a monstrous exaggeration.'

'What did she say, exactly?' Denys asked.

Richard was flummoxed, all the more so because he couldn't remember *what* Lucilla had said. In itself it was nothing, he was certain: just the crest of the iceberg – but below it trailed all that stuff about Denys not being a real Aspin. What *did* it matter if he wasn't? – yet how could he say to Denys, 'Miss Distington thinks you are an impostor'? It would have been easier to accuse him of murder.

'What did she say, exactly?' Denys repeated.

'Oh, Denys, it was absolutely *nothing*, just that your name was mentioned. One *has* to mention names, doesn't one, or conversation would be impossible. I'm sure you sometimes mention mine.'

'Yes,' said Denys, 'but there's this difference. When I mention your name, Richard, I do it – if I may say so – *affectionately*. I gathered from Mrs. Cuddesdon that when you mentioned my name to Miss Distington, or when she mentioned it to you – or when you both mentioned it together! – you didn't do so with affection.'

Terribly distressed Richard tried to keep his end up.

'My dear Denys, we didn't say *anything* that you could possibly have minded hearing. I don't know what Mrs.

Cuddesdon may have told you, of course, and now we can't ask her.'

'Why not?'

'Because she's gone.'

A running frieze of expressions, impossible to interpret, flitted over Denys's face.

'Why did she go?'

It's no use hedging any longer, Richard thought.

'She went because I taxed her with telling you about, well . . . all this that we've been discussing.'

'And what did she say?' asked Denys, lightly.

Richard took a breath long enough to blow away any other thoughts he might have had, and said with all the firmness he could muster,

'She had nothing to say, of course. But she took umbrage, Denys, you know how people of that sort do. They can't bear to be found out, and they can't admit they're in the wrong. So she marched off, then and there, hoping I suppose to put me to inconvenience, as she well might have, seeing how hard it is to get hold of daily women.'

'What an odd way of putting it,' said Denys, looking more relaxed.

'You know what I mean, though you thought once, and I thought too, that she had a slight *tendresse* for me. What nonsense, at our ages.'

Denys's next remark made Richard colour.

'I don't suppose one's ever too old for that,' he said.

'But anyhow she's gone.'

'So how have you been managing?'

95

'Oh, not too badly. Jimmie, the porter, found me some-one else. Such a nice woman. Mrs. Stonegappe, she's called.'

Richard couldn't tell whether Denys was pleased by this news, or not.

'What an odd name. But I expect she'll turn out to be just like the other one.'

'Well no, because she's deaf.'

'That's something in her favour *re* the telephone, but in any case you won't need me.'

'My *dear* Denys!'

'You say that,' said Denys sombrely, 'but I don't think you mean it. Talking of *meaning*, Miss Distington means more to you than I do.'

'Oh, Denys!'

'She does. And if I come back, *if* I come back, I should like to think you won't see so much of her.'

Richard stiffened.

'I'm afraid I can't promise you that, Denys. Lucilla has been very kind to me, especially during this last week, while you were away. I don't take exception to any of your friendships, and I don't think you should take exception to mine.'

'Then you don't want me to come back?' Denys said.

'Of course I want you to come back, but on the old terms – that you have your friends, and I have mine.'

Denys thought for a moment.

'It isn't as simple, or as fair, as you want it to sound. None of my friends dislike you – they hardly know you. You've never been very welcoming to them, have you? Whereas Miss Distington does dislike me, I'm sure of it.'

'Why are you sure?'

'From what Mrs. Cuddesdon told me.'

'Oh, Denys, all that is such nonsense. The wretched woman, she just lives for gossip. That and the telly are her two main interests – and her pay-packet, of course. If I'd listened to everything she said – well, I shouldn't have a friend left in the world.'

'That means she said something against me, I suppose,' said Denys.

Richard tried to parry this.

'Well, nobody escaped. She thought it made her interesting, you know, running people down. But anyhow why worry about it? She's gone, now.'

'And I've gone, too,' said Denys.

'I hoped you were coming back.'

'I wanted to, but there's such a feeling of suspicion and mistrust here now – what *they* call an "atmosphere". I don't like it. Once you trusted me absolutely – now you don't.'

'Of course I trust you, Denys.'

'Then why don't you offer me a drink? You're drinking yourself, although the doctor told you not to.'

He always puts me in the wrong, thought Richard.

'My dear chap, I'm sorry. In the surprise of seeing you, I forgot. Help yourself, you know where everything is.'

Denys knelt down by the cupboard which contained the drinks. There was a sound like a dog scratching for admittance, and then he slowly rose.

'I can't open the door – you must have locked it.'

Again Richard felt caught out.

'Oh, so I have, it was after what you told me about Mrs. Cuddesdon and her dram at breakfast. And you were quite right; after that I noticed the whisky disappearing, and I took your tip and marked the bottle, not right-side up, they're sure to spot that, but at the level of the whisky when it's upside down – they don't suspect that. So now I lock the cupboard, whenever I remember to, though I'm sure Mrs. Stonegappe doesn't take it, and sometimes I lose the key, which is a nuisance. Where is it now?' After some searching Richard produced it from a pocket, and handed it to Denys. 'And by the way,' he added, 'how did you get in?'

'Get in?' said Denys, on his knees again. 'How do you mean, get in?'

'I meant, get into the flat.'

'I had the key,' said Denys, slowly straightening himself, bottle in hand. 'I don't lose keys. Why, do you think I ought to have returned it?'

'Not if you were coming back. And you had the car-keys, too.'

'Yes, I forgot about them, I admit. I left in such a hurry. You don't know what it is to act on impulse, do you? I was hurt, I saw red and so I buggered off, if you will pardon the expression.'

'In my car?'

'Well yes, it was handy, and I knew you couldn't drive it, so I didn't think you'd grudge it me.'

'Not if you were coming back. Did you come back in it?'

Denys took a hasty look round the room, as if seeking inspiration.

'Well, not to tell a lie, I did. You see, taxis are very expensive and I am so hard up. You don't mind, do you? I wasn't depriving you of anything. I wouldn't have done that, of course.'

'You deprived me of yourself,' said Richard, beginning to feel he was more in control of the situation. 'But have you been using the car in the meantime? I haven't been out much, but one of the porters told me he couldn't see it in the Square.'

'I took it out once or twice so that the battery shouldn't run down, you know. That was for your sake more than mine. It doesn't do to leave a car too long unused, especially in winter-time. All sorts of things might happen to it – it might get frozen up.'

Richard knew that he knew nothing about cars, and would never learn; he didn't know much about Denys, after all these years; but he had learned something.

'What do you intend to do now?' he asked.

'Now, this minute?'

'No, in the immediate future.'

'You make things so difficult for me,' said Denys, sipping his whisky. 'To begin with, I don't like other people knowing my business—'

'Your business?' said Richard. 'I didn't know you had any.'

'Well, in a sort of way I have,' said Denys, 'here, with you, and a good many people know about it – more than you would think.'

'You mean they know that I am your employer?'

'That – and other things.'

99

'What else is there? Our relationship is perfectly correct.'

'I know, but sometimes you look at me in a funny sort of way, and people think—'

'What people?'

'Oh, just people. People in the Square, for instance. They see us going about together, and they think—'

'Oh, *let* them think!' cried Richard, 'if they *can* think, which I doubt.'

'It's all right for you,' retorted Denys, 'but I have all my life before me.'

'Don't be too sure,' said Richard. 'I might outlive you yet.' But he didn't like the turn the conversation had taken, and to change it, said: 'I can't understand why you're so hard up, Denys. Only a little while ago I gave you—'

'I know you did, but I have to keep my end up, and any little dinner costs a fiver.'

'Not for one, surely?'

'I didn't say for one.'

Richard didn't follow up the subject of Denys's little dinners. He said:

'Is that why you came back?'

'Why I came back?' repeated Denys. 'I don't follow you.'

'I meant, to strengthen your financial situation.'

'I haven't come back,' said Denys. 'What makes you think I have?'

Richard was not prepared for this, and his idea of Denys as the Prodigal Son was rudely shaken. What an anti-climax, if the Prodigal Son had turned on his heel and refused the Fatted Calf! He had convinced himself that Denys had come back with his tail between his legs. This vision of a 'tails-up' Denys was most disquieting. It called his bluff. It conflicted with, if it did not destroy, his vision of the situation restored to what it had been, with Denys a gay, faithful, affectionate companion, who would see him through to the end, which might happen at any time. The courage, coming from he knew not where, that had carried him over the week of Denys's absence and might have carried him further had Denys not come back, suddenly failed him, sapped by the vision of what might have been. He could have faced his loss; he couldn't face the disappointment of having his loss made up and then repeated. The prospect of a Denys-less future – 'I thought you had come back,' he lamely said. 'Of course it's up to you.'

Denys shrugged his shoulders, one of which was higher than the other. In times past this had seemed a distressing physical defect among Denys's other perfections; now it seemed a blemish to be regarded with affection.

'All right, then, I will,' said Denys, as one who yields a point with a good grace. 'But you'll remember what I told you, won't you?'

'You said so much,' said Richard with a flash of spirit. 'I can't remember everything.'

'Well, the general gist. And you don't mind me taking your car to bring my things back?'

In imagination Richard saw Denys's room re-occupied, with his clothes and his personal effects, which were pitifully small, littering chairs and tables.

'Very well,' he said. 'Anything to re-charge the battery. No symbolism intended.'

'See you again soon, then,' said Denys and got up and left, with more alacrity than was usual with him.

Richard remained in his chair, nor did he leave it until, an hour or so later, he heard the outside door open, and the heavy, irregular footsteps of someone weighted down with luggage. Then from the bedroom beyond his came the muffled thuds and softer thumps of things being put back in their accustomed places. How sweetly sounded on his ear these proofs of Denys's return! And later, when, nearer at hand, the bathroom became vocal with re-occupation, what pleasure was his! At last the *status quo* had been restored. Richard could wait no longer, and knocked at Denys's door.

'Come in!'

Richard went in and the sight of the familiar room, just as it used to be and with Denys in it, almost made him weep. Indeed it wasn't till then that he realized how much he had missed Denys.

'You young rascal!' he said, suddenly betrayed into effusiveness. 'I'm glad to see you back!'

9

'*What* a good thing,' said Lucilla, when next Richard dined with her. 'So all's well that ends well?'

The note of interrogation was still lingering in the air when Richard answered: 'Oh yes, I think so. I fancy he's learned his lesson. He won't do it another time.'

'I should hope not,' Lucilla said, with more warmth than she intended. 'I mean, it was too inconsiderate, his going off like that. He might at least have warned you.'

Richard rose, though he did not spring, to Denys's defence.

'Oh, the young, you know, they see things so differently from us. From me, I should say,' he corrected himself, with a glance at Lucilla, who at that moment, whether from art or nature, looked surprisingly young. 'I don't think they recognize the word "ought". They follow their natures, and obey the impulse of the moment. I couldn't do that, nor I expect could you, though you're so much younger than I am. But isn't it perhaps better to behave so, in accordance with your nature, than act a kind of part, which may take in other people, and yourself, giving yourself, and them, the idea that you are different from what you really are?'

'I should have to think about that,' Lucilla said, 'and I rather mistrust generalizations about the young – often they don't have much in common except youth.'

'They're honest at least – you know where you are with them.'

'You may know where *you* are,' said Lucilla mildly, 'but you didn't know where Denys was, did you?'

'No,' Richard confessed.

'He didn't tell you *why* he went away?'

Oh dear, thought Richard, honesty belongs to the young, not to the old. I needn't tell Lucilla everything.

'It was because of something the daily woman told him,' he said. 'You know they're terrible mischief-makers, they haven't anything else to think about. She told him something, and he, being young and touchy, just walked out.'

'And then *she* walked out?'

'Yes, because I taxed her with it. Perhaps I ought not to have (excuse the "ought"!) but I wanted to get to the bottom of it.'

'And did you?'

How far need an old person, a dotard you might say, be honest, truthful?

'Well, not quite. He felt he'd been insulted, that was it. He said the daily woman, Mrs. Cuddesdon, was a nosey sort, if you know what I mean. She used to read my letters too, apparently, and when he caught her at it, all she said was "How can I keep up to date unless I do?"'

Lucilla sighed. 'How lucky I am to have darling Nellie, who has been with us for twenty-five years. She's so fond of you, Richard; she doesn't really like London – it frightens her, she says, but she always cheers up when she hears you're coming.'

'Not more than I do, when I know I'm coming.'

'Ah,' said Lucilla, 'but you have Denys again now, I am so glad of that.'

If she had said, 'I am so sorry for that,' Richard would have thought she was being hard on Denys. But her sympathy made him wonder if Denys was such a great asset, after all.

'Of course I do depend on him,' he said, 'he's, well, a familiar friend, and without him I am rather stuck, I realized how much last week, while he was – wherever he was. He knows my ways, and I know his – at least I used to think so. But how difficult life is, Lucilla, if it depends on other people!'

Lucilla thought for a moment.

'I suppose it has to,' she said.

'Well yes, it has. One can't be absolutely independent, can one? Certainly an elderly bachelor can't be. It's easier, in some ways, for a woman.'

She didn't answer at once, Richard felt it had been a flat-footed remark, unworthy of a retired novelist who was supposed to know about human nature, and they talked of other things.

When the acute joy of Denys's return had worn off, their old relationship was renewed, but, Richard felt, at a lower level. A question-mark hung over it. At one time he had always wanted to confide in Denys; now he didn't always want to, the area of uncertainty was so large. Where was the bull's-eye, the real heart of Denys, at which his confidences had been aimed? Not at the scion of the ancient house of Aspin, for seemingly Denys wasn't one: nor at the blank, the nothing of a week or two ago when, apparently, he hadn't been anywhere. Now Richard could see him in the flesh, as large as life but only half as natural as he had been for three years. Often Richard caught himself on the point of telling Denys something, and then not telling him, because it didn't seem to be quite worth while. But there was no one else to tell it to, no one, except possibly Lucilla – and with Lucilla he still had to edit what he said, thinking, will it interest her? Will it amuse her? Will it bore her? – in deference to the usages of London life, to which, though she was a newcomer to it, Lucilla, in his mind, belonged.

To live in the memory of past associations would need Proust's passion for the past. But how compare, in magnetic attraction, a girl drowned in Fen-water with a madeleine dipped in tea?

Every now and then he wished his old friends wanted him; but it wasn't an urgent feeling. He had Denys, who meant less to him than he had once, he had Lucilla, who meant more. How lucky he was, compared with most men of his age, who hadn't anyone who meant much to them or anyone to whom they meant much. And he had his reputation as a novelist, a reputation of many years ago, a tattered cloak, but he could still wear it to keep out some of the winds of change.

Meanwhile he must try to find again in Denys the companion of former days, and this shouldn't be difficult if each of them showed regret; Richard for giving offence, and Denys for taking it. There must be the interchange of self-sacrifice essential to the marriage of true minds.

What could Richard give up? Lent was not in season, and Christmas, which was not far off, was not an occasion for self-denial, for him or for anyone else. Rather the opposite. Still one's private abstentions were dependent on the spirit of Christianity, not dictated by the feasts of the Church. He could give up expecting Denys to spend his evenings, or even his nights, at the flat. He had done that before, sometimes rather grudgingly. Should he give Denys *carte blanche* to stay away as long as he liked? He didn't want to – Denys was, in a way, his nurse. Did one give one's nurse leave to stay away as long as she liked? Most nurses would welcome that arrangement, but it wouldn't be realistic; even in these days people ought to do something of what they were paid to do – unless the word 'ought' had really become archaic, corresponding to none of the processes of the modern mind.

It was no use denying himself something, impersonally, for the good of his soul, which indeed would be for the good of his health, and therefore a self-regarding action. He must give up some obligation in which Denys was involved.

This was much harder, for Denys owed him a great deal besides money. Affection, love, and all that went with that. Should he disregard them, and treat Denys as an electronic operator, devoid of any feelings which could be exercised towards him, Richard, in the flat?

But those feelings, with their attendant actions, were just what he had engaged Denys for – to make the rest of his life, which might end at any moment, bearable and even interesting, on a human plane. To forgo them would be a complete abdication of himself as a person, and he might almost as well be dead.

There was one thing he wouldn't give up, and that was Lucilla. When he thought he might have to choose between Denys and Lucilla, his mind refused to work and he got up and walked about the room until he calmed down.

What Denys might give up, wasn't for him to say. As Lucilla had told him, one couldn't make generalizations about the young – but one thing he felt sure of, they didn't and couldn't be expected to see life in terms of self-sacrifice. Self-sacrifice was for the old; it was much easier for them; it was almost a condition of their existence – their rather useless existence. Self-sacrifice is compatible with looking backwards, not with looking forwards. Perhaps he ought not to expect – even for the renewal of their friendship – self-sacrifice of any sort from Denys. A friend of Richard's, a professor of moral philosophy, had told him that in brief the rule of ethics was, that one could only wish for oneself to be good, and for other people to be happy.

It did seem rather unfair.

For a few days Richard and Denys got on well enough. They seemed to be settling down into their old ways. If Denys stayed out all night, Richard made no remark and if Richard lunched or dined with Lucilla, or, as more rarely happened, she lunched or dined with him, Denys made no comment, either.

It was over Mrs. Stonegappe that the trouble started. Richard had introduced her to Denys with due formality, and they appeared to take to each other. But presently Richard noticed a cloud – a counterpart of the fog outside – obscure rather than darken Mrs. Stonegappe's features. Her lips tightened. From showing a slight tendency to mother Richard, which he had taken in good part, since it involved no toe-brushing, or other signs of physical encroachment, she began to hold herself aloof. Her customary parting salutation – 'See you again tomorrow' – suddenly ceased. This he did mind, for though he was not aware of nuances of behaviour, and in his novels had invented rather than observed them, he was sharply aware of any current of feeling. Had something upset Mrs. Stonegappe? And if so, was it his fault? He was quite abnormally worried by the thought that something might be his fault. Was it something he had said or done? He would have liked to question Mrs. Stonegappe about it, but her compressed lips and hardening eyes offered him no encouragement.

'Oh dear,' he thought, 'these people! Their ways are past finding out.'

It was Denys who first enlightened him. Lucilla's revelation, if it had been one, had troubled his vision of Denys, the down-at-heel aristocrat, without substituting another for it; his ageing, unadaptable mind couldn't find a satisfactory image for the present Denys. Nor, apparently, could Mrs. Stonegappe. She treated him, he complained, as a 'half-sir', without the usefulness of a servant or the dignity of an employer. Worse than that, he complained that she was an expert and persistent pilferer. If he and Richard went away for the week-end, as they sometimes did, to stay at an hotel by the seaside, or if he went away alone, as he put it for a break, he came back to find the fridge had been rifled and there was nothing left to eat. Worse still, when Mrs. Stonegappe ordered the groceries, as she did if Denys happened to be away, she would order on his account, but for herself, a whole lot of eatables and packets of cigarettes, too, for she was a heavy smoker, as Richard must have noticed. Mrs. Cuddesdon might have listened in to the telephone, but at any rate she hadn't robbed him.

Richard didn't know what to do. Since his illness, his natural lethargy had grown upon him. Always, throughout his life, he had had to do by force of will what other people did by impulse or inclination: he dared not relax his hold upon himself for fear of becoming absolutely static. He didn't need his mother to tell him that will-power would be useful to him in after life. Now that he had no after life in prospect he had let himself go; why make the effort to wrestle with practical affairs when Denys was there to make it for him?

All the same, he didn't want to get rid of Mrs. Stonegappe. Domestic help was hard to find, and though the burden of this would fall on Denys, Richard would have to share it, take up references, be present at interviews, and in the end, *decide*, a thing he found more and more difficult. He hadn't asked Mrs. Stonegappe for a reference, and this was the result – or was it? If they came 'out of the pocket' references were notoriously misleading;

probably they were composed by the applicants them-selves. The only safe way was to ring up the employers, who might or might not tell the truth, according as to whether they feared the law of slander or thought the tele-phone might be tapped by an eavesdropper. Come to that, he hadn't had a reference with Denys: but Denys was quite different; he was a companion and a friend, and a member of the ancient house of Aspin – or so he said. They had met at a party – a quite respectable party – and had taken to each other at once, and had then and there agreed to throw in their lot together. If their relationship had dete-riorated during the past weeks, the fault might be his as much as Denys's. Yet he couldn't quite forgive Denys's defection, even if he didn't take such a dim view of it as Lucilla and the two or three friends who still came to see him took. Lucilla had been quite indignant on his behalf until he showed her, by the excuses he found for Denys, that her indignation was misplaced. Then she accepted his attitude to the episode, or seemed to, for she never disagreed with him for long. He could not disguise from himself that the occasion of Denys's return had been one of his happi-est moments of his later life.

Yet he didn't want to oblige Denys by getting rid of Mrs. Stonegappe, in spite of the depredations which she, in common with others of her kind, was alleged to commit. He only had Denys's word for it, and the evidence of the empty fridge. He didn't doubt Denys's word, but there were other people who came into the flat besides Mrs. Stonegappe, window-cleaners, electricians, gas-men, the head porter, who had a key. Need he pin the thefts on her? If he sacked her it would get round among the porters – the whole square was a whispering gallery, buzzing with gossip: the place might get a bad name, and potential dailies, always a sparse tribe, might give it a wide berth and where would he be then, where would Denys be, for that matter? Denys wouldn't take kindly to making his own bed, or Richard's – and as for 'doing' the flat!

Meanwhile the atmosphere of suspicion and mistrust thickened, faces were long and set, and Richard would wake up in the morning with a feeling of oppression, as if something disagreeable was going to happen. The smog outside was not nearly as poisonous as the smog inside. If only Richard had had some compelling, over-riding interest to put this really trifling discomfort in its true proportion! But he hadn't; he couldn't brush it aside, age and circumstances compelled him to play a waiting game.

It had been bad enough to accuse Mrs. Cuddesdon of eavesdropping; it would be much worse to accuse Mrs. Stonegappe of stealing. It was unthinkable; the words simply wouldn't pass his lips. Besides, he liked her. He realized that the tightened mouth, the hard eyes, the altered manner, were not aimed at him. Justice was justice, the most important thing still left in the world – if it was still left. But the air *must* be cleared.

One evening Denys said to him, with an exaggeration of his languid manner, 'You know, Richard, I can't go on if Mrs. Stonegappe stays here. She hates my guts, and to tell you the truth I hate hers, if she has any, and I think she must have, considering the amount of time she spends in the loo. Much longer than she does dusting or carpet-sweeping, or whatever she's supposed to do. Besides, she's a thief. Our household bills have been up by two or three pounds a week since she came. You may not mind that, but I do, and what's more, I won't be implicated in it, I tell you straight.'

'Do you mean I shall have to choose between you and her?' asked Richard.

'It might come to that. See you again soon,' said Denys, and without giving Richard time to answer he rose and hurried out.

10

It was then that Richard began to feel the need of his old friends. Where were they, and why didn't they come to see him? For three years he hadn't missed them much. Denys gave him everything he wanted, above all what he wanted most and most felt the lack of – the opportunity to give. Had he had anything to give besides himself when he knew Lucy, he would have given it to her. His nature demanded it then, this pouring out of all he had; it had never demanded it since, till he met Denys. Denys's givability was his great attraction; it was a passport to felicity, renewable with every gift. Richard wasn't aware of wanting an exchange, for Denys was himself the exchange. With his friends he exchanged presents, but there was little emotional release in them: he had to think what they would like, just as they had to think what he would like. He was glad if his presents pleased them, disappointed if they didn't; but no spiritual outgoing took place on either side; they were just tokens of friendship. On the material plane, most of his friends had everything they wanted, just as he, Richard, had most things that he wanted. It wasn't really possible for him to confer a benefit on them, or they on him, except as an expression of good-will – a formality almost.

Whereas everything was grist to Denys's mill – a cheque was enough to make him happy – if not as happy as it made him, Richard.

His friends were not bound to him by presents, they were bound by other, more intangible ties, and it was only now that he asked himself why he valued them, and what had occurred to loosen them. Alternative or allied answers stared him in the face. Either his friends recognized his absorption in Denys, and left him alone to enjoy it; or they recognized but didn't like it, and therefore left him alone: it came to the same thing. Not one of them had made any comment; not one of them had told him he might not have chosen the best way of being happy. Why should they? His mother or his father would have told him soon enough; Aunt Carrie might have suggested something, as she had once before, when he was too far gone with Lucy to take heed. But now he was too old to be scolded or even advised. They had only one course, to withdraw: and they withdrew.

He still had one friend left in whom he could confide – and she was a comparatively recent friend. To Lucilla he told, as lightly and ironically as he could, the story of his domestic troubles.

'It seems so childish to complain of them,' he said, 'when practically nobody has them, domestics, I mean, not domestic troubles – but you can't have one without the other. You see, Lucilla, I do want to make people happy. It isn't an affectation when I say so. But as soon as they realize this – or so it seems to me – they want to take advantage of it, and at my expense, in more ways than one. If I could be a martinet, a proper disciplinarian, I think they would like it better. But I can't be.'

'When you say "they",' Lucilla asked, 'do you include Mr. Aspin? He isn't exactly a servant, is he?'

Richard didn't like this question.

'Well no,' he said, 'he isn't of course. I employ him, but he's a friend. I meant Mrs. Cuddesdon and Mrs. Stonegappe. Mrs. Cuddesdon didn't, and Mrs. Stonegappe doesn't, like him. Why, I don't know, except that he's a gentleman and therefore not of their class.'

'Mrs. Cuddesdon said it was he who listened in to the telephone,' Lucilla reminded him.

'Yes, but not until I had taxed her with doing it. You know what those people are – they cannot admit they are in the wrong, or they lose face, and, among each other, never hear the last of it. They *have* to be in the right. You couldn't expect Mrs. Cuddesdon or Mrs. Stonegappe to admit they weren't.'

'But you haven't asked Mrs. Stonegappe whether she has taken things, have you?'

'No, I haven't, Lucilla. I can't bring myself to. But I suppose I shall have to, or Denys will be walking out again.'

Lucilla was silent for a moment: then she said:

'Does Mrs. Stonegappe know that you suspect her?'

'I think she must,' said Richard. 'Otherwise, why should she be in such a black mood all the time? She never smiles and hardly ever speaks – she's been a different woman since Denys came back. I feel sure she has tumbled to it that he knows and has told me.'

'There is another possible explanation.'

'What's that?'

'She might be jealous,' said Lucilla, slowly.

'Jealous? But who of?'

Lucilla gave him a long look.

'Of Denys, I suppose.'

'Of Denys, but why?'

'Because of his friendship with you.'

Richard stared at her. The idea that he could occasion jealousy in any breast was so new to him that he didn't know what to make of it. As an ex-novelist, of course, he knew about the passions, and not altogether at second-hand: he could still remember what it felt like to hold Lucy in his arms, and perhaps the most operative part of his life had been spent in two contradictory efforts – to recover, and to root out, that feeling. But jealousy, no. Experience had never put jealousy in his way. Denys had had his nights out, and his week away; but Richard hadn't felt jealous – he had put it all down to Denys's youth and need to be amused. His behaviour had been inconvenient and inconsiderate but, good heavens! It hadn't hatched the green-eyed monster. Moreover, Richard disapproved so much of jealousy – that most destructive and unrewarding of emotions – that he didn't feel he could ever be guilty of it. And as for being the cause of it, that too was unthinkable. Poor old Richard, with one foot in the grave! It was almost indecent. Jealousy, he had nearly forgotten there was such a thing. And to put Mrs Stonegappe in the same class with Othello!

Out of the mists of his bewilderment, he said,

repeating his thoughts aloud, 'But, Lucilla, how could I make anybody jealous?'

She replied with a gulp: 'You underrate yourself. You are too modest.' And to his amazement and horror he saw tears filling her eyes. Presently they dried; and Richard was able to attribute Lucilla's momentary lapse to one of those unaccountable gusts of feeling to which women are subject.

Afterwards she applied herself wholeheartedly to his problem. 'Who orders the food?' she asked. 'You or Denys or Mrs. Stonegappe?'

'Not I,' said Richard, 'it's one of the others.'

'But don't you know which?'

'I suppose it's Denys, as he does the cooking.'

'Really you are hopeless,' said Lucilla with a mock severity of manner that he hadn't noticed in her before. 'I shall have to come and do your housekeeping for you.' She gave him a moment to reply to this, and when he didn't, went on. 'My advice is that you and Denys should make a list every night of all the eatables in the fridge, and the cupboards too, and check it the next morning, when Mrs. Stonegappe's gone.'

'Couldn't Denys do it by himself?' asked Richard, to whom anything in the nature of a list was an abhorrence.

'I suppose he could,' she answered, 'but I think you ought to share it with him, just to satisfy yourself. It takes two people to make an inventory, you know, one may always overlook something. And then if you find that things *are* missing—'

'Yes?' said Richard.

'Then you'll have to speak to Mrs. Stonegappe.'

'If you knew how I hated that!' said Richard.

'I do know, and I think it's a pity that your mother, who wisely told you of so many things that would be useful to you in later life, didn't tell you that sometimes you would have to be disagreeable, for the good of all concerned. But perhaps she did.'

'I'm sure I'm often disagreeable,' Richard said, 'but not often deliberately.'

'Well, this time you must steel yourself, or you may have Denys leaving you for good, which would be a calamity, wouldn't it? I quite understand how he feels. When there are two people, suspicion must fall on both.'

'You don't suspect Denys, do you?' Richard asked.

'No, but I sympathize with his wish to clear himself.'

'Oh dear,' said Richard, 'now you're taking his side.'

'Only,' Lucilla said, 'in this particular instance. I haven't always, have I? I know how valuable he is to you – or should I say, invaluable? You couldn't get on without him, could you?'

'I did, for a week,' said Richard.

'Yes, I know, but you were miserable. No, that's too strong a word, but could you envisage the future without him – I mean, and not feel too depressed?'

Truthfulness had been enjoined on Richard as a child, and he tried to answer truthfully.

'Really, Lucilla, I don't know. You see, I'm not quite well, as I told you, it's nothing much but sometime it might be. So I want to have someone about in case – well – it should get worse. And someone to run the flat, too.'

'I quite see,' Lucilla said, 'how much you count on Mr. Aspin. He was with you, wasn't he, long before I knew you. I can't think he'll leave you, Richard, over such a trifle as a dishonest daily woman – tiresome as it is, and many people besides you have found it so. But whether he's an Aspin or not' – she smiled – 'his future is wrapped up in you, isn't it? For his own sake, and in his own interest, he couldn't be so silly as to throw all that away. Who would he find to look after him as – as lovingly as you do? He's young, I know, but he hasn't been brought up to do anything, has he? Anything money-making. He must know on which side his bread is buttered.'

'He does know,' Richard said, 'only too well.'

'Well, that's a good thing, isn't it? Only don't let's be cynical – you know him so much better than I do – but he is very fond of you, isn't he?'

'I've always thought so, Lucilla, and he's always said so.'

'Then that's all right . . . he couldn't be such a fool . . . but supposing he was – supposing you found yourself without him, what would you do? Would you try to replace him?'

'I should have to have notice of that question,' Richard said. 'Sufficient unto the day—'

Lucilla sighed, and the tension that had crept into their conversation relaxed somewhat. 'I was putting a hypothetical case. It won't ever happen, but if it did, I should like you to feel I was at hand, as a sort of stop-gap, you know, until something better and more permanent turned up.'

For the second time that evening Richard answered Lucilla's words and tried to ignore the feeling behind them.

'If I'm left in the lurch again you may be sure I'll call you in,' he said.

'Is that a promise?' asked Lucilla.

'Of course it is.'

'Then I shall hold you to it.'

After that they talked of other things, but the conversation limped, for Richard was aware of inadequacy and also of insincerity. He wouldn't have given Lucilla the promise if he hadn't been sure that Denys would stay. Still it was partly her fault for cornering him. With some vague idea of making it up to her he lingered longer than usual; trying to modulate their intercourse back into its old key, in which neither demanded more of the other than a friendly exchange of feelings and ideas at an emotional level not far below the surface. As an ex-novelist he could more easily enter into other people's feelings than have them or express them on his own account. Chameleon-like, he took on the colour of his interlocutor's mood and could not show himself in his true colours, for what were they but a reflection of those being offered to him? Whereas with Denys he could play the part of a solo instrument, and hold his own, and more. With Denys he did not feel at a personal disadvantage, as if he was receiving benefits he could not return.

The longing to see Denys increased with the slowly passing minutes; at length he rose to take his leave. But he still felt he owed Lucilla something, some more positive expression of his regard than any he had given her yet; and as he was saying goodbye he leant across, for she was much the same height as he, and kissed her. It was the second kiss he had given her, and, like the first, a token kiss, not like the real kisses he had given Lucy, but its effect must have been real, for she stood still and speechless, and her good night only reached him on the doorstep.

The next morning it was Mrs. Stonegappe who brought Richard his early morning tea. As it was Denys who usually performed this office he was a little disappointed, but not surprised, for when Denys slept late, or spent the night out somewhere, Mrs. Stonegappe did it for him.

She drew the curtains, helped him into his bed-jacket and said:

'I think I ought to tell you, sir, but Mr. Aspin has gone.'

'Gone?' said Richard. 'Gone? But he was here last night.'

'I don't know anything about that, sir, Mr. Aspin's movements are no business of mine. But he's gone now – his room's quite empty. I thought you ought to know, sir.'

'I suppose I should have found out,' said Richard, hardly knowing what he said, 'but thank you all the same.'

He lay back in bed and awaited the symptoms which any emotional shock was liable to produce; when they didn't come he got up and went into Denys's room, not so much to confirm what Mrs. Stonegappe had said as to see and feel for himself. Denys's room was indeed empty, doubly empty, if emptiness could be doubled, for the second loss was more bitter and more depriving than the first. His bed was unmade; sooner or later, no doubt,

Mrs. Stonegappe would make it. How badly he must have slept, for the lower sheet was furrowed like a ploughed field: and the whole room which Denys's presence had animated, and re-animated, resembled its former self as much as a corpse resembles a living body. The drawers pulled open, the sliding doors of the wardrobe thrown back, the writing-table denuded of writing-paper – it looked like the scene of a burglary. And a burglary it was – even if the thief had only stolen himself.

Passing the kitchen, where Mrs. Stonegappe, with averted head, sat smoking her first morning cigarette, he saw through the sitting-room doorway, something white and something gleaming on the end of the oval dining table, which at this hour was usually cleared. Gingerly, with a presentiment of unpleasantness to come, he advanced towards it. The gleam came from a row of keys – he recognized them – the keys of the flat, the keys of the car, the key of the wine-cupboard, sundry other keys which Richard didn't know that Denys had in his possession. The white object was an envelope, and for the first time Richard found himself resenting the fact that Denys always used his writing-paper, and remembered, again with resentment, that Denys had taken away the writing-paper from his bedroom. The keys lay in almost martial array, the envelope beneath them. For a minute Richard hovered round it, yielding to his besetting habit of putting off something disagreeable, afraid too, and annoyed with himself for being afraid, of the shock it might give him. At last he tore open the envelope and read:

Dear Richard,

I am sorry to have walked out like this but it seemed the only thing to do in view of the way you have been behaving to me lately. I suppose it's natural you should prefer Miss Distington's company to mine, but you can't expect me not to feel sore about it, when we have been together so much. Besides that, I've come to think that you don't trust me. I've been with you all these years and yet you take the word of the daily woman against mine – don't tell me you haven't, because if you haven't, why are you keeping her on? I know you listen to what she says about me. And there's another thing, more important, how do you think I can live on this beggarly salary you give me? A common unskilled navvy makes more money than I do – and I have to keep up appearances as well as I can, take friends out to meals, and so on. It may surprise you to hear it, but some of your old friends sometimes ask me out, and I have to ask them back. I know you've given me money from time to time, but I can't count on that, and you seem to have been rather tight-fisted since you met Miss Distington. One or two of your friends have spoken to me about her, and expressed amazement that you should neglect me after all I've done for you, and all the things you have told me that you were afraid to tell anyone else.

So I've no alternative but to look for a better job, and I only hope you'll find somebody to look after you as well as I have. It's no sinecure, I can tell you, dancing attendance on you, though it wasn't so bad before Miss D. came along. I shall be coming round in a day or two to return your suitcase, which I borrowed, and collect some money which I think is owing to me. Till then good-bye and take care of yourself.

Denys.

When Richard's anger at this letter had cooled, he began to think again. Even if Denys had grossly exaggerated his grievances he still had something to complain of. He had been Richard's mainstay for three years, and no doubt, as he said, it was no sinecure. Lucilla had reminded Richard of the power of jealousy in human relationships, suggesting that Mrs. Cuddesdon and Mrs. Stonegappe might both have succumbed to it. Evidently (a thing she had not foreseen) Denys had succumbed to it, too. All this would have been flattering if Richard had had more amour-propre to flatter; lacking that, he merely felt that the three of them were working on his feelings. 'Thank goodness Lucilla isn't jealous,' was his passing thought. 'That would really be the *end*.' Still jealousy was a basic human emotion and Denys was as much entitled to it as anyone else. Indeed, if he hadn't been jealous it might have proved that he had no real affection for Richard. Richard had no patience with a great many of the excuses that people put up for themselves, and had put up for them nowadays; that they were suffering from diminished responsibility, that something came over them, that they didn't know how it happened, but they found they had a knife and had stuck it into somebody. Hurrah, boys, we are all of us human. But jealousy was a classical emotion, as old as the human race, and anyone who was the victim of it had a right to compassion – that misused, misapplied and over-worked word. So he mustn't be as hard on Denys as Denys had been on him. He could honestly say that jealousy didn't enter into his feelings for Denys. Those nights out, whatever they were for, or about, didn't arouse it.

So Denys's behaviour could be put down, mostly, to the 'jealousy account' – a substantial, ancient overdraft on which that part of humanity who wanted to justify them-selves had always drawn. Mostly, but not altogether. There were other charges not so easily disposed of. The incon-siderateness of leaving him, Richard, so suddenly in the lurch without any chance of finding the quick replace-ment which the condition of his health needed, was one; the borrowed suitcase was a trifle, but it irritated; and the suggestion that Denys had been discussing his affairs with some of Richard's friends did more than irritate, it alarmed.

Which of them? Richard wondered. Who was the trai-tor? From love's shining circle the gems drop away, so the old song says. They had dropped away, Richard sometimes suspected, on Denys's account; they didn't like him. How strange it was, and how disquieting, that some of them should have kept up with Denys, listened to him, and gleaned from him things that Richard wanted to keep private, not *one* thing, of course.

Then there was 'the money owing' to Denys. What exactly did that mean? Richard owed him nothing – rather the opposite – for Denys had drawn his salary two days before he left. Richard paid him monthly: was he going to claim for those two days?

Mrs. Stonegappe was in his bedroom, wielding the carpet-sweeper. Tiny as she was, she often contrived to get in his way, and sometimes she literally cornered him with this instrument: back to the walls, imprisoned in an inexorable right angle, he had no escape. Meanwhile, she pushed the carpet-sweeper with vicious thrusts towards him.

Awaiting his release he said:

'Mr. Aspin went away early, didn't he, Mrs. Stonegappe?'

'I don't know anything at all about that,' she replied, almost stubbing his toes with the carpet-sweeper. 'I do know that he was gone when I came at eight o'clock.'

She obviously didn't want to pursue the subject, but Richard couldn't let it drop.

'He didn't say anything about going when I saw him last night.'

'He often did things without saying he was going to do them,' said Mrs. Stonegappe, putting Denys into the past tense. 'The other time he took himself off he didn't tell you he was going to.'

'I know, and it does leave me in rather a hole.'

'Mr. Aspin doesn't mind about that, if you ask me,' Mrs. Stonegappe said.

'Yes, I'm afraid he is rather inconsiderate,' Richard said.

'Inconsiderate isn't the word for it,' said Mrs. Stonegappe, retreating a little and allowing Richard to escape. 'He's just about as selfish as he can breathe.'

'If only he had let me know!' wailed Richard.

'You needn't think you've lost him,' said

Mrs. Stonegappe grimly. 'He'll come back as soon as he wants some money.'

Her words struck a chill, for they reminded him of Denys's letter. How much did Mrs. Stonegappe know? Had she steamed the letter open?

'Mind you,' she said, as if answering his thoughts, 'I don't know anything about him. I never talk to him, never. It's the only way.'

Richard took leave to doubt this, for he had often heard her conversing with Denys, during the *longueurs* of his morning toilet. A sense of loneliness came over him and overcame him; how could he face the empty life ahead?

'Mrs. Stonegappe,' he said, raising his voice above the angry gasps of the carpet-sweeper, 'I don't suppose you could come in now and then and cook me a meal?'

Mrs. Stonegappe's face became utterly expressionless.

'I should like to see you out,' she said – sinister words – 'but of course, like other people, I have myself to consider. I have to look ahead. It might be the thin end of the wedge, you know.'

'Oh well,' said Richard. 'It would depend on you entirely, when you came.'

'I don't deny,' said Mrs. Stonegappe, 'that you have treated me well. There's many a time I've said to myself, "If it wasn't for Mr. Mardick, I shouldn't stay here another minute, I've been that fed up. You wouldn't understand it, sir, but there are things that a person like me can't take. I mention no names. I make no allegations, it's just that. There are things that don't go with flesh and blood, if you take my meaning. But I should like to see you out, sir, and I'll come in sometimes, not in the evenings, of course.'

'Of course not,' Richard said mechanically.

'I have to preserve my leisure, don't you see. And of course not if he's here – but you wouldn't want me then.'

'I don't expect he will be,' Richard said.

'You never know, there's many a bad penny that turns up, and I'll say that for him, he knows which side his bread is buttered. Or if he doesn't, he ought. Well, sir, I'll be off now, or else I shall be to seek, as someone said. But I'll come in tomorrow and cook your lunch. Would a mutton cutlet and a nice rice pudding do?'

'A nice rice pudding would be very nice,' said Richard.

'A gentleman told me that you can't get them in London now, except at the Ritz,' said Mrs. Stonegappe. 'Well, bye-bye, sir, see you again tomorrow. Can't come today, I've promised to look after my daughter's baby, such a sweet little thing, sir, she reminds me a bit of you, she has such taking ways.'

So Richard had to go out for lunch and dinner, which he regarded as a hardship. And the expense! The Brickworks would pay for that; but Richard had enough of his mother in him to deplore an uncalled-for extravagance. He wasn't hungry, but he couldn't do without food, he supposed.

Meanwhile his mind ranged this way and that, seeking some new attitude to Denys, some way of liking or even loving him again. Not to be able to do either was most painful. It was his nature to feel in the wrong, just as it was Denys's to feel in the right – a basic difference between many people. This trait now came to his aid; he could remember many occasions when he had put upon Denys, or taken his services for granted. Perhaps he hadn't welcomed Denys back after his first defection as warmly as he should have. He tried to forget the wounding wording of the letter, natural enough in someone who felt sufficiently aggrieved to leave his home before daybreak.

Meanwhile three letters had come for Denys, one on the day he went away and one on each of the succeeding days. They bore the postmark Stockport and were written in the same handwriting – a handwriting which Richard didn't know. Richard worried about this; he felt he ought to send the letters on but how could he, not knowing where to send them? The fourth day no letter came for Denys – perhaps Denys had given his correspondent a forwarding address – but a letter came for Richard. It was the grocer's bill for the past month and was truly astronomic. A family of six would have been well fed on it, and it would have kept them in cigarettes, too. Richard blinked as he looked at it, and automatically invoked the succour of the Brick-works. Then he remembered Denys saying that Mrs. Stonegappe ordered foodstuffs on his account – I must have it out with her! he thought, but half-way to the kitchen, he changed his mind. Counsels of prudence prevailed. For one thing he couldn't afford, at this juncture, to get rid of Mrs. Stonegappe or even to alienate her, and for another, he must examine the account more closely. He took the bill into his sitting-room and forced himself to scan the separate items. He couldn't imagine Mrs. Stonegappe eating caviare or foie-gras, and though she smoked like a chimney she didn't smoke like a volcano. But what astonished and perturbed him most was a consignment of goods ordered for the 12th December. Consulting his diary – for his mind refused to count the days – he discovered it was the day before Denys went away.

None of this was inconsistent with Mrs. Stonegappe having ordered the goods for her private ends, but it would be an odd coincidence if she had.

He spent the day trying to think out a formula by which he could bring the subject to her notice without upsetting her. In vain. Mrs. Stonegappe was touchy, and never more touchy than where Denys was concerned. She would fly off the handle, she would go up in smoke, if he so much as questioned her about the grocery bill.

And why hadn't Denys shown him the invoices as they came in? True, Richard had never asked him to and Denys never had; partly from laziness, mainly from laziness, he had left all that to Denys. And he remembered that Denys had told him that Mrs. Stonegappe sometimes did the ordering.

The next day came without bringing a solution for him, or a letter for Denys, but it brought something else: a telephone call. The telephone speaking with its own voice, as it were, or at any rate on its own account. And what an account!

A woman's voice said she was speaking for the Telephone Manager. 'He apologizes for troubling you but he would like to know when you intend to pay your telephone account.'

'Oh,' said Richard, 'I'm very sorry but I've never had it.'

'According to our records,' said the voice with a shade of severity, 'the account was sent to you three weeks ago and you have had two reminders since.'

'I've no recollection of seeing them,' said Richard, not feeling on sure ground, for he had a bad habit of not opening envelopes which he didn't like the look of; 'I should have paid if I had. Please tell me what the amount is and I'll send you a cheque at once.'

'A hundred and fifty-four pounds, three shillings and two-pence.'

'What?' cried Richard, aghast.

Inexorably the voice repeated the sum.

'I can't understand it,' said Richard, more to himself than to her. 'I can't understand it.'

'Would you like me to send you another account?'

'Yes, please,' said Richard, and then a thought struck him. 'And can you itemize the account, showing where each separate call was to?'

'We can, but it will take time and there will be an extra charge.'

'I don't mind,' said Richard recklessly, again involving the Brickworks, which this time seemed to turn a deaf ear.

Mrs. Stonegappe had not yet gone and before he had time to turn tail he summoned her.

'Oh, Mrs. Stonegappe, I've had such a large bill from the grocer's, I can't understand it, can you?' and he put it in her hand.

She looked at it expressionlessly.

'Mr. Aspin ordered this lot, I didn't,' she said.

'I didn't think you had,' said Richard, not quite truthfully, 'but where has it all gone? Look, on the 12th the stuff ordered was over nine pounds' worth.'

'That was the day before he went away,' said Mrs. Stonegappe.

'Why, so it was,' said Richard, affecting surprise. 'There's hardly room in the kitchen for all that food. The fridge must be full to bursting.'

Mrs. Stonegappe opened the fridge door.

'Look for yourself,' she said.

The cupboard wasn't quite bare but it was very sparsely furnished.

'All that's there,' she said, 'I ordered, and I don't deny it, for your meals. You've got to live on something. The day he left there wasn't anything, except some cheese that wouldn't tempt a mouse.'

'It's her word against his,' thought Richard, and a fog descended on his spirit, for he would still rather have believed Denys. But the borrowed suitcase – had it been stuffed with groceries, bulging with caviare and foie-gras? If I believe this, he thought, casting his mind away from Denys into the world around, I shall have to believe so many things I don't want to believe. And if it's Denys, it's worse, for Mrs. Stonegappe owes me nothing.

He took the bill back from her.

'Well, I shall have to pay it, I suppose,' he said grudging but resigned. And then he had another idea. It was most distasteful, but better to get it over, while he was on the subject. 'And there's something else,' he said. He didn't mean to sound portentous, but Mrs. Stonegappe who, during her long lifetime, almost as long as his, must have been inured to shocks of one sort and another, raised her eyebrows. 'There's a really' – he sought for an adjective that might impress her – whacking – smashing? no, in these days smashing was a term of praise – some derivative of a four-letter word like effing? – no, better not – 'a really *ghastly* bill for the telephone. I simply can't understand it.' He stopped, mortified to think how much of his conversation, both with Mrs. Stonegappe and himself, turned on things which he didn't understand.

Mrs. Stonegappe stiffened.

'I hope you don't mean—'

Richard cut her short. 'Of course not, Mrs. Stonegappe,' he interrupted her, 'of *course* not. You mustn't think that anything I say is meant personally. I know quite well you *never* use the telephone. That's why I'm so surprised by this . . . this *tremendous* bill—'

'It hasn't anything to do with me,' said Mrs. Stonegappe. 'I never touch the telephone except to dust it. I hate the thing.'

'Oh yes,' said Richard, hastily, 'I quite appreciate that. But someone has been using the telephone in . . . in . . . quite an irresponsible way. I wonder who it can have been?'

'I can guess,' said Mrs. Stonegappe.

'Who?'

'I won't say the name, sir, it wouldn't be lucky. But you know quite well who I mean. He often used the telephone before you was properly awake, sir, and able to look after your own interests. Whether this person used the telephone later in the day I couldn't say, not being there owing to pressure of work. But he knew quite well when you would be in and out, sir, being a gentleman of such regular habits, if I can put it like that.'

'I do have a nap in the afternoon, that's quite true,' Richard said, feeling that that truth, if it ever came to light, ought to be recognized. 'And then I have a little walk if the weather's fine.'

'That's just what I mean, sir, and no doubt he knew it too, and took advantage.'

'I think you may be right,' said Richard, unwillingly. 'And I know he had a good many friends in London – he often went out to see them. But all these long-distance calls, that's what I can't under—' He bit the word off.

'You can't understand, sir?' said Mrs. Stonegappe, finishing it for him. 'Well, if you can't, I can.'

'Tell me, then.'

'He was phoning to his wife.'

'His *wife*?'

'Didn't you know that he was married? Ah, he was a sly one.'

After a long pause, Richard asked:

'How long has he been married?'

'About three months, he told me.'

'He *told* you? But you said you never talked to him.'

'You have to be civil to those you're working with,' Mrs. Stonegappe reproved him. 'I couldn't pretend I didn't hear him, could I? A man will say things to a woman that he wouldn't say to a man – especially if he thought the news wouldn't be welcome, as it wouldn't be to you, sir.'

Richard saw the force of this.

'Perhaps that explains the telephone calls. But what I still don't under— what still puzzles me, is why I never received the original bill, or the reminders.'

Mrs. Stonegappe looked at him pityingly.

'*He* always looked at the letters when they came, sir, before you were up.'

'You mean he saw the bill and the reminders, and destroyed them so that I shouldn't see them?'

Mrs. Stonegappe compressed her lips without speaking.

'And then went off before I could find out?'

Comment was needless, and Mrs. Stonegappe made none.

'He certainly never told me that he was married,' Richard said.

'No, sir, and there were a good many other things he didn't tell you. As I've said before, you're too easy with us, that's what it is. You let yourself be imposed on. I don't suppose you'll see him again unless he wants some money. . . . You must look out for someone else. Now, sir, I've got a nice steak for your lunch.'

But Richard couldn't eat it.

12

'You must look out for someone else,' Mrs. Stonegappe had said, but for the moment Richard didn't try to. Instead he tried to analyse his feelings, and think what he should say to Denys when Denys came to see him.

At first the suspense was almost unbearable, but as the days passed and nothing happened, the acute agitation dwindled to a chronic anxiety which was worse in the early mornings. Some of his senses were sharpened; he could hear the telephone-bell, or the door-bell, or the sharp, startling rap of the letter-box, or the dull murmur of the rising lift, sounds which before hadn't always pierced his consciousness; while things that depended on his mental grasp often eluded him. Had he written this letter? Had he signed that cheque? The gradual process of ripening and decay, before the fruit fell off its tree, which he had expected and accepted, was suddenly disorganized – hastened here, retarded there. These new experiences sometimes made him feel a stranger to himself, and he should have been quite familiar with himself at seventy.

Why, after all, shouldn't a man get married? It was nothing to be ashamed of. Men had always done it, often without consulting their nearest and dearest. If Denys had kept his own counsel, about that and, as Mrs. Stonegappe hinted, about other things, had he, Richard, any right to be angry? He might have got married himself, he had had opportunities – he still had an opportunity and would he have refrained for fear of leaving Denys in the lurch? No, and in his case it would have been a worse betrayal, for he had enough to live on, and Denys hadn't. The fact that it was a hypothetical case – his dreadful experience with Lucy had put marriage, or anything of that kind, for ever beyond the pale – made no difference; he might have done it, so he told himself, without first consulting Denys and Denys would have been left high and dry. Denys had no Brickyard at his back.

But the telephone calls – and there would be more in the coming account – how could *they* be excused? The dishonesty, the calculated cheating, landing him in for hundreds – it was rather much. No Aspin would have done it. But Denys wasn't a real Aspin, he was only a nominal one – at least the signs pointed that way. He came from who knew where? – he might have been a proletarian child, and the proletariat, so Richard had been told, though he couldn't quite believe it, had totally different standards of morality from those of the middle and upper classes. Their standard (if standard it could be called) was that you were entitled to take from anyone what that person could afford to lose. It was very inconvenient at the moment for Richard to fork out capital, but he supposed that the Brickyard would foot the bill.

Discarding these sordid and cynical considerations, couldn't Denys's conduct be put down to the 'friendship-account'? People talked of an 'experience account', to which they debited unpleasant or unsuccessful happenings – inferring that these happenings were worth it, if they added to one's knowledge of life. A friend of Richard's, who didn't agree, had once referred to this as the 'life-ist' heresy – meaning that mere 'life' took precedence, as a way of looking at things, to any system or theory, derived from a contemplation of life. Life was the source, the river, the sea, and could absorb, and apparently purify, anything one chose to put into it. An unavowed marriage, an exaggerated telephone bill – what were they but a drop in the ocean, the great disinfectant ocean, which receives and whirls into a kind of sewer-bed of 'activated sludge', all our deeds and misdeeds?

But to hell with all that! All's fair in love and war. The love-hatred relationship was a fact of old standing but the idea that the two emotions could be hyphenated was new, – new to Richard. It was just too bad, and he must take care not to make the same mistake another time, if there was one. It would be interesting to know about, and perhaps meet (but would he ever meet her!) whoever it was who had made on Denys such an *éclatant* effect that he was prepared to throw up a good job for her, with no prospect of another job, as far as Richard knew. Or did Denys mean to combine his present situation with marriage, bring his wife into the flat, perhaps, where there would be just room for her?

Whatever happened Richard must be generous, generous in word, thought and *deed*, remembering that Denys had all his life before him, whereas he, Richard, had but a very limited amount of time.

But in spite of his mental and emotional preparations for Denys's arrival, he was completely taken by surprise when Denys did arrive. Denys hadn't written or telephoned; he just walked in, at half-past eleven in the morning. Richard opened the door to him, thinking he was the postman bringing a parcel – and his first reaction on seeing him – gladness – was the same reaction he had always had on seeing Denys. 'Well, how are you?' he said, as he would have said to his old friend, and led the way into the sitting-room.

Their greetings over, Denys appeared a little sulky, but perhaps that was just embarrassment.

'How have you been getting on?' he asked. 'No heart-attacks, I hope?'

'No,' said Richard.

'I begin to think your heart is as sound as a bell,' said Denys, stretching out his long legs and beginning to look more like himself. 'Sounder than mine, I shouldn't wonder.'

An unfeeling remark, but it gave Richard an opening.

'How is your heart?' he asked, with more solicitude than Denys had.

'Oh, it still ticks away.'

'I had an idea,' said Richard, trying not to sound arch, 'that something might have happened to it.'

'Because I went away, you mean.'

'Yes, that and other things.'

Denys didn't quite know how to take this.

'The same things as before?'

'Yes, I suppose so.'

Richard couldn't help showing that he felt hurt.

'You know, Denys, I think you imagine them. If you mean Lucilla, isn't it really rather a relief to you that I go out sometimes? After all, you go out quite a bit yourself, and if I was always in—'

'You were not behaving as an invalid should,' said Denys. 'An invalid should have a familiar friend, but not necessarily a familiar female friend.'

'Think of your remembering that quotation,' said Richard, admiringly. 'But you have familiar female friends, too, Denys.' He took a plunge. 'I have some letters for you, don't let me forget to give you them.'

'Letters?' said Denys, in his tiredest voice. 'Who from?'

'I wouldn't know, and I couldn't send them on, because I didn't know where you were.'

'Letters are a curse,' said Denys. 'They sometimes need answering. But I suppose that as I'm here, I may as well have them.'

Involuntarily he stretched his hand out, and Richard, for once able to find something, gave them to him.

'Hm,' Denys said.

Richard took another plunge.

'Don't think me inquisitive,' he said, 'but the postmark is Stockport, and since you went away I've had the telephone bill.' He paused to let this sink in.

'Oh yes, you would have had,' said Denys calmly.

'It was absolutely staggering. So I asked to have the separate items sent to me. As a matter of fact, they came this morning.'

'Oh,' said Denys, 'so what?'

Richard didn't like his tone, but he had made a plan for the course this interview was to take, and he meant to stick to it.

'At least three-quarters of the calls were to somebody in Stockport. That's nothing to do with me, of course, but the bill is, because I've got to pay it.'

'You always let me use the telephone,' said Denys. 'It was one of my perks. I didn't think you'd object.'

'Well,' said Richard, 'I don't actually object, but I think you might have told me before you ran up such a big bill. Just imagine, sometimes the calls came to over four pounds a day, and quite a lot of the charges were reversed. I think your interlocutor might have paid for those.'

'He did offer to,' said Denys, 'but he's as hard up as I am. You used to like to do me a kindness and I thought you still did.'

'I did and do,' said Richard, trying to infuse into his voice more warmth than he felt, and put out of his stride by the unexpected sex of Denys's friend. Where do I go from here, he asked himself. How do I get back on to the main line?

'I didn't know your friend was a man,' he said. 'That makes things different.'

'Why?' asked Denys, jauntily. 'Can't I have men friends? After all, you have them, or you did have, until a certain lady turned up.'

Richard agreed. 'But somehow I didn't think that you, or anyone, would telephone so often to a man.'

'What an extraordinary idea. Are men never called up? Are they outside the range of telephone activity?'

Richard laughed.

'Oh yes, they are called up quite a lot, but mainly on business, don't you think? At least, they call each other up on business, but as a rule they don't take long over it, they listen for the pips. But if a man calls up a woman, or vice versa—'

'Yes?'

'Well, then they don't take so much account of time.'

'Certainly I've heard you having quite long pow-wows with Miss Distington. I didn't hear what you said, of course, but the telephone has been on the batter quite a long time.'

'What strange expressions you use,' said Richard. 'Where did you pick them up? I thought that "on the batter" meant something else. But to go back to what I said – it does make a difference, if it was a man.'

'What sort of difference?'

'Can't you see? If it was a woman you were so devoted to that you wanted to telephone to her all the time – well, I thought it must be a romance.'

'And if it had been?'

'Oh then,' said Richard, making a great effort, for his plan had been to lead up to this – in fact the conversation had been like the parlour-game in which one competitor tries to get in a given sentence before the other can – 'in *that* case I should have wanted—'

'Yes?' said Denys when Richard hesitated.

'To mark the occasion in some appropriate way.'

'How?'

'To put it crudely, Denys, by a wedding present.'

'That's very kind of you,' said Denys, at last. 'You take my breath away. Not many presents have come my way just lately. My fault, perhaps, but someone else's too. What form was the present going to take?'

'Oh,' said Richard, a little nettled by Denys's casual, not to say, cavalier reception of his offer. 'Well, I hadn't quite thought what you and she might like.'

'What makes you so sure it is a "she"?' asked Denys teasingly. 'Men have been known to have men friends.'

'Yes, but they don't marry them,' said Richard rather tartly. 'At least, I've never heard of them getting wedding-presents. That's what I meant by saying it would make a difference. If you are going to be married, or have been married, Denys, well, I wish you joy, and all its accompaniments. If it's a man—'

'Then you wouldn't feel so generous?'

'No.'

'It's a woman,' Denys said. 'But who told you I was married?'

'Oh, a little bird,' said Richard, and thinking of Mrs. Stonegappe he added hastily, 'I mean, everything pointed to it – your . . . absences, and the telephone-calls and one thing and another.'

'Your little bird was wrong,' said Denys. 'I'm not married, but I'm as good as married, if you take my meaning.'

'I think I do,' said Richard.

'Well, that's how it is. Pat and I have been in love – in love, you know, for some time now. You must meet her, she's heard a lot about you – she's a splendid girl, and any little present you could give us would be very useful.'

Richard was irritated by this speech, irritated and hurt. To have his magnanimous gesture (for such he conceived it to be) greeted in this casual fashion! In the circumstances no doubt, he couldn't expect Denys to have much feeling for their past relationship but he might have paid lip-service to it, or shown some recognition of it.

'Another thing you could do,' pursued Denys, 'would be to put us up here for the time being. The only snag is, Pat won't be separated from her dog. She simply dotes on it. I tell her it means more to her than I do. But you wouldn't mind that, would you?'

'Mind what?' said Richard, bewildered. 'Mind the dog, or mind her caring more for it than she does for you?'

'The dog, of course,' said Denys patiently. 'Bungy is very well behaved, but he's a corgi and they're trained to snap at people's heels. Not people, cattle – but it's much the same thing. But I'm sure we could train him not to regard you as a Friesian.'

Richard's emotions were sluggish, and as far as they moved at all, it was in a one-way street with traffic-lights ahead. To reverse or make a U-turn was impossible for him. But at any rate he could slow down, and he did now.

'I don't believe it would work, Denys,' he said, 'even if your wife, if Pat' (he remembered the present generation's insistence on Christian names), 'wanted to live in a bed-sitting-room, it would be too cramped for her – and for you, I should have thought, not to mention the dog.'

'Oh, he could doss down anywhere,' said Denys, 'anywhere where there's heels. But you wouldn't keep us out of your sitting-room, would you? I mean, we could all muck in together here. If you can't muck in nowadays, you're nowhere. Pat and I aren't choosy, but we do want to be *somewhere*.'

The traffic lights turned red.

'Of course, of course,' said Richard, 'you must be *somewhere*, but do you really want to be *here*? I've never been married, as you know, but I imagine that married people want a certain amount of privacy – they want to be by themselves or what's Heaven for?, as Browning said.'

'Well, you're not in all the time,' said Denys, reasonably. 'Quite often, very often, you go out to lunch or dine with Miss Distington.'

'Oh, yes, I do,' reflected Richard, 'and then you would have the place to yourselves, such as it is. But I still feel that you would be happier on your own.'

'Are you turning us out?' said Denys, with a faint hint of truculence.

Richard made an effort.

'My dear boy, you haven't yet come in.'

After a silence, Denys said:

'Does that mean you don't want us?'

'Oh *no*,' cried Richard, who hated being put into the position of seeming to do someone a bad turn. 'I simply think it wouldn't work, that's all.'

'Then what,' said Denys, elongating himself still further in the chair, 'do you propose to do for us?'

This was a facer, and Richard, who all along had been trying to ward it off, realized that, as Cleopatra said, the exigent had come. Irritation, even temper, came with it.

'I'll do anything for you that I can,' he said, rather shortly.

'But what does that mean, Richard? You owe me a great deal, you know. Three years and more of faithful service, the best years of my life, and then to be turned out into the street—'

'Oh, Denys,' said Richard, 'that is most unfair. I admit that I have got more out of you than you have out of me, but even so you can't complain that I am turning you out. You are married or going to be – that's fair enough; but you can't expect to go on living here too.'

'Why not? I can still go on looking after you.'

'Oh, Denys, you must see it wouldn't do. Besides, I don't pay you enough – you said I didn't.'

'It would be enough if you were giving us board and lodging. Pat's got a job as a shorthand typist. She could do some work for you too, in her spare time.'

'It wouldn't work, Denys, I'm sure it wouldn't,' said Richard fretfully. 'For one thing, she wouldn't like it.'

'Pat does like it,' Denys said. 'We've talked it over and she likes the idea of it very much. She's tired of Stockport and wants to settle in London.'

While Richard was racking his brains for some objection to the project that wouldn't sound offensive towards Pat, Denys was saying:

'Pat's a splendid cook, much better than I am. Her cooking would add years to your life. And she's a very good conversationalist too, you know, no holds barred. You'd find meal-times much more amusing than when we're just chatting together.'

The prospect of this intimate *ménage à trois* became more and more distasteful to Richard. He felt he would never hold his own in conversation with Pat – his mind refused to accept her Christian name, she was always 'she' or 'her'.

'But I don't like dogs!' he suddenly exclaimed. 'At least, I only like *some* dogs. They *can* be so noisy and rampageous, and in a small flat like this—'

'But you'd love Bungy,' said Denys. 'The Royal Family likes corgis, so why shouldn't you? He does bark a bit, I have to say, but he'd be a protection against thieves and there are a lot round here.'

One by one Richard's arguments against cohabitation with Pat and her dog were being demolished and he could think of nothing to say that wouldn't seem not only a reflection on her but on the whole institution of marriage.

'Of course we wouldn't ask you,' Denys said, 'if it wasn't that accommodation in London is so terribly difficult to find, especially for penniless people like Pat and me, with a dog in tow. Of course here everyone has dogs, but in the kind of places we could afford the landladies won't look at a dog.'

'I wish it had been a cat,' said Richard, playing for time.

'Oh, but I know you'd love it, and Pat too,' said Denys. 'Do come and see them, they're just outside the door on the landing.'

What could Richard do but say yes?

As soon as the door on to the landing opened, a salvo of barking and the frantic twistings of a small, thick-set, tubular body made Richard recoil. 'Sit, Bungy, sit!' its owner admonished him, but any idea of sitting was far from Bungy's mind. In the whirl of teeth and tail and voices, human and canine, it was quite impossible for Denys to introduce his wife, if wife she were, to Richard. Bungy needed no introduction. 'Silly Billy, Silly Billy,' she kept saying to him, in tones of affectionate reproach, but the words sounded as if they were addressed to Richard and annoyed him too by their inadequacy as a reproof to Bungy. When at last the clamour ceased he was in such a state of irritation that he could only splutter, 'I do think you might have more consideration than to bring that nasty vicious little brute here. Please take it away at once. I'm not well and you have upset me very much.'

No sooner were the words out of his mouth than he regretted them, and all the more because the girl, who was an Irish type, tall, dark and dressed in green, with a handkerchief over her head, gazed at him in wide-eyed disbelief and burst into tears. She said nothing but moved away towards the lift dragging the dog, which now showed an embarrassing desire to make friends with Richard, after her. Denys put his arm round her still shaking shoulders and went with her to the lift and pressed the button. Richard watched them from the doorway of his flat, thinking he was seeing the last of them. 'Good-bye,' he said. But when the lift arrived Denys bundled Pat and Bungy into it, and came back to him.

13

'I'm sorry about that, Denys,' Richard said. 'I didn't mean to be rude, but people with hearts are apt to be irritable, I believe.'

'I don't think you have much heart,' Denys said.

The knowledge that he had been guilty of bad manners made Richard angry with himself and, unfairly, with Denys too.

'I don't think you have any right to call me heartless,' he said as they re-entered the sitting-room, and he was going on to enumerate the reasons why Denys should be grateful to him, but stopped just in time.

'It was the dog,' he said. 'It startled me.'

'Bungy is always a bit suspicious of strangers,' Denys said. 'Most dogs are, that's what they're for. But I don't see why you should have turned on Pat. She's terribly sensitive about him.'

Richard longed to say, 'She has every reason to be,' but again stopped in time. 'It's being startled,' he said, 'that puts one off. But I'm sure she understood.'

'She didn't understand at all,' said Denys. 'She was terribly upset, as you must have noticed. You won't see her again in a hurry.'

'I don't want to see her *in a hurry*,' said Richard, with some spirit. 'I should like to see her with time to spare.

But I'm truly sorry, Denys, that it turned out so awkwardly, and I hope you'll apologize to her for me.'

'I'll give her that message,' Denys said, 'but I don't think she'll accept it, she's so terribly sensitive, as I told you, where Bungy is concerned. She thinks the world of that dog. And of course any idea that we should come to stay with you is off.'

Richard's heart leaped up, as far as its enfeebled state allowed it to, but he had the sense not to show it.

'Oh dear,' he said. 'Well, perhaps it's for the best.'

'You seem to forget,' said Denys, 'that we have to live, and have to live *somewhere*, I don't know where that will be. But you were talking of giving us a wedding-present, Richard, so perhaps you can help us out.'

Why did I ever like this man? thought Richard. Then he reproved himself. 'You *must* take into account changed circumstances.' But his own reasoning didn't convince him and he said:

'There's one present I could give you.'

'What is that?' asked Denys, and a light flickered in his eye.

'The telephone bill for your calls to Pat – to Mrs. Aspin. It will come to something like £200.'

After a pause in which Denys seemed to be considering this, he said: 'I thought we agreed that I was entitled to use the telephone.'

Still ruffled by the events and questions of the morning, Richard answered:

'You may have agreed. I'm not sure that I did. Two hundred pounds is quite a lot, you know.'

'It isn't like you to strain at a gnat,' said Denys. 'I was hoping for something more substantial.'

'Such as?'

'I hadn't thought of any particular sum. Our relationship hasn't been on those terms, has it? I thought that Pat and I would be welcome here, but it seems we aren't.'

'Well, not with Bungy making such an unshadowy fourth,' said Richard, disingenuously.

'I didn't think you'd object to a poor dumb animal.'

'Dumb, he wasn't dumb!'

'It was only his way of being conversational. You don't expect a guest not to utter, do you? You weren't very talkative yourself.'

'I couldn't hear myself speak,' said Richard.

'Well, we could have heard you. I own I was disappointed, Richard. I thought you had my welfare more at heart.'

Richard said nothing.

'It would have been such a good arrangement,' Denys went on. 'Pat to cook for you, me to look after you, Bungy to protect you and the flat from burglars. But that's over. Now what can you do for us?'

'I don't think I can do anything.'

'Oh come, Richard. It isn't everybody's job, you know, working for you. I get asked a lot of questions about it, and they're not always easy to answer.'

'What sort of questions?'

'Oh, I don't know. Why should a young chap like me give up all his time – and so on.'

'You don't give up all your time – at least you haven't lately.'

'That's just it – it was to show them, and myself, that I can stand on my own feet.'

'Instead of on mine?'

'Which isn't comfortable for either of us. I take it that you still want to retain my services?'

'It depends on what conditions.'

'I thought you might say that. Well, since you obviously don't want us on the premises, we shall have to find somewhere else – which so far we haven't been able to. You know about the housing problem, of course.'

Richard said he did.

'Then you see the jam we're in.'

'I do,' said Richard. 'But I'm afraid I can't do anything to help you. When we were engaged – when I engaged you – you were a single man, at least I thought so. It's different now you're married.'

'I see,' said Denys, 'you didn't reckon with the powers of Nature.'

'Well no,' said Richard, 'nor did you give me any indication that they were affecting you in that way.'

'I hardly could, could I?' Denys said. 'Not a physical sign, at any rate. There were other signs. Who was the little bird, by the way?'

Richard was too angry to answer.

'But we do want some money,' Denys went on, 'if you won't take us in. I've got to write that memoir of you, which will take me some time, and we can't live on air while I'm doing it.'

'It needn't be long,' Richard said.

'I suppose a publisher will pay me for it. But when?'

'Your guess is as good as mine,' said Richard, shortly.

'You've seemed a good deal better lately, I'm glad to say,' said Denys. 'What fun if you outlived me. But the damned thing will take time, even though it is a labour of love, and all the more if you're not there to help me.'

'No – yes, I mean,' said Richard.

'How much did you think of giving me for it?' was Denys's next question.

'I hadn't thought,' said Richard. 'At least I had – I thought the fee would be included in the money I was going to leave you.'

'You were *going* to leave me?' echoed Denys. 'Have you thought better of it?'

'You haven't given me much time to think.'

'Oh, but Richard, I have! You've had three years and more to think about it. And I'm not used to writing. I shall find it so difficult – I mean, deciding what to put in and to leave out.'

'I told you I relied on your discretion, Denys.'

'But I'm not very discreet – I might put in something that you wouldn't like.'

Somewhere below Richard's conscious mind a warning bell sounded, but he didn't heed it.

'You can show me what you've written and I'll vet it for you.'

'But how could you, Richard? I hate to say it, but by that time you would be . . . well, you wouldn't be, I mean, anywhere where you could use a blue pencil.'

Richard smiled.

'My ghost might perhaps direct you, Denys.'

'But are ghosts punctual? Hamlet's father, so I seem to remember, spoke too late in the day.'

'Yes, but what he said went. Anyhow, he had been murdered. You won't have murdered me – at least I hope not.'

'You never can tell, Richard. You never can tell. You mustn't try me too far. At any rate I don't want to murder your reputation – I could, you know.'

'How?'

'Well, I know something about you that other people don't know.'

'You don't mean—'

'Of course not, Richard, but I'm sure you'll agree that my silence has a certain value.'

'Are you a rogue?' asked Richard.

'Of course not, I'm only very hard up, and clutching at any straw.'

'Are you asking for hush-money, Denys?'

'Don't put it like that, I'm only saying that this job is going to be a bit of a headache, and I think you ought to take that into account.'

'I have taken it into account.'

'Yes, I know you've made a provision for me, but what I should like is something *now*, for me and Pat and Bungy, in that order, of course.'

'I'm afraid I can't do anything for you, Denys, I'm overdrawn as it is.'

'Overdrawn my hat, Richard. Think of the Brickworks.'

The reference to the Brickworks annoyed Richard intensely, as Denys thought it would; for it recalled to his mind the Brickfield, where Lucy and he had played together; oddly enough he had never connected them in his mind, for one was a symbol of calamity and the other of prosperity.

'Are you trying to make me angry?' he asked.

'Of course not, Richard. Only realistic. When I'm writing about you, I want to be in the mood to do you justice.'

Richard had the sensations attributed to a drowning man. The scenes succeeded each other – the pool in the Brickfield which he had seen with his eyes, the grave in the Abbey churchyard which he had seen so often with the eyes of dream, but even in dream could never identify – until they reached Lucilla, the inheritor and climax of all this. But though they followed each other, waxing and waning in distinctness, they also made a synthesis of thought and feeling, desire and dread, which was: none of these things must ever come to light, and above all – suddenly he felt this with overwhelming force – must never come to the knowledge of Lucilla.

'I suppose it's a question of a cheque,' he said, and got up to look for his cheque-book, which for once was at hand. 'How much, Denys?'

Denys named a sum.

'Denys, do you really mean that?'

'I am astonished at my own moderation, as someone said,' said Denys.

Richard wrote out the cheque and handed it to him.

'Thank you,' said Denys, putting it folded in some pocket which his long figure, rising to its feet, had made available; 'this will do for now, but Richard, if I should still feel that, in the interests of posterity, still more of the truth ought to be told – for we all owe posterity the truth, don't we? – I'll come to you again.'

'I never want to see you again,' said Richard.

'Oh, but you will,' said Denys. 'Hullo, Richard, anything the matter?'

Richard had slumped in his chair. 'My tablets, Denys!' he gasped, feebly struggling to get up, making little circles with his hands, clutching at the air as though it could support him. Denys saw the tablets on the chimney-piece, but didn't move in their direction. He glanced down at Richard, whose efforts to keep his mind afloat had ceased, sapped by the power-cut in his breast. 'He won't get over this,' Denys thought, 'he's had it, but I have the cheque, and with luck the legacy.' And with much more alacrity than he usually showed, he tiptoed from the room.

14

But Denys was wrong: Richard hadn't had it. Mrs. Stonegappe, coming in to cook his lunch, found him still breathing though unable to move. Her tongue clicked at the sight, but she did not lose her head, for she had had much experience of illness, and she did not regard the difference between life and death as so fundamental as some people do.

She knew Dr. Herbright's telephone number, it was written on the pad beside the telephone. Soon he arrived and between them they got Richard into bed; she did not shrink from his inert sagging body, indeed with the doctor's help she handled it expertly.

'Get him a hot water-bottle, will you?' said the doctor, 'and I'll give him an injection.'

Coming back from the kitchen she asked, 'Is he conscious?'

'I don't think so,' said the doctor. 'But he's coming round. Where's his secretary, I wonder, Mr. Aspin?'

'Mr. Aspin has been away now for some days,' said Mrs. Stonegappe, through stiff lips. 'I couldn't tell you where he is, I'm sure.'

'That's a pity,' said the doctor, 'I don't like to leave him, and I don't want to send him to a hospital – he would hate that.'

'What's wrong with a hospital?' asked Mrs. Stonegappe in her blunt way. 'They don't cost nothing, do they? You don't have to pay.'

'No, but he dreads it,' said the doctor. 'I've known him for a long time and I respect his wishes. But somebody must look after him. What's happened to Mr. Aspin?'

'Gone,' said Mrs. Stonegappe shortly. 'Slung his hook, walked out, as you might say.'

'You don't say so!' exclaimed the doctor. 'Well, that does surprise me.' Curiosity overcame him. 'Not a very gentlemanly thing to do, was it? Had they had a row, or something?'

'I wouldn't know,' said Mrs. Stonegappe, and her tone implied reproof. 'I don't interest myself in the affairs of those I work for. Some think it's smart to take the mickey out of anyone that employs them, and Mr. Aspin did, if you ask me. He said he was a gentleman, but in my opinion, he's no more a gentleman than you or I are.'

The doctor let this pass.

'In that case,' said he, 'we shall have to get in a hospital nurse.'

Mrs. Stonegappe's face fell, and the good-nature which found a precarious lodging there went out of it.

'A hospital nurse,' she said. 'A hospital nurse. Oh, then, I couldn't stay.'

The doctor, who knew human nature as well as she did, was ready for this.

'Why, what's wrong with a hospital nurse?'

'Well, for one thing, they're no more use than a sick headache, and for another, they're a pain in the neck.'

'Perhaps you've been unlucky with them,' said the doctor.

Mrs. Stonegappe shrugged her shoulders.

'I wouldn't give myself the chance to be unlucky with them, no, nor lucky neither. When I see one of them sort coming, well, I'm off. Let them get on with it, I say.'

The doctor looked down at Richard. He was breathing better, and his colour was beginning to come back. How could Mrs. Stonegappe's antipathy to hospital nurses be got over? It was obviously so deeply-seated that questions of life or death would not affect it. Working-class prejudices were stronger than other people's principles. Could he play on them? He tried another tack.

'If he dies here,' the doctor said, 'they won't like it, of course. I mean, the owners of the flats won't, and the other tenants will – well, they'll protest. You live in a flat, I expect, just as I do, though I have my surgery in another place. Flat-dwellers don't like anything out of the ordinary – they don't like noise, except their own noise, they don't like a kitchen sink overflowing, unless it happens to be theirs, they don't like babies being born, because it means a hurry, and somebody pushes past them – and they don't like people dying, because a coffin takes up the lift, if the lift's wide enough. They don't want to be reminded of *death* – well, I can sympathize with them. I don't like it myself, and being a doctor, I often get blamed for it.'

'It's true what you say,' said Mrs. Stonegappe, 'at least some of it is. Some of the people round me – well, you wouldn't think they'd heard of a dead body. Anyone who can't bear the sight of a dead body, well – they're not fit to live in this world, so I say.'

'I say so, too,' the doctor said, 'and I dare say I've seen more dead bodies than you have. But if we keep him here they'll be up against us – supposing anything should happen.'

'I'd like to see them try,' said Mrs. Stonegappe, warmly. 'I'd like to see them stopping me from dying, or doing anything else I wanted to.'

'That's just it. Whatever happens Mr. Mardick must stay here. The hospitals are overcrowded, anyhow. I might not even be able to get him in. But we must have a nurse.'

Dr. Herbright said this in his most conciliatory and persuasive voice, and thought that he had won the day. But he was mistaken.

'Then I'm leaving,' Mrs. Stonegappe said. 'It isn't that I don't like Mr. Mardick. I like him very much, as far as he goes. But I don't like hospital nurses. They never do a hand's turn, in my experience – not that I've had very much experience of them, for when they come, I'm off. They want waiting on, and having cups of tea made for them and cooking for – who'll cook Mr. Mardick his supper, by the way?'

'Perhaps Mr. Aspin will come back,' the doctor said.

'What a hope! He's got other fish to fry, if you ask me. And if he comes back, where is she to sleep?'

'On the sofa in the sitting-room.'

'Catch one of them doing that.'

'I know of one who would,' the doctor said, 'and cook for him as well,' he added, reasonably but rashly.

'I like that! Then where do I come in? It's taking the bread out of my mouth, that's what it is. I'm picking up £6 a week now, with all the extra work I do for Mr. Mardick. Not that I grudge it him, mind. I'd work my fingers to the bone for him. But I don't see why I should be stood off, just because a hospital nurse is coming.'

Dr. Herbright was taken aback by Mrs. Stonegappe's sudden change of front.

'There was no idea of standing you off,' he said to Mrs. Stonegappe, who seemed very much to be standing on her dignity, 'just the opposite in fact. I'm sure Mr. Mardick wouldn't want to dock your wages. I dare say he would pay you more.'

'I doubt it,' Mrs. Stonegappe said. 'I very much doubt it. Between you and me, Doctor, I doubt if he has the money he gives out he has, and there's others besides me thinks the same. He often has an overdraft in the morning, when he's been on the jolly the night before.'

'On the jolly?' repeated Dr. Herbright. 'If he has been, it's against my orders. But he always pays his bills, doesn't he?'

'Oh yes, he *pays* them,' said Mrs. Stonegappe, as if there were ways of paying and paying. 'He *pays* them, I admit that. But I don't think he's too well off, not like some gentlemen I've worked for, who would be just the same even if we went into the Common Market. Those bricks, you know—'

'Well, what about the bricks?' said Dr. Herbright, surprised that Mrs. Stonegappe should know about Richard's chief source of supply. He supposed that she must read his letters – Richard was always careless, leaving them lying about.

'Well, there's steel and there's cement,' said Mrs. Stonegappe, shrewdly. 'Soon there may not be any call for bricks, then where will he be? If I asked him for a rise, being as the hospital nurse is coming, he'd certainly say yes, but could he, when Friday comes?'

'Did you think of asking him for a rise?' asked Dr. Herbright.

'Well, I should be a mug if I didn't, shouldn't I? What with the inconvenience and the extra work.'

'I don't know what you'd be,' said Dr. Herbright, wearily. 'You're the best judge of that.'

'There's no need to be rude about it,' Mrs. Stonegappe said. 'Civility costs nothing, not even a doctor's fee,' she added, nastily. 'And with him leaving everything about' – she glanced round Richard's untidy bedroom.

'How does that come into it?' asked Dr. Herbright. 'It's your job to tidy up for him, I should have thought.'

Mrs. Stonegappe raised a warning finger. 'As I've just told you, civility costs nothing, and even a doctor has to be civil sometimes. What I meant is, it isn't fair to people to trust them – it's putting temptation in their way.'

'In whose way?' asked Dr. Herbright.

'In the way of anyone who might come unknown and unexpected to the flat – and unwanted, too,' she added.

'Oh, is it?' said Dr. Herbright. He glanced down again at Richard, off whom, it is only fair to say, he had never once taken his eyes since he began to talk to Mrs. Stonegappe. 'It's a pity, all this,' he said, trying to sum up

164

Mrs. Stonegappe's grievances, Richard's illness, his own overdue obligation to go on to the next patient, and the human predicament, all in one breath. 'It's a pity,' he repeated, fumbling in his pocket and bringing out his note-case. 'It's a pity, but he's conscious now' (he was aware that the words didn't mean what he intended them to mean) 'so we must stop talking, or he'll go back again. At any rate,' he said, drawing a five-pound note out of his pocket-book, 'please accept this. I know you've done a great deal for him, whether you want to do any more is up to you.'

Mrs. Stonegappe took the note, and almost at the same moment Richard opened his eyes.

'Hullo, Hal,' he said feebly. 'I must have had one of my attacks.'

'You did, my boy,' the doctor said, 'but only just a mild one. All the same, we shall have to keep you quiet for a bit. Mrs. Stonegappe and I have been having a chin-wag. You're off now, Mrs. Stonegappe, aren't you?'

'I never said so,' Mrs. Stonegappe answered.

'Oh well, that's up to you. You have the keys of the flat, haven't you?'

'I couldn't get in unless I had, could I?' asked Mrs. Stonegappe, tight-lipped.

'Of course not. But someone else might want to get in – I don't mean a burglar. These are yours, Richard, aren't they?'

He picked some keys up from the bedside-table.

Richard nodded, weakly.

Dr. Herbright put them in his pocket. 'They will do for me, or someone else. You won't need them anyhow, Richard, for a week or two. Now I must give you a pep-talk. Good-bye, Mrs. Stonegappe; see you again soon, I hope.'

'Perhaps, when you've calmed down,' said Mrs. Stonegappe, and the door shut behind her.

'Now, Richard,' said the doctor, looking down at his patient, 'whatever *have* you been up to? Have you been disregarding my advice, never to get annoyed with anybody?'

'Sometimes it's forced on one,' said Richard. 'I suppose life would be less interesting if it wasn't.'

'Yes,' said the doctor, 'but it wouldn't last so long.'

The words slipped out. He regretted them, they were unprofessional; but who knew if it was better to warn a patient or to encourage him? Seeing a shadow on Richard's face he added, 'Isn't there a friend you would really *like* to see? You mustn't let your capacity for liking things, or people, dwindle. Isn't there anyone who might share your problems without adding to them? It's bad for you to feel that people are against you and might lead to persecution-mania.'

'Just because there is such a thing as persecution-mania,' Richard said, 'it doesn't follow that there isn't such a thing as persecution.'

'Of course not,' Dr. Herbright answered testily, 'only we must keep the two distinct. The nearest are not always the dearest – as you seem to have found. Isn't there some-one towards the periphery who might help?'

Richard's thoughts flew to Lucilla. 'Yes, there is.'

'Well, I should contact him or her, if I were you. But warn whoever it is that you are persecution-prone.'

'I'm not!' protested Richard. But the moment Dr.

Herbright's back was turned, he rang Lucilla up, only to be told that she was going abroad.

Going abroad, he thought, and without telling me? Suddenly he felt aggrieved, as if she had no right to go abroad without telling him. He knew he was being unreasonable, but although as a rule he could make his feelings listen to reason, in this case he could not. Didn't Lucilla realize how ill he was?

'Where is she going?' he asked, almost rudely, for it was no business of his where she was going.

'To the South of France, sir,' said the maid.

'To the South of France?' repeated Richard, as if such a destination was quite unheard of.

'Yes, sir, to stay with a friend.'

What friend? thought Richard, suddenly assailed by jealousy. She never told me she had any friends who lived abroad. As he realized how unreasonable he was being his resentment mounted. But he managed to curb it, and at the same time to excuse himself: people with bad hearts were notoriously irritable.

'Did she leave an address?'

'Yes,' said the maid, and spelt it out to him. 'But I think she has written to you, sir.'

'Oh she has, has she?' said Richard, mollified but still menacing.

Next day he got her letter.

Dear Richard,

I feel a little guilty for going away without telling you – though I don't know why, for why should either of us mind? Certainly not you, who have already more on your hands than you can cope with, in the way of domestic troubles. I wish I could help you, but how can I? If I could have helped you, I dare say I should have stayed here, but helping is an art, isn't it? – I mean, it needs practice. I like to think I helped my parents in some ways, but I once overheard my father say to my mother, 'I wish Lucilla wouldn't try to pull me out of my chair, it makes me feel so *helpless*,' and after that I had to watch him struggling – what else could I do? And one can doubtless be more officious with a parent than one dare be with a friend – even with such a dear friend as you are. I wouldn't have tried to pull you out of bed! only to smooth your pillow, but I expect there are others to do that for you, and if you had needed my assistance (I won't say 'help') you would have told me. So now I am going to Fréjus [she didn't give her address] for a few weeks, or for as long as I am wanted. (I almost wrote needed, but who can tell if they are needed, or wanted either, for that matter?) However, if you should want (or need!) me, you have only to say so, and I'll come back. Naturally, I hope that such a contingency won't arise, but if it should, you will let me know, won't you?

Ever yours,
Lucilla.

Richard snatched up the telephone and broke into incoherent speech.

'You mean you don't want me to go abroad?' interrupted Lucilla, and when his silence gave consent she added, 'I'll cancel my reservations now.'

'She is just what you, the doctor, ordered,' exclaimed Richard. 'She likes me, and I like her. She will increase my powers of liking, ha-ha!'

'But you're not fit to see anybody,' Dr. Herbright said.

'Not fit?' cried Richard, offended. 'But you told me I was to find a familiar friend for . . . for therapeutic reasons.'

'I can't remember every silly thing I said,' said Dr. Herbright, rising. 'I have a lot of patients and you, as far as I know, have only one doctor. As a doctor I would gladly meet your wishes – any doctor would. But women are notoriously hard on the heart – not hard of heart, please don't mistake me – but hard on the heart as an organ. You can write to her, of course, but until this slight set-back is over, I'd rather you didn't see her.'

'Oh dear,' cried Richard, 'but she has given up her trip abroad just to – I mean, just to—'

But his plea got no further than the door, which had closed on Dr. Herbright.

15

Dear Lucilla,

Thank you for those lovely, lovely flowers. I only wish I could have thanked you in person, as they say, although, in my case, *what* a person! Dr. Herbright still doesn't want me to see people, which is too idiotic of him, because I *have* to see people and generally people I don't want to see! One glimpse of you would do me far more good than I get from interviewing X and Y and Z, which I have to do, because you can't *engage* someone, any more than you can become engaged, without first seeing them, though I believe they did that in the Middle Ages. The trouble is, I have to have someone to live in, or at any rate to sleep in – Denys used to, as you know, but he's buzzed off and I don't even know where he's gone to – cherchez la femme! Dr. Herbright (who is my friend as well as my doctor) doesn't think I need two nurses, and I'm glad of that, for what a lot they cost! And though he told me he would find one who could cook, he hasn't been able to, so she comes by the day, and leaves after she has put me down for the night – if you know what I mean. This happens earlier and earlier, last night I was put down at half-past seven – I fancy she had a date she wanted to keep.

She and my daily, Mrs. Stonegappe, aren't on speaking terms, of course, which is such *fun*. They refer to each other as 'that person', or 'the other woman', or if it's more serious, 'someone you know about'. They accuse each other of all kinds of dishonesty, and naturally, lying on my bed, I don't know who to believe. But because neither of them can see me through the night, or they declare they can't, I've had to look for a man with cooking and nursing qualifications. They aren't hard to find, if you put in an advertisement, but *what* they're like, when found! I've already had two – in, what is it? a fortnight. The first had marvellous references, both from himself and from people who knew him or who had employed him – I thought he would be an angel in the house. He was an old public schoolboy, and so nice to talk to. He spoke the same language as we do, to put it snobbishly. But he hadn't been here a week before I was rung up by the police, to say that he had been driving my car to the public danger, without a licence, and under the influence of drink. A stalwart detective came, and stood beside my bed – he apologized for the intrusion, but of course illness doesn't really affect them, in the execution of their duty – and I told him all I knew about this character, which wasn't much. The policeman was sympathetic but as they often are, a little stern. 'Where is Mr. Kinklecross now?' he asked me. 'But isn't he *here*?' I said. 'He was here this morning. Have you looked in his room?' 'With your permission I will,' the policeman said. He didn't ask me where it was, he seemed to know. In a moment he was back and said with an impassive face, 'He isn't there. Did he live in, sir?' I said he

did. 'Well, his bed isn't made and all his gear has gone.'
'You don't say so!' I exclaimed. 'And is the car there? It
should be in the Square, not far from the door.' The detective said he would go down and have a look, and while he
was gone Mrs. Stonegappe arrived and with her the hospital nurse, Miss Tranter – Miss Tantrum, as Mrs.
Stonegappe will insist on calling her. I suppose they had
come up together in the lift – it must have been rather
embarrassing for them, and I shouldn't have known they
were both here, if I hadn't learnt to distinguish between
their footsteps – one becomes sensitive to all sorts of
sounds, lying in bed. They both come at 10 o'clock, but
according to Mrs. Stonegappe (though how does she
know, since they are not on speaking terms?) there is a
sort of dispute as to who should first come in and see me,
so they take this privilege by turns. This morning it was
Mrs. Stonegappe's turn. I asked her if she had noticed
that Kinklecross had left, and she said No, she hadn't
noticed, because she wasn't particularly interested in him,
but she wasn't surprised by anything he did – any more,
she added, than she was surprised by anything Mr. Aspin
did. I told her about the policeman, but she merely shook
her head. A moment later there was a ring at the door, and
of course it was the policeman coming back. I heard raised
voices, and then Sister Tranter burst into the room in a
state of high indignation and said the constable wanted to
see me, but she wouldn't let him, because by doctor's
orders I wasn't to be disturbed. Disturbed! I ask you,
Lucilla. I said, as coldly as I could, that the police had to
be admitted, it was the law; they had to be admitted to

hospitals, as she must well know, to watch cases of attempted suicide, in case the culprit should have anything to say. At this she got still more angry, and said, 'Well, I'm not responsible if anything happens!' (I knew what 'anything' meant.) So the policeman came in, quite calm and collected, and took his helmet off and put it on the bed. 'Oh, don't do that!' I said, for by this time I was rather nervous, 'it's unlucky!' 'Unlucky for whom?' he said, smiling blandly. 'Unlucky for you,' I said, 'it doesn't matter about me, I'm about finished anyway.' Then he took the helmet and put it on the dressing-table, where there was a space between the medicine bottles. 'I'm sorry to have to tell you,' he said, 'that your car isn't there. But never fear, we shall get it back for you.' I was rather touched, because he did seem quite concerned for me, so I thought I would ask *him* a question for a change – they must get tired of always asking questions. 'How did you know,' I said, 'about the car, and Kinklecross, and me and everything?' 'Oh,' he said, 'it was just a routine matter. The chap he ran into took his name and address, and the number of the car, and then I came round, sir. It's a pity about all these motoring offences, they take up our time, sir, and then the public thinks we aren't bothering about proper criminals. But we'll get the car back for you, I promise you that, and we'll get him too, most likely. I suppose you want to charge him?'

'Oh dear, officer,' I said, 'I suppose I ought to – what do you think?'

'You ought to, strictly speaking,' said the policeman, 'but being as you're not in the best of health—'

At this moment Dr. Herbright was announced by Sister Tranter, who wore a discreet air of triumph. He asked the policeman to have a word with him outside. Soon after he came back alone and said: 'You know, old boy, I think you have too many people looking after you, and would be better off in hospital.'

I protested strongly. 'Why,' I said, 'should I have to go to hospital simply because three people whom I was paying handsomely, or fairly handsomely, were too quarrelsome, or too dishonest, or both, to take care of me? I'm no trouble,' I said, 'I'm here on my bed, and all they have to do is to look in from time to time and see that I'm not dead' (forgive this ridiculous exaggeration, Lucilla, I'm not at all ill really, but that makes their behaviour all the more annoying, and they *think* I'm ill which gives them less excuse). 'I'm no strain on the kitchen, I only have the simplest food – it couldn't be simpler in hospital! – And I lighten their labours by doing certain things for myself which are forbidden to bed-ridden patients. Any one of them,' I said, referring to these wretched employees, 'could do the job better than the three of them do' (I say three, but Kinklecross is an absentee until the police round him up). 'I agree,' I said, 'that all these goings-on do agitate me; and how absurd it is that I shouldn't be allowed the visitors I most want to see', you, Lucilla, in particular, 'when people foam and fret around me, sending up my blood-pressure, if I have one.' 'That's exactly what I mean,' he said, 'you would be better off in hospital.' 'But how do I *know*,' I argued ('calm yourself,' he said), 'that I should get on any better there? I am a mild-mannered man to the point of insipidity yet wherever I go, or stay, I seem to be a storm-centre – people literally howl around me, so why shouldn't they in hospital? You told me yourself,' I said, 'that there was something about me that brought out the worst in people.' 'I don't think you are very good for people,' he said, 'Sister Tranter (you shouldn't call her Nurse, by the way) had an exemplary record until she came to you. But you wouldn't be such a corrupting influence in hospital because they're under discipline, and so would you be.' This annoyed me. 'Discipline!' I sneered. 'Why should there be so much need of discipline in the Welfare State? I thought people were so happy they did everything for love. In my young days, when everyone was downtrodden, including myself (you needn't laugh, I told him, you don't know what parental pressure is) the ill and the old were respected, they weren't turned out of house and home just because people regarded them as a nuisance. At my uncle's house near Rookland there were three useless mouths – Aunt Carrie's, Mrs. White's, and mine, and my Aunt Ada didn't pull her weight, though she threw it about, and he wasn't at all well off then, yet neither he, nor his wife who would have liked a gayer life, shopping at Harrods, and so on, ever quarrelled over us, or with us, or talked of turning us into the street or sending us to hospital though hospitals were privately run then – they didn't have the resources of the State behind them.' 'Now, now,' he said, 'you've told me all about that, but as the Latin poet said, times change, and we change with them. It isn't so easy to be ill now as it was, or to be old, either. I'm not sure that a hospital would take you anyway, you're too argumentative. But I know of an agency where they have male nurses and men-servants, all guaranteed free from police records. I'll send you one from there, if Kinklecross doesn't come back.'

'But can I have visitors now?' I asked – thinking of you, Lucilla.

'I don't advise it,' he said, 'you have quite enough on your hands already.'

So you see. Forgive this long epistle, my next will be much shorter. And thank you again for the divine roses. They at any rate don't play me up.

Yours,

Richard.

My dear Lucilla,

I can't remember what day it is, but I feel much better though why I should I don't know! Yes, I remember now, it's because of that heavenly white lilac you sent me. What a benefactress you are! Sister Tantrum (but I must learn *not* to call her that) will take them out of my room at night, which is so silly, for what harm can they do me, compared with what X & Y & Z do?

X & Y you know about; Z is the man Dr. Herbright sent me. I had to have somebody. The police found my car, as they said they would: it had been abandoned somewhere in brightest Brixton, with no greater damage than that the wireless set (which I never liked much anyhow) had been half torn out, so that it wouldn't work. As I couldn't fetch the car myself, the police very kindly brought it back for me. But though they brought the car they didn't, as Sergeant

Davis ruefully admitted, bring Kinklecross. 'He's been a bit too smart for us,' he said, helmet in hand. 'But we shall get him back for you, never fear.' I told him that the return of Kinklecross was the last thing I wanted: 'You can keep him,' I said, trying to be facetious.

Here followed several lines crossed out. Richard went on:

Sergeant Davis gave me a brief but illuminating lecture on the duty of employers to their employees, whether they, the latter, were criminal or not. (He was too tactful to suggest that the former might be.) I tried to copy it out 'for your information and necessary action, please,' as we used to say in the First World War. But these domestic problems don't exist for you – lucky you!

'O fortunatos nimium sua si bona norint, Agricolas!'

So I have deleted the sergeant's homily in favour of 'a perfect and absolute blank!' These allusions are to prove to you that I was once a literary man.

So much for Kinklecross. Too much, I hope it's the last of him, as far as I'm concerned. Sergeant Davis said I shouldn't have to be present at his trial – if they needed my evidence, they would take it at my bedside. How considerate they are.

For the next two days I had no 'evening meal', but how I longed to take you at your word, and ask you to come and cook for me! But Dr. Herbright is adamant. No visitors! (What does he think the police are?')

Mrs. Stonegappe cooks my lunch, and Sister Tranter, before she goes, leaves me a cup of Horlicks – one doesn't want much to eat in bed. Then there arrived the man

Dr. Herbright had found for me from the Prorogue Agency (so-called because they don't demand a booking fee until the employee has given satisfaction for at least a week). This man also had a strange name, Ladbroke Grove, it was his stage name, he said, and he adopted it because he had been born there. I didn't ask him about his stage career – I think it's better, don't you, Lucilla? *not* to inquire too much into people's past lives. At the same time it seems rather inhuman, and perhaps *unwise*, not to show *some* personal interest! However, I didn't – the Agency vouched for it that he had no police record. He said his previous employer had called him Lad or Laddie, but I didn't think I could, so I called him Grove, which is a nice name with musical associations – *The Ash Grove* and *Grove's Dictionary*. Well, he arrived with fifteen suits – would you believe it? and complained there was no hanging-room for them. He said he liked to wear a different suit every day for a fortnight, and then to have one over. I know how keen young men are nowadays about their clothes – they have to be in the fashion, even more than women do – so I tried to give him the necessary space, partly in my wardrobe and partly in the airing cupboard. He had two huge white leather suitcases (so Mrs. Stonegappe told me), and some of his suits he carried on his arm. It took him at least three hours to settle in – of course I couldn't show him the vacant spaces, being in bed. However, he gave me a nice meal in the evening, invalid's fare – and I quite took to him, but so I had to Kinklecross. He asked me if I would mind his having a friend in now and then, and I said of course not.

Being such a dressy man, I naturally didn't expect him to wear the subfusc clothes that menservants wore in olden days, but all the same I was astonished by the number and frequency of his sartorial transformations. For calling me in the morning he wore a loose-fitting bath-robe with sandals; nothing else, as far as I could see. At nine he brought me my breakfast, and then, according to Mrs. Stonegappe who regarded him with amused disfavour, he retired to bed, and reappeared about eleven wearing jeans and a heavy knitted pullover. When he brought my lunch he was wearing a serving coat and narrow trousers with a knife-edge crease; he had four of these coats, he told me, to go with his suits; sometimes he wore shoes and socks, but more often sandals on bare feet. In the afternoons, so Sister Tranter told me (she rather liked him, perhaps because Mrs. Stonegappe didn't, at any rate he caused her pleasurable if shocked excitement), he either went out dressed to kill, or took a nap for which he wore some kind of slumber suit that wasn't exactly pyjamas which suggested bed but could be worn for open-ing the door – though as you know, Lucilla, very few people ever come to the door, except tradesmen and the postman and the porter. Sister Tranter says that when Grove opens it to them, dressed, or undressed like this, they recoil in horror, and the porters have a name for him which she wouldn't tell me – 'though I don't know *why*,' she added, 'because he's always quite *decent*. It's partly the way he *walks* – someone ought to tell him about that.' Actually he didn't walk so much as *glide*, keeping his legs and shoulders stiff.

'Well, I thought he rather égayéd our dull lives, and it simply is *no* use, is it, Lucilla, to blame the young for not behaving, or dressing according to the ideas of *our* generation (mine, I should say, since you are *so* much younger). But alas, two days ago, he carried this principle of égayement too far. I don't know when it began, because I was asleep having taken the usual two tablets that Dr. Herbright prescribes, but gradually the noise from the sitting-room came through to me, and having been a subdued murmur, a sort of sound-dream – it became a roar. Musical instruments – rather like those in the prophet Daniel – and under, or over it, the trampling of feet – thudding, stamping, stopping and starting, continuous, rhythmical, arrhythmical, every variety of foot-noise you can think of. I looked at my watch: it was half-past one. I'm not supposed to get out of bed for any reason, but I simply had to. In the tiny lobby outside my bedroom door was piled half the furniture from the sitting-room and, now that only one door divided me from it, the din was deafening. I put my hand on the knob meaning to go in, but when I thought of the scene that would follow, and how bad it would be for me, I cravenly crept back to bed. They'll have to stop it soon, I thought, but they didn't, not till four in the morning.

My tea didn't appear, nor did my breakfast: at ten o'clock I heard an altercation outside my door. I gathered it was Mrs. Stonegappe and Sister Tranter arguing as to who should go in first.

Mrs. Stonegappe won, or lost, at any rate it was she who appeared. She drew the curtains, she didn't answer my good morning, but merely said:

'They've made a fine mess of your sitting-room.'

'Oh what?' I said, and added disingenuously, 'I heard some noise going on in the night.'

'Noise, I should think so! The whole place is in an uproar, and it'll take the best part of a week to get it straight. And the things they've broken! Some of the things you like the best, like that funny little woman's head on the mantelpiece, that I've always been so careful not to break. I'm thankful you're too ill to go and see it, sir, though you really ought to, it's such a shambles. Some of them didn't know how to hold their drink either, but I shall clean that up as best I can. It's heart-breaking, when you've worked as hard at a place as I have here. It's enough to make you want to give notice, it really is.'

'Oh, I hope you won't, Mrs. Stonegappe,' I cried.

'Well, I shall think about it, but it isn't what I'm used to, having always worked in well-conducted houses.'

'Where is Grove?' I asked at last.

'Sister Tantrum could tell you better than I could, sir. He's in his bedroom, I suppose. It's my belief that she cares more for his interests than she does for yours. I dare say she's looking after him, but I must go and get your breakfast ready. There has to be somebody in the flat to do things.'

While I was having my breakfast there was a ring at the door, and Mrs. Stonegappe told me that the couple in the flat below (mine, as you know, is on the top floor) wanted to see me. 'Miss Tantrum has told them that you're too ill to see anyone,' said Mrs. Stonegappe.

'I will say this for her, she knows how to tell people where they get off. They train them to be like that in hospitals, I suppose, because they get all sorts there. But they're going to write you a letter, lodging a complaint I think they call it.'

Later, Sister Tranter brought me the letter. It was short and to the point. 'We are sorry to hear that you are ill, but after what happened last night we are not altogether surprised. Parties such as you give are not health-giving, to say the least. We would draw your attention to the clause saying that tenants must not be a nuisance to their neighbours and we have no doubt that the agents of the flats, to whom we have already written, will write you to the same effect.

Yours faithfully.'

I saw Ladbroke Grove again for a moment, he was wearing his bathrobe and looking very much the worse for wear. I said he must go, at once. He had only been with me five days, but he wanted another week's wages in lieu of notice, and spoke about his stamps and his P.A.Y.E. I felt it would not be good for me to continue the discussion so I referred him to my solicitor, and at eight o'clock Sister Tranter, bringing me my Horlicks, told me he had gone. 'He will come later to collect the suits he left in your wardrobe,' she said, 'in the circumstances he preferred not to ask you to release them. I think you were rather hasty with him,' she added, and there was emotion in her voice. 'Youth will be served, and there are many worse than he, much worse.'

I rather look forward to telling Dr. Herbright about his protégé!

With much love,

Richard.

P.S. This letter isn't as short as I meant it to be, but it is a transcription of life, and, in spite of the proverb, life is sometimes longer than art. How long, O Lord, how long!

16

Dearest Lucilla,

Thank you for the lovely, lovely lilac – it has made my day, my week, my month! and thank you for your letter too – but I am so terribly sorry that you feel hurt with me. It is most understandable, after what I've told you about the goings-on here (at much too great length, but it was a relief to tell you) – that you should wonder why I am not allowed to see my best friends – and especially my *best* friend, who, one would have thought, could do me nothing but *good* – interest me, soothe me, help me to *relax* (a word to conjure with, nowadays). I have pleaded with Hal Herbright and he's anything but a martinet-doctor, that he should lift the ban, at any rate on you! I got into quite a state about it (which I'm not supposed to), but I simply couldn't persuade him. 'I know what you feel,' he said, 'and I know what you've been through (though I agree with Sister Tranter that you were hasty over Ladbroke Grove, he seemed to me a nice fellow and boys will be boys – those people in the flat underneath must be very stuffy), but these things are cumulative and what you really need is to *be left alone*. If friends come you will have to make an *effort* to entertain them, and effort is bad for you.'

Here Richard laid down his pencil. Was this a true account of what had passed between him and Dr. Herbright? What Richard had actually said was, 'There's a great friend of mine who wants to see me, Hal.' 'Is it a man or a woman?' 'Why, what difference does that make?' 'Speaking medically, it might make a difference to your heart.' 'Oh, my heart is quite sound, in that sense.' 'But is *hers*? You say she wants to see you so much.' Richard hesitated. He had taught himself to believe, it suited him to believe, he wanted to believe, that no woman could ever entertain a tender feeling for him. More than once the idea had crossed his mind that Lucilla might be attracted to him, but he had dismissed it. It could do nothing but harm. Once was enough! Once was enough to have destroyed Lucy's life and blighted his. His did not matter now, but Lucilla's did. At any rate it was easy to argue that way; and what other way was there to argue?

'She does want to see me,' he said, 'and she takes it badly that she hasn't been allowed to come. I've told her about the things that have been happening here—' 'I expect you exaggerated them,' the doctor said. 'They are only what happens in every house that is lucky or unlucky enough to have staff. How do you suppose I manage? I have a daily help who comes in twice a week, and I have an arrangement with the telephone to answer my calls when I'm out – otherwise I have to do everything for myself.'

'Yes, but you haven't a bad heart,' said Richard.

'I soon should have,' the doctor said, 'if I encouraged every nice-looking woman who probably had nothing wrong with her (and there are some, I can assure you) to call me up every time she wanted to. The fate of bachelors is hard – you're one of the lucky ones, if you could only realize it.'

'So you advise me not to see my friend?' said Richard.

'I most certainly do,' the doctor said, 'unless you want to make your life more complicated than it is already. She might play you up worse than these other scoundrels have. And in that connection, Richard, let me tell you, as someone who sees more of the world than you do, that unless you can lower your moral standards to meet the requirements of modern behaviour, you won't be happy here.'

'Here?'

'I mean in this life. You may have a wonderful time in the next.'

For the first time Richard's precarious hold on life seemed more like a promise than a threat.

'So you don't want me to see Lucilla?' he said.

'Who?'

'Oh, that friend of mine.'

'I'll put it bluntly,' said the doctor. 'For your sake as well as hers I don't.'

Remembering all this, Richard took up his pencil, and tried to arrange the blotter to rest evenly against his thighs. 'I must make it sound as well as possible,' he thought, 'and above all I mustn't hurt her feelings.' Had he been better versed in the art of love, he would have known what a dangerous step this was. 'She knows how ill I am,' he thought, 'or doesn't she? I've always played it down to her. Who wants to appear a crock, anyhow? Better appear a crook. I expect she thinks

I'm shamming, and that's upset her. Well, perhaps I am, but the doctors don't say so!' He remembered his mother's Victorian dread of illness: they were all going to die, he was going to die, his father was going to die. Aunt Carrie was going to die. Aunt Carrie still survived – at least he supposed she did. Was he lingering, or just malingering?

Of course it isn't a question of 'entertaining' each other in the social sense, is it? I mean we don't have to, you and I, we don't have to think, 'Now I must say something, or he (or she) will feel let down.' With us, it's just a question of being together, isn't it? and that's why I feel, well, frankly so *resentful* of Dr. Herbright's attitude. But there it is. One must obey one's doctor, mustn't one? He says that any extra strain (as if it was a strain!) would be bad for me. You see it's this 'heart condition' as they call it – such an odd phrase, I don't know what it means, and I don't want to alarm you, still less myself, about it. But as I said he's adamant. So I hope you don't feel disappointed with me, dear Lucilla. If only you were *here*, you could manage things so much better than I do.

To change the subject (but it isn't really changing the subject), I've found a successor for Ladbroke Grove. He doesn't call himself Bayswater Road, or anything of that sort, he is just plain John Chinnery and instead of having fifteen suits, he has, so my spies tell me, only one, so I shall have to get him a couple of serving jackets to wear in the house, but they will have to be outsize, for he is an outsize man, not specially tall but very big-built, with a large red face to match, black or nearly black eyes, and a moustache:

if the moustache was longer and more whiskery, he would look like Puss in Boots. Mrs. Stonegappe seems to like him, she says he is a real man, which couldn't be said so confidently of Ladbroke Grove. I don't know what Sister Tranter thinks. When I asked her if she liked my latest acquisition she said she hadn't noticed him particularly.

As if she could help noticing him, when he takes up all the space there is! He told me he has been a big-game hunter (he is a man of about 45), and there is evidence of this. Although he himself has only one suit, he has innumerable *skins*. Against doctor's orders I got up and peeped into his room and saw what I took to be the pelts of leopards, jaguars, pumas, ounces, ocelots – not however a lion or a tiger – overlapping each other on the floor, and hanging and hugging each other on the walls. And there was, unless I imagined it, what I can only call a *feral* smell, as if the room had been somehow joined on to the Zoo.

Sister Tranter told me that it turned her stomach, but Mrs. Stonegappe said she rather liked it, because it reminded her of jungle life.

I wonder. Someone said you ought to practise believing a dozen impossible things before breakfast, but my advice is just the opposite – try to disbelieve a dozen possible things, not only before breakfast but at any hour of the day. I am by nature very credulous, unlike my father who was just the opposite. If one told him some interesting or startling fact, that a lioness had whelpèd in the streets for instance – he would say, 'I should like to have further evidence of that.' It wasn't the same as calling you a liar – though some people thought so, and took umbrage – he dissociated the statement from the speaker, and thought that on *à priori* grounds it was inherently improbable and needed confirmation. It wasn't only that, working in a bank, he learned to suspect people's veracity, for there's nothing, I've been told, they lie about so much as money. His nature was sceptical and his outlook scientific: he always wanted *proof*. I'm sure that Kinklecross wasn't what he made himself out to be, nor was Ladbroke Grove, though I'm not sure *what* he was, and Denys (but I won't go into that) may not have been a real Aspin. If Chinnery was a real big-game hunter, he must find me very small game. There was a play, do you remember? called *The Skin Game*: perhaps he plays at that.

But isn't it rather boring, and disquieting, after all these years to find that people, apart from you and me, are so very untruthful? Men more than women, of course, for women lie with an object in view, negative or positive, whereas men lie for the pure love of lying (perhaps pure isn't the word!). When Sister Tranter and Mrs. Stonegappe tell me lies, I sometimes know what's behind it, a man they like or don't like – cherchez l'homme! But men seem to love misrepresentation as such: perhaps that's why so many modern painters can't look facts in the face, they veil them in abstractions, meant to mislead. But enough of this, I am doing my best to work on Dr. Herbright's feelings as a man, and his knowledge as a doctor, to let you come and see me. Surely, a little of what you fancy does you good – though I should like a *lot*.

Much love,

R.

Dearest Lucilla,

What you wrote in your letter, and told me on the telephone this morning, has disturbed me very much. Of course I'm not trying to keep you at arm's length, why should I? Arm's length, as a measure of distance, is quite close, isn't it? But not close enough. Thinking about this, I long for you to be *very* near, within arm's reach, not at arm's length, but what *can* I do? I was brought up by my mother to have this great respect for doctors – they were *gods* to her, and somehow it's in my blood. Does he think you are a sort of Medusa, who would turn me to stone if I set eyes on you? You seem to think I'm stony enough already – but really, Lucilla, I'm not. I only wish you could come here with your flowers – yourself a fairer flower (I quote from Milton). I suppose I'm lucky that Dr. Herbright hasn't forbidden me to have flowers on the ground that they might over-excite me!

With much love, and praying for our immediate reunion,

Richard.

Darling Lucilla,

I have been inexcusably long in writing to thank you for the freesias – what a heavenly scent they have – and for your sweet, forgiving letter though it's Dr. Herbright, not me, who really needs forgiveness.

The reason I didn't write sooner is that there has been another domestic crisis, you would think that I must be hardened to them by now, but I am not. It has arisen over those skins I told you about, that John Chinnery brought into the house. Apparently he has been *selling* them, and this has come to the ears of the agents of the flat. I don't know if it's the same with you, but the tenants of these flats are forbidden to carry on any trade or profession in them (on the premises, I mean). I can't imagine you wanting to sell anything – *buying* is much more in your line. How the flower shops must flourish on you! Well, I had quite a stiff note from the agents, saying didn't I know it was against the regulations, and would I please stop selling the skins, at once. I replied, as was the truth, that I wasn't selling the skins, and (as was also the truth) I didn't know that they were being sold. And I promised to stop this iniquitous traffic at once.

But to do that, as you realize, I should have to *make a scene* with Chinnery, and any kind of scene has been expressly forbidden me by Dr. Herbright (which makes it so idiotic that he doesn't want me to see you, for *you* would *never* make a scene). So I kept putting off 'speaking' to him about it, and then a worse, a much worse thing happened. The police rang me up. It was Sergeant Davis again – very nice, as usual, saying he would like to come and see me about something. I couldn't say no: I suppose that even on one's death-bed (perhaps especially not then) one couldn't refuse to see the police.

Sister Tranter brought him in, and I fancy that her manner made him a little embarrassed, hard-boiled as he must be. He had the effect he always has, of making the room seem smaller. Taking off his crash-helmet (I suppose he had been riding a motor-bike) he carefully deposited it between a photograph of my father and mother and a silver cup which (would you believe it?) I had won at school for the long jump. Then he assumed a graver air than was usual with him, and said, 'I take it you don't know what I've come about, sir.' 'No, Sergeant,' I said. (Sergeant-Inspector is such a mouthful.) 'You've had no complaints here, recently?' 'Complaints,' I echoed, 'complaints? My dear Sergeant' (I hastily withdrew the endearment and substituted Sergeant *tout court*), 'I've had nothing but complaints. Mrs. Stonegappe, my daily help, complains of Sister Tranter, my nurse, Sister Tranter complains of Mrs. Stonegappe, they both complain of Chinnery, my man-servant, so-called, and now the agents of the flat, Messrs. Jenkins and Dobody, have complained of him too.' 'On what grounds, may I ask?' 'Oh, Sergeant,' I exclaimed, 'surely you don't want me to tell you *all* they have complained about? I will, if you like, but it would be a complete waste of your time.' Sergeant Davis smiled. 'No,' he said, 'I'll spare you that. It is the complaints about Chinnery we want to look into.' 'Oh,' I said, and the feelings of guilt the police always arouse took hold of me. 'It's a tiresome matter but it's trifling, and I don't think, with all respect, that it comes into your department, at least I hope not.' Then I told him about the skins and how Jenkins and Dobody had complained of Chinnery's using the flat for commercial purposes. 'I shall have to tell him not to, but I keep putting it off,' I confessed, 'because I suppose it means he'll go, and then I shall have all the trouble of finding someone else. I have to have somebody to look after me because I'm not quite well.' 'You needn't worry about that,' the sergeant said, as if he meant my illness, though I knew he didn't, 'we don't *want* you to tell him.' 'Not tell him?' I exclaimed. 'But what will Jenkins and Dobody say? They'll turn him out of the flat and very likely me as well.' A wave of misery swept over me, then I noticed the sergeant was still standing and begged him to sit down. 'Draw that chair up,' I said, indicating the only one that was unencumbered.

The policeman complied and sat down quite lightly for so heavy a man. 'I may as well be frank with you' (my heart turned over, for I never expected to hear such words from a policeman's lips), 'we don't want you to tell Chinnery because we want to keep him under observation. We want to know *where he is*, if you take my meaning.'

I did. 'But is it illegal to sell skins?' I asked. 'I know that Jenkins and Dobody don't like it, but—' 'We've been in touch with them,' the sergeant said. 'Not to worry, as far as they're concerned. No, it isn't illegal to sell skins – you could sell your skin, if you wanted to, and I could sell mine' (and he glanced at the back of his hairy hand), 'but we aren't sure that selling skins is what Master Chinnery is really up to. We think he may be selling something else besides skins. I won't say what – I leave it to you to guess. And we're not sure what he's getting in exchange. Something the Government might be interested in – Security, you know. That's why I came round, to ask you to carry on as usual.'

'Oh thank you,' I said, much relieved. 'I always want to carry on as usual. It was only when Jenkins and Dobody—'

'We are in touch with them, Mr. Mardick.' He made 'in touch' sound sinister. But who wants to be out of touch?

'Do you mean that Chinnery's a dangerous criminal?' I asked.

'Oh no, no,' said the sergeant, rising briskly from his seat, as if it was only a stepping-stone to higher things. 'And in any case, we have our eye on your place – you only have to ring us up. You've been in touch with us before, you know the number?'

'Oh yes, oh yes,' I said.

The sergeant took his helmet from the dressing-table, and adjusted it, rather to my surprise, in the looking-glass. 'Keep us informed about anything unusual that happens. But not to worry – we have another line on him as well. The chief thing is not to let him know that you suspect him – or that we do,' and with a smile and a salute the sergeant left.

So here I am, Lucilla, a sort of jailer, which is quite a new role for me. If this flat is a prison, as I sometimes think it is, all the criminals have escaped, except me, and Mrs. Stonegappe and Sister Tranter, and they could get out, if they wanted to, but I can't, unless I go to hospital, which I don't want to, and I doubt if I *could*, after what the police-man said. I might be regarded as Chinnery's accessory! I wish he had told me what Chinnery was suspected of – is he a drug-peddler, a blackmailer, or just a murderer? I quite like him, and he is a good cook, as far as he goes; but not ideal for an invalid, as he cooks everything in wine – my wine, I suppose. I know it's stupid, but after what the sergeant told me, I shan't sleep at night unless I lock my bedroom door. I can't see why Chinnery should want to kill me, he has nothing to gain by it, but he may be a homicidal maniac!

It's odd, at my age, to be involved in so many experiences, when I never expected to have any more, of any sort! The fact that chiefly concerns me is that I'm ill, or supposed to be, but no one but you takes this into account. For the police, I am a stooge, and for Sister Tranter and Mrs. Stonegappe, just a cog in the machinery of their grievances! And I sometimes feel that for you I am not the ray of light that I should like to be – and that you are, for me.

But some of my old friends have been writing to me and ringing me up. They seemed quite surprised when I answered – I think they thought I was dead! Of course I can't see them, any more than I can see you, but it's nice to know that one is still in people's thoughts – if nowhere else.

I'll write again. Bless you and thank you for the freesias,

Richard.

P.S. I hate to say this, but I think I ought to tell you that some of the flowers you gave me haven't lasted very long. I believe that in certain shops they *do* something to them, I mean, to shorten their lives, so that they will soon have to be replaced. I mind for you more than for me, much as I treasure the flowers, but apart from the personal question, one wants value for one's money, doesn't one?

17

Darling Lucilla,

So many things have happened since I wrote to you – the only pleasant one was the arrival of your tulips, which, believe it or not, are still flourishing! I suppose Sister Tranter must be given some of the credit – she always takes them out of my room when she goes away in the evening so that I cannot infect them, nor they me! She picks the vase up with the air of saying, 'This is a disciplinary action.' It isn't only that she feels that flowers are the enemy of health; she also feels, I think, that the money spent on them should have been spent on *her*, and resents it. The tulips are extra-professional, they don't help me to get better. Not that she thinks of *me* in that sense; I am not a person to her, I am just something on which to unload her grievances. I don't think that if I were *dying* at closing-time she would stay a moment longer, because that would be to let down the side, the side for whom regular hours are the be-all and the end-all. Especially the end-all. So when she removes the flowers she is saying, in effect, I am asserting my right to go. What a lot can be said with flowers! – and what a lot you have said, but much more pleasantly. To nurses, nursing is a routine employment: not a vocation – they squeeze every penny out of it they can. Or am I being unjust to them? They don't get paid much, and aren't well enough organized to strike . . .

Illness is demoralizing – it makes one feel the world ought to revolve around one – as indeed it did, in the old days. I remember my mother's anxious face, when I was ill, or my father, or Aunt Carrie. Nothing else seemed to matter – except that we should get well. And my Aunt Esther, who wasn't so illness-conscious – less than she should have been, my mother thought – what trouble she took for all of us lame dogs at St. Botolph's. I can still hear her saying, 'What shall we find for Richard to *do*?' – so sweet of her!

(Richard laid down his pencil, for this was dangerous ground. How had he arranged with his conscience, his nervous system, or in whatever place the sense of guilt resides, to write such things to Lucy's half-sister? Didn't it suggest sclerosis of the moral arteries, a deterioration, not just physical, of the heart? 'I must have gone downhill further and faster than I thought,' he told himself. And then, in self-excuse, it was the gradualness of our friendship that made such a thing possible – that, and the fact that it all happened so many years ago. And then he thought, again in self-defence, 'Can there be some affinity between me and Lucilla, as there was between me and Lucy, that is stronger than I am, and more deep-seated than my thoughts?' He took up his pencil again.)

What I meant was, one *counted* in those days more than one does now – except with you, my dear Lucilla, who have done so much for me, and would have done still more, if Doctor Herbright hadn't been so uncooperative.

Well, Chinnery has gone. He was marched off yesterday morning about half-past ten. I heard voices and heavy footsteps, but nothing more until Sergeant Davis came in and told me they had arrested him – for, of all things, receiving stolen goods. None of those nice skins, at which I once had a peep, belonged to him. 'I didn't let you know before,' Sergeant Davis apologized, 'for reasons which you will appreciate. I know you wouldn't have warned him, but it would have put you in a difficult position – all the more so if you liked him.' I scented a trap in this. Friendly as the sergeant had always been, it would have helped him a little in his career, perhaps, if he could have made me an accessory. 'I did quite like him as a matter of fact,' I said, 'I've liked them all, to begin with. I'm getting to know quite a lot about criminals, but you must know more' – he smiled – 'and I take it that plausibility is part of their stock in trade?' 'You are quite right,' he said, 'the average confidence-man – and there are some in private service as in other walks of life – has to be plausible. They see a gentleman like you, sir,' he went on, looking down at me, 'and say to themselves, "Where is his weak spot? How can we have him for a mug?" The majority of them just want bed and breakfast, but some of them want more. You might be luckier with a foreigner. They haven't learned the ropes.' 'Do you mean,' I said, 'that no man is to be trusted?' 'Oh no, sir,' and the sergeant sounded shocked. 'But there are so many temptations in this line of business. At least, that's what we find. But it's all in the day's work, and I suppose if it wasn't we should be out of a job. And what are you going to do now, sir?'

'My doctor would like me to go into hospital,' I said.

'And very good advice, too,' said the sergeant. 'In hospital they can't get at you, see? Nice, comfortable beds. There are many worse places than hospital, in my opinion, and I've had some experience.'

I found this conversation terribly depressing, and all the more so because the policeman obviously wished me well.

'But even in hospitals,' I argued, 'you sometimes find undesirable characters.'

'Oh yes,' the sergeant said. 'You're dead right there. Quite often men break in and steal the nurses' wages. You'd be surprised how many dodges they're up to. If I was you I shouldn't take much money with you, I'd keep it in the bank – it's safer there. Well, sir, I must be off, but I thought you'd like to know what's happened.'

'Will they want me to give evidence?' I asked.

'Oh no, I don't suppose so. It's just bad luck it's happened on your premises, so to speak, and being as you're an invalid—'

When he had gone I rang the bell – not an electric bell, for as far as I know, flats don't have them – but a brass hand-bell that had once belonged to my grandfather.

There was a slight altercation outside the door, then Mrs. Stonegappe came in.

'Oh, Mrs. Stonegappe,' I said, 'what's been happening?'

'Happening?' she said, with well-assumed surprise.

'Well, I know that Chinnery's been arrested – the

sergeant told me that – but I just wondered what actually took place.'

'To tell you the truth, I didn't pay much attention,' Mrs. Stonegappe said. 'I was busy hoovering the sitting-room, not that it's much use, seeing you never go there. I heard the door-bell ring, of course, and Sister Tantrum, who was nearest, let them in. Two policemen and the sergeant – but I didn't notice specially.'

If she wanted to disappoint me, she was quite successful.

'Oh, I thought you might have seen what happened,' I said. 'If he offered any resistance or not, or what he did. But you didn't see it, and it's of no importance.'

'But I did see it,' Mrs. Stonegappe said. 'You don't suppose I could be in a flat as small as this, and not see what was going on? Naturally, I didn't *want* to see it – I had my furniture to polish – that Mrs. Cuddesdon had let it go disgraceful. So I just looked up with the duster in my hand—'

'I thought you were hoovering,' I couldn't help saying.

'I don't know which it was, but they rang, and I answered the bell, seeing as Sister Tantrum never does.' 'I thought she let them in,' I said, but Mrs. Stonegappe ignored this. 'So they said, "Is Mr. Chinnery here? We want to see him." I said, "Mr. Mardick is here, but he's in bed" – I didn't want to get mixed up with it. Then they asked again, and I showed them Chinnery's door – you have to do what the police tell you, don't you? They opened it but he wasn't there, he was in the toilet shaving, I ask you, at half-past ten in the morning! I didn't listen, of course, but I heard them say – the sergeant it was, "Are you Mr. Chinnery?" and of course he couldn't deny it. So then the sergeant said, "I'm afraid we shall have to ask you to come with us." He cautioned Chinnery not to say anything, so Chinnery only said, in that posh voice he sometimes uses, "I think you must have made a mistake. What do you want me for?" I didn't listen, of course, but I couldn't help hearing the sergeant say "for receiving stolen goods", or something of that sort. Then I went into the kitchen, for I didn't want to be mixed up with anything of that sort, so I said to Sister Tantrum who was making her face up (I hate her doing that in the kitchen, it's so dirty), "It seems they've got him, I always knew that there was something fishy about him." I won't tell you what Sister Tantrum said because she's so uneducated, and you can't hear what she says anyhow when she's talking through her lipstick, so I just went out into the passage again because Chinnery isn't a bad sort and anyone can be unfortunate. I didn't want to look, of course, but I saw them taking him away, so I only said, "See you again sometime," or something like that, not to demean myself, but just to say good-bye, seeing as *you* couldn't, being in bed, and perhaps didn't want to, as none of us want to be mixed up with things of that sort. The policemen didn't stop him from turning round to say good-bye – they're human, after all. But of course I didn't really see or hear anything at all, I was too busy hoovering, and trying to hear what Sister Tantrum said.'

So you see, dear Lucilla, I am back where I was, and the question for me now is, shall I try again, after those rather dismal experiences, or shall I go to hospital, supposing Dr. Herbright could get me in? That is what he thinks is best, I know, but I do cling to my freedom, such as it is.

If only I could find somebody *honest*! But I gather they are the exception in this walk of life. At least the men are. You have said, and my friends who sometimes ring me up have said: 'Why don't you have a woman?' (Excuse the expression, dear Lucilla, our language is so ambiguous, but you know what I mean.) Women are much more honest than men, they say, and it is true, in a way; they don't pride themselves on their dishonesty in the way that men do. Men of a certain type don't feel themselves to be men unless they have cheated you. It is their badge of manhood, so to speak, as the *toga virilis* was to the Romans – only they acquire it much earlier in life than those antique Romans did.

Women are expert pilferers, but they are more practical and their operations are on a smaller scale. For them it is a routine proceeding and I don't think inspired by motives of prestige.

One thing I'm sure of, which is that when 'they', male or female, accuse each other of certain peccadilloes, it means they are doing them themselves. Such a simple stratagem – but I'm always taken in by it, and I suppose I always shall be. It's not an amiable trait, on my part, because it shows a readiness to believe the worst that people say about each other, but it isn't quite as subjective as that – it's an instinct of self-preservation, one has to protect oneself even on one's bed – especially on one's bed – and when I hear them billing and cooing, and then one or the other comes to me and says, he or she has broken this or that, or taken this or that, and that there's nothing left to eat, or eat out of, or that the car isn't there, and where is it? – or when I'm told that it has used ten gallons of petrol since yesterday, and where have they gone to? – I can't help feeling that whoever is obliging enough to tell me this *must* have good grounds for his or her suspicions – whereas the fact is, I'm practically sure, that the informer himself (or herself) is the culprit. I don't know whether Sister Tranter has a driving-licence – how can I know, unless I ask her? And equally, how *can* I ask her? – but before Chinnery 'left' (rather a euphemism for his enforced departure) each accused the other of using it. What I think *may* have happened is this: that Chinnery took them both (not at the same time!) for joyrides, and Mrs. Stonegappe, who is a nicer character, I think, than Sister T., and according to Sister T. is susceptible to the pleasures of a pub-crawl, was grateful to him – as she showed unmistakably in her account of his arrest – (though of course she didn't see or hear it). Since he 'left' there have been no more complaints of unauthorized car-using. We shall see what happens when Alberto Ferrero, from the Peerless Domestic Agency, arrives. Peerless, I suppose, because peers don't use it.

How much does all this matter, do you think, Lucilla? Or to put it more personally, how much should one mind it? There is the monetary loss, of course. The Bible says, 'Thou shalt not muzzle the ox that treadeth the corn,' but I don't believe that the Israelites of those days (or of these) would have let the ox have his head unless he was doing a lot of treading – whereas Sister Tranter and Mrs. Stonegappe don't do much treading, at least not much footwork – to judge by the long silences that re-echo through the flat. Now that I am no longer there to chase, Mrs. Stonegappe doesn't seem to use the carpet-sweeper, and as for the hoover, I have her word that she was using it when Chinnery was marched off, but I've never heard it wailing with my own ears.

So, as oxen, I don't think they ought to be utterly unmuzzled, that is if their depredations are as great as they say each other's are – being in bed I can't check up on this – but the cheques I have to sign do seem rather large, especially the grocers', which last month included 500 cigarettes – Chinnery's, I suppose, but I don't know, for they all accused each other of being heavy smokers. One consolation is, that now he is gone, I shan't have to pay those astronomic bills for petrol – Chinnery said the car drank up petrol, and when I told him it was supposed to do twenty-five miles to the gallon, he said that in London, what with starting and stopping, it only did eight – I imagine that he used it for collecting stolen goods and taking Mrs. Stonegappe to her favourite haunts – but perhaps he didn't use it at all, but asked the garage to make out a bill for it, and shared the proceeds with them. I believe that's quite a common practice. You might say why did I let him, or any of them, use the car – they would be sure to take advantage of it. To which I reply that for one thing it's better for the car to use it, and for another, I genuinely wanted them to be happy. But the moment you let them know that, you are lost. And they don't like you any the better for it, they just think you are a mug and find new ways of imposing on you.

I'm afraid it's partly laziness too, I don't want the trouble of keeping them up to the mark – even if I could, being in bed. Somebody said to me, 'You must trust somebody, or life becomes impossible.' But it's equally impossible if you do, not that I ought to complain when I lie so composedly here in my bed – to quote Edgar Allan Poe – one of my favourite writers. Not so composedly as all that, though.

But to go back to what I was saying. How much does it really matter, this dishonesty which seems to be the rule nowadays? The human race is much too old, or much too young, for me or anyone to try and reform it. And think of the fate of so many reformers, Savonarola, for instance. An attitude of acceptance is more becoming, isn't it, and much more comfortable. The trouble is, dear Lucilla, that being brought up as we were, it is almost impossible for us to take dishonesty for granted, as we must if we are to live happily in the modern world.

How lucky we are not to feel the need, the necessity, the obligation to deceive people – not even each other, not even ourselves! I don't like to think that this immunity is due to having a private income. Some people would say it was, but even if it is, it doesn't affect us, you and me, for we don't have to pool our incomes, as married couples have to. It's so unfair. Keep single, keep single!

My next letter will be far more cheerful.

With much love,
Richard.

True to his word, Richard began his next letter to Lucilla in a more sanguine vein. He counted, and recounted, his blessings. 'Besides one, that you know of! – I have the prospect of a nice Italian who is coming "to do for me" (our language is so ambiguous, especially when one ventures into idiom). He comes from Udine, where, unlike the people of the Bas-Italia, they have a high reputation for honesty, at least the Peerless Domestic Agency says so. They also say that he has no "police record", but they say this of everyone on their books, and as he hasn't been long in England, he may not have had time to get one.

'I am in a state of mind which it is fashionable to call euphoria. But it is bed-time now, I will write again to-morrow.'

He didn't write the next day, but the following day, after a rather half-hearted effort to count more blessings (the weather, the unexpected punctuality of the post, the kindness of the milkman, who, Mrs. Stonegappe reported, had asked how he was getting on – 'and he doesn't do that for *everybody*,' she added) he wrote a postscript; but the pen, no less than the tongue, goes to the sore place. After a short mental struggle, in which he convinced himself that a correspondent would rather hear bad news than good news, he went on:

Before I close (ominous word – though many things, like shops and flowers, open again after they have closed), I should like to tell you of another incident, if you can bear to hear it – something that happened since Denys left (I haven't heard from him again, by the way: *that* chapter seems to be closed, even if *I* am not). I have all the time in the world to write, but you may not have much time to read, and I wouldn't bother you with it if it didn't provide objective proof that I am not a victim of persecution-mania!

Well, one morning (these things always seem to happen in the morning) Sister Tranter came in with a stiff, expressionless face and said, 'There's a person to see you, Mr. Mardick.'

'Oh,' I said, 'who?'

'He didn't give a name,' said Sister Tranter. 'He said that in any case you wouldn't know who it was.'

She paused.

'Is that all?' I asked.

'No, Mr. Mardick,' she said, using my name as if it was an imprecation, 'it isn't all. I told the person that you were ill and not allowed to see visitors, but he said it was very urgent and a matter of Government importance.'

'What did you say then?' I asked.

'I told him to *wait*,' said Sister Tranter impressively.

'And is he waiting?' I asked.

'Yes, Mr. Mardick, he's in the passage but he hasn't taken off his hat.'

'Oh, is he wearing a hat?' I asked inanely. 'I mean, so few men do, nowadays.'

'I thought he might have taken it off in the presence of a lady,' said Sister Tranter, 'but I can't altogether blame him, because the daily woman leaves so much dust on the side-table it's quite a disgrace, though I haven't liked to tell you.'

'Couldn't you ask him,' I said, 'to hang his hat on the peg in the airing cupboard? It wouldn't get dirty there.'

'I shouldn't like him to see inside the airing cupboard,' replied Sister Tranter. 'It's not very nice, and besides—'

'Besides what?'

'Oh, nothing.'

To keep myself from wondering what that nothing was, for it sounded the gravest of Sister Tranter's charges, I said:

'Oh, do bring him in, he may be in a hurry.'

'Not if he's anything to do with the Government,' said Sister Tranter, shrugging her shoulders as she shut the door.

A moment later she opened it, and holding the knob as if it might escape, announced: 'The gentleman to see you, Mr. Mardick.' The gentleman proved to be tall and thin and dark, with a hair-line moustache; he was still holding his hat, and looked exceedingly embarrassed.

'My name is Macpherson,' he said with a strong Scottish accent. 'I am an Inspector of Pensions and National Insurance. I am extremely sorry to trouble you, Mr. Mardick, but this is a rather important matter.'

'Do please sit down, Mr. Macpherson,' I said, 'and put your hat down, too.'

He looked round, but all the available surfaces seemed to be covered by medicine-bottles, or books, or clothes, and he was preparing to lay his hat on the bed when my silly superstition about putting hats on beds pricked me, and I warned him.

'Oh, don't put it there. It might bring you, or me, or both of us bad luck. Put it on the top of the wardrobe.' (The wardrobe is a tall Victorian mahogany edifice, embellished with an arcading of three arches in low relief. I don't think you've ever seen it.) He stretched up and put the hat on the ledge, and then turned to me.

'Please draw up a chair,' I said, 'and throw all those things' – indicating the miscellaneous objects that littered the chair-seat – 'on the floor.'

'Shall I put them on the bed for the moment?' he said. '*They* won't bring bad luck.'

I agreed, and he sat down and opened his brief-case, bringing out a formidable assortment of documents, the topmost of which was headed, '*Urgent, for Immediate Prosecution.*'

I didn't at all like the look of this. He noticed my eyes straying towards it and said,

'Don't let that worry you, Mr. Mardick. It won't concern you per-r-sonally, unless—'

I waited for him to go on.

'Unless things turn out otherwise than I expect. But perhaps I should explain the purpose of my visit.'

The purring 'r' sound was getting on my nerves.

'Please do,' I said.

He fingered his files.

'I understand you had an employee by the name of Ladbroke Grove.'

'I've had so many employees,' I said, 'but yes, I think you're right.'

'Did you pay your share of his insurance stamps?'

I searched my memory, which isn't very good now.

'Oh yes, I'm sure I did. I always paid their stamps – my share and their share, too. The whole boiling.'

'You shouldn't have done that,' said the Inspector. 'The upkeep of the Welfare State is their concern as well as yours. By your thoughtless, though excusable generosity, you undermine their sense of civic responsibility.'

'I didn't know they had any,' I retorted. 'But why do you ask me about Ladbroke Grove?'

'Because,' said the Inspector, drawing his chair nearer to my bed, 'he says he's lost his stamp-book.'

'I'm sorry to hear that,' I said, trying to remember what Ladbroke Grove had looked like. 'But I expect it does happen to people, doesn't it?'

'Only too often,' said the Inspector, grimly. 'But, as you will appreciate, the loss is sometimes – what shall I say – a *convenient* loss – convenient to the loser, I mean.'

'I understand,' I said, not quite understanding.

'Perhaps you will have noticed, Mr. Mardick, that the working class – perhaps every class – is not over-anxious to pay their contribution to National Insurance, in spite of the benefits they derive from it?'

I said I had noticed.

'Well,' said the Inspector more briskly, 'Mr. Grove said he had lost his stamp-book. He needed it when he applied for a position with the United Universal Paper Mills. He did not, I think, ask you for a reference?'

I said he hadn't.

'Perhaps he had his reasons, Mr. Mardick. He asked the U.U.P.M. to arrange for him to be issued with a new stamp-book. Many firms do this as a matter of course, there is such a shortage of labour nowadays. Mr. Ladbroke Grove said he was familiar with the techniques of paper-making. But the U.U.P.M. is a conservative firm, and without a reference, and without a stamp-book, they hesitated to employ Mr. Ladbroke Grove. So they consulted us, and on further inquiry – carried out in the most tactful way, as you can imagine – Mr. Ladbroke Grove discovered that he had discovered his lost stamp-book.'

'What a blessing!' I exclaimed. 'I thought you might want to look for it here – and you see what a chaos my papers are in. So now everything is all right, isn't it?'

'I'm afraid not,' said the Inspector, turning his eyes downwards to the file headed *Urgent, for Immediate Prosecution*, 'and this is where *you* come in.'

Whereupon he brought out a National Insurance stamp-card, and handed it to me. I glanced over it – there were the stamps, all in order, marked with appropriate squiggles.

'Yes, Inspector?' I said, forgetting that Macpherson was his name.

He drew his chair still nearer, and fixed his eyes on mine.

'Did you ever see such *dreadful* stamps?' he demanded.

'What's wrong with them?' I asked. 'They look O.K. to me.'

'What's wrong with them?' he repeated, appalled and horrified by my ignorance. 'What's wrong with them? Everything's wrong. They are someone else's stamps. They were bought on the Black Market, probably for a quarter of their real cost.'

'The Black Market,' I exclaimed rather excited, as one

is apt to be, at the thought of a new crime. 'Is there a Black Market in insurance stamps?'

'You didn't know?' repeated the Inspector, incredulously. 'You didn't know? You must have led a very sheltered life.' He paused, looking round the room, which wasn't open to the elements, and perhaps thinking he had said too much. 'It's one of our chief headaches,' he went on. 'We lose hundreds of thousands of pounds every year because of the illicit sale of insurance stamps. They get them in all sorts of ways – through dishonest cashiers of companies, for instance, who mark them off with a rubber stamp which isn't easy to detect, or from Irishmen who come over to work in England, and when they go back have some spare stamps by them – and in all sorts of ways. We have experts, of course, who can detect them, but it takes time, a lot of time. Deserters from the Services are always trying to get hold of them. These' – he studied the card in his hand – 'are from Ireland, I should guess.'

'But how does this affect me?' I asked.

'It affects you in this way,' said the Inspector, patiently. 'Ladbroke Grove says, in his defence, that you never paid your share of his stamps, and so, being hard up, he had to buy them on the Black Market.'

'But I did pay for them!' I protested. 'As I told you, I gave him the money to pay for his share as well as mine.'

'But did you *see* him put the stamps into the book?' The Inspector fixed on me a gimlet eye.

'I didn't actually *see* him,' I said, 'I assumed he had.'

The Inspector looked horrified.

'You *assumed* he had? But you should have made sure. It was your duty as a citizen either to affix the stamps yourself, or else to see that he did.'

'I don't see why,' I answered angrily. 'This is a free country, or supposed to be. I can't compel a man to put stamps on his card. Every single man (don't misunderstand me), or every married man whom I've employed during the last year or two, has raised every conceivable objection to having his cards stamped. I'm not well, as you see; I can't always go out and buy the stamps myself. Can I never trust the men to put the stamps on? Is this the result of all the money we spend on the education of what used to be called the masses? Am I supposed to be an unpaid Government watch-dog, and *force* them (supposing I was able to) to put the stamps on? If we lived under a dictator, no doubt I could.'

'All the same, I'm afraid it was your responsibility,' said the Inspector, rebuking by his mild manner my indignation. 'That is the *law*.' He paused, and again consulted his file of papers. 'He ought, of course, to pay his share,' he went on.

'I should think so!' I said, still simmering with resentment.

'He ought to,' continued the Inspector calmly, 'and by rights he ought to go to prison. Are you aware, Mr. Mardick, that offences of this kind carry very heavy penalties?'

'For him or for me?' I asked.

'For him, naturally,' replied the Inspector, ignoring my sarcasm. 'Very heavy penalties, a long term of imprisonment. But in the circumstances the Ministry has decided to waive the prosecution.'

'Oh,' I exclaimed, disappointed. 'Why?'

'Mr. Ladbroke Grove had a very good war record in the S.A.S.,' said the Inspector, 'but he is a highly-strung man, and the Army Welfare Officer of his district is of opinion that his experiences as a paratrooper have affected the balance of his mind.'

'Are you sure that he was a paratrooper?' I asked. 'He didn't look like one.'

'We have made inquiries,' said the Inspector, 'and it seems certain that he served in the Parachute Regiment, though probably under a different name. You may not appreciate this, Mr. Mardick, but to men of a sensitive temperament, any form of Commando training, involving as it unfortunately does the practice of violence, is unsettling mentally and may lead to crime.'

'Crime I grant you,' I said, 'but mentally unsettling, no. While Ladbroke Grove was here, he seemed quite on the spot – metaphorically, I mean, for he often absented himself without warning. And doesn't the fact that he knew how to get hold of these stamps argue a certain degree of sanity?'

'Indeed it does not,' said the Inspector warmly. 'Most criminals are kinky in one way or another. These stamps are easy to get hold of, though it needs an expert to detect them. We have a special department for it. You wouldn't believe how smart some of these fellows are – but sane, no. It takes a sane man to be honest.'

'So what are you going to do about Ladbroke Grove?' I asked.

The Inspector glanced at me and then looked away.

'We don't want to be hard on him, Mr. Mardick. We have to recognize that a large – an increasingly large – section of the community earn – make, perhaps, is a better word – their livings by crime. Crime is beginning to pay. The police do what they can, but they are in a minority. As the general public grows more criminal – more anti-social, I should say – they have less and less use for the police, and tend to regard the man in blue as an enemy. I myself, though only a Civil Servant, have been threatened, I may tell you. As a law-abiding Scotsman I regret this, but what are we to do? We can't segregate the criminals from the rest of the community, as we once did; we have to try to absorb them, and raise their standards, even at the cost of lowering ours. We have to adjust ourselves to the new outlook on crime, and the better-off part of our national collectivity, which on the whole is less criminal than the rest, will have to bear the brunt.'

'What sort of brunt, Inspector?'

Again he looked away from me.

'You may not like what I am going to say, Mr. Mardick, but I hope you will take it in good part. The most important compromise is between the sense of right and wrong. You would agree, wouldn't you, that the conceptions of right and wrong are based on human behaviour, and are not abstractions invented by a divine law-giver, unrelated to human needs and impulses?'

'I must have notice of that question,' I said.

'Without being in any way personal, I can assume that we have all of us, at one time or another, blotted our copy-books?'

'Some of us have, Inspector, otherwise you wouldn't be here.'

'Ah,' countered the Inspector, 'if employers would only make sure that their employees' stamps were properly affixed, I might be out of a job.' He let this sink in. 'But to return to our friend, Ladbroke Grove—'

'He's no friend of mine,' I said.

'There you go, Mr. Mardick, making yourself out holier than he—'

'I can assure you, Inspector,' I interrupted, 'that in this day and age the danger of spiritual pride is so remote as to be non-existent.'

'Spiritual pride takes many forms, Mr. Mardick. In his case it would be the rever-r-rse of what it might be in yours. Do you suppose he loses face with his pals because he buys his stamps on the Black Market? On the contrary, they respect him for it and it boosts his ego. In his world it's the right thing to do. I have to chase him because it's my job, just as it's the greyhound's job to chase the hare. But what we all have to realize is that morality is made for man, not man for morality. I earn my living by rounding him up, but I don't blind myself to the fact that more and more men – I don't say more and more women – are think-ing and acting as he does – and therefore, we must adjust our moral conceptions accordingly.'

'But where is all this leading to?' I asked.

'I was coming to that, Mr. Mardick. The authorities have decided that as Mr. Ladbroke Grove is a poor man' (again the Inspector consulted his file headed *Urgent, for Immediate Prosecution*) – 'he only picks up £8 3s. 4d. a

week working in a garage – and as he has people dependent on him—'

'What sort of people?' I inquired. 'I didn't know he had
any ties. He told me he was alone in the world.'

'I am not at liberty to divulge his private affairs,' said
the Inspector snubbingly, 'but in the circumstances he
hasn't much left over for beer and cigarettes.'

'I should hope not!' I exclaimed.

But the Inspector was more tolerant. 'We all have to
live,' he said. 'In the ordinary way he would be sent
to prison. Perhaps you think he ought to be?'

'I do indeed,' I said. 'Society should be protected from
rogues like him.'

'What is Society?' asked the Inspector, and Pilate-like
he would not stay for an answer. 'He is a member of
Society, just as you and I are, and in view of his war record,
and the damage to his ner-r-rvous system, the Ministry
has decided to be lenient with him.'

'Oh well,' I said. 'Good riddance to bad rubbish.'

'I'm afraid you're not altogether rid of him,' said the
Inspector. 'You will appreciate that he owes the State a
certain sum of money. The State cannot forgo this, even if
it wished to, for accounts have to be balanced and Her
Majesty's Government has to be carried on. You, Mr.
Mardick, are well-to-do—'

'Well-to-do, possibly,' I said, 'but not well.'

'I appreciate that,' said the Inspector, looking down at
me with more sympathy than he had yet shown. 'But the
Government cannot take into account an employer's state
of health.'

'But in the case of an employee it can?' I sneered.

The Inspector was unmoved.

'Yes, that is – how shall I say? – the feeling of the times. You, Mr. Mardick, were at fault for not taking the trouble to see that Mr. Ladbroke Grove put the stamps on his card. By this omission you committed an offence. This offence we are willing to overlook, and take your word for it that you gave him the money, but you did not fulfil your duty as a citizen.'

'But if I was not well enough to?' I objected.

'I'm afraid the responsibility still rests with you.'

'Then besides having paid his share of the stamps, I am to pay my own share twice over?'

'Not only your own share twice over, but his share, too. You will appreciate, Mr. Mardick, that Governments do not live on air.'

'I never thought they did,' I said.

He ignored my petulant outburst and with the air of someone who has got a disagreeable duty over he said, rummaging in his brief-case,

'I thought it might be a convenience to you, Mr. Mardick, if I brought the account with me, so that you could settle it on the spot, and save postage. Ah, here it is. The total amount payable is £7 9s. 4d., and I can show you the details by which this sum is arrived at, if you wish.'

'I don't wish,' I said rudely, trying to stifle the anger that was rising in me. Steady, now, steady! 'How *can* it be as much as that?' I demanded. 'As far as I recollect, Ladbroke Grove was only with me for the inside of a week.'

'Have you a note of when he came and went?' the Inspector asked.

I confessed I hadn't.

'He claims to have been with you much longer,' the Inspector said, once more consulting his file. 'Six weeks and four days – the four days, of course, would count as another week.'

'I remember now,' I cried. 'I had to sack him, because he threw a party and my neighbours complained of the noise. Does that make a difference?'

'I'm afraid not,' the Inspector said. 'It's your word against his, and as he has a record of the dates, and you haven't—'

'I'm sure I could prove it,' I said, searching my mind. 'Sister Tranter or Mrs. Stonegappe might remember, supposing they were here when he was here. Shall I ask them?' I continued, unhopefully, for though they were both full of information, it was always coloured by prejudice.

'I shouldn't bother to ask them, if I were you,' said the Inspector, 'unless the money is a matter of great moment to you. Mr. Grove has his story pat, as so many of them have, and if you contest it,' he added a little wearily, looking down at the wodge of papers in his brief-case, 'we should have to start all over again. It might take months, and even then you would not be sure of satisfaction. A poor man, mentally disabled by war-service, is sure of a sympathetic hearing.'

I gave up.

'If you would be kind enough to look on the top of the

chest of drawers,' I said, pointing to it, 'you will find my cheque-book.'

The Inspector rose and fumbled vainly among the letters, prescriptions, medicine bottles, nail-scissors, razor blades and other oddments that had accumulated since I was bed-ridden.

Forgetting doctor's orders, conscious of my gaping pyjamas and invalid's general disarray, I pounced on the cheque-book and, with the jealous possessiveness of a cat with a mouse, took it back to bed. Then I remembered something.

'You couldn't oblige me with a pen?'

'Cer-r-r-tainly I could oblige you with a pen.'

'To whom shall I make out the cheque?'

'To the Ministry of Pensions and National Insurance.'

'Not to you?'

'What would be the point of making it out to me, Mr. Mardick?'

'I only wondered,' I said, as offensively as I could.

His face became expressionless; he moved his hands from his knees to his thighs and back again. Shall I or shan't I, I thought. I decided that I would, and with pen poised I said,

'Listen, Inspector. You have said a good deal to me, and now there is something I want to say to you. Supposing I take this case to the Law Courts?'

'I'm afraid your chances of success would be very slender, Mr. Mardick. The Court would naturally be in favour of Mr. Ladbroke Grove, with his services to his country and their detrimental effect on his mental health, whereas

your – your negligence in failing to supervise the affixation of his stamps would certainly go against you. I think
you would be well advised not to take legal action.'

' "Affixation" is a new word to me,' I said, 'though no
doubt you could find it in the dictionary. Asphyxiation I
know, of course. But there are one or two things I should
like to say, before I sign this cheque. It isn't that I object to
paying three, or is it four times? as much as I need have, on
behalf of Ladbroke Grove. It is because of your attitude in
the matter, and your cynical disregard of the difference
between right and wrong. Here is a man to whom I did
several kindnesses, besides giving him the money for his
stamps; and how has he rewarded me? By fleecing me.
And yet you back him up, or the Government does. How
convenient for him! Is it your theory that all criminals
suffer from mental ill-health?'

'Anti-social attitudes are a sure sign of mental instability,' said the Inspector. 'The properly integrated man is
not at odds with Society.'

'I am sorry for you,' I said. 'I am sorry for you having to
spend your time, or perhaps I should say, waste your time,
among people of that sort. If I am adopting an anti-social
attitude now,' I said, leaning forward in bed and reaching
for a hard-backed book to write out the cheque on, 'would
you say I was suffering from mental instability?'

'You have been provoked, I know,' said the Inspector
soothingly, 'but I am sure it will pass.'

As I handed him the cheque I saw his eyebrows lifted in
relief, and he jumped out of his chair with an alacrity that
surprised me. Did he think I might become violent? He

was obviously anxious to take his leave; he had collected his brief-case but he was still looking for something. I knew what it was, but for the moment I wouldn't help him. How childish one sometimes is.

'Your hat is on the wardrobe,' I said.

He gave me a grateful look and reached up for it. It was a black felt hat and there was a thick layer of whitish dust under the brim. He flicked at it with his handkerchief, and as he turned to go he said, 'Thank you for telling me. It's quite an event to find an honest man nowadays.'

I suppose he thought I meant to annex his hat.

A minute or two later Sister Tranter came in.

'Has the man gone?' she asked, looking round the room, as if the Inspector might be lurking somewhere. 'I was so busy wondering about you – if he had done you any harm, I mean – that I didn't notice. I'm sorry. It isn't my business to see anyone to the door, but you never know with people of that sort.'

Such is my life, dear Lucilla. I hope yours is going on *oiled wheels*.

With much love,   Richard.

18

With the coming of Alberto Ferrero things began to look up for Richard. Alberto – Berto as he liked to be called – was an Italian, and his attitude to Richard, and to his illness, was quite different from that of his predecessors. Richard could talk Italian, not well, but better than Berto could talk English; and this was a source of unfailing delight and surprise to Berto, who was constantly in and out of the room, practising his English on Richard and having Richard's Italian practised on him. He appeared to take the greatest interest in everything to do with Richard, and was always asking him how he felt, sometimes at such short intervals that Richard could not say whether he felt better or worse, but he liked being asked, for none of the others had ever done so – they appeared to regard Richard's illness, if they recognized it at all, as a tacit reflection on themselves better ignored. The same was true, more or less, of Sister Tranter and Mrs. Stonegappe; for though Sister Tranter made routine inquiries – 'How are we this morning?' – she did not wait for an answer, whereas Mrs. Stonegappe alluded to his state of health obliquely, by telling Richard of people she knew, or had heard of, whose plight was much worse than his – indeed it often ended, or was about to end, in death. Berto, on the contrary, knew cases of *mal di cuore* almost as bad as the signorino's, in which the patient had made a rapid recovery to the astonishment and delight of all his friends and relations, especially of his mother, who always doted on him. Berto did not seem to think it was his mission to be a ray of sunshine; the desire that everything should go well for everyone bubbled up in him naturally, and made a dramatic contrast, on which he much enjoyed dilating, with his horror of the English climate. The winter was, indeed, particularly severe and prolonged, and although Richard assured him that he remembered similar winters in Italy, Berto, who had been brought up with the Italian's unalterable (and generally correct) view of the English climate, wasn't to be convinced. But he didn't try to make Richard responsible for its shortcomings; indeed he seemed to think that anyone who had such a hardship to contend with needed especial sympathy and care.

In spite of his disappointments with Berto's forerunners, Richard was predisposed in the Italian's favour, and any little thing he could do, from his confined position, to make Berto happy, he tried to do. This wasn't much: a present now and then, the means to get a handkerchief or a tie, since he couldn't get them himself, for which Berto was touchingly grateful. He would appear wearing the object, whatever it was, as if his *raison d'être* was to display it. And the more that Richard did for him, the more anxious he was to do something for Richard. As he was quite intelligent enough to see that the choice of wearing apparel for the bed-ridden is strictly limited, he contented himself with giving Richard a bed-jacket, of a hue so vivid that only Italian sunlight would have made it suitable for an elderly invalid. All the same it had a curiously reviving effect on Richard's spirits, and whenever he saw Berto brandishing it like a bull-fighter, his face puckered with concern lest Richard should put his hand into the wrong armhole, he felt his hold on life increasing. It didn't seem to occur to Berto that because he, Richard, was in bed he might as well be in his grave, which had been the attitude of the others. The others thought that one good turn deserved another, but from Richard, not from them; any kind of reverse motion was unthinkable to them. But not to Berto, who delighted in giving as good as he got, and was much more imaginative in the ways of reciprocity than Richard was. Richard could think of concrete, material benefits that Berto might be in need of; but he hadn't the gifts of looking, acting and speaking in a friendly fashion that came so naturally to Berto. Berto brought his inheritance, his country's civilization, with him, which included an instinctive sympathy for the old and the infirm.

Berto was a personable young man of twenty-eight, with very nice manners, and it never occurred to Richard that he could be other than acceptable to Sister Tranter and Mrs. Stonegappe. Besides, he was so active! It might not be corn that he trod, but his to-and-fro footsteps could always be heard, even between eleven and eleven-thirty, that period sacred to relaxation. By now Richard was experienced enough not to ask either of those ladies, without taking due precautions, what they thought of Berto. Needless to say, they neither of them gave Richard a lead; perhaps they would never have mentioned Berto, if at last he hadn't.

'You mean the Italian?' Mrs. Stonegappe said. 'I expect he is all right, I don't go much on foreigners myself.'

Richard was annoyed by this.

'We have to remember,' he said, pompously, 'that everything is strange to him. He has to adapt himself to our ways. In Italy they have different ideas from ours – not necessarily worse, but different.'

Mrs. Stonegappe shrugged.

'Sister Tantrum and I,' she said – and it was the first time Richard had ever heard her align herself with her arch-enemy – 'don't think much of Berto, as you like to call him. It doesn't seem a name to me. Not that we think about him, of course, we have so many other things to think of.'

'Such as?' said Richard, goaded past endurance.

'Oh, nothing much – keeping the flat clean and tidy, and looking after you – it's more than one person's job, as Sister Tantrum said, but you wouldn't notice, being in bed, and this Italian being in and out the whole time, making work.'

'Does he make work?'

'I don't speak for myself, but Sister Tantrum says he's the untidiest man she ever came across – if he is a man.'

'I daresay she hasn't come across many men, in *that* sense,' Richard said, rashly.

'I don't know what you mean by "in that sense",' said Mrs. Stonegappe. 'Men are all made the same way, aren't they, although you can't be sure with foreigners. I'm only telling you what Sister Tantrum says. We were thinking of you, sir, we don't want you to be imposed upon. Being in bed you can't see what's going on same as we can, who have time to look about, not that we should ever use it for that purpose.'

'I'm sure you wouldn't,' Richard said mechanically. Into his mind came a picture of Sister Tranter and Mrs. Stonegappe hand in hand, employing their time to better purpose than spying on poor Berto. But his imagination couldn't tell him what actually they *were* doing.

Towards midday, when the beat of corn-treading hooves had died away, when Mrs. Stonegappe had departed, when Sister Tranter had gone round the corner for some refreshment (as Mrs. Stonegappe, in her anti-Tranter days, had assured him that she did) and when Berto had gone out *per far le spese*, Richard got out of bed. He was now allowed to do this, to visit the loo. The visit made a break in his long day. Why not, he thought, by-pass the loo and take a peep at Berto's room, which was only a few steps further? If his heart could manage the one, it could surely manage the other. Not to spy on Berto's arrangements, of course, but just to see if the aspersions on his tidiness were justified. And they were not. No skins, thank goodness; nor the blow-lamps and revolvers which Chinnery was credited with having; nor Ladbroke Grove's fifteen suits. All was neat and orderly. On the dressing-table stood a very large photograph of Berto's mother, in a silver frame; a smaller one, also framed in silver, of his father, and a still smaller one (in which his mother and father also figured) of himself and his five brothers and sisters – all dressed in their Sunday best and staring at the camera with a fixed intensity, as if it had frightened them or they meant to frighten it.

There was really nothing wrong with the room at all. A visiting sergeant-major, intent on finding fault – knife, fork, spoon, toothbrush, button-stick, clean razor and shaving-brush, namestamp – would have passed it. It had a foreign air, because Berto's belongings (and they were few) came from Italy, where they made things differently, and, some people would have said, better. Berto's walking-out shoes had pointed toes, and his mufti suit, nestling on the coat-hanger, might once have been condemned as 'loud'. But not today; today young men peacocked and preened themselves as much as women did, and they adopted Italian fashions, too. Only a fanatical xenophobe, Richard felt, could have disapproved of Berto's accessories, or him.

He tiptoed back to bed, and presently Berto came in from shopping, breathing rather hard. '*Ho fatto un corso*,' he said, meaning he had hurried; 'I made several bargains, for I do not wish the signorino' (Richard was always touched at being called 'signorino', though he knew it was a reference to his unmarried state, not to his youth) 'to be deceived. Many of the magazines round here' (Berto had not mastered the word 'shops') 'think they can take advantage of a foreigner. *Cosa vuole?*' and he shrugged his shoulders tolerantly. '*Il mondo è paese*,' a favourite phrase, by which he meant that as far as dishonesty goes, the world is the same everywhere. And how was the signorino? Would he be able to eat the *pollo alla cacciatora* that Berto was preparing for him?

Richard was so unused to being inquired after, and having his wishes consulted, that he sometimes suspected that Berto was putting on an act, but he didn't think so and didn't want to think so, for Berto's solicitude increased his sense of well-being. It was easier to get well if someone was interested in your recovery.

Berto, he felt, had been wronged and next morning he tackled Mrs. Stonegappe. 'I looked in Berto's room,' he said, 'and it all seemed quite tidy.'

'You looked in the room!' said Mrs. Stonegappe. 'But the doctor said you weren't to get out of bed.'

'I have to, sometimes,' Richard said, with all the dignity that he could muster. 'And Dr. Herbright says I can.'

'Sister Tantrum won't be pleased when she hears that,' said Mrs. Stonegappe, grimly. 'She sees to that side of things for you, and you can take it from me, sir, if I hadn't tidied that room you couldn't have got into it, let alone looked at it. You have to be behind him all the time.'

'I could look at it without going into it,' said Richard, repressively, but he didn't feel sure of his ground: Mrs. Stonegappe *might* have tidied up after Berto, he couldn't prove she hadn't.

A little later Sister Tranter came in. 'We don't look so well this morning,' she said, 'and I hear we have been out of bed.'

Annoyed by her use of the royal plural Richard snapped: '*We* never have been in bed, that I can remember.'

Sister Tranter gave him a nasty look and on pretence of straightening the sheet, gave it a vicious tug, which sent his wrist-watch (he sometimes laid his wrist-watch on it, for the compression of the strap seemed to tire him) flying into a distant corner of the room.

'That's a way we nurses have,' she said, retrieving it.

Holding it to his ear to make sure it was still going, Richard said: 'Then I think you ought to mend your ways.'

Sister Tranter retired in good order, and presently Berto appeared, his shining morning face a little overcast.

'What's the matter, Berto?'

'Oh, nothing.'

'Yes, there is.'

'La sorella Tranter and Mrs. Stonygappy don't like me,' Berto said.

'You mustn't pay any attention to them,' said Richard.

'They are jealous of me, I think,' said Berto, 'because my service seems to please you. It is the same in Italy. Italian women are very, very jealous,' he added with some pride.

They discussed jealousy for a while, Richard maintaining it was a barren and profitless emotion which had never done anything but harm, Berto saying it was the sign of a generous nature and inseparable from love.

'But Sister Tranter and Mrs. Stonegappe don't love me,' Richard said, 'so why should they be jealous of you?'

'Ah!' said Berto, '*Le donne!* we men can never hope to understand them. But I am not sure that la Signora Stonygappy is not a leetle bit – *un pocchino, pocchino* – a little bit in love with you, signorino.'

'*Ma chè!*' cried Richard, hoping that this exclamation could express, among its many other meanings, absolute disbelief. 'If she is in love with me, she has a very strange way of showing it.'

'Excuse me, signorino,' Berto said, 'but the ways of love *are* very strange. It often happens that people we love behave badly – *molto, molto male*. But one must always excuse them,' he added. 'Otherwise, how would the world go on?'

'In that case, you ought to excuse Mrs. Stonygappy,' said Richard, falling into Berto's way of pronouncing her name.

'I do excuse her,' Berto said magnanimously. 'But women have so many ways of making a man miserable.'

Two days later Mrs. Stonegappe, wielding the carpet-sweeper – she could not corner Richard with it now that he was in bed – paused in mid-sweep and said:

'Sister Tantrum can't find her cigarette-case.'

'Oh dear, I'm sorry. When did she last have it?'

'Yesterday afternoon. She doesn't smoke much, of course, nurses aren't supposed to, but she'd just had one and was good enough to offer me one and she put the case down on the dresser, and that was the last she saw of it. It was a good case, silver and all that – a present from a grateful patient, she told me.'

'But you said this was in the afternoon,' said Richard. 'She'd gone by then, hadn't she?'

Mrs. Stonegappe's face stiffened. 'I can't remember exactly, but that was the last time she saw it. She's very upset about it, of course, because of its sentimental value.'

'She may have lost it going home,' suggested Richard.

'No, because she looked for it in the bus, and it wasn't there. She must have left it here, she says.'

As Mrs. Stonegappe seemed to expect a comment, Richard said: 'I can't understand it.'

'You can't understand it?' Mrs. Stonegappe repeated. 'It seems quite plain to me.'

'You mean that someone has taken it?'

Mrs. Stonegappe nodded.

'Who do you think?'

'Well, I mention no names, but someone not a mile from here.'

Cutting the cackle, Richard said: 'You mean Berto?'

'I don't mean any special person,' Mrs. Stonegappe said. 'But who else could it be?'

'The window-cleaner or the porter or the electrician.'

'People of that sort don't steal,' said Mrs. Stonegappe. 'They have their livings to get.'

'Well, so has Berto.'

'If you call it a living,' Mrs. Stonegappe said. 'I should call it something else.'

Richard didn't ask her what she meant, and she resumed her labours with the carpet-sweeper.

'Oh, Berto,' said Richard, a day or two later, 'do show me again that nice cigarette-case of yours – the one your mother gave you.'

Berto produced it with pride. 'It is a design altogether Italian,' he said, *'molto elegante, non è vero?'*

Richard agreed that it was very elegant. 'But in England, too,' said Berto, 'you have very nice cigarette-cases, especially for women.' Berto was always making distinctions between England and Italy, and trying to do justice to both countries. 'In England women smoke more than they do in Italy – it is the climate, I expect.'

Richard saw his opportunity.

'Sister Tranter has lost her cigarette-case, I believe,' he said.

Berto opened his eyes wide.

'*Ma scusi*, signorino, you are mistaken. A moment ago la sorella Tranter gave a cigarette to Mrs. Stonygappy, who smokes like a chimney, *proprio*, and Mrs. Stonygappy said, "That's a nice cigarette-case, *stia attenti* that nobody steals it," and they both laughed, because there are a lot of thieves in England, just as there are in Italy.'

For a moment Richard was too angry to speak; then he said, 'Send Mrs. Stonegappe here.'

After a decent delay, to show that she was not always on tap, Mrs. Stonegappe appeared, and stood in the doorway, her hands folded in front of her.

'Yes, sir?'

'Mrs. Stonegappe,' said Richard, 'I understand that Sister Tranter has found her beautiful cigarette-case, or did she never lose it?'

For a moment Mrs. Stonegappe was obviously at a loss: then she recovered herself.

'Sister Tantrum has discovered her cigarette-case,' she said, 'it was under a pile of mending that she was doing for you in her spare time – goodness knows how it got there. I was just coming in to tell you when Berto informed me that you wished to see me. Was it about that, sir?'

'You know it was,' said Richard, trying to keep his anger below the danger-mark. What a fool they must think me! he told himself. What a bloody fool! The thought inflamed his anger still further; he felt it boiling up in him, but for the sake of his health as well as on Christian principles he damped it down. 'Never get angry! Never get angry!' Dr. Herbright had dinned it into him. 'If you do I can't answer for the consequences.'

'Very well,' he said to Mrs. Stonegappe. 'But the next time you try to plant something on Berto, do it more cleverly.'

He heard her sniff as she left the room – but whether from tears or indignation he couldn't tell.

19

Lucilla was his first unofficial visitor. He hadn't seen her for a month and had almost forgotten what she looked like. While the flowers – yellow roses this time – were being put in water she sat down beside his bed.

For a while they seemed to have nothing to say to each other but small talk – expressions of undying gratitude on his side, resolute disclaimers on hers. 'It was nothing, nothing at all, less than the least I could do.'

'But there were the books as well,' said Richard, embarrassed by the multitude of his obligations. 'You shouldn't . . . you shouldn't have done all that for me, Lucilla.'

He knew it wasn't the right thing to say; it sounded as if he was squaring the account with his conscience, instead of thanking her.

'It was nothing,' she repeated. 'But I have one grievance against you, Richard – one little bone to pick.'

Richard's heart sank. How unattractive, how ignominious it was, to have to consider in personal relationships the physical, rather than the emotional condition of one's heart.

'What bone is that?' he said, as lightly as he could. 'A funny-bone? A wish-bone?'

'A wish-bone, I suppose,' Lucilla said. 'Only a tiny wish-bone, no bigger than a wren's. But I do think you might have let me know how ill you were.'

'I didn't want to bother you,' said Richard and again he knew it was the wrong thing to say. For his heart, that miserable organ, told him, and not for the first time, that Lucilla *wanted* to be bothered. Her answer confirmed this.

'You shouldn't have denied me the privilege of worrying about you,' she said. 'I lead a rather empty, lonely life, and worrying about you would have helped to fill it.'

Again Richard took refuge from the particular in the general.

'My mother used to say, "If you do this, or that, I shall worry about you—" It was a kind of threat, or blackmail – I must never, never do anything to make her worry. And of course, worry is an occupational disease of our age, isn't it, Lucilla? Especially of the unoccupied!' He saw how tactless this was, and added, 'The anxiety neurosis – I wanted to spare you that!' He laughed as heartily as he could. 'Besides, I don't *know* if there *is* any reason to worry about me, only the doctor says so.'

'I think it depends on who the person is,' said Lucilla, leading Richard away from the topic of anxiety in the abstract, 'as to whether one *wants* to worry or not. I can't conceive not wanting to worry about someone I am fond of. I'm like your mother in that. I'm not a bit grateful to you, Richard, for trying to save me from worrying about you. I even thought at one time that you didn't want to see me. That did worry me. I should have worried much less if I'd known how ill you were.'

'How different women are from men,' said Richard, grasping once more at a generalization. 'I should have worried very much if I'd known you were ill—'

'Would you?' said Lucilla, half sceptical, half-eager.

'Yes, and if I had been told you were so ill you couldn't see me, I should have worried more. Isn't that logical?'

'It didn't work like that with me,' Lucilla said. 'I'm happier not kept in the dark. I agree that in principle out of sight is out of mind, and one would rather not be told. But in special cases—'

'Am I a special case?' asked Richard, feeling he could avoid the issue no longer.

'Of course you are. Surely I don't need to tell you that?'

Richard muttered something about how kind she had always been to him.

'Not kind at all,' Lucilla said. 'Kindness is not a failing in our family, but love is. Do I make myself clear?'

Richard felt a cold air blowing round him, and pulled his bed-jacket across his chest.

'I won't say more,' Lucilla said, 'perhaps I have said too much, but this seemed the moment to say it. But now let me turn to something quite, quite different. How is your domestic situation? I'm afraid you've had a lot of trouble there?'

Richard agreed, but added that since Berto came things had improved. 'He really seems to take an interest in my welfare – the only one who does, except for you and Dr. Herbright. The others, Sister Tranter and Mrs. Stonegappe, I don't know, I wouldn't say they exactly hope for my death (not that there's any question of *that*,

Lucilla), but they feel I'm something like the weather, that they can't affect, and that the worse I am, in a way, the more news-value I have, do you see? They seldom ask me how I am, in case I should disappoint them by saying I feel better. Those scoundrels I had – you know about them. But the women are nearly as bad, they want a crisis, like the men do, and they don't like Berto, because he sees me as an individual, not part of a cosmic upset with headlines in the evening papers.'

'This Berto,' Lucilla said, 'I don't imagine he will be with you very long. Italians aren't allowed to stay, are they? I was wondering, Richard, whether for your convalescence—'

The word had a delicious sound. 'Yes?' said Richard.

'You wouldn't come and stay in my flat for a bit – I have a spare room, as you know, that is never used, and a staff of one and a half, which for the moment is quite faithful to me. You wouldn't have the worries you have here – you could relax, and I shouldn't have the anxiety of feeling you weren't being properly looked after. I'm sure you'd get better quicker away from all these automatic hindrances to recovery. We could park out Berto somewhere, since you and he seem to like each other – and as for the rest – you haven't any obligations to them, have you?'

Richard said he hadn't.

'It could be just a temporary arrangement, for as long as you liked, and no longer than you liked – though for me, the longer the better. Do consider it, Richard, do give it a thought.'

Richard said he would.

'I seem to have talked so much,' Lucilla said, 'but can you blame me, when I haven't seen you for a month, and it seems like a year. Did you miss me, Richard? I can't help hoping you did.'

'Of course I did, Lucilla.'

'Are you quite sure? Your voice on the telephone sounded so far away sometimes. I knew you were tired, of course, so I didn't ring you up as often as I wanted to – but . . .'

'I was always bad on the telephone, you know,' said Richard. 'I can speak to people's faces more easily than to their voices.'

'You say "people" so often, Richard. When you say it, do you include me?'

'Well, you are a person, aren't you?' Richard countered, knowing how wrong this answer was. 'What I mean is, I fade, I die away. I peter out into silence – I cannot think of anything more to say – heaps of people have complained of it.'

'There you go again – people.'

'Well, a habit is a habit, isn't it, you can't alter your nature, can you, for the sake of some one person, however much you'd like to.'

'No,' said Lucilla slowly. 'I suppose you can't. But *I* could, Richard, I could alter mine for you.'

What Richard's subconscious mind had always known, and what his waking consciousness had always refused to acknowledge, now clamoured to be heard, but he tried to silence it.

'It is sweet of you, Lucilla,' he said, 'to ask me to stay

with you while I'm getting better. Of course I'll consider it, though I think it's unfair on you.'

'Unfair on me – why?'

'Well, in these days people – no, I mustn't say that – but no one wants to have a semi-invalid about the house. I've told you how it is here, I pay them to look after me. And yet, except for Berto, they really resent my being ill – that is, as far as they believe I *am* ill. It was different in the old days, before your time, Lucilla! – when I, and my aunt Carrie, and old Mrs. White – all invalids more or less, two of them half-bedridden – we all lived at the expense of Uncle Austin – at least I didn't, but the others did – and there was Aunt Ada, too – she was a drag on the household, being so critical and so unpunctual. We were as much of a bind to him and to Aunt Esther as we were to the housemaid and the cook. We were a nuisance without a nuisance-value, but none of them, I swear, thought of us as such. Whereas nowadays – but you've heard all this so often—'

'Ella and Mrs. Gumbridge won't think you a nuisance,' said Lucilla, 'and I shall only think you a nuisance if you don't come. What is there to keep you here, Richard? Two women in league against you, and this Italian servant – they'll get the better of him, somehow. Wouldn't you like to settle down for a time, and wouldn't it be better for you, in a place where all these cares are taken off your shoulders? What is the good of nominal independence, when you are not really independent, but the slave of your own household? "A man's foes shall be those of his own household," it says in the Bible. Well, they wouldn't be your foes in mine.'

'It is too kind of you,' Richard murmured.

'I've told you before, it isn't kind, it's what I should *like*. I'm not being altruistic about it, I can assure you. I know you were brought up on a theory of self-sacrifice, so act on it, don't think of yourself, think of me, and the pleasure it would be for me to have you – officially or unofficially, I don't care which. I don't pretend to be well educated, but surely, Richard, I could give you something that your hospital nurse, who you tell me is leaving soon, and your daily help, can't give you – am I vain in believing that? As for Berto, who could perhaps do things for you that we couldn't – valeting and so on – I could find a room for him, I'm sure. Won't you get lonely and crusty and misanthropic here by yourself? It was different, I know, when you had Denys, but he has gone, hasn't he? You are not expecting him to come back, are you? Do you ever hear from him? You told me he was married, or nearly married.'

It wasn't so much what Lucilla said, it was the vehemence of her utterance that surprised and frightened Richard. What have I been hatching for myself all this time, he thought, what trouble have I been brewing? Lying on my bed, sometimes better, sometimes not so well, keeping the least possible communication with the outside world – and yet all the time these feelings have been piling up – not due to anything *I've* done, Heaven knows! And then there flashed across his mind, possessing it utterly, a vision of his future life as Lucilla had planned it for him – no more domestic cares and troubles, no working himself up over trifles! Never again those pointless, undignified, ridiculous, ignominious, acrimonious altercations, all about nothing! Not quite about nothing, for 'they' wanted to assert their equality, no, their superiority.

In the few moments that it takes a dream to re-construct the feeling of a lifetime, in those few moments between what Lucilla had said to him, and what he must say to her, he had a vision of the remainder of his lifetime as she would organize it, and the way it was organized, or disorganized, now.

'What did you say, Lucilla?' he asked. 'I'm afraid my mind wandered for a moment – it does, sometimes, now.'

She gave a troubled look. 'It was nothing, Richard. I hope I haven't tired you. I think I asked you if you had heard from Mr. Aspin.'

Richard apologized again.

'No, I haven't, he seems to have quite gone out of my life.'

'I only wondered,' Lucilla said, 'I know how attached you were to him, and I wondered what had happened. I meant to have asked you before, but somehow I forgot to. Now I mustn't stay any longer, but remember, my dear, if you should be looking for a Convalescent Home, or any sort of home, my flat is always at your service, for as long a time or as short a time as you wish.'

Why didn't Richard say, 'I'll come *now*'? He had plenty of time to say it while Lucilla, collecting this and that of her belongings, gradually assumed the perpendicular; height was the dimension that he associated her with: she never sprawled or sank, she was always upright, and perhaps that was why, feeling he couldn't live up to her standards, feeling he might fail her in more ways than one, he didn't take advantage of her departure preparations to say he would join her for as long or as short a time as suited her.

'You are too kind,' he murmured.

For answer, she bent down and kissed him, and it was then there came a knock on the door, and Berto said, '*Scusi*, signorino, but there is a Mr. Aspin who would like to speak to you.'

Lucilla left the room as Denys entered it.

20

It was so long, by certain measures of time, since Richard had seen Denys, that he didn't quite know what, or even whom, to expect. His first impression was that Denys, usually so spruce, looked down at heel.

'Well, old boy,' Denys said, when they had broken whatever ice there was to be broken, 'I'm sorry to find you like this.'

'Oh, I'm much better, Denys,' said Richard, who hated to admit that he was ill, or in need of pity. 'It's just one of my attacks that went on rather longer than usual.'

'I heard about it,' Denys said, sitting down on the chair so lately occupied by Lucilla, 'that's why I came, to find out how you were and to offer you my sympathy.'

'Oh, I'm still above ground,' Richard said, subconsciously recalling all the jokes he had had with Denys, 'still above ground and very pleased to see you.' This was less than the truth. '*Comment ça va?* How goes married life?'

'Oh,' said Denys, 'it has its ups and downs, you know, just now one of its downs.'

'I'm sorry to hear that,' said Richard. 'I hoped that with Pat and the dog – Bungy is it called? – that little corgi that was so vociferous—'

'Yes,' said Denys, 'but you've forgotten the baby.'

'The baby?' Richard repeated. 'I never knew there was one.'

'Oh yes,' Denys said. 'We wondered if you'd like to be its godfather.'

'Its!' said Richard. 'I didn't think a parent of your experience would fall into that error. Is it a boy or girl?'

'A boy,' said Denys. 'He will be the staff of my old age, but meanwhile I have to be the staff of his infancy. What do you think of making yourself responsible for his moral welfare, Richard? Or any kind of welfare, for that matter.'

'I'll give him a mug, of course,' said Richard. And then he couldn't help laughing. 'I might give him myself.'

'You're not such a mug as you make out,' said Denys. 'Not in my view, at any rate. We're going to call him Richard, and we hope he'll take after you.'

'Are you married yet?' asked Richard. 'I couldn't be godfather to an illegitimate baby.'

'We nearly are,' said Denys, 'we can't quite afford it yet, because of the Income Tax question. You wouldn't know about that, Richard, but when people are married their incomes are lumped together for tax purposes. And of course Bungy doesn't earn his living except by keeping burglars away.'

'I should have thought he kept everyone away,' said Richard.

'You didn't like Bungy, did you?' Denys said. 'He's a grand dog, really, and Pat dotes on him. But of course he's expensive. Everything is expensive, I'm sure you realize that.'

'Even being ill is expensive,' Richard said. 'They used to say it's a poor disease that doesn't keep itself, but it's not true now.'

'Poor Richard,' Denys said, 'but not really poor. Richard is rich by definition.'

'And poor by definition, too,' said Richard.

'Oh, surely not. I've thought so much about you all this time, and would have looked you up, only I had a sort of feeling that I shouldn't be so welcome married as I was when I was – well, single.'

'But are you married?' Richard asked.

'That's just a technicality. What I meant to say was, could you help us – Pat and me and the little one and Bungy, over a rather difficult patch?'

'But I helped you a short time ago,' protested Richard.

'I know you did, but I'm afraid all that's gone. Pat's a splendid girl and most economical, but of course we don't live like hermits, and we have little Richard to provide for now, as well as Bungy. And there's another thing.'

'What's that?'

'Well, your biography. You see I'm not used to that sort of work, and it will take me a long time, during which, I need hardly say, I shan't be able to follow my own occupation.'

'Which is?' asked Richard.

'A motor-salesman. When I'm on the job, I hardly get any time to myself and what time I do get, I like to spend with Pat. She's a good girl and doesn't nag me, but she doesn't like to be left alone too much, can you blame her?

And I don't want her to be – for obvious reasons. None of us are perfect, are we? You see I haven't your mastery of English – but I do want to make a good job of the memoir, and I don't want to put into it something unsuitable – was it Miss Distington I saw as I came in?'

Richard said it was.

'I should hate to say anything that she wouldn't like and I'm sure you would, too. You depend on her a great deal, don't you?'

'In what way?' Richard asked.

'Oh, I don't mean that she's just a useful bread-ticket, although I remember you used to take a good many free meals off her.'

'That was partly to leave you some free evenings'

'Oh, I doubt it, Richard. At one time, before you met her, you much preferred staying in with me, and didn't care if I had a night out or not. When you met her you started going out, leaving me to my own devices, so then I had to console myself, of course.'

'The dates don't bear that out,' said Richard. 'It was I who had to console myself when you were courting Pat, and Bungy. But don't let's argue. Lucilla is a great friend of mine, of course.'

'That's just what I meant,' said Denys. 'I don't want anything I say to upset her or any of your friends – you have so many.'

'Not so many now,' said Richard, 'not so many now. Death has thinned their ranks, for one thing. You'd be surprised, Denys, how many people I've outlived who I thought would outlive me.'

'A creaking gate, eh?' Denys said. 'You might outlive me too! – and that's another thing. I have Pat and little Richard and Bungy to provide for. You may not be as fond of me as you used to be, but you wouldn't like to see us starve.'

'But what has this to do with Lucilla?' Richard asked.

'Only that as she seems to have taken my place in your life, you wouldn't, nor should I, want her to find anything in your biography that was prejudicial to you.'

'We went into all that,' said Richard. 'You were just to suggest – nothing more – that my life hadn't been quite such plain sailing as it seemed. People who still read "The Imperfect Witness" would otherwise get a wrong impression of me. It doesn't really matter if they do – but you were to suggest that there was an emotional experience – a trauma, if you like – that made it possible for me to write the book. I wrote several more, as you know, and they seemed all right to me, but they didn't come off because everything I had went into the first one. I thought that was all understood between us, Denys.'

'Oh yes, it was,' said Denys, 'but that was before Miss Distington had appeared on the scene. Miss Distington, Lucy's half-sister. She owes her life, or at any rate her birth, to you, doesn't she, Richard? There would have been no Lucilla if you hadn't somehow – no one quite knows how – disposed of Lucy?'

'What are you getting at?' said Richard. 'If you don't want to write the memoir, by all means don't, but in that case give me back the money I gave you to write it.'

'Oh no, Richard, don't misunderstand me. I want to write it, to preserve your literary reputation, which won't be difficult, and your personal reputation, which may not be so easy. As I see it, Miss Distington is our chief headache. The others – let's call them posterity, though you're by no means dead yet – won't worry very much over what your emotional entanglement exactly *was* – though I dare say they will speculate, as they did and do about Jane Austen and Emily Brontë. No, the only person who *will* be curious is Miss Distington, because she thinks such a lot of you and would be so horrified if—'

'If what, Denys?'

'If she found out something, or guessed something, that made you seem less of a hero in her eyes.'

Richard said nothing, and Denys went on: 'You haven't told her about Lucy, have you?'

'No.'

'Why didn't you? It would have been more straightforward, and easier for you in the long run.'

'I don't know what *you* mean by straightforward,' Richard said. 'And as for the long run, there isn't one, in any case.'

'That's what you say, Richard, that's what you say. But it's you I'm thinking of. If Miss Distington found out about you—'

'But how could she? You wouldn't publish the memoir, presumably, till I'm dead.'

'If my circumstances don't improve, Richard, I might have to – I mean, we have to live, the four of us – even if you—'

249

'You might make yourself liable to libel.'

'Liable to libel – there's the old stylist coming out. No, I shouldn't risk that. The only danger is, Richard, and I'm looking at it entirely from your point of view – that whether I publish the memoir before or after your – your decease—'

'She still might recognize me as the villain of the piece?' Denys nodded.

'Dead men tell no tales,' said Richard. 'But they can have tales told about them.'

'That's just what I'm afraid of,' Denys said. 'You gave me a most difficult assignment, Richard; to say something, and yet not to say it. Oh, how I wish you'd inflicted it on someone else! And that Miss Distington had never come into your life! If something I said made other people tumble to the facts – your relations in the Fens, for instance – it wouldn't matter much. But if Miss Distington—'

'Don't bother to write the memoir, Denys,' Richard said. 'I'd far rather you didn't. I hadn't realized what a worry for you it was going to be.'

'Oh, but I must, Richard! It's a charge you've laid on me – a sacred trust – or does that sound too pompous? All I'm afraid of is that I might injure you—'

'You needn't,' Richard said, 'unless you want to.'

'Oh, but I beg your pardon. The least word in the wrong place! Of course it would all have been plain sailing if Miss Distington hadn't come along.'

'Forget her,' Richard said, turning his head on the pillow.

'But how can I forget her, when everything hangs on her! If it hadn't been for her I should never have—'

'As I told you before,' said Richard, 'the dates don't bear that out. You were married, or half-married, or as good as married, weeks or months before I met Lucilla.'

'But if that is so, which I don't admit, it makes things all the worse for me, don't you see? By worse, I mean more expensive. We've had to scrape and save all this time. Surely, Richard, if you have no regard for my happiness, or yours, you must respect Miss Distington's. She has built up such an image of you – I don't know how – as a cheva-lier *sans peur et sans reproche* – that if it was taken from her, and you were taken from her—'

Almost for the first time during their interview, Richard looked hard at Denys, and saw the sweat standing on his forehead.

'Bring me my cheque-book, Denys,' he said in quite a different tone. 'You know where I keep it.'

Denys came back, not only with the cheque-book but with a pen.

'How much do you want?' asked Richard.

Denys named a sum.

'You don't mean that?'

'I'm afraid I do,' said Denys. 'You see we have to live.'

'And what about me?' asked Richard, letting the pen slip out of his fingers on to the sheet where it left a spread-ing stain. 'Don't I have to live too?'

Denys smiled.

'Well, not as long as we have to, Richard, not as long as we have to. Dying has always been your *métier*.'

He spoke lightly, and once Richard would have laughed, but now he didn't feel like laughing, and only wanted to bring Denys's visit to an end. Denys got up from his chair, but didn't seem able to take his leave. He hovered about on his long legs, looking round him, and said experimentally, 'How familiar all this is!'

'Yes,' said Richard, 'and no.'

21

After Denys's visit Richard had a relapse, and for a few days was forbidden visitors. He was allowed to see his solicitor, however, indeed he had to see him. The price of Denys's silence was so heavy that he had to review and revise the whole of his financial situation.

Financially, Richard had been very lucky – so lucky that he had never had to bother about money. His first novel had come out in the twenties, when it was still possible for an author, or anyone else, to keep the bulk of his earnings from the clutches of the Inland Revenue. *The Imperfect Witness* had been filmed and dramatized; all told, its earnings made a considerable nest-egg. Richard's subsequent novels, though respectfully received by the Press, didn't make much but they made something. He didn't have to feel that he had failed to be what his mother's family, with all their other ideals, rated very high, a good business man.

But he had to admit that when he enjoyed the 'warmth' that money gives, he didn't get it from his own efforts but from the smoking chimneys of the brick-kilns at Fosdyke of which his father had seen the possibilities, when other people shook their heads. Walter was a clever man, they all recognized that; but the sacred appellation, 'a good business man' they would never allow him. Even when events had proved them wrong, they still thought that the Brickworks owed its success more to good luck than to good management.

However that might be, the Brickworks had provided Richard with an unfailing income, which was no doubt partly why, when his earnings from authorship fell off, he acquiesced in their decline, instead of asking himself, 'How can I please the public better?'

But the Brick Company was a private company, the shares were difficult to dispose of; whoever sold them felt he had been given too little, and whoever bought them thought he had given too much. And besides this practical difficulty of marketing the shares, there was the fact that to his father in his later years the Brickworks had become sacrosanct. It was his creation; he believed in it when no one else had, and continued to believe in it when no one else did; he had nothing at all to start with, but thanks to the Brickworks he died well off. He was far too detached and philosophically-minded to rejoice in this as some men would have; it was the cause he valued, not the effect. The Brickworks was almost a religion to him, the money was not.

He didn't own the Brickworks but he was one of the largest shareholders, and he bequeathed the bulk of his shares to Richard. He didn't stipulate that Richard shouldn't sell them, but Richard knew he didn't want him to; they were to be an heirloom. His wife had persuaded him to give some to Aunt Carrie; she, too, in a small way, was a pensioner of the Brickworks. Most of them he had handed over to Richard years before he died; and he had asked Richard to pay the death duties on his estate out of his other securities, leaving the Brick shares intact. When this had been done there were not many liquid assets left; Richard would have had to live almost on a fixed income, without any capital he could touch, but for the modest nest-egg laid for him by his first novel. His father had been proud of this success, but though he knew less about the literary world than his son did, he knew more about life, and perhaps more about Richard, and he did not think Richard would be able to repeat the success of his first book. 'Two lucky hits,' he said, coupling, as Richard guessed, the Brickworks with *The Imperfect Witness*, 'are all we can expect.' Richard, pen in hand, basking in recent glory, didn't believe him; but his father was right, as he was right about so many things.

Cutting up the figurative nest-egg was an easier operation than if it had been a real one, but all the same it was distasteful. Like other men who live chiefly in their imaginations, Richard was unrealistic about money. Not indifferent to it – quite the contrary. He held it in superstitious awe, and had all sorts of *idées fixes* about it. One was that he must keep enough liquid capital (as his father had) to pay the death duties on his Brick shares, which must be handed on inviolate. It must be maintained at a certain figure – not so much on account of the Inland Revenue as because this particular sum was the one his imagination had seized upon to see him out. If it should fall below the danger-point, what might not happen?

But Denys would have to be paid off.

Rather to his surprise, Mr. Smallcross appeared to take the proposed inroad on his nest-egg much more lightly than Richard did. 'I think you are very wise,' he said, 'to unload some of your capital now. So many of my clients leave it till too late. Let's hope that after the statutory five years you will be laughing heartily at the discomfiture of Her Majesty's Government.' He took another look at Richard, propped up on the pillows, and said with less assurance, 'I am quite certain you will be.' When Richard smiled rather wanly he went on: 'And we must be practical. Let's face it, we're none of us getting younger, but with each year that our expectation of life . . . er . . . decreases, we are, on the financial side, so much the better off. Ha-ha, you see what I mean. It isn't as if you were in your first youth, blueing capital that you might need in after life.' (The phrase struck a chord in Richard's memory; how often had he heard it on his mother's lips!) 'No, I think you are very sensible to give some person, possibly younger than yourself, the benefit accruing from this money. Cast your bread upon the waters, and – who knows? It isn't a very good moment to sell, of course, but it might easily be worse later. And you have your income from the Brickworks – we must go into that. And talking of bricks, how is that nice young fellow – I forget his name – your secretary?'

'Denys Aspin?' said Richard, as casually as he could. 'He's left me, you know, to get married. Young men will do that, one can't blame them.'

'No, indeed, but what a pity. He seemed ideal for you, in many ways, and in these days responsible young men are as rare as rain in the desert. My wife and I – but I won't bore you with our domestic adventures. I take it that you have someone looking after you?'

'Oh yes,' said Richard. 'There's my nurse, Miss Tranter, and my daily help, and a nice Italian boy. Foreigners appear to find this kind of job, well, less degrading than our people do. They seem to want to please you.'

'Oh yes, how right you are. Well, hold on to him. I'm sorry about Aspin, though, he seemed so promising – and he was what used to be called a gentleman, wasn't he?'

'I suppose so,' Richard said.

'Now,' said Mr. Smallcross briskly, 'I don't want to bother you with details of the securities we shall have to sell. You'll leave that to me, won't you? All the same, I think I ought to have your O.K. on what we decide to do. These problems take some sorting out, especially when a rather large sum is involved. They are not exactly invalid's fare. May I ring up and make an appointment?'

'Whenever is convenient to you,' said Richard.

'And next time, Mr. Mardick,' the solicitor said, rising suddenly, 'I hope we shall meet more on all fours – what am I saying? – I hope that when we next meet we shall both be *upright*.'

Richard said he hoped so, too, and Mr. Smallcross bowed himself out.

Upright! – how very different from supine, or prone, or prostrate, or whatever position one assumed in bed. Upright! In faraway Fosdyke 'to live upright' had no moral connotation: it meant living on an unearned income, as he, Richard, had lived. Upright! Well . . .

'A fool and his money are soon parted,' said the proverb. It was true that Richard in his palmy days (whenever they were) had quite enjoyed parting with money. It gave him a sense of generosity, a sense of power, and a sense of freedom – almost as if, on a hot day, he had thrown off a coat that was too heavy for him. Something that he was glad to get rid of went with the money, especially if it went to someone he liked, or to buy something he wanted. But even if it was to pay a bill or his Income Tax he felt lighter, freer, less encumbered, for getting rid of it. Did that make him a fool? He supposed it did, for a fool is someone out of touch with reality, and money is the most undeniable of all realities.

He had to admit that the occasions in the past when he had given money to Denys were some of the happiest of his life. If he had suspected that Denys wasn't blue-blooded, as he professed to be, would it have made a difference? Richard didn't think so.

But it made a difference now, when the money was not being offered but demanded, and demanded with threats, when it was blackmail, to use an ugly word which the modern age, with all its sympathy for criminals, hadn't quite succeeded in making sound pretty. 'Never, never let yourself get used to anything ugly,' his mother had implored him: 'don't look at "the M!"' There was an M in blackmail as there was in money, but he would have to get used to it.

It is one thing to be relieved, another to be fleeced – to give up under pressure – immediate, irresistible pressure – something which one would much rather keep and can't indeed, considering the magnitude of the contribution asked for, afford to lose without a great deal of distress. A purge, but not a purge that did one any good.

Well, this was the last time he would have to pay Denys hush-money. He would not see Denys again, and if Denys wrote to him, the letter would go straight to the police. That was the way with blackmailers.

His secret was safe at last. But at what a cost, not only financially but spiritually and morally, for he had invested a much greater sum in Denys than the money Denys had extorted from him. Who steals my purse steals trash, but whoso taketh from me my good name, enricheth not himself and leaves me poor indeed. Richard had saved his name from Denys: but the Richard-Denys relationship and what it stood for in the way of affection, had gone forever. 'My bonds in thee are all determinate,' just as surely as the material bonds they symbolized.

If Richard could have hated Denys it would have been easier and given more point to the past. The fact that he didn't and couldn't seemed to take the meaning out of the whole affair, and make it seem trivial. If they had quarrelled and had words, if they had parted on some high note of emotion, some sharp clash of will or temperament, bringing out the essence of each, it would have been better, it might even have been tragic. But to be bled white by a trickster, so that not a drain of feeling was left: how ignominious it was.

Better a heart swelling with anger than a vacuum in the breast which did not even ache. Better emotionally, but not physically; physically anger and all its concomitant emotions were against doctor's orders. They were harmful and might be fatal. They were against Richard's temperament too: it could not entertain them. How much more meaningful his life would have been if he could have got into a temper as most men did when their wishes were crossed! More meaningful and to the average person more attractive; for what appeal had someone who could scarcely harbour hostile feelings, much less get into a rage! How could murders be done, how could wars be waged, how could nuclear armament flourish, how could anything newsworthy ever take place, if everyone felt as he did? He owed his life to his passivity, perhaps; his heart, that most important of all the organs, wouldn't otherwise have lasted out. But it was neither a virtue nor a fault in him if he found it easy to obey his doctor's orders. Heredity and example had enjoined it on him. His father, in spite of his moods of irritability, was much too sensible to let his feelings get the upper hand for long; he would have thought such indulgence merely silly; while his mother, who was the creature of her emotions, had brought him up on the legend of Aunt Carrie's selflessness.

So by the example of one parent and the precept of another Richard was excused from anger. Excused! The word came into his mind before he was aware of it. It wasn't only that his self-accusing nature demanded an excuse; he didn't, in spite of religious teaching, believe that anger was necessarily wrong. To the famous question, 'Doest thou well to be angry?' he would have answered, 'In certain cases, yes.' The whole of his present predicament, he told himself, came from his inability to feel and show anger. But now he would not need to; for had he not Lucilla on the one side, and Berto on the other, to keep away the Furies, which are so much more dangerous inside than out?

22

Alas, alas! No sooner had Richard begun to entertain these consoling thoughts than they were rudely dashed. The day after his interview with his lawyer Berto came in with a face so transformed that Richard, who was better at portraying such changes on paper than at recognizing them in the flesh, stared at him in alarm.

'O Berto, *cosa è successo?*' he asked, and then, in case his Italian hadn't penetrated, 'What's the matter?'

'O signorino!' cried Berto, and was struck speechless.

'*Mi dica*,' Richard urged. 'Tell me.'

At that Berto plunged into a long and incoherent story, partly in English, partly in Italian, the gist of which Richard only gathered after repeated questioning that evidently seemed to Berto like a cross-examination by a hostile counsel, though Richard was far from meaning it that way.

'Ah, *le donne, le donne!*' he exclaimed at last, shaking his head and spreading out his hands.

By this time Richard had understood most of what he meant, and he knew that to the male Italian mind women, though infinitely forgivable, gave infinite cause for forgiveness.

'But what have they done to you, Berto?'

'They have not done me anything,' said Berto, 'how could they, being only women? But either they do not speak to me, or they say I speak badly of them to you.'

'Speak badly of them?' said Richard. 'What do they say that you say of them to me?'

Talking to Berto Richard often found that English failed him and Italian did not come to his aid. Justifiably puzzled by the accumulation of pronouns, Berto said:

'Pardon?'

Richard tried to explain, more successfully this time, what he meant and Berto, always anxious to understand, at once caught on.

'Mrs. Stonygappy says that I tell you that she does not clean out properly the other bathroom, and that she does not use *quella macchina*, to clean the *tappeti* – the carpets – how does it call itself—?'

'The Hoover.'

'Yes, yes, signorino, the Hoover, because it is too heavy, and she is too old to use it, and that you *si lagna della polvere* – you complain of the . . . the . . .'

'Dust.'

'Yes, yes, dust, which is everywhere in London. And you complain that the flat is *sporco*, feelthy—'

'But you never said anything of this to me.'

'No, signorino, but she says I did. And I have said it to her because I do not think she ought to advantage herself of your being ill in bed.'

'I see,' said Richard, 'and what does Sister Tranter say to you?'

'O signorino, la Sorella Tantrum, she also says that I am a spy, and that I tell you when she goes out to the *bettola* – how does one say it?'

'The public-house.'

'Yes, the public howoose, when instead she ought to be here in case you should be *colto da malore*—'

'Taken ill.'

'Yes, signorino, though I hope that will never happen.'

'But I don't understand, Berto. You have never told me this.'

'No, signorino, but I have told them and they think I have told you, or they make pretence to think so. And otherwise they do not speak to me, because they say I am an Italian, and *per quello* – for that – I must be a spy.'

Richard had a brief vision of Berto's position, vis-à-vis the two women. It wasn't enviable.

'But I thought they didn't like each other,' he said. 'They certainly did not, before you came. They were scarcely on speaking terms. Each of them was always telling me she would leave unless the other did.'

'Yes, signorino,' Berto agreed, 'but since I came they have become great friends, one sees. They have made a *camorra* against me, because they know you like me, and that I wish you well. They are jealous, like so many women are, even in Italy.'

Richard remembered hearing someone say that though you cannot be in love without being jealous, you can easily be jealous without being in love.

'Berto,' he said, wearily, 'don't pay any attention to

them. They're just a couple of silly women, who have nothing better to do than neglect me and try to make you miserable. Ignore them, if you can.'

'I cannot, signorino. I cannot support it. I must go, because if I stay I might do them an injury. In Italy we do not allow ourselves to be insulted by types of that kind. *Canaglia!*'

For once Richard made up his mind quickly.

'All right,' he said. 'Sister Tranter must go.'

Berto stared at him in stupefaction. Then smiles broke out on his face.

'*La sorella Tranter va via?*' he said, with a wide gesture of his arm towards the door, to indicate her departure. '*Allora, si sta meglio!*' And he did at once look better, completely different, as if a word had cured him.

Richard had some difficulty in arranging with his doctor for Sister Tranter's departure. 'I'm afraid you're not out of the wood yet,' he said dubiously. 'You ought to have someone about you who knows something about nursing, even if it's only during the day.'

'But what good is Sister Tranter if she's always at the pub?' said Richard.

'You only have the Italian's word for that,' said Dr. Herbright. 'And they're not notoriously truthful.'

'I'd back his word against hers,' said Richard.

'Perhaps so,' said Dr. Herbright. 'But with many people, I find, you have to consider not what they say, but what makes them say it. This Berto has evidently got his stiletto into Sister Tranter.'

When Sister Tranter left she asked him for the first time

how he felt. Before she had always told him, associating her own health with his. Better or worse, for better or for worse, they were together, an indissoluble plural. We.

'How do you feel?' she asked.

'Better,' Richard said.

'You may feel better, but I don't think you are,' she said, looking at him hard, 'and it's my impression that Doctor thinks the same. You're still a nursing case. If you have a relapse, I'm afraid I shan't be available.'

'I'm sorry about that,' said Richard.

'I have so many patients lined up. And if I hadn't, I shouldn't want to come back. I don't like the way things are run, and done, here. I've worked with foreigners before, of course, in hospital but never in a private house. And they have been really black, not just dagoes.'

'I'm sorry,' said Richard, 'if Berto has given you any reason for complaint.'

'He hasn't,' said Sister Tranter, 'I mean I couldn't be affected one way or the other by a man of *that* kind. And Mrs. Stonegappe feels the same. She often says to me, "I don't mind Mr. Mardick, he doesn't give much trouble, but I can't stand that Italian, he's so nosey for one thing, and then he has dirty habits."'

'What sort of habits?'

'The sort of habits they all have. She says she's fed up.'

'Is she leaving, too?' asked Richard, rashly.

'She hasn't told me. I'm not in her confidence, of course, and she's not one to gossip, but I think she is. You see there are lots of places where they don't have Italians sneaking round.'

Richard's relief at Sister Tranter's departure was mitigated by the shadow of Mrs. Stonegappe's. What would he do if *she* left? While he was considering this problem, Lucilla arrived. When they had talked for a minute or two, he said:

'You're the exception to the proverb, that one swallow doesn't make a summer.'

She seemed pleased with this and smiled for the first time since her arrival.

She had never been very liberal with her smiles, but this time her gravity had struck him, and the thought crossed his mind, 'Am I the cause of it?' and he felt guilty, just as he used to feel as a small boy when he wasn't well, and his mother came in with her strained bedside face.

'I'm afraid you have been rather ill,' she said, confirming his suspicion. 'I didn't want to worry you – I have a feeling you don't like being fussed over.'

'There you're wrong,' said Richard, 'I do quite like being fussed over – at least by certain people – you, for instance.'

Her face lit up and he wondered if he had said too much. But he had been alone for a long time and in spite of Berto's unvarying kindness the unsympathetic attitude of Sister Tranter and Mrs. Stonegappe still rankled. He didn't realize how much it had rankled until he began pouring it out to Lucilla.

Throughout his recital her indignation mounted.

'What dreadful women!' she said, when he stopped.

Having got it off his chest, and received Lucilla's sympathy, he felt more tolerant towards them.

'Oh, I don't know. They disliked each other heartily until Berto came, and then they joined forces against him. I suppose it's human nature. They weren't so bad as that succession of male crooks I had – not so dishonest, anyway. The trouble was their feelings were engaged, which couldn't be said of the men, who were just out for what they could get.'

'And Mr. Aspin?' Lucilla said.

'Oh Denys!' All these subsequent pin-pricks had been a counter-irritant to the real wounds dealt by Denys – the wound to his feelings, the wound to his purse, the wound to his faith in human nature – at Lucilla's question they bled anew.

'Don't let's talk about Denys,' he said, 'I'd rather not, if you don't mind.' To speak of Denys to Lucilla embarrassed him: it seemed to show lack of tact, and worse still, lack of taste. But having said he didn't want to talk about Denys, he proceeded to do so.

'Of course Denys has been my great disappointment,' he said as casually as he could. 'I had staked a lot in . . . on . . . him, and he has let me down, properly – or improperly. It seems he isn't really an Aspin of Aspin Castle, either, though that's a small point. It was you who told me, wasn't it?'

'Yes, but I never was quite sure.'

'It all ties up with the rest of his behaviour, there isn't a grain of truth in him anywhere.' Richard thought of telling Lucilla about Denys's behaviour, but decided not to.

'If he *had* been an Aspin,' he contented himself with

saying, 'it would still have been in character – they were just Border-robbers who ought to have been hanged for sheep-stealing, and perhaps were. But that Norman door! When I looked at it, and thought of Emily Brontë looking at it (I know, dear Lucilla, that she couldn't have), something stirred in me – I suppose it was a sense of the past, not to give it a more snobbish name. You never liked him, did you? – Denys, I mean.'

'I thought he took advantage of your good-nature,' said Lucilla.

'Yes, but I wanted him to, until . . . until . . . But now he's "out", as they say. I never want to hear of him again, and I sincerely hope I shan't. Have you ever put your trust in somebody who's let you down?'

'No,' said Lucilla, 'I don't think I have. You know, Richard, I haven't had a great deal of experience. My parents saw to that. They had a sort of horror of the world – all because of something that happened when they were quite, quite young. It had to do with Rookland, I believe – that's why I go there – but before that, too, there was something. I have an inkling of what it was, but I don't really want to know what they didn't want to tell me. Your connection with Rookland has been a bond, a strange bond . . . But now, Richard, may I say this? I don't feel altogether happy about you – or should I say, *comfortable* about you. You seem to be at the mercy of a lot of people who haven't your interests at heart—'

'You're telling *me*,' said Richard, smiling.

But Lucilla didn't smile back.

'I know what you're going to say – that you won't find any honest person in that walk of life, and it isn't worth while trying. And that it is a greater sin to put temptation in people's way than it is to yield to it. You say that is the modern view—'

'Did I say so, Lucilla?'

'Yes, but I'm old-fashioned and I don't agree with it. I think you've been unlucky. There may be something in you that tempts people to take advantage of you – I'm not saying there is. I hope you're not offended?'

'Of course not,' Richard said, though he was, a little.

'But I'm sure that if you tried long enough you would find someone as honest as you are yourself.'

'That shouldn't be difficult,' said Richard.

Lucilla passed this over.

'But as I said, it might take a long time, and you aren't well, and shouldn't be subjected to the strain. What I propose is this, and please give it your consideration, Richard. You need someone to look after you, and who have you got? This daily woman, Mrs. Stonegappe, who tells you she is going to leave—'

'She won't,' interposed Richard, 'now that her other worser self, her *âme damnée*, Sister Tranter, has departed.'

But Lucilla swept on.

'She hasn't been very satisfactory, has she? And then there's this Italian—'

'I won't hear a word against Berto,' said Richard, feeling that in defending Berto he was somehow defending himself. 'Berto is really a jewel—'

'Yes, but you know what these Italians are,' Lucilla said,

clearly unwilling to concede Berto's good points, 'all charm one moment, and the next they're off! I don't want to discourage you about Berto, Richard, but what I want to say is this: leave your flat, or let it, and come and stay in mine till you are better. I shouldn't worry you – even if I worry about you.'

Lucilla fixed her eyes on him – her healthy eyes – alight with vigour and determination.

'You are too kind,' he murmured, 'much too kind, Lucilla.' He let her name linger on, stroking the air as if it was a charm, while he thought of an excuse. Suddenly he felt very tired – nowadays even the shadow of an impending decision tired him. 'It's such a wonderful prospect – wonderful. May I really think it over, and let you know?'

'That means you won't come,' said Lucilla, with disappointment, almost anger, in her voice.

'Oh no, it doesn't. I have so many things to think about – my will for one, and will-power, of any sort, is just what I haven't got. Where there's a will there's a way, but where there's a way there isn't always a will, unfortunately.'

He smiled wanly at this pleasantry.

'But couldn't you make your will staying with me?' Lucilla asked. 'I could witness it for you, and then no one could accuse me of having had undue influence.'

Richard saw the implications of this.

'Oh, but I should want to leave you something, and if you witnessed it, I couldn't.'

'Then make your will, and come to me afterwards.'

'I will, I will,' said Richard, hardly knowing what kind of will he meant.

'You mean you won't,' Lucilla said. She stooped over the bed and kissed him gravely. 'But I shall go on hoping.'

23

Soon more swallows came to complete Richard's summer.
Old friends, they came from all dates and directions in the
sunny climes of the past. Some he had almost forgotten,
and was astonished that they had not forgotten him. Now
that he was up and about again, and surprisingly well, he
could receive them in the spirit in which they came; and
he was so pleased by this recrudescence of his old life,
amounting to rejuvenation, that he forgot to ask himself
why, after such a long absence, they had come back. All
excused themselves on various pleas for their neglect of
him.

'It wasn't that we'd forgotten you,' said one of them,
taking refuge in the plural, 'but you seemed so happy as
you were, leading an idyllic life with your young friend –
one might call it an Indian summer, only you are much too
young for that. And of course we didn't know you had
been so ill – you kept that from us, Richard, or we should
have come in shoals and almost besieged your bed. It
really was rather naughty of you not to tell us. But I expect
you would have, if you hadn't been so well looked-after.
How is the young man, by the way? Stupid of me, but I
forget his name.'

'Denys,' said Richard, 'Denys Aspin.'

'Oh yes, of course. It seemed such an ideal arrangement, we didn't like to butt in on it. And then we heard a rumour that it had somehow come to an end. Is that right?'

'It is,' said Richard, 'he's gone.'

'Oh dear, what a pity. And yet we had an idea it might not last. Young people are so fly-away, nowadays, they don't know when they are well-off. Was it you who got rid of him, or did he—?'

'He got married,' said Richard, briefly. 'At least I think he did.'

'But you're not sure? You know I never quite trusted him – I don't think any of us did. He was very attractive, of course, and no doubt to women, too, but we felt he had his eye on the main chance. We got the impression that he wanted to make you dependent on him – at any rate he didn't want you to be dependent on *us*. He made that rather clear.'

'I hope he wasn't rude to you,' said Richard.

'Oh never! But he had – what shall I say? – an air of quiet possessiveness that rather warned us off. "Hands off Richard, while I'm here!" It seemed a bit like that. And it wasn't for us to interfere, when you both seemed so happy.'

'I wasn't very happy latterly,' said Richard.

'Oh dear, I'm sorry. It's always painful when some old attachment comes to an end. One blames oneself, often unreasonably. Still, it's an ill wind that blows no one any good – and we'll do our best – our united best – to fill his place. How are you fixed now, I mean domestically?'

'Oh, I've got a daily help and this nice Italian, Berto.'

'So you're not too badly off?'

'Oh no, I'm really very lucky.'

But Richard wasn't as lucky as he thought. A few days later, when he had begun to feel happier, and better, than at any time since Denys's defection, and to have recovered his pre-Denys outlook, convinced that there was more safety in numbers than in one, the first blow fell.

'Can I speak to you, sir?' said Mrs. Stonegappe, resting her hands on the handle of the carpet-sweeper with which she had just cornered him.

'Why yes,' said Richard, extricating himself. 'What is it?'

'I'm afraid I must give in my notice, sir.'

'Oh, but why?'

'I can't stand it any longer, sir, this Italian being about the place. I know you like him, sir, but you don't see what I see.'

'What do you see?'

'There are some things best not told, and I shouldn't dream of telling you. But he isn't what you think he is, and so I'm handing in my notice.'

'Won't you reconsider it, Mrs. Stonegappe?'

'No, sir, I'm not one to change my mind. I only hope you'll find somebody else to do for you what I have.'

Richard was slightly hurt but not unduly dismayed when Mrs. Stonegappe left. She had been one more drop in his cup of disillusion, but she did not make it overflow. Once he had been fond of her; of all his toilet requisites, so to speak, she had seemed the best. Now he was not; she might be the best, but the best of a bad lot. She had seemed to have his interests at heart, and perhaps she had, if her tell-tale tongue, so quick to report the faults of the others, was anything to go by. How often had she said that this one and that one of her colleagues was taking advantage of him. Berto was her latest suspect; on Berto's account she had made it up with her former *bête-noire*, Sister Tranter. She had made this unholy alliance just to do Berto down.

So he didn't attach too much importance to the vague aspersions she had cast on Berto. Nor, as a cleaner, was she any loss. One of Richard's more outspoken friends had remarked that the flat could do with a good clean. Berto could do it all on his head, so to speak, using the Hoover which Mrs. Stonegappe, wedded to her favourite weapon, the carpet-sweeper, always said was out of order. Berto, though far from being *mauvaise langue*, had sometimes said that Mrs. Stonegappe swept the dust into a corner – just as she swept him, Richard; but he could get away, whereas the dust couldn't.

So he wasn't unduly dismayed by her departure, while Berto was obviously relieved. All Richard's friends liked Berto, and congratulated him on this new acquisition. Left to himself, Berto scrubbed, scoured and polished the flat: it gleamed and glowed, reflecting the smiles that Richard's old friends, once estranged, now turned on him. Only Lucilla who sometimes came with them, but more often alone, inferred that their rejoicing might be premature.

They didn't know her, most of them, but they welcomed her as a new element in Richard's life. 'You could do worse, you know,' said his old friend, Lewis Charleston, the novelist, who had retained the public's favour longer than Richard had, 'than throw in your lot with her. If I were you I should regard her as a godsend. She's a nice woman, and just right for you. She seems disposed to accept us, and we certainly accept her. She isn't exactly our sort, perhaps, but we should learn, and she would learn. I haven't been to her flat, but others have, and they say the bib-and-tuckery's quite wonderful. Why do you hesitate?'

'Oh, my dear Lewis,' Richard said, 'there are a hundred reasons. Besides, what makes you think she likes me enough?'

'Of course you're a bit old for her, aren't you, but women are very considerate in those matters, so why not try your luck? Together you could start a salon, and we old-stagers would flock to it. You could be Mme du Deffand, and she could be Mlle de Lespinasse.'

'I don't see why we should hit it off better than they did,' Richard objected.

'That is because you're wedded to this idea of an arm's-length relationship. If I may say so, it's what's wrong with all your books except the first, which everybody liked, and why? Because in it you showed people coming together, and being together – since then, you've always shown them hungering for each other across vast desert spaces. Your youthful self knew something about human nature that your adult self didn't, or forgot. I don't know what you felt for Denys Aspin – whatever it was I'm sure he wasn't worthy of it – but whatever it was it's over, and now you have this wonderful chance. We shall rejoice. We didn't like Denys Aspin – let's be frank – and didn't very much like coming while he was here, but we *do* like Lucilla – though I ought not to call her that – and we shall welcome her with open arms – not at arm's length – if you do. I know it's said that when a confirmed bachelor of old standing marries, he loses all his friends, especially his women friends; but I can promise you, Richard, that you won't. We shall all rally round you, and if there's to be any chucking out it's you who'll do it. I long to think of us as a large happy family again, presided over by you and your . . . your consort. Haven't you proposed to her yet?'

Richard was startled.

'No, of course I haven't.'

'Do you swear that you haven't suggested that you should . . . combine in some way? Make your orbits touch? Legitimize your – how shall I put it – your loose relationship?'

Richard thought a little, and remembered Lucilla's offer of sanctuary in her flat.

'Well, I suppose—'

'If you haven't, you must. For your sake, not for hers. You have made a desert and called it peace. You look across the Sahara of your life and think, "Oh no, Lucilla, that would be to spoil something very, very precious." Now aren't I right?'

'You are right, in a way,' said Richard, unwillingly.

'I knew I was. So do come off it, as they say, and make everybody happy.'

'But at my age—' protested Richard. 'And apart from that, I'm not a very good life, you know.'

'Is any of us? Haven't we all one foot in the grave? In any case, that's her affair. If she consents to take you on—'

'I'll think about it,' Richard said, 'I'll think about it.'

24

Richard didn't think about it very much, for his heart and mind were lulled into a sense of security and well-being that he had never known since Denys was paid off. Getting Denys out of his system had left a hole in his financial position, and an ache in his heart; but Richard was too unrealistic to mind about the first, and as for the second, the sense of having been wronged – which can reduce the strongest affection – had half obliterated even his visual memory of Denys. Why remember a black-mailer whose whole meaning to him had been so completely different from what he thought it was? Of all the emotions, love is the least amenable to reason; but in the end it learns to cut its losses, especially if they can be screened or made up from other sources – as Richard's had been. Like Mr. Veneering, he had his friends rallying round him, to keep off the cold draught of indifference; he had loyal Berto to look after him and minister to his immediate needs; and in the distance – quite at what distance he couldn't decide – but why decide? – he had Lucilla. In every way he was provided for – even his health, that incalculable factor, seemed to reflect the improvement in his general style. Seventy, and going stronger and stronger!

But the river is often at its most placid before it reaches the weir.

Berto's face, bent over his early morning tea-tray, was never more a study in the art of giving and receiving happiness, than it was that morning. Anxiety lest he should drop the tray, anxiety lest this anxiety should impede his smile of welcome, were, as always, in conflict. The signorino must not be greeted with a *muso duro*, a hard, shut face, still less with a salvo from the tea-pot, a vessel which Berto was never quite at home with. Having safely deposited it, he drew the curtains, praised the day – as he always did however little the day deserved it – helped Richard into his bed-jacket with the utmost solicitude, and tiptoed out.

Oh, what a treasure Berto was! Richard never thought of him without making a mental act of gratitude. More than any other single person – except one, except one – he had contributed to Richard's recovery.

As the Welfare State got more into its stride, so did the post arrive later and later – as if to show that lateness was a sign of communal well-being. Early morning breadwinners had to wait for their letters until they came home in the evening. Richard was not a breadwinner, he could afford to await the postman's knock. While he was in his bath, Berto would steal in and lay the letters on his bed.

Richard emerged from the bathroom but found no letters on the bed. Later than usual, the postman was. During his relapses Richard had tended to regard his letters as addressed to a posthumous self. Letters implied a continuity of existence: why bother to write answers which might not arrive before he was dead? He remembered how, in the first war, and in the second, letters he had written had been returned to him, with a note to say that the addressee was no longer alive. In the valley of the shadow men's puny efforts at communication were a mockery to be ignored. But as each false alarm ceased to reverberate, he found himself returning to the world of normal relationships and obligations, one of which was the receiving and answering of letters. Seeing none on the bed, he was disappointed.

He went on dressing, vaguely listening for the sounds of Berto's movements, and his customary morning cough, for which, so Berto said, the English climate was to blame. But he listened in vain. Richard wasn't a man to be surprised by a failure in routine; but at last, fully dressed, he went out into the passage.

The letters, quite a pile of them, lay on the console table. And there was a sound, coming from Berto's room – a sound he hadn't heard for ages – and couldn't for the moment recognize. When he did recognize it he knocked and went in. Berto was sitting on his bed with his back to Richard. His shoulders were twitching, and only his neck and the back of his head were visible. His hands were invisible; and his stuck-out elbows suggested that they were pressed against his eyes. At intervals sobs shook him, mingling with broken breaths.

The gay, care-free Berto, whose philosophy of life reflected his own temperament, reduced to this!

He hadn't heard Richard come in, and Richard's first impulse, as always when a strong emotion was forced upon his notice, was to withdraw: people should be left to their own grief. But not Berto, Berto the man of feeling, whom no difference of nationality, age, class, upbringing or outlook had been able to dehumanize.

Richard coughed and shuffled, and when these demonstrations had no effect, he said: 'What's the matter, Berto? *Cosa hai?*'

Berto jumped up from the bed, and turned a startled, even terrified face to Richard.

'O signorino!'

It's no good, thought Richard; I'm too old to respond to these violent feelings, whatever they are about. But at any rate I can be sympathetic.

'Something has upset you, I can see that,' he said lamely, feeling – for at the back of his mind the particular always merged into the general – how much better an Italian painter would have treated the situation than he did. 'Can you tell me what it is?'

Berto shook his head violently.

'No, *nossignore. E una cosa che non posso dirle*. It is something that I cannot tell you – that I cannot tell to anyone, for they would not understand.'

Richard, who rather prided himself on his power of understanding, if not on his power of emotional response, replied: 'All the same, tell me.'

Berto burst into speech. At first he was quite incoherent; even a fellow-countryman, thought Richard, wouldn't have known what he meant. Two names kept cropping up – La sorella Tantrum and Mrs. Stonygappy: they were responsible for all this, whatever it was.

'But they have both left,' said Richard, when at last he could get a word in. '*Sono partite, Berto, sono andate via, sono – non so dove.* Why do you worry about them?'

Berto agreed that they had gone. 'But do you know why they went, signorino?'

'No,' admitted Richard.

'Because they had laid a trap to ruin me.'

How the Italian temperament dramatizes everything, thought Richard. But perhaps that was too simple an explanation.

'What sort of a trap, Berto?'

'They have written – or made to be written – a letter to *mia mamma*. They said the most terrible things about me.'

'What sort of things, Berto?'

'O signorino, I could never tell you. They are so shameful, and so untrue. All women tell lies of course (and we Italian men are habituated to that). But I had never done those two any harm, so why should they tell lies about me?'

'You haven't told me what they did say, Berto.'

'*Nossignore.*' The effort of finding words to express, or suppress, his thoughts had pulled Berto together and he began to look more himself, in token of which he jumped off the bed in confusion – '*Scusi, signorino!*' and begged Richard to be seated. 'I am so *commosso*,' he apologized, 'that I have forgotten my manners. But no, signorino,' he said, recollecting himself, 'I could not tell you what those ill-educated women said. You are *troppo buono e troppo ammalato* to hear such things.'

The idea that being good and unwell excused him from being told an unpleasant truth was so utterly un-English, at any rate so foreign to his recent experiences of his own countrymen that tears came into Richard's eyes.

'Don't disturb yourself for me,' he said, attempting the Italian idiom. 'I am old and ugly enough to look after myself. I shan't be shocked by anything you tell me. *Ma forsè non ci entro* – perhaps I don't come into it?'

Berto's face began to work, and Richard was sorry he had spoken, for to him, and evidently to Berto, nothing was more embarrassing than to find a middle way between truth and falsehood. None of Berto's predecessors in Richard's household had been worried by this problem; they did not think there was one.

'Signorino,' said Berto at last, 'you are a signore' (How can I be both, thought Richard, flattered none the less), 'and you would not understand how these women's minds work. I am an Italian, and I do understand.' He paused, whether to let this sink in, or to gain time, Richard did not know. '*Tutto il mondo è compagno* – the world is all like itself,' he translated, with difficulty. 'Therefore, they say and do what they should not say or do. We Italians are habituated to that. But the signorino is not. It is bad enough for me to have to go away—'

'Go away, Berto?'

'Yes, signorino, I must go. I could not stay, and my mother would not wish me to stay, would not allow me to stay, after hearing what those women said. But at least I can go away without being too inconvenient to you.'

'But how could they have found out her address?'

'Because, signorino, she writes to me every day, and I did not think it necessary to conceal her letters. And they know how well she wishes me, and how well I wish her, because I showed them her photograph more than once when first I came. They were obliged to admit that she was a beautiful woman.'

Richard agreed that she was a mother of whom any man might be proud. 'But how could they write to her,' he asked, 'when they don't know Italian?'

Berto shrugged his shoulders and spread out his hands.

'There are many Italians in this quarter, signorino,' he said, 'who would write a letter for a *mancia* or even for a drink.'

'But I still don't understand why you have to go away,' said Richard, whose mind could not take in this calamity, and who had forgotten what a decisive part Italian mothers played in the lives of their sons.

'You would if I told you, signorino, and that is what I must not and cannot do. I must go back to Italy and perhaps I shall be able to persuade my mother that what those women said was false.'

'But can't you write to her?'

'*Nossignore*, because a letter would not be enough. It is different when one talks to someone. When she sees me she will believe me. I shall implore her to believe me.'

Berto broke down again and became speechless. Richard watched him helplessly. There was nothing he could do or say.

*

Richard persuaded Berto to stay on another week, ostensibly to give himself time to look for another man but really hoping that Berto would change his mind. But Berto did not change his mind, nor did Richard try to find anyone to replace him. The thought of starting all over again with another man and another daily help, even if he could have found them, depressed him too much. He hadn't the energy. Reviewing what had happened since Denys left he felt utterly let down and forlorn. He had made a complete mess of things. He could not run his own life or get anyone to do it for him. He was a bad chooser, no doubt; he got hold of the wrong kind of people. He was not alone in that; many of his friends had fared no better than he had. But they were for the most part younger than he was, and did not have illness to contend with. For them hope continued to triumph over experience; they were always ready to have another go. Richard wasn't. His age had caught up with him, thrown him on to a reef and left him stranded. He didn't tell his friends that Berto was leaving him, he couldn't bring himself to; they had heard the saga of his domestic troubles too often. Berto himself was no consolation; he was present but he was utterly changed. He never smiled and seldom spoke. Sister Tranter or Mrs. Stonegappe, or both, had done their work well.

What had they got out of it, Richard wondered, what had any of them got out of it, from Denys onwards? Denys, yes, he had got a lot out of it; he had got enough to live on. The thought of Denys was the bitterest of his thoughts, for in Denys the failure of his life was personified. Often he found himself seeing himself through Denys's eyes. He could not get the picture out of his mind; surely, he argued, there has been something in my life more worth-while than my paternal attachment to that wretched fellow? The feelings he had had for Denys were not like the feelings he had for Lucy, but in terms of emotional output they were the best he could do. But they had been utterly misplaced; they had left him nothing but debts.

And as for the other men and women who had been in his employ, they too had depleted him as far as they were able to and with no advantage that he could see except the momentary satisfaction of their greed or spite. He had started off, he told himself, with the best intentions towards all of them: he had shown them such kindnesses as he could; but the moment they realized he wanted them to be happy, from that moment he was lost. 'He's easy, that's what it is,' he had overheard Mrs. Stonegappe say. If only they hadn't been so difficult!

He grew more and more low-spirited as the time for Berto's departure drew nearer. With Berto in his present mood his departure would be no great loss; but he depended on Berto for the machinery of living: he would have to take some practical steps, but he couldn't.

Meanwhile he tried to find some rationale to explain his present plight. It didn't suit him to think that all these set-backs, major and minor, were fortuitous; he would rather believe that something had caused them – something inside himself, rather than something outside, a pattern of life which fate had forced on him.

Responsibility – he didn't want to shirk it. And he had shirked it, he knew. He had buried the Lucy episode under a mass of excuses and half-truths: he had even persuaded himself that he could evade its consequences to himself by treating Denys as a father-confessor. Denys, of all people! And the fact that Denys had betrayed him, and black-mailed him, had seemed an additional expiation. It wasn't, of course, it was just another pretext for not feeling really sorry, a substitute for repentance. All his life he had tried to believe that what had happened at the Brickfield wasn't his fault, tried to believe that as long as people didn't know about it and couldn't blame him for it, he needn't blame himself. His compromise-confession to Denys, by which he hoped to get rid of the guilt, without openly disclosing the fact, was a cowardly subterfuge, and he deserved what he had got. He should have told Denys to make a clean breast of it, and let his friends think as badly of him as they liked. And he shouldn't have let the revela-tion wait till he was dead and couldn't feel the shame and disgrace of their disapproval. That would have been a real expiation, and if they avoided him, as they surely would, his conscience would be the clearer. How had he come to let himself live this lie?

Richard didn't realize to what extent his present posi-tion, bereft of domestic help and the will to find any, had encouraged these despondent thoughts. He believed that he ought to be miserable; but he was miserable apart from that, and he still had enough come-back in him to try to escape his misery. The way was open and he knew it. Why had he hesitated so long? It seemed inconceivable that

Lucilla should want to marry him, but if she married him, all his major problems would be solved. He would spend his last weeks, months or years in comfort, and perhaps one day, one day, he might even bring himself to tell her the truth.

Just before Berto was due to leave he wrote to her.

Dearest Lucilla,

A little while ago you were kind enough to ask me to come and stay with you. I didn't accept your invitation at the time because I didn't think you could really want to be saddled with a semi-invalid. But now I feel that you knew your own mind well enough to take the risk. I still feel it isn't fair – you have so much to offer me and I have so little to offer you. But if you are still of the same mind [he knew she would be] this is just to say that I should love to come, any time you like, as soon as you like – it cannot be too soon for me, or last too long.

With my love, Richard.

If he realized how disingenuous the letter was, he didn't care. The relief of having at last made his mind up, the blessed release from indecision, the tremendous tonic of action, made him feel a whole man at last.

25

When he came back from posting the letter he found that Berto had admitted two of his old friends, Lewis Charleston, and Eddy Stapleford, a dramatic critic. Old friends, but younger than he, and in touch with modern trends in art and literature and public taste that he knew nothing of. They had an air of subdued excitement, and looked at him with curiosity, he thought.

'You know, Richard,' said Lewis, who was the chief spokesman, and accepted as such, in any gathering of Richard's friends, 'it's really time you wrote us another novel. You've been slacking all these years, living the life of Riley. You should pull yourself together and tell the world what you have been thinking about.'

'I haven't been thinking about anything,' said Richard, 'that could possibly interest the public.'

'That's what you say,' said Lewis, 'but it's because you don't know what interests the public. The public today is interested in a lot of things that you were never prepared to tell them. They liked your first book because it chimed in with something they were feeling at the time, and you went on in the same vein when they had begun to listen for something else. That was a mistake. Now you should rectify it.'

'But what experience have I had,' said Richard, 'that would be more palatable to them now than it was then?'

'That's for you to say. But couldn't you let your hair down a bit and tell them some of the incidents of your murky past? I'm sure you've had them – every man has.'

'My dear Lewis,' said Richard, uneasily, 'you know how quiet my life has been. I've used up every ounce of experience I had.'

'Are you quite sure?' said Lewis. 'Couldn't you make something out of Denys, for instance? I believe he wasn't altogether an exemplary character, but he was the sort of man the public of today finds sympathetic – an anti-hero, if you like.'

'He certainly was that,' said Richard.

'He must have had some good points, or you wouldn't have put up with him so long. But don't give him too many, that was your mistake in the past, portraying characters who were sound at bottom. The reader of today doesn't want to hear about them. He wants to hear about someone who's as bad as he is or a little worse so that he can feel sorry for him, and compared with him a good chap. Denys would be ideal – why not write him up – instead of letting him write you up?'

Richard was startled.

'But what makes you think he's going to write me up?'

'Well, there's a rumour going about to that effect.'

'Has anybody seen him, then?'

'I haven't, but Eddy has.'

Eddy, who was slight and fair whereas Lewis was tall and dark, said rather casually:

'Oh, at some wild party, you know, I don't remember whose. I didn't specially want to talk to him, because, between ourselves, I never liked him much, and I have an idea that he didn't treat you very well.'

'He didn't,' Richard said.

'I shouldn't have spoken to him, but he came and spoke to me, so I couldn't help myself. He said he hadn't seen you, and asked me how you were.'

'Did you say all the better for not seeing him?'

'I couldn't, could I? I didn't really know what terms you were on.'

'We're not on terms. I don't even know where he lives.'

'Really? Well, in the circumstances I had to be civil to him. He was more than a little sozzled, but then most of us were.'

'He always liked his glass,' said Richard reminiscently.

'Well, he had had more than one, that evening. And then he told me you had commissioned him to write about you.' Eddy stopped and looked at Richard inquiringly.

'Yes, I did.'

'He said that, and then he said he had something to say about you that would surprise your friends.'

'Surprise my friends?' echoed Richard, stupidly.

'Yes, that was why Lewis and I thought it would be a good idea if you got your blow in first and wrote about him. He might sue you for libel, I suppose, but I doubt if he'd want to. The sad thing is, from the point of view of sales and public interest, that he isn't as well known as you are.'

Richard tried to conceal his agitation.

'I may have been once, but I'm not any longer. Did he say when he meant to write the book?'

'Now, I gathered, while Richard was still news.'

'I could stop him doing that, couldn't I?'

'Yes, I should think you could, especially if he puts in what he says he's going to put. It would make the book sell – there's no doubt of that – it would bring you back into the picture, as an anti-hero, you know. It would be a free advertisement. I think you'd be unwise to try to stop him. And if you wrote about him too, think of the sensation it would cause.'

Richard looked from one to the other, and then straight in front of him.

'Did he say what he was going to put in that would surprise everybody?'

It was now the two friends' turn to exchange glances.

'Well, yes, he did,' said Eddy. 'And that's why we came round hot-foot – to congratulate you.'

'To congratulate me?'

'Why yes, because we didn't think you had it in you. We thought you were someone who had always lived outside of life, and got your knowledge of it at second-hand. But this explains why your first book was such a good one, because it was written while the experience was still working in you.'

'What experience?' said Richard. 'My first book may have been prophetic, because it was about someone who let down a friend, but it didn't come from any experience I ever had.'

'Are you quite sure? Are you sure it wasn't a transposition of some experience, and that you changed the forms but kept the essential meaning? From what your young friend told us, it could have been.'

I must hear the worst now, thought Richard. No good trying to put it off.

'What did he tell you?'

'Well, as I said, he was pickled and not making much sense, but the gist of it was this – that when you were a boy, seventeen I think he said, and living with an uncle at a place called Rookland, to learn farming, you got a young girl into trouble and she drowned herself. No one ever knew why she did it, because no one knew you had been meeting her, and naturally you never told. In fact you came in for a lot of sympathy, because it was you who found her body, and it upset you, as it would have upset anyone.'

Richard sat with his face in his hands.

'My dear fellow,' Lewis said, 'I expect the memory is still painful, but don't you see how it adds to . . . to your stature as a human being? You've had a gift for friendship, we all know that, though latterly you canalized it in a way that some of us regretted – not that we disapprove of such friendships, Heaven knows, but in this case it kept us out: we couldn't see you, the dragon wouldn't let us. And so you got a name for being a good fellow, but not really *counting*, if you see what I mean, either as a man or a writer – just repeating, over and over again with slight variations, the same pattern of literary good manners. The public felt it too: they liked the taste at first, but with each repetition it grew fainter and then they tired of it. *We* never tired of *you*, but then you're not a book: you respond to a person in a way you don't respond to a blank sheet of paper. You take in – that's why you're such a gift to egoists – but you don't give out. Now we know this about you you've become real, you don't just reflect, you shine with your own light like a lighthouse. Everyone, except a few old stagers, will think the better of you, because you're somebody to whom something has really happened. Why don't you write a book about it? It's what the public wants, the raw stuff of experience, and the rawer the better. Experience doesn't need justifying: it's its own justification, in life as well as art. That's why we came to congratulate you – on being the person, the real live human being, that you've so long concealed. And you'll find that everybody will feel as we do: they'll hail you, not as a purveyor of old-fashioned literary wares but as a real, live, gay seducer – an archangel a little damaged, as someone said of Coleridge.'

But Richard could bear no more. 'Go away, go away, go away,' he repeated, without looking at them, and when at last he did look they had gone.

26

Events moved quickly, hardly giving Richard time to take in the full measure of Denys's perfidy or to reflect on the extraordinary reaction of his friends to the disclosure Denys had made. In a way, he told himself, he would have preferred their downright disapproval; he would have known how to deal with it, it would only have added another bitter but salutary draught to his cup of repentance. As it was, their reception of the news left him hopelessly bewildered. They had said they actually liked him better for what he had done, and so would other people. Was it true? If it was, it made nonsense of his entire interior life since the day when he had found Lucy drowned in a muddy pool in the Brickfield. Had there been some revolution in ethics which in all those years he had never noticed – a revolution that dethroned traditional morality and made obedience to impulse – whatever impulse it might be – the sole criterion of merit? Had self-control and consideration for other people's welfare ceased to be virtues?

He couldn't believe it, yet how gladly he would have believed it, for he realized that the obligation to think badly of himself had poisoned his life, or if not poisoned, distorted and frustrated it. If only he could have thought himself the hero – the anti-hero, as they called it – of the episode – he would have been another person – not Richard Mardick at all.

Experimentally he tried to think of himself as an anti-hero, someone who had had the guts to follow his own inclinations and proclaim his personality for what it was. He *had* done it, and for a short time he had been that person, and it was – he didn't disguise it from himself – the happiest time of his life. If he had accepted the consequences, if he had told the Coroner's Court, 'I did this, I'm to blame but I'm not ashamed of it' – wouldn't he then have emerged as a whole person, taking what he would from life, instead of a pretence person, an amalgam of evasions and subterfuges fabricated by his fear of public opinion?

Now that the cat was out of the bag was there still time for him to be once more the Richard of the Brickfield, admired for what he was, instead of tolerated for what he was not? Then he would still have something to look forward to with hope instead of back on with despair. Richard the seducer! The violator of young girls! The elderly gentleman, seemingly so innocent who had once had the courage of his passions, who had come to grips with life, instead of declining its challenge, and who still bore the scars of the encounter! Richard who had known that a personality is hollow until it has realized itself in action, an action entirely self-regarding, untainted by moral scruples, an action with no suspicion of compromise in it, a perfect instance of pure self-expression! Richard who had the courage to be himself without regard to the claims of other people; Richard the Lion-Heart!

Going to sleep with these brave thoughts he woke up with others, for the thought-patterns of a lifetime are not to be blurred or erased by one single stroke from without, however violent. For hours, it seemed, he lay in utter wretchedness, facing the world's opinion, as if he was a prisoner in the dock, and the world was arraigning him – Richard the sneak-thief, the seducer, the murderer. How would he dare to go out into the street, when every passer-by would stare at him with horror, and point the finger of scorn at him? How would he dare to show his face, as the saying is? What had he to look forward to but the promise of death, the promise that had been so often offered, and so often withdrawn?

But gradually, as the daylight began to shine behind the curtains, so were his thoughts shot through with brighter gleams, for today was to be the day of his deliverance, one sort of deliverance at any rate, deliverance from his immediate material problems. Today would come Lucilla's letter, offering him the haven, the refuge, that his body so much needed. And who knew if the spirit might not take its cue from the body? He began to think of Lucilla, not only as someone who had given him endless hospitality and companionship, but as his one great benefactor, his bulwark against the world and against himself. Because he could not return her love in the same measure and quality in which it was offered, he had shied away from the thought of it and her; it was a charge upon his feelings that his feelings could not return. He had taken her devotion for granted because it was the easiest way out; if he could not return it he could at any rate spare her the knowledge that it was not returned. And he defended himself by thinking that she understood this, without any explanation from him, and acquiesced in it; she would accept the half a loaf that was better than no bread. Once or twice she had intimated that she didn't accept it, that she wanted to be more to him than she was – the 'more' that, if any law of reciprocity governed the affections, she had every right to be. Those occasions had frightened him and filled him with an unbearable sense of personal inadequacy; but somehow he had shuffled by them, relying, in cowardly fashion, on the fact that a woman of Lucilla's conventional upbringing would never allow herself to say the one thing that would break off their relationship. So he had maintained the status quo, disregarding the axiom that no relationship ever stands still, it must wax or wane.

Now she appeared to him not as the figure of love that he would have liked her to be, but still as far the most important figure in his shrinking universe, a star of the first magnitude. *Nil desperandum*, while she was there to comfort and sustain him. And his heart overflowed with a gratitude to her and for her that was akin to love. If Richard hadn't believed that he was more undeserving than deserving, he could more easily have accepted Lucilla, that infinitely precious windfall which he certainly did not deserve. In his present mood he almost felt he could accept her, as one accepts the beauty of a summer's day which one has done nothing to bring about, still less deserve.

Berto came in with his tea, not with his letters which would not be forthcoming for at least an hour. Berto's sensitive pale face was still hag-ridden, and it still gave Richard a pang of guilt as well as sorrow. It wasn't Richard's fault that the two women had destroyed Berto's peace of mind and with it Richard's independent life; he needn't have felt guilty if he hadn't been constitutionally prone to find blame easier to take than credit. But as he asked Berto the question he asked him every morning, and sometimes during the day as well – 'Have you changed your mind, Berto?' – he didn't shrink from the negative that he knew would come as he had shrunk in the past, before he had decided to throw in his lot with Lucilla.

Supposing Berto had changed his mind, what then?

But he hadn't; he didn't say no, he only shook his head, helped Richard into his bed-jacket and arranged his clothes on the chair.

Coming out of his bath, Richard saw the letters lying on his bed, where Berto always put them. There were only two, and neither was from Lucilla. Richard tried to brush away his disappointment. Perhaps she had gone away – she did go away sometimes, and this was about her time for going to Rookland Abbey. But in that case why hadn't she told him? She always let him know her movements. He almost felt hurt with her for not telling him.

He opened the typewritten letter first. It was from his solicitor, asking if he might come and see him the next day. It was a long letter and he read it twice, once to take in, and the second time to digest its import.

Richard's grasp of money matters had never been strong. They did not touch his emotions, which were the seat of his anxiety; even the large sum he had paid out to Denys affected him chiefly in its personal aspect, the ingratitude it represented, the cruel breach of friendship. In the same way the confidence he had always placed in the Brick Company was a reflection of his confidence placed in his father as a business man. Whatever uninformed people might say, and perhaps all the more because they said it, he was convinced that his father could not go wrong in matters of business.

Mr. Smallcross's letter concerned the present and the future, in their most material aspects; but they touched off in Richard a long reverie, bringing back his youth and his relations with his parents through the years, sweet though in sadness. He remembered times when his father had been anxious, and when he asked his mother why, she would always say, 'It's about something you wouldn't understand, my darling – something to do with money' – for she always felt that Richard must share her ignorance of such matters.

And then occurred to him, what had never occurred to him before, the parallel between the Brickfield at Rookland and the Brick Company at Fosdyke. He had not connected them because the one had been a symbol of failure and the other of success. Geographically they were within a few miles of each other, but spiritually they were poles apart – life and death, truth and falsehood, day and night, were not more antithetical to each other. Yet now they seemed to have come together.

Perhaps everything tended to coalesce as one grew older. Distinctions were blurred or ceased to exist with one's inability to feel them. Even wealth and poverty did not seem so different. Richard would now be less well off, much less well off, but did that matter when he had Lucilla? To do him justice he had never thought of her as that kind of nest-egg, he hadn't needed to; it was the successive deprivations of his emotional life that had made the thought of her so precious. Was the thought of her more precious than she was herself? He could not tell but he could feel the warmth of it about his heart, that tired but most resilient organ.

Should he ring her up and tell her of the latest change in his affairs? He longed to, and he had no one else to confide in. Yet a scruple held him back: the next move must come from her: he must await her letter.

27

Mr. Smallcross arrived on the dot, with a shining morning face which he immediately shed for one subdued to the solemnity of a sick-room. After greeting Richard, and inquiring after him, his visage was furrowed with lines of still deeper gravity.

'I'm not altogether happy,' he said, 'about your shares in the Fosdyke Fundamental Brick Company. It is true that the Company has an excellent record, and that for sentimental reasons – your father's interest in it for one – you are attached to them. To the average investor, with an evenly diversified capital, Fosdyke Fundamental is still an attractive share. But as I have said to you before, it is not good policy to put all your eggs in one basket. Supposing a substitute should be found for bricks? Plastic bricks, or bricks made from the clay between coal seams? Many unlikely things are made from coal – sleeping-pills, for instance – so why not bricks? And there is the danger of foreign competition, bricks imported from Belgium, and these complete, fully-fashioned Self-Help Homesteads from Scandinavia.'

'I never heard of them,' said Richard aghast.

'Possibly not, but did you attend the last Fundamental Board Meeting?'

'No,' said Richard guiltily. 'My doctor said I wasn't well enough. But I've read the Minutes, and I'm almost sure there was no reference to Belgian bricks, or to Scandinavian Self-Help Homesteads.'

Mr. Smallcross smiled.

'If you'd had as much experience of board-room procedure as I have, Mr. Mardick, you would realize that a good deal is said on such occasions that does not find its way into the Minutes – for fear of alarming the shareholders, and for other reasons. I have no doubt that the question of Scandinavian Self-Help Homesteads *was* discussed, and the threat that they constitute to the building industry here. These Self-Help Homesteads are of all shapes and sizes, from a three-roomed bungalow to a palace; they are brought over in sections and can be pieced together within a few weeks at any spot you like to choose.'

'Good Heavens!' said Richard. At once he had a vision of the English countryside peppered with Scandinavian Homesteads, all much more desirable than ours, being the product of a more highly socialized conception of human needs. 'What am I to do?'

Mr. Smallcross sighed. 'You could find a cheaper flat, no doubt, but it would mean moving and many other inconveniences which at your age and in your state of health—'

'I know, I know,' said Richard, appalled at the thought. 'I should have to find someone to look after me – and no, I really couldn't. Please think again, Mr. Smallcross, and so will I, and perhaps between us we can work out something.'

Mr. Smallcross shrugged his shoulders.

'Life isn't too easy in this day and age for elderly people with dwindling incomes. Would you consider an Old People's Home? I believe that some of them are well-run and quite pleasant, and there is the social factor, which is so important nowadays, you wouldn't have to live for yourself—'

'Myself!' cried Richard. 'Whom else have I to live for? But seriously, Mr. Smallcross, please tell me what you think I ought to do.'

Mr. Smallcross folded his hands across his waistcoat.

'I think you would be well advised,' he said impressively, 'to sell the greater part, if not all, of your holding in Fosdyke Fundamental.'

Naturally suggestible, and especially in money matters, Richard at once saw his Brick shares as a rapidly wasting asset, a financial death-trap.

'What should I invest the proceeds in?' he asked. 'Proceeds' was a word with a professional ring, there were no flies on proceeds.

'I would suggest Juvenile and General Hair Stylists,' replied Mr. Smallcross promptly. 'Hair-stylists have a great future before them, because of the interest that teen-agers of both – we might say of every – sex take in what is for them an all-important subject, the hair-do. You, Mr. Mardick, belonging to another generation and yourself not over-well thatched, if I may put it so, may not realize what hair-distribution means to the rising generation. A hair out of place! – for them it means the difference between a successful evening out, and, well – total personal failure. They are prepared to pay large sums – very large sums – for a particular hair-style which will, so to speak, add lustre to their appearance and enhance their personality. Juvenile and General Hair-Stylists are setting up a chain, a *network* of studio-shops to meet this demand, and the Company offers exceptional prospects of development and capital appreciation.'

Richard said rather grandly, 'I will instruct my stock-brokers to sell out all or nearly all my securities in Fosdyke Fundamental, and invest the proceeds in – what is it called?'

'Juvenile and General Hair Stylists.'

Richard went to bed feeling that his financial future was secure; but at the back of his mind lingered a doubt which would not quite declare itself. His thoughts troubled him, and like Pharaoh of old he dreamed a dream. Two people were talking; he didn't at first recognize them, for their voices were clearer than their faces, but they were talking about him, for he heard his name bandied to and fro in a tone of disapproval which they would hardly have used if they had been aware of his presence. 'He has done us a great injury,' one of the speakers said. 'He might at least have told us what was in his mind. By putting this large block of shares on the market he may have given investors the impression that there is something wrong with the Company. *We* know there isn't, but *they* are not to know. And besides discrediting us, he may have opened the way for Leonard Bumfontein, who already has far more shares than we like, to get a controlling interest in the Company, and then where shall we be? Taken over, no doubt, by Balbus Building Projects (Ltd.), and thrown out on our ears.'

The other voice said, 'The boy must have taken leave of his senses. I grant that he had a bad start, his mother's concern for his health was a handicap to him, just as her concern for my health would have been a handicap to me, if I had let it. She meant well, of course. But he was slow getting off the mark, and then there were these novels. His mother enjoyed seeing his name in print more than I did; women like that sort of thing. But where would he have been, I ask you, without the Brickworks?'

'The Brickworks?' interposed another voice, deep, grating, and angry. 'Which Brickworks do you mean? The Brickfield at Rookland, or the Brickworks at Fosdyke?'

'Can you be so stupid as to ask such a question?' Richard's father answered, for now he knew it was his father. 'The Brickworks at Fosdyke, of course. The Rookland Brickfield was a miserable failure. It made some nice-looking bricks, I was told, from which some of the farmhouses round about were built, including St. Botolph's Lodge, my dear wife's home. Otherwise it did nothing, except to spoil a few acres of good agricultural land. We had some excellent duck-shooting there, I admit. But why on earth, Soames, do you bring up the Rookland Brickfield?'

'Your son could tell you, Mardick, and so could my daughter, if she were alive.'

'They were children then, and collected caterpillars, I seem to remember. I hope they got some fun out of it. My boy was lonely, he wasn't born to be a farmer, and I dare say your girl—'

'I'd rather you didn't mention Lucy, Mardick.'

'Oh yes, I remember, it all comes back to me. Life is cruel, Soames, but accidents do happen. They happen on the roads, they happen everywhere; men get killed nowadays in brickyards, even at Fosdyke. They don't take precautions, they are careless.'

'Was your son careless, Mardick?'

'I've no idea; your daughter was careless, wasn't she, poor girl, when she slid into the pool. I understand your feelings, but no money was involved, as the Rookland Brickfield was quite derelict. It is Richard's behaviour *now* that we were talking about before you butted in.'

'Oh please don't blame Richard!' said a woman's voice, his mother's. 'I'm sure he acted for the best. He had such a sweet gentle nature—'

'I never said he hadn't,' said his father, irritably, 'but in this case he has acted for the worst, as Rainsworth, our Chairman, has just told us.'

'But if he wrote to Mr. Rainsworth *very nicely*,' and now Richard could see his mother leaning forward at what his father used to call the 'apologetic', or the 'persuasive' angle, 'if he wrote to him *very nicely*, and explained—'

'How can you write *nicely* about something which isn't nice? The most he can do is to apologize, and hope that the other Directors will take a lenient view. At the next Board Meeting his name will come up for re-election. By then Richard will have, I suppose, turned seventy, and in view of what has happened, they may well make this an excuse for not re-electing him. He has never been a great asset to the Company, and there are plenty who will be willing to take his place, and the emoluments that go with it, or that went with it.'

Here his mother's voice rose in inarticulate protest, as it always did when she had exhausted her arguments. The other voices became inarticulate too, baritone and bass to her soprano; they made a sort of fugue around the word 'emoluments', which repeated itself meaninglessly in Richard's consciousness, turn over though he might in bed, and was only silenced by the arrival of his early-morning tea, and even after that it recurred, now as a shape, now as a sound, now as a colour, disturbing the tenour of his thoughts.

With each day that passed he drafted a fresh letter to the Chairman, finding new forms of apology for the damage he had done to the Fosdyke Fundamental Brick Company. But however he worded it, the more he pleaded poverty, or illness, or mere ignorance of money matters, the less the apology seemed adequate to the offence. He began to feel that all the mistakes and wrong-doings of a lifetime were summed up in his betrayal of the Brick Company.

He dared not, at first, consult the Stock Exchange list, in case his worst fears should be confirmed, but at last, acting on the principle that disaster is never so bad as one's apprehension of it, he did, and let his eyes slide down the F's – F for fool, F for fornication. He didn't think the shares would be quoted now; the Company would have gone into liquidation. At last he found them, and they stood at 21s. 6d., two shillings higher than when he had sold them, who knew how many days ago?

Relief followed incredulity, but there must be a catch in it somewhere, a misprint, eleven for twenty-one; nowadays compositors were not infallible. And if it wasn't a misprint, the explanation could only be that Balbus Building Projects, Ltd. had made a take-over bid for the Company, which had somehow sent the shares up. From the personal angle, this would be almost as bad as bankruptcy; the Chairman and the Directors, including himself, and his father's ghost, would have been sacked without notice, and replaced by Mr. Bumfontein's nominees. For several days he followed the fortunes of the Company, and the shares continued their wayward and intermittent upward trend. When they had reached 24s. he suddenly thought of his investment in Juvenile and General Hair Stylists. He took it for granted these shares would have soared, and only a queasy conscience had kept him from looking to see how much his finances had benefited by his perfidy to the Brick Company. They stood at a quarter, less than a quarter of what he had given for them. He wrote to his solicitor who replied, 'The collapse of J. and G.H.S. is as unfortunate as it was unforeseen. I advise you to sell out before the Company goes bankrupt.'

Richard complied, and the transaction cost him several thousand pounds.

The one consolation in all this was that he had not, apparently, done the Brick Company any harm. He need no longer write the Chairman that letter of apology, that very nice letter, the composition of which had occupied him for so many days. Not yet, at any rate. But what about the take-over bid threatened by Mr. Bumfontein and Balbus Building Projects, Ltd.? It no longer worried him as it once had, for anxiety, like an allergy, can wear itself out. But there remained the fear that the fate of the Brick Company, being such a small affair, would not have found its way into the papers, or that if it had, he might have missed it. So he wrote the Company's Secretary a non-committal letter, regretting that financial stringency had forced him to part with so many of his shares, and at the same time expressing his satisfaction at the Company's continued prosperity. 'As a matter of interest,' he wound up, 'I wonder if you would be kind enough to tell me the names of the buyers who took up my shares.' This would settle the question of the take-over bid.

He awaited in trepidation the Secretary's reply, and when the familiar envelope, with 'Fosdyke Fundamental Brick Company' stamped on the flap arrived, he could not at once bring himself to open it. Those pills, of which Denys never remembered the whereabouts – he must have them handy. As if they were still offended by Denys's neglect, he could not immediately find them; when he did he had no further excuse, and opened the Secretary's letter.

It was a charming letter, and began by saying how very sorry the Secretary was that he, Richard, had had to sell his shares in the Company. He said he felt sure that all the Directors, when they knew the circumstances, would feel the same sympathy that he did; and should Richard be well enough to attend the next Board Meeting, he would receive an ample assurance of their regard. Richard's name, on the list of Directors, had been an ornament to the Company for many years, and had doubtless helped to win the public confidence in its stability which had been recently shown in the satisfactory rise in the value of the shares. Should he wish to resign his directorship, as the Secretary hoped he would not, he would receive 'a golden handshake'.

Bewildered and astonished, Richard raised his eyes from the letter. Instead of being a financial Jonah, he had seemingly been a kind of mascot. The idea that his public image was so much brighter than his private conception of it almost took his breath away – the breathlessness of relief, that needed no pill to counteract it. Nothing about his having ruined the Company! Nothing about ingratitude, faithlessness, deserting the sinking ship! He read on:

'I only hope that the sale of your shares does not imply immediate financial embarrassment, and that you will have been able to invest the proceeds in a concern that is doing as well as, or better than, Fosdyke Fundamental. As regards your last question, I must tell you that the public interest shown in your shares, when they were put on the market, was most gratifying: numbers of small investors – I will give you a list – were interested, but the bulk of your shares were bought by Mr. H. T. Smallcross, who acts, I believe, as your solicitor in London. Using your name, as he told me you had invited him to do, he made inquiries about the prospects of the Company, which happily I was able to answer to his complete satisfaction.'

A list of minor investors followed.

Richard leaned back, while conflicting tides of emotion swept over him. Was it better, for one's peace of mind, to look a fool or to feel a knave? He needn't feel a knave, for he had acted on expert advice, as anyone was entitled to do, in the furtherance of his own interests: and in the event it turned out that he had done the Company more good than harm. But a fool he *must* look, to others and above all to himself; he had missed the rise in Fosdyke Fundamental, and got caught in the fall of Juvenile and General Hair Stylists. For both he had Mr. Smallcross to blame. Mr. Smallcross had owned that for someone with an evenly diversified capital (which Richard's wasn't) Fosdyke Fundamental was still an attractive share. But was J. and G.H.S. evenly diversified? The thing that above all Richard was forbidden to indulge in began to mount in him: rage. He hated Mr. Smallcross's guts. For a short time, keeping his eye on the pill-bottle, he let the sweet poison of adrenalin, the strongest of stimulants and intoxicants, surge through his system. He felt *capable de tout*; if he met Mr. Smallcross now, he would strangle him! Then all at once he burst into tears, tears of self-pity. It seemed so sad that he, Aunt Carrie's nephew, who in a former life had had so many good friends, that he who had lived in his thoughts of them and been sustained (perhaps) by their thoughts of him, should find his greatest satisfaction, the pinnacle of his personal fulfilment, in an impulse of blind rage. Most people admire a martyr, but who can sympathize with a victim? Richard didn't need telling to which category he belonged.

Wearily he heaved himself out of his chair, and began a letter to Mr. Smallcross which he knew he would never send. For what was the use of crying over spilt milk? He pushed the writing-paper away, and it was then that he saw, topping a pile of unsorted papers, the envelope with the ill-formed handwriting that he had received, how many days ago? – and hadn't bothered to open. It was easier for him to act from disinclination than from inclination. Between the two evils of writing what he did not want to write, and reading what he did not want to read, he chose the latter.

So, averting his eyes from the date of the postmark, he opened the envelope.

Dear Mr. Mardick, he read,

I thought I ought to write and tell you that Denys has had a serious accident. He was sitting in a café quite quietly doing no harm to anybody when this teddy-boy or whoever he was set on him. He beat him up terrible and Denys is now in hospital and they do not know whether he will get better or not. I am only allowed to see him for a few minutes every day. At first he did not know me but now he does and he asked me to write to you as he cannot write himself. He cannot do anything himself, everything has to be done for him. So he asked me to write to you and say, Please Mr. Mardick we are terribly short of money. All the money you gave Denys when he left you he put into a garage which has unfortunately failed and left us destitute. I have no money even to pay the rent of this flat which is expensive because Denys did not want us to live in a tumble-down place.

So, Mr. Mardick, you will see what a position we are in. You have always been good to Denys so I hope you will see your way to sending us some money.

Yours truly,
P. Aspin.

Richard's first reaction to this letter was the old familiar one – 'I mustn't let myself get angry! I mustn't let myself get angry!' Once again he felt the thermometer of passion rising. He dared not read the letter a second time but left it on the table and went into his sitting-room to be as far away from it as possible. But in a looking-glass in which he had tried not to look, for he hated his face in these moods, he saw that he was still undressed, and even in his fury this gave him an uncomfortable sense of incompleteness. Besides Berto (where was he?) would want to 'do' the room before he went out to do the day's shopping. So he returned to finish his toilet. Denys's wife was a cheap piece, just as Denys was, for all his Aspin airs and the money his adoptive father had wasted on his education. Cheap, cheap, that's what they both were, and now this letter! Could cheek go any further?

It was all a tissue of lies, of course, just another way of playing on his sympathies and bleeding him! It must be untrue; had Denys ever told him the truth when a lie would have served him better? Had any of them, any of that long procession of rogues, male and female, who had battened on him?

Better not answer the letter – that was the most dignified course, though what did dignity count, in the state he had got himself into? But he knew what they were like; if you didn't answer, if you let your case go by default, they thought you had nothing to say, and Richard had plenty to say. Indignation swelled in him; he paced up and down, re-living the whole Denys saga, from its earliest beginnings to the blackmail, and the betrayal, and then this!

It would be better for him in every way, and better for them too, if he got it off his chest. At any rate they would know what he thought of them, which was something he had never told them, and he would be tethered to his chair while he was writing, which would be better for him than this tiger-prowl up and down his sitting-room.

Hardly had he seated himself when Berto came in – Berto with his sad, anxious face.

Madam, he wrote,

Your impudent letter has just reached me. Even if I believed a word that you and/or Denys said, I would not send you a single penny. You have had too much from me already, you lying, cheating rogues.

R. Mardick.

Having written this, and addressed and stamped the envelope, he felt better. But soon he began to take himself to task. What if this letter should be the last written utterance he sent out into the world? Did they really represent him, these few words, feeble for all their fury? Were they all he had to say? The thought that some stranger might get hold of them and judge him by them was most painful. How I have gone downhill, he thought, been pushed downhill, perhaps, but surely I could have stopped somewhere, made a stand? He thought of many wrong turnings he had taken, many places where the way hadn't been as slippery as he thought, but self-reproach brought him no comfort. Does it really matter what sort of person I am? he asked himself at last. Does it matter if no one is the better for me, or the worse? When he tried to think of himself as valueless (for good or bad), in a world without values, his mind wouldn't function, and for a moment he thought he was losing his identity. Perhaps he had lost it, he was so little like the self he used to know; perhaps he would never get it back.

Berto was standing beside him.

'A letter for the post, signorino?' he said.

Richard pushed the letter toward him.

'Yes please, Berto.'

'And what will you have for lunch, signorino?'

'Oh, anything you like, Berto.'

'A nice risotto, perhaps?'

'That would be perfect.'

'And for dinner?'

'Whatever you think best.'

'Some chicken, perhaps. *Pollo alla cacciatora*?'

Richard agreed.

'*Il signorino non sta molto bene*,' said Berto – adding, when Richard didn't answer, 'isn't very well?'

'Yes,' said Richard. 'I mean no, not very well.'

'I was afraid not,' said Berto. 'Perhaps you had some bad news this morning.'

'I never seem to have any good news,' Richard said. 'By the way, Berto, you haven't changed your mind – about going away, I mean?'

Berto shook his head sadly.

'*Nossignore.*'

28

The next morning brought no letter from Lucilla, but it brought one from Lewis, which enclosed two newspaper cuttings, a short one and a long one. Richard looked at the short one first.

It said there had been a fight in a restaurant in Soho, in the course of which Alfred Baker, 21, builder's labourer, had attacked and severely injured Denys Aspin, 32, garage proprietor, described as of Chelsea. How the fight started no one seemed to know, but it was generally agreed that Baker was the aggressor. The police were called in and arrested Baker, and an ambulance took Aspin to hospital, suffering from multiple injuries.

The longer cutting was a report of the proceedings in the Magistrate's Court in which Baker came up for trial. He pleaded Not Guilty.

His solicitor said that this was a curious and pathetic case, but he felt sure that in view of the facts the Court would feel great sympathy with the accused. The facts were these. Baker was sitting in the café having taken two or three drinks to which he was not accustomed, when a young man, very well dressed and of somewhat effeminate appearance, came into the café and sat down in a chair opposite him. This man, whose name was Denys Aspin, was alone. He ordered a drink and then proceeded to stare fixedly at Baker. This piece of bad manners, Baker, as many young men of his type do, and who shall blame them? – resented, and he more or less politely requested the newcomer to look in another direction. Aspin seemed surprised and for a short time complied with Baker's request, but soon he began again to fix Baker with his offensive stare. At this Baker, as any young man of spirit would have done, took umbrage; he rose and accused Aspin of trying to get off with him – that is to say, making a homosexual advance.

Here the solicitor explained to the Court that Baker stated that in early youth an infamous proposal of this kind had been made to him, which had left a lasting scar on his subconscious mind. His home life had been unhappy as his mother and father were at loggerheads, and he suffered from an acute sense of social inferiority, which was inflamed by the sight of Aspin's flashily expensive clothes and arrogant manner. 'We live in a democratic age,' said the solicitor, 'but unfortunately some of the more privileged members of the community do not always respect the feelings of those less fortunately placed than themselves.'

All this must be taken into account in relation to what followed. Aspin replied to Baker's accusation with a sneering remark, and then, Baker said, 'something came over me and I went for him'. He knocked Aspin down, banged his head several times on the floor and then kicked him in the face, knocking out most of his teeth and incidentally breaking his jaw before two or three waiters came in and pulled him off. Shortly afterwards the police and the ambulance arrived.

'I submit,' said the lawyer, 'that the accused acted under intolerable provocation, and only did what any young man of his age and social group might have done. Violence is always regrettable but it is, unfortunately, much more prevalent than it used to be. It is also better understood by psychologists, and in a young man of Baker's type can almost be accepted as a normal pattern of behaviour. Baker would have lost face with his fellows – he would have forfeited their respect – if he had acted otherwise. Unfortunately he went too far, but he did it in defence of his honour. It must not be forgotten, either, that he has a wife and child.'

The Chairman of the Bench also showed himself sympathetic towards the accused. 'Violence,' he said, 'is only an exaggeration of natural human behaviour. We may regret it, we must regret it. But it is in a different category from the offence against which this young married man believed he was defending himself. I say believed, for none of the witnesses is prepared to say that the offence was offered, and unfortunately the injured man is too ill to give evidence himself. But I think we may give the accused the benefit of the doubt when he says he did believe it, and if that is so he was defending himself by natural means, his fists, and his feet, against something which is wholly unnatural and un-English and abominable and ought to be stamped out or kicked out. No man has a right to take the law into his own hands, but if ever there were extenuating circumstances, Baker, in my opinion, has a right to claim them. We must commit you, Baker, for trial at the Assizes, but I am sure that there they will take as lenient a view of your case as it is possible to take, and I hope for your sake that the man you handled so roughly will survive, although men of that sort – if he was a man of that sort – are of no use to anyone, indeed they are a menace to society.'

Attached to the report was a picture of Baker, a good-looking young man, flanked by his wife with a baby in her arms. No other reference was made to Denys.

So it was true what Mrs. Aspin had said. Richard had believed their lies a hundred times. Now, when he, or rather she, spoke the truth he hadn't believed it.

He didn't feel sorry for Denys. Denys had got what was coming to him. But the episode at the café brought back a vivid picture of him – sitting in the chair opposite the one in which Richard was sitting, and fixing Richard with that blank, unseeing stare which had so often made Richard offer him a penny for his thoughts. He always answered that he hadn't any, but sometimes Richard gave him the penny just the same. It was odd to remember the days when complete trust seemed to exist between them and, radiating from that focal point, extended to everyone. Untruth had been as much a mirage then as truth was now, and when he met the latter he didn't recognize it.

The telephone bell rang and he took up the receiver.

'Lucilla! Is it really you? Come to see me? Why yes, come any time. Come now, come to lunch, come to dinner . . . To dinner then, but it seems so far ahead . . . Oh yes, I'm all right, but are *you* all right? Did you get my letter? I thought I should have heard from you? You did? I thought you might have been away . . . Things to discuss? Of course there are, but when have there not been? You meant to write to me? Why didn't you, then? I got a little anxious . . . Talking is easier? Oh yes, of course it is, and so much pleasanter. We'll talk and talk. But you sound a little sad. I hope you aren't?'

Before dinner-time came, Richard had had many dinners with Lucilla. In his imagination they all took place, strangely enough, at her flat. He had vacated his, and though he kept returning to it in spirit, he returned as a stranger. His familiar possessions, on which he had set so much store, had an unfamiliar air, as though they belonged to someone else; he was critical of them, he noticed faults in them, faults which reflected faults in his own taste, in the taste of his parents, from whom he had inherited most of them. His parents had some nice pieces, or they had seemed nice at the time. His father had been innocently proud of them, and used to draw people's attention to their points – this bit was Sheraton, this Chippendale. He had an eye for furniture, his father had, but he had collected them when he was first married, and had no money. Richard could have replaced them, but he had kept them out of piety because they reminded him . . . Now, when he went to Lucilla's flat, he might have to sell them, for he would be poor – not as poor as his father had been at the time of his marriage, but poor compared with her. With all my worldly goods I thee endow. How would his furniture look alongside hers? She wouldn't want anything material from him at all; but he must make what contribution he could to the housekeeping expenses. Housekeeping! All those troubles would be taken off his hands and with them the thing that most of all had made them irksome and distasteful – the whole nimbus of dishonesty which for years had enveloped him like a bad smell, poisoning the air he breathed, infecting the springs of life, so that he could never trust anyone. Even the trust he put in himself was tainted and suspect; for trust is mutual, and can't exist without its counterpart or reflection in those around one.

At Lucilla's all would be confidence and trust, and his nature would expand again.

At Lucilla's!

But even if she didn't want money from him, since she had more than she needed, she would want something: he couldn't stay with her simply as her guest. She would want something, and what would that be?

'Dear Lucilla, dearest Lucilla, darling Lucilla, but I can't accept all this from you, it isn't fair! You must tell me now what you would like me to do and be! I'm not an ornament, I know, I'm not even a useful piece of furniture. I'm not very well, I'm not even an author whose name anyone remembers, I am *nothing*! You must give me a *raison d'être*, since I can't give myself one!'

'Dear, dearest, darling Richard, please don't talk in that way. You are *my raison d'être*, isn't that enough?'

'No, darling Lucilla, it isn't. I must do and be more than that.'

'But what do you want to do and be, darling?'

325

'First let me tell you what I don't want to be. I don't want to be a drag on you, I don't want you to feel you must be always trailing me about, I don't want your friends to say to each other, "Here's Lucilla's Richard Mardick again. What a bore he is. What can we do about him? We must try to be nice to him! If only we could see what she sees in him!"'

'My dear, you have far more friends than I have. Nearly all the friends I have I made through you. When they come to my flat they'll come to see you, not me. You have enriched my life with your friends – doesn't that satisfy you?'

'I didn't know you saw them. I've been so out of things, Lucilla, these last weeks.'

'Yes, and we talk about you, which is one of my great pleasures. Not such a pleasure as it is to talk to you, but when you are with me, I shall have both, and I shan't have to feel I've cut you off from your friends. They say that when men marry—'

'Marry, Lucilla?'

'Yes, because we are going to be married, aren't we?'

'Do you really want to marry me, Lucilla?'

'Yes, darling, of course I do. It's what I've always wanted.'

'And you still want to?'

'Well, yes.' In his vision of her Lucilla seemed a little hurt.

'How wonderful, how marvellous. But you were saying—'

'I've forgotten now.'

'You were saying something about men when they marry—'

'Oh yes, that they lose their friends, their men friends. But you wouldn't – I should see to that. Besides, we have so many friends in common, as I told you – they welcomed me for your sake, so why should they drop you now?'

'Lucilla, you are wonderful but I still feel you are doing much more for me than I can do for you. What can I do for you to make you happy?'

'I've told you over and over again you *do* make me happy.'

'Yes, but what can I do more than that?'

'Nothing, except, perhaps,' and here the Lucilla of his interior dialogue halted.

'Yes, Lucilla?'

'Love me.'

There were many versions of what happened next. One after another he rejected them – they did not satisfy him and why? Because he felt they would not satisfy Lucilla. They were not what she desired or what she deserved. And the more he thought of what she desired and deserved, the more closely the thought of what she meant to him enveloped him, the more acutely he realized the emotional richness of his life with her compared with the poverty, the barrenness of his life without her. His feelings soared on wings towards her. His earth-bound, self-bound spirit became air-borne, conscious of power lost for over half a century, the power to meet a beloved human being on any terms she chose. While his ecstasy mounted his sense of her presence was as actual as if she had been physically in the room with him, holding his hand. There was nothing now to restrain him, no inner resistance to any claim she might make. Instead, there was an overwhelming desire to meet that claim, to strengthen it, encourage it, embrace it. And he did actually stretch his arms out in an enfolding gesture towards the air that seemed full of her, deliciously, fragrantly, corporeally full – a consummation and he heard himself say the words out loud:

'Yes, Lucilla, I do love you and I shall always love you. Darling, darling, darling Lucilla.'

He was still holding her image in his grasp when she came into the room. But she was not like herself, nor like his picture of her. He missed her smile, he missed her kiss, he missed the myriads of little movements which established her identity. He missed *her*, and missing her he missed himself.

He knew what was wrong before she told him, he knew it from the start, and at first his object was to prevent her telling him: he felt he could not bear to hear it from her lips. But as the meal went on, with jerky interchanges between them falling flat and dying out, he felt he could not bear that either. Speaking or silent he was equally unhappy, and so, he saw, was she.

'Something has happened, Lucilla,' he said at last. 'Won't you tell me what it is?'

'You know what it is,' she said, and her lip trembled. 'If only you had told me yourself, Richard, and not let me hear it from someone else!'

'But why should I tell you, Lucilla, when it could only grieve you?'

'You should have told me, you should have told me,' she repeated.

'But why, when it was all so long ago? Before you were born? How does it affect us now?'

'If you don't understand, I can't explain,' she said, turning away from him.

'But, dear Lucilla, one isn't bound to tell people the . . . the worst about oneself. Life would be impossible if one did. You may have done something yourself – I'm sure you haven't – that you'd rather not tell me or anyone – and who would blame you? Your parents—'

'Oh, don't talk of them!'

'Yes, but I think we should. They did things they didn't want people to know about, and they didn't tell, and do you blame them? Would anyone, nowadays at any rate, blame them? I don't.'

'You can't compare the two things, Richard. What they did was for the sake of love—'

'But wasn't what I did for the sake of love? I don't know who your informants were or what they said. And I myself don't know what really happened – no one does.'

'I was told that you seduced my half-sister Lucy, and when she found she was pregnant, she drowned herself.'

'Who told you?'

'Does it matter? He appeared to know what he was talking about. He was a friend of yours, and a friend of Denys Aspin's. It was through you I met him.'

'Whoever it was, did he say that Lucy was your half-sister?'

'Oh no. Surely he wouldn't have said what he did say if

329

he had known. He said she was some girl living in the Fens. But he knew, of course, that I knew you.' She paused a second and her tone changed. 'He didn't think it was to your discredit, he thought it was rather a feather in your cap, and that you were, or had been, more human than people thought. Indeed,' Lucilla went on, 'he said explicitly that he wouldn't have told me, since I was a friend of yours, unless he had thought that I should see it the same way he did.'

'But you didn't?'

'I'm afraid not, Richard.'

They both sat silent, looking down at the untasted food on their plates. Berto will think we don't like it, thought Richard, and he began to peck at his, and swallowed some wine.

'What else did he say?'

'Oh, Richard, must we talk about it? I'd so much rather not.'

'I'd like to hear the rest.'

'Well, he said it had always haunted you, and somehow spoilt your life. The whole thing came out during a conversation we were having on changing views of morals. He said that today no one would have fussed about what you did, it would have been taken as a matter of course, and you were unlucky to have lived at a time when it was supposed to matter. He didn't blame you in the least – he wasn't being malicious or disloyal.'

'But you do blame me?' Richard persisted.

'Yes, I can't help it.'

'I suppose one might say your parents were unlucky to

have lived at a time when people thought it wrong for unmarried people to live together as man and wife.'

'Perhaps,' Lucilla said. 'But even then they wouldn't have thought it so bad to live in . . . in sin as to seduce a young girl and make her drown herself. *That* was almost murder.'

'Oh, Lucilla,' Richard exclaimed, 'I can't bear us *arguing* about this. Please, please listen to me. It didn't happen in the cold-blooded way you think. It *grew*, it grew out of a lot of circumstances that we couldn't help – loneliness on both sides, on hers perhaps more than on mine. It was a boy and girl friendship that turned insensibly into love. It was my fault, I know, I knew what I was doing and she didn't – but I was ignorant, too, I didn't even know that unmarried people could have children. I'm sure I never did anything she didn't want me to, because we were united to each other in a way that I should still think beautiful if my conscience would let me. And she wasn't pregnant when she died – that came out at the inquest. I know it makes no difference really. She wasn't but she might have been – it was the governess who made her think she might be. And another thing, Lucilla, it could have been an accident, her getting drowned. There was that long skidmark on the clay – I can see it still – she didn't *throw* herself into the pool. Why should she have, when she came to the Brickfield to meet me – even if it was only to tell me she couldn't see me any more – just as you, I'm afraid, have come tonight to tell me the same thing.'

Richard broke down under the pressure of these painful thoughts, but Lucilla was still articulate.

331

'If I hadn't been so fond of you, I shouldn't have minded so much. You went to Distington like a private inquiry agent and ferreted out my parents' unhappy story. Why didn't you ask me if I was Lucy's half-sister, and save yourself that trouble?'

'But did *you* know?' asked Richard, wretchedly. 'It always seemed to me that you didn't know whose grave it was that you laid flowers on in the churchyard of Rookland Abbey.'

He saw that he had disconcerted her.

'I did know, and I didn't,' she said. 'My parents never told me, though I guessed something. But what difference does it make? You didn't ask me, you preferred underhand, underground methods, just as you did long ago, when— Why do you have to do everything by stealth, Richard? If I had suspected you of having had anything . . . to do with Lucy, I should have asked you – I should have *had* to ask you. I couldn't have gone on being friends with you with that . . . that question-mark hanging over us.'

'And if you had asked me?'

Again Lucilla looked embarrassed. 'Oh, what can I say? How can one tell what one's feelings would have been if something had happened that didn't happen? You can't *foresee* your emotional reactions; they are quite unpredictable. Pressures make you what you are; but shocks unmake you – for the time being, at any rate. I don't feel the same person I was before I heard about . . . about you and Lucy. It's different for you, Richard. You have lived so long with the memory that it must have grown indistinct with time.'

'You're wrong,' said Richard. 'It hasn't.'

'No?' said Lucilla, incredulously, and Richard wondered, for the first time, if his feeling for her, and hers for him, hadn't blinded him to a streak of insensibility in her make-up. 'Well, in that case,' she went on, 'perhaps you agree with your friends, whoever they were, who seemed to think you had done Lucy a good turn.'

'No, no,' said Richard. 'Please don't talk like that, Lucilla. Believe me . . .'

'But how *can* I believe you?' cried Lucilla, at last giving rein to her indignation. 'You have deceived me from the beginning, just as you deceived Lucy. You wormed your way into her affections – oh yes, I heard all about it, they didn't spare me – and persuaded her to go with you. Oh yes, I know. You laid a trap for her, as you did for me.'

'That's most unfair, Lucilla,' protested Richard. 'I never laid a trap for her, as you call it. I took the first step as what man hasn't? and after that—'

'You needn't tell me what happened after that,' Lucilla broke in. 'It isn't a pretty story, whatever your sophisti-cated friends may say! The least you could have done was to steer clear of me, and leave me to my ignorance – I was happy then.'

Unwisely, Richard tried to defend himself.

'But it was *you* who wanted to be friends with *me*.'

An unchivalrous remark, and Lucilla treated it as such.

'I didn't know who you were, and if I had known—' Her hands made a despairing gesture.

Richard translated it into words. 'You wouldn't have had any truck with me?'

She looked down her lowered eyelids at him.

'I think,' Richard began, 'I think . . .' He stopped, not knowing what he thought, but hoping to gain time.

'If I hadn't been so fond of you,' said Lucilla, 'I shouldn't have minded so much.' She had said this before, blackmailing him with her affection for him. 'And if it had been anyone but Lucy, I shouldn't have minded at all.'

She spoke a little judicially and Richard resented it: what right had she to sit in judgment on him, as if he had let her down, whereas it was she who had made the running? She felt that the strength of her feelings gave her an advantage over him, but it was an unfair advantage. She had the unconscious arrogance of wealth, just as her parents had. She thought, as they did, that the possession of money entitled her to say what she had no right to say. He muttered something.

Lucilla noticed the flicker of rebellion, and laying her hand on his said hastily: 'Oh please don't think that I was blaming you. I was only trying to excuse myself for having feelings which . . . which perhaps you wouldn't understand.' She gave him a questioning look and added, 'at least I hope not.'

She is trying to tell me, thought Richard, that I mean more to her than she does to me, and a feeling of hopelessness came over him, and a sense of grievance too, not so much against Lucilla as against Fate, which, do what he might, would always put him in the wrong. He watched her changed face shrouded in sorrow and it reminded him of Lucy's face at their last meeting when they had nothing to say to each other and could only, across a widening gulf, exchange signals of farewell. Lucilla and he were friends, not lovers, parting, and they knew what they were about, which he and Lucy hadn't known; but did it seriously signify – was friendship so much less precious than love that it could be renounced without a sigh – a sigh for him and perhaps a tear for her, to mark the inequality of sacrifice?

His hand was still in hers when he said with an effort such as one makes on waking to recapture, and retain, the substance and feeling of a dream:

'Can't we forget about it?'

But even as he spoke he knew they couldn't, for the facts of the past were far more powerful than the feelings of the present, which compared to them were as the mirage to the desert.

Lucilla withdrew her hand and looked vaguely round her.

'Forget it?' she said. 'But then we shouldn't know each other; we should be like strangers. We have nothing between us but remembrance.'

'I'm sure you're wrong, Lucilla,' Richard said. 'No one exists by permission of the past. You have a life in the future; even I have. What has happened doesn't dictate to us what may happen. If you have been happy with me in the past—'

'It wasn't with you,' she said, 'it was with somebody I didn't know. My Richard isn't you. All this is real' – she glanced round the room – 'but I only recognize the portrait by its frame.'

'You shouldn't say such things, Lucilla,' Richard cried. 'You'll hurt yourself by trying to hurt me.'

A portrait trying to escape the scrutiny of an unfriendly eye, but trapped by its frame, he strove to blot her out of his vision, to look anywhere but where she was. And he was so far successful, that when he looked towards the place which she had occupied beside him on the sofa, she was gone. Only her bag remained, to testify to the abruptness of her flight.

It was a black bag with a gilt monogram, the sort of bag that many women have: and the thought came into his empty mind, Why did she choose this one? Did it in some way represent her? Women's bags were as personal as men's ties – more, perhaps. Anyhow, she would be lost without it. She would not come back to reclaim it, he would have to send it to her.

'Berto!'

Berto came into the room, wearing an expression that was at once surprised, diffident and anxious.

'The signorino called me?' he asked.

'Yes. La signorina—'

'She has gone?' asked Berto, looking round the room, puzzled and distressed. '*Scusi*, signorino, but I did not hear her, so I could not open the door for her.'

'She has left her handbag behind,' said Richard, holding it up by the strap rather gingerly, as though he might infect it, or it him. 'Will you take it back to her?'

'Tonight, signorino?' asked Berto, anxious and eager.

'No, not tonight,' said Richard, distressed by the hollows of fatigue in Berto's face. 'She will know where she left it, and besides' – he glanced at the clock, his constant but inexorable companion. It was making its way to midnight. 'She will probably be in bed.'

'But supposing she has left the key of her flat in her *borsetta*?' Berto asked.

Richard hadn't thought of this. 'We can soon find out.'

He opened the bag and rummaged among its contents. He hated doing it, it was like a violation of her personality, akin to the one that he had forced on Lucy. Why did one ever have any relation with another human being except a wave of the hand in the street? Various intimate objects came to light, things to make up her face with, that somehow he had never thought of as made up. And three letters in his own handwriting, from which he averted his eyes. Last of all, hidden by all these, there was a key – a key to who knew what? To the Universe, perhaps. But for her, at the moment, the shelter of her flat was more important.

'Will you ring her up, Berto?' He couldn't face the telephone himself.

He heard the exchange of voices, English and Italianate, without paying much attention. They stopped.

'The signorina says that *tutto va bene*,' Berto said. 'The *portiere* has a key, and he has let her in.'

'Thank God for that,' said Richard. He had a vision of Lucilla pacing the streets, like an orphan of the storm.

In the morning Berto duly started out with Lucilla's bag, to which he managed to give the air of a treasure that he would defend with his life, tucked under his arm. The minutes passed, half an hour passed, an hour passed, and still Berto did not come back. All Richard's thoughts were of Lucilla. They were divided between reproach and self-reproach. She had left him so abruptly, so unkindly! – but at the same time he had an uneasy feeling that she had gone because she couldn't bear to stay. As the hands moved slowly round the clock-face, 'Am I so disastrous,' he wondered, 'that I have undermined the manners of a life-time?' – for Lucilla was invariably punctilious in the technique of arrival and departure. 'What have I *done*?' he asked himself, and the self-interrogation was none the less wearisome because so many other people had suffered from it.

At last Berto returned. Of late his features had been so careworn that it was difficult to tell what, apart from his personal predicament *vis-à-vis* his mother, he was feeling. 'The signorina asked me to stay,' he said, 'while she wrote you a *biglietto*. That is why I am so late.'

Of all Richard's employees during the last years, Berto was the only one who had the wish or the ability to apologize. 'Of course it doesn't matter, Berto,' he said, 'your being late. *Non importa, fa niente.*'

Berto looked relieved, and handling the envelope with the tenderness which he accorded to everyone else's possessions, gave it to Richard. Overcoming his reluctance to read anything that he thought might upset him, Richard opened it at once.

'Dearest Richard,' Lucilla had written, 'I can't tell you how sorry I am about last night. I hated going away when you were not well, but what could I have done for you if

I'd stayed? And you had Berto with you. What a weight off my heart it was when he told me just now that you were better! I am sorry I forgot my bag – I suppose it was a subconscious wish to leave behind something of myself, a token of the friendship which has meant so much to me and will always be a precious and treasured memory.

How gladly I would retract the things I said. Anything that was hurtful in them I do retract, and ask your forgiveness, which is all that I can ask you for.

Circumstances alter cases. I wouldn't put it more personally than that. If only one's feelings would take the easiest way, the way one wants them to! But they won't.

With my love always,
Lucilla.

Berto withdrew while Richard was reading the letter. He read it three times before he realized how final it was.

29

The next day, which was Berto's last day, Richard moved into a small hotel not far from his flat. The long winter was over at last. It was June, and his spirits would have risen to greet it, but they were tired and numb. He could not decide what he would need to take with him and asked Berto to choose for him. Poverty, or relative poverty, was new to him and he was ashamed of it, and ashamed of being ashamed. He didn't know where to look for pleasure, or even peace of mind, for all the avenues seemed closed.

He still had one hurdle to surmount – Berto's departure. This he dreaded, for it would leave him quite alone; but when it came he did not mind it at first so much as Berto seemed to. But soon he caught the infection of Berto's grief, for Berto, who was in tears, kept reminding him, with unintentional cruelty, how bad his lot would be without him, Berto. Who would see to his clothes? How would he get the kind of food he liked? Who would look after him if he was ill? Why had he not gone to Miss Distington, as he said he would? (Richard had told Berto of this project, hoping it would cheer him almost as much as it cheered himself.) Richard had never liked Berto more than he did at this moment: in all the unhappiness of his obsession about his mother, and his dread of meeting her, he still was able to enter into Richard's feelings and convey his sympathy.

But Richard could not help being relieved when he was gone – Berto the latest, if not the least, of all his failures.

Lucilla was so much the greatest, that his mind could rank the others in a sort of descending scale. Of her he tried not to think – and trying not to, thought of her the more. Why had he taken her devotion so much for granted? Why had he not realized she was his life-line? Why had he clung to his independent life, long after it had ceased to nourish him, long after it had ceased to bring him anything but trouble? He had thought she could never be to him what he, conceivably, was to her. But he had never really tried, never taken the situation seriously in all its implications, he had let his ingrained habit of bachelorhood keep her at a distance. He had waited till too late to find out that all the time he could have been to her *something* of what she wanted him to be: the knowledge had come to him under the direst pressure, but it had come too late.

How easy it would have been, he now thought – not perhaps at their first meeting but at some quite early stage of their relationship – to have broached the matter to her!

'Miss Distington, there is something I want to tell you before . . . before we go any further. Long ago, longer than I care to think, I had a boy and girl love-affair with your sister, your half-sister, Lucy. We were both ignorant of the facts of life, as were most young people of our age and class in those days. She was completely ignorant, I had

had a slight grounding from a friend in the more elementary details of the business, but I still believed you could not have a child unless you were married. Well, Miss Distington, we became lovers, and all might have gone well, for your father and mother (Lucy's stepmother) both liked me. Unfortunately they engaged a governess who rightly thought that Lucy's sexual education had been much neglected. What the governess told her we shall never know. Probably she had missed a period and the governess said this might be the result of sexual intercourse with a man. I don't for a moment think that Lucy told her about me, but she knew herself that she had this relationship which the governess no doubt all too graphically described (though how she could have known about it beats me). Lucy was naturally upset, and for several days she kept away from me, in every sense of the word, and when we did meet, her manner towards me had changed completely. She did make one more appointment to meet me at our old rendezvous, an abandoned brickfield, and it was there that I found her at the edge of one of the brick-pits, drowned. Whether she slipped in, or threw herself in, goodness only knows. Your parents left the district and I, after a brief breakdown, resumed my education. I used to feel uncomfortable about it, but in the light of modern thinking I see that I was wrong to. What we did was *natural*, completely natural; it needs no defence, still less blame. The blame attaches to our parents (though Lucy's mother, as you know, was dead) for not telling us what conduct of this kind was likely to lead to. Today we should have armed ourselves with contraceptives and be living happily as man and wife, with several healthy children to our credit.

'I thought I ought to lay my cards on the table, Miss Distington, because it appears to me that we like each other, and for that reason the ground between us should be cleared of any misunderstanding. Now we can go on from there.'

'Oh, oh, oh, oh! Let me think, let me think, let me think! And while I think, please hold my hand.'

Or,

'How splendid of you, Richard, to have told me this. I always liked you, as you know, but I wondered if you possessed moral courage, which is the quality I most admire in a man. Now I know you have it, for it can't have been quite easy for you to tell me all this especially as some of it concerns my parents, who, in the fashion of those days, were secretive about it. I didn't know there was this air to clear, but now that it is cleared I love you more than ever, and I respect you too, which I'm not sure I did before. The fact that you were my half-sister's lover is an added bond between us and completes the pattern of our lives, which began so strangely at Rookland before I was born or even thought of. Why, I may owe my very exist-ence to you, for if Lucy hadn't died, my parents might have never had another child, they were so wrapped up in Lucy. They might not even have got properly married; perhaps they only did it, when the law allowed them, so that they might have another child, a replacement for Lucy, born in wedlock. Oh, my dear, how happy this has made me. You'll move into my flat at once, won't you, and we'll be married as soon as it can be arranged – not in church, I think, we're rather old for that, besides, it takes longer, and the ceremony might tire you.'

But sometimes their colloquy followed the lines of the real one, not in sorrow so much as with argument and recrimination.

'Dishonesty, Richard, dishonesty! You are always complaining that the people you have lived among have been dishonest. Isn't that a good deal your fault, for not having had the sense to choose them better? And as for dishonesty, who has been more dishonest than yourself? All these years you have lived a lie – well, that was your concern. But when you made me part of it, it became *my* concern. You sailed under false colours, you persuaded me to trust you, when you well knew that if I had known the truth about you, I couldn't have borne the sight of you, much less eaten in your presence – every crumb would have choked me.'

'Careful now, Lucilla! You accuse me of dishonesty, but what about your parents, what about yourself? Didn't they live a lie all the time they were at Rookland, pretending to be man and wife? Didn't they live a lie afterwards when they changed their name (it was Soames once, you know, not Distington) and moved to another part of England, hoping that no one would know who they were – and nobody did know, till I found out – oh yes, perhaps I never told you, but I went to Distington in Cumberland and pieced together the whole story! You say you didn't know it, but I wonder. You knew, you must have known that there was something fishy, when you used to go to

344

Rookland, to lay flowers on Lucy's grave! You must have smelt a rat somewhere, unless you are stupider than I think you are! *You* sailed under false colours – you tricked me into loving you – because I did love you, if you want to know – and you have spoilt my life, what little's left of it. I know you think I suffer from persecution-mania, but people *have* combined to persecute me, and you are the worst of the whole lot! Dishonesty, indeed! *You* should know what it means.'

Richard emerged from these encounters with Lucilla's shade utterly exhausted. But gradually they wore themselves out, his imagination could think up no new make-believes to torture him with, and the old records scratched and wobbled and from repetition lost their power to hurt.

An ache and a void remained. He settled down to life at the hotel where, if dishonesty existed, as he felt it must for his whole consciousness was steeped in it, it affected him no more than would have a suspected escape of gas in a distant street. He began to see that life without emotion might have its advantages after all.

His doctor gave him a good report. 'With cases like yours,' he said, 'one never knows, one simply can't tell. The troubles you've been through' (for Richard had told him some of them) 'may have increased your hold on life. I congratulate you on not letting yourself get angry – your chief danger – but happily your temperament doesn't express itself that way. Interest without excitement is your chief need. I'm afraid you'll find that living here will pall after a time. Why don't you try to find someone else to run your flat? Don't you miss having your own things round you?'

'I miss the things,' said Richard, 'but not the people. I had about fifteen attendants of one sort and another, and they were all rogues except one.'

'Perhaps no one but ourselves is strictly honest,' said the doctor.

'Perhaps not,' Richard answered, 'but there are degrees. I refuse to associate myself, still less you, with any of those people.'

'Aren't you in danger of spiritual pride?'

'I'll take the risk. At the moment I don't feel like a person at all – I'm just the sum of my frustrations and annoyances and mistakes.'

'Perhaps what you really want,' said the doctor, 'is not someone to look after you, but someone to look after.'

'I can't see anyone volunteering for that post,' Richard said, 'but if you know of any nice invalid or cripple—'

'I'll keep my eyes open,' the doctor said. 'Someone who might profit by your attentions, and be grateful for them.'

'I should at any rate know how to cheat him or her,' said Richard. 'You couldn't beat me at that.'

Dr. Herbright smiled.

'It will be interesting to see how you shape as a criminal,' he said. 'Meanwhile let me congratulate you again on having made your misfortunes beneficial to your health.'

30

Richard hadn't formally notified his friends of his change
of address – he hoped against hope it would be merely
temporary – but many of them knew it, and some of them
dropped in to see him. He didn't much encourage these
visits, he knew he was poor company as well as poor.
Entertaining he was not, and as for more concrete kinds
of entertainment such as drinks at the bar (if drinks could
be called concrete) with strangers chattering around, they
were even less satisfying than a cocktail party, while meals
in the restaurant – especially after his solicitor's warning
– alarmed him by their expense.

But not everyone knew where he was, and letters sometimes came which the porter forgot to forward, so he had
made the habit of going round each morning to the flat in
case there should be any. Sitting there he felt more kinship
with his old self, or with *some* self – he conjured up a sort
of personality out of the familiar objects round him, and
being alone, he had a say in which personality it was to be.
Sometimes the telephone rang – quite an event – and he
would answer it with an animation that the receiver could
conjure up better than a friend's face. With each visit the
dust lay thicker – the telephone-receiver was its favourite
resting-place – and he remembered he must ask the porter

to find him a woman, to come in once a week, but each day he put it off.

These little expeditions gave him something to look forward to: they made his day and he never thought how extravagant it was to be using his flat as a sitting-room.

Now here was a letter – two indeed, one marked Air Mail from Australia in a handwriting he knew well, the other with a Rookland postmark, in a handwriting he took to be his cousin's. Aunt Carrie's missive was thick and pulpy; his cousin's thin and stiff.

It was nearly a year since he had heard from Aunt Carrie. Once the most regular of correspondents, latterly she had been remiss; she hadn't answered his last two letters. She lived on in his memory, but more faintly with the passage of time and all the impressions and experiences which had been forced upon him. Now the sense of her personality flooded his vacant mind and was almost as vivid as if she had been in the room.

He opened her letter first.

My dearest Richard, for you are still that to me, after more than fifty years. Yes, it is more than half a century since I came to live here, and I expect you have a very dim picture of your old aunt, if any impression at all. You were only seventeen – but I remember you so vividly – standing with the others outside the white gate of St. Botolph's, waving till we were out of sight. Not out of mind; as long as your dear mother and Ada and Florrie and Austin and Esther and Hal were alive we always wrote – I believe I wrote to each of them once a week – perhaps not so often to Hal, for he was never a great letter-writer, and I didn't want to bore him. And you were so good at writing, Richard, in more ways than one, if I may say so, that I always felt in touch with you. But when you had left the family circle, and gone to make your own life in London, I couldn't see you as distinctly as I saw the others, and wondered if the small annals of my life with James at the school outside Sydney – now long ago inside it – could be of any interest to you. Not from anything you said or didn't say, my dear, dear Richard – my dear boy, I nearly wrote, but you are a boy no longer! – but from a feeling I have always had that circumstances must be respected, and it is no good trying to impose our wishes on them, indeed, it may do harm.

As you will remember, we were a most devoted family – the Holy Family, as Austin called us – and what happened to the others was of intense interest and concern to each of us – to your dear mother and Florrie most of all. Do you remember how your mother – darling Mary – worried about your health and your father's health, and my health? She felt that a breeze would blow us away, yet your father lived till he was eighty, cheating the undertaker, as he used to say, and you and I are still alive.

And that made it sometimes difficult for me, and I daresay for you – to tell the others what was really happening to us in case it should worry them. It's true to say that your mother lived more in other people's lives – three other people's at any rate – than in her own, until the end when she became so nervous about her own health. One had to edit everything one said to her, in case she should misinterpret it. I didn't tell her that I was going to marry James, or that I was coming out here. I knew that it would grieve her, whether I told her or not, and she *was* hurt that I had kept something from her – something that the others knew, for Ada at once guessed why James was making a long stay at St. Botolph's. Your mother didn't, partly because she thought my heart was in the grave with Arthur (in which she wasn't altogether wrong) and partly because, as you remember, she didn't often come to see us at that time: Medehamstead was so far from Rookland!

If she had come oftener she would have realized that you were lonely, as we all did, I think, especially Esther. But you were like the rest of us, you kept it from her, and it was only when she couldn't bear your absence any longer that she called you home – too late.

They told me, of course, what had happened, but only in outline and in such a guarded way that even reading between the lines I could not guess what it had meant to you. But I knew there was more in it than they said, because of the message the girl gave James for you. She told him not to tell anyone and he didn't, only me. At once I felt you were involved in something serious – serious to your feelings, I mean, and it was that that made me, when we had our last talk together, which I so well remember, try to warn you against setting too much store by any single person. I don't suppose you remember it! You seemed so surprised and said: 'But aren't you going to be married, Aunt Carrie?' – as if that could only mean setting too much store by a single person. You caught me out, I couldn't say any more.

Should I say any more now? You may well ask. I don't know, I might. I wasn't in love with James when I married him, I loved him and afterwards I fell in love with him. I wanted to get away, that's how it was. I felt my continued presence was like a spell, almost a curse upon St. Botolph's, and for myself that I should never get well while I was there. Too many people were watching. And you, too, Richard, you must have felt the tension in that household, that could never be expressed, and I don't doubt that you suffered from it in your mind and spirit. It was better for everybody that I should go away, certainly better for me, for as soon as I got to Australia those tiresome symptoms began to abate, and I was able to lead an almost normal life. I kept house for James, of course, and taught a little in the school – I even taught the piano. It was a great joy to go back to that and feel that I was contributing something instead of always being contributed to, for helplessness is a drag on the spirits and gratitude can become a burden, especially when you have no hope of repaying kindnesses.

I only taught elementary subjects, and in an elementary way, for in those days there wasn't much demand for higher education: Australia was utterly different from what it is now. It was in many ways a primitive country, now it is in the vanguard of all kinds of progress, and has left me far behind, but that didn't come for many years. For a long time I was looked upon almost with awe as a bluestocking – just think of it! – and felt I must adapt my mind to meet their meaner apprehensions. Certainly time does bring in its revenges.

Those were very happy years, and I made many friends. Their outlook wasn't the same as mine, but mine, I know, was special and constricted, a sort of family endowment, with a family approach to things and perhaps a family way of talking – I don't mean *accent* – though for a long time that did make a sort of barrier. I even tried to learn the Australian accent, but on me it sounded affected, and James begged me not to. I may have caught it now, involuntarily, but one doesn't hear one's own voice.

But my heart never lost touch with you all, and my friends at Westerbridge and in London with whom I could still talk, on paper, without translating what I meant to say.

But I couldn't talk quite freely, just as I couldn't when I was in England, and I will tell you why. You are the only one left who remembers what my problems were. Victor may have heard something about them from Florrie, but I never knew him, he was only a child when I emigrated. He is too kind, as I'm just going to tell you, but we never knew each other. Well, James and I never lost the happiness we had together – but it was clouded, clouded by the mental illness that came on him oh, twenty years ago. I didn't tell the people at home much about it, your mother would have worried terribly – Austin and Esther were the only ones who knew how serious it was, and your father, and they were angels to me. They helped me with money while they were alive, and left me money after they were dead – as you would know, being an executor. That is how we were able to live when James had to give up his work at school.

Austin wanted us to come back to England, but for many reasons I didn't want to – I didn't want to inflict another invalid on those dear people. They would have taken us in, I know, just as they did before, but – perhaps it was partly pride – I couldn't bear the thought of it. And another thing. In those days psychiatry was in its infancy and people thought that a nervous breakdown was one's own fault or something to be ashamed of – they might have thought the same about my breakdown, if it hadn't been physical. They might have thought that James should have pulled himself together, which I knew he couldn't do. They never had a very high opinion of him, because he didn't make his way in the world as they did – he wasn't a business man. They would have been kind to him but they would have been impatient with him – or so I thought, and even sorrier for me than they always were.

And so we stayed here, and I used to talk to him and try to calm his fears, of which he had so many – but the worst were his religious fears, and his feeling that he had somehow offended God – though why, why, when he was always such a good man? Threatening texts used to start into his mind – 'The wrath of God has fallen upon the sons of disobedience' – things like that, and darken his mind for hours and even days. How often have I got up in the night and searched the Bible for other texts, texts of promise and forgiveness – which might reassure him. Sometimes they did, sometimes they didn't, I always felt that I could have done more. When he was dying the cloud lifted from his spirits.

It was a sad time and I won't say any more about it, except just two things – the things that helped to keep me going. One was, that the worse he got the more I loved him – I don't know how that happened. No illness – no invalid – is especially lovable; a neurasthenic is always turning his least attractive side towards one. Yet love him I did, which halved the burden – made me even love the burden. How did that come about? I can only believe that God's grace helped me; but I shouldn't have realized it unless his illness had been founded on religion – not founded, for it was a perversion of religion, but thinking about it, and trying to help him, and above all reading the Bible over and over, as I had to do, gave me a glimmering of what religion means – a glimmering that still grows brighter and brighter. I never was religious, as no doubt you know, though I was brought up in a religious family. I suppose that friendship with its joys and obligations was my religion; I never felt the need of any other. But alone with James I did, and it came to me, and I hope I shall never lose it.

And now to come to the end of this too long letter. There has been a wonderful instance of God's working for us. Your cousin Victor wrote and offered me – what do you think? – St. Botolph's! His tenant has left. He doesn't want to let it again, anyhow for a time, but he wants someone to occupy it. I never meant to return to England, but now I do, old as I am: I feel it would complete my life and give it a meaning, such as nothing else would. Victor says the house is only half the size it used to be, his foreman lives in one part. But it would be big enough for me, much too big. Won't you come and share it with me, Richard, anyhow for a time? You would bring back to me the past that I most love to remember, and perhaps to you I could be something that I couldn't be when we were last together. Do think about it, Richard, and do please say yes! Already after writing in this way to you, though I am ashamed of much, perhaps all that I have written, I feel an extraordinary lightening of the spirit, as though we were at last together again, and could speak freely to each other, without reserves of any kind, which I have never been able to do to anyone, in all my life.

I shall sell all my things here and come by plane – my first experience in the air. In a week or two I shall be in England. I could not believe it if I did not now believe so many things I once thought incredible – and one is that you will stay with me at St. Botolph's.

For this I hope and pray,

Your old but loving aunt,
Carrie.

The other letter, as Richard thought it would be, was from Victor, and in the course of it he said:

You really would be doing us a kindness by coming to St. Botolph's, Richard. For one thing we've seen far too little of each other in late years, but Time marches on, and blood is thicker than water: you and Aunt Carrie are the only relations I have left on Mother's side. You know how devoted Mother was to Aunt Carrie, and your mother was, too. Between them I think they must have driven the poor old thing half batty, though of course she wasn't old in those days. All the family worshipped her, I don't quite know why, even that old sour-puss Aunt Ada did, it was something to do with her being so unselfish. And of course she was very clever, or would have been, but for her illness. I was only five when she got married to that rather hopeless man, but I can still remember the tone of awe in which they spoke of her, even your father did who wasn't easily impressed and thought most people fools (he was quite right).

Mother used to say you didn't like it at St. Botolph's. You weren't well and were being made to be a farmer against your will, and then a girl got drowned and you were in on that. But it was all so long ago and the whole place is so changed you wouldn't recognize it. I quite understand your wanting to be in London, leading a gay life, but I believe you haven't been too well yourself, so perhaps it would do you good to vegetate a little in the Fens. You might even give us some wrinkles about farming! The boys and I farm like mad. Two of them are married now, and the other two soon will be, I daresay, but till that happens St. Botolph's, or what remains of it, will be at your disposal and Aunt Carrie's, and I needn't say how pleased we shall all be to see you. The boys haven't set eyes on you for ages, nor has Margaret for that matter – we were only saying so the other night, and wondering how it had happened, but if any ghosts from the past have kept you away, I assure you they are all exorcized by now.

As for the business side – the maid of all work our late tenants had is still available. She's a country girl, not very bright, not up to your standard, I'm afraid, but good and honest, and if you and Aunt Carrie would pay her, and the gardener who comes in twice a week, you wouldn't have any other expenses, except your keep. And by the way Aunt Carrie isn't too badly off – her brothers and sisters saw to that – and she has her pension, so you needn't have any scruples about asking her to pay her whack – if she's still like what we were told, she'll want to pay the lot! Self-sacrifice, you know, and you mustn't thwart her. But one thing I must warn you about. From the way she wrote to me, she seems to have taken to religion in a big way – she has bees in her bonnet in the shape of texts. I'm sure she is quite harmless, poor old girl, but she *may* be a bit crackers.

She's coming in about a fortnight. Why don't you come first, and welcome her with a suitable text? – 'Blessed is she that cometh—' But I mustn't be blasphemous.

Well, that's about all, I think. Of course it may not suit your plans to come here, in which case don't give it another thought. But if you can come, dear old boy, it will set us up no end.

Love from us all,

Your affectionate cousin,
Victor.

It didn't take Richard long to decide that he could come. Indeed the two letters brought him such an access of energy that the tasks of settling his affairs in London, 'assigning' the flat, and so on, which had seemed quite insuperable, turned out to be child's play. When the last link with London was broken and he stood on King's Cross platform, which hadn't changed much with the years, he knew what it meant to feel like a new man.

31

Victor was right. St. Botolph's had changed, Rookland had changed, the whole Fenland had changed. Not the landscape, of course, or not very much. The flatness, the featurelessness, the trees dotted about, the wide sky, they were the same. But not the roads teeming with cars, nor the dykes, which now seemed designed on a different principle. They had been scoured and deepened; instead of brimming water, thick with scum and weeds, which had given a feeling of fullness almost to overflowing, a thin trickle ran between high, steep banks denuded of all verdure. St. Botolph's drain, that mighty waterway, was like a crevasse in a dry season. But it was in the bridges that he found the greatest change. Gone were those ancient, humpbacked, red brick structures, the only hills in the Fens; they had been replaced by flat road-connecting units of white cement, which Victor's car hardly noticed as it crossed them.

How kind Victor had been, meeting him at Medehamstead, taking him to his own house in Rookland where quite a number of the clan were gathered to welcome him, the long-lost cousin; he might have come from the moon. And after tea, driving him to St. Botolph's: 'It will only take five minutes,' Victor said. Five minutes, and it used to take twenty-five. 'Go slowly, Victor, please go slowly! I want to look at the Abbey.' There it was, the great West Front, unchanged, save that the blue clock had been newly painted. Now they were skirting its north side, and Richard suddenly remembered that he mustn't look. He heard his mother's voice in tones of anxious almost anguished warning, 'Don't look, my darling, please don't look! It's the M, you know, and it's so ugly. You must never, never look at anything ugly.' And he was turning away, to fix his eyes on the Council School with its slender spire (which hadn't changed, either), when all at once the car stopped and he heard Victor say, 'I'm going to show you something that *has* changed since your time, Richard. The Abbey tower. Do you see any difference?' Thus appealed to, Richard had to look, though not without a lurking sense of disobedience. 'But, Victor!' he exclaimed. 'Ah,' said Victor, disappointed, 'you *have* seen, and I was hoping to spring a surprise on you.'

'Heavens above,' said Richard, unable to believe his eyes. For the M was gone, gone were those great flat buttresses that had been such an eyesore to his mother, and instead he saw a glorious traceried window, more than half the height of the tower. 'But *how*?' he asked. 'I don't understand.' Victor chuckled. 'One day, I don't know when it was, they found those buttresses weren't pulling their weight, or pushing it, and took them down, and uncovered the window which had been there all the time – a beauty, isn't it? You must see it from inside the tower, it's wonderful.' Richard agreed, but perversely he couldn't reconcile himself to the removal of the buttresses. 'What if the tower fell down?'

'Not to worry,' said Victor, confidently. 'Towers don't fall down, you know.'

In silence they started on again. Richard felt a lightening of the spirit. All my life, he thought, I have been turning away from something ugly, and now it isn't there! At some time, without my knowing it, it must have gone. How pleased his mother would have been could she have known that her bugbear was demolished. She couldn't have known, or she would have told him. Did it mean that evil had vanished from the world?

He was divided in his mind between desiring change and dreading it. The windmill that used to stand beside the road beyond the Abbey, that had gone: even the mound on which it stood had been levelled. And further on, to the left, the long line of poplars, leaning crazily to the north-east, away from the wind, was no longer a line: they had been reduced to two or three stragglers, with irregular intervals in between, like gaps in a once good row of teeth.

Now they had reached the flat, crownless successor to St. Botolph's Bridge, and the sharp right-hand turn which brought St. Botolph's Lodge into view. But where were the five straw-stacks behind which it used to nestle?

'We don't need them now,' Victor explained. 'We haven't any horses except one or two old stagers we keep more from sentiment than anything. Farming's been mechanized since your time. And a good job too. And there's been another change since you were here – but I'll leave you to find out what it is.'

How quickly speed out-stripped conversation! Once you could have had a long talk, settled down to it, between

St. Botolph's Bridge and St. Botolph's Lodge; now, after exchanging a few sentences, they were turning into the white gateway of the house. 'Don't knock down both gateposts at once!' Richard almost said. But he had no time to notice outside changes before Victor had taken him inside and was showing him the new arrangements.

'We've turned the dining-room into the drawing-room,' he said, conducting Richard from the one to the other. 'The drinks are here, you must need one, and then I'll show you the rest of the house.'

'How kind you are,' said Richard for the tenth time, as he gratefully accepted the drink that Victor offered him.

They sat down together and Richard felt that their relationship had been as continuous in time as it had been in blood. 'Why,' he asked himself confusedly, 'did I spend all those years in London when I might have spent them here?'

The tour of the house upstairs showed still more changes. 'All this part's shut off,' said Victor, pointing to a door on the left, as they stood at the top of the curving staircase; 'so, there are only five bedrooms, and one of them is Edna's, leaving four, but they'll be enough for you and Aunt Carrie, won't they? Or will you be having masses of visitors?'

Richard truthfully said he couldn't think of one.

'Would it amuse you to have a look at the rooms?' said Victor. 'They haven't changed since your day, except the old spare room, the Lilac Room, which Uncle Austin built on to. Which room did you have?'

'This one,' said Richard, opening the door.

'Oh, that was Uncle Hal's room, wasn't it? A small room for a big man. If he had been a farmer, he might be with us still, being a wine merchant didn't agree with him. In those days there was a feather bed in here, but that went long ago. It's nice, the view of the Abbey.'

More curious than beautiful from here, the strange lop-sided shape rose above the tree-tops, a beggar holding out a tattered cloak on a stiff arm. It hadn't lost its power to sway Richard's thoughts.

'We had to do away with all those groups with Uncle Hal holding a football and a cricket-bat and so on,' said Victor, looking round the walls. 'He must have been quite an athlete in his day, poor old chap. I was quite fond of games myself, but this room gave me an inferiority complex. Did you feel it too?'

Richard admitted that he had.

'I don't think you'll want this room,' said Victor, closing the door and leading Richard across the landing, 'too poky, for one thing. Nor this one either,' he said, turning another knob, 'it used to be the Pink Room, and there's still a swallow nesting under the eaves – they always did, if you remember. It faces east, and looks on to the crew-yard. My mother had it once, now Edna has it, and she seems to like it.'

He shut the door and went to yet another, the middle one of three. 'This was Aunt Ada's room, do you remember how untidy it used to be? I never liked going into it, because of some scent she used – too sweet, it was, not like her nature, poor old dear. She wanted to be worshipped and adored, just as Aunt Carrie was, but she went the wrong way about it. I don't suppose you'll want to use this room, the other two are nicer. Did you like the Lilac Room? Let's go in . . . You see it's still lilac, though a different shade, and we kept the old four-poster. And there's the picture, too, of Tam O'Shanter. I should have this room if I were you . . . which room did Aunt Carrie have?'

'The room opposite,' said Richard, 'at least it was hers until old Mrs. White came. Then she moved into the one your mother used to have.'

'That stuffy little hole? Unselfishness again, you see. You must give her scope to exercise it, so I should bag this one, the Lilac Room. But perhaps you'd like to see the other?'

'I should,' said Richard. 'It's the only room in the house I've never been into.'

'Never been into? Why was that?'

'Because . . . because it was Aunt Carrie's, I suppose, and I wasn't allowed . . . at least, I never went. And then old Mrs. White had it. It was always a bit of a Blue Chamber to me.'

'Let's see if it is still.' Victor opened the door and Richard, conquering his reluctance to cross the threshold, followed.

'It's not blue, you see, it's white,' said Victor, 'and there's the old brass bedstead, not very comfortable, but I should think original, one of the early furnishings that has survived, like the four-poster in the Lilac Room. And there's this hanging cupboard – quite convenient, let's see if there are any corpses of dead wives in it.'

364

There weren't; it was swept if not garnished, but Richard felt relieved when they were out again on the landing.

'Well, now,' said Victor, 'the grand tour is over, and I've nothing more to show you except Edna, who will be in the kitchen cooking dinner, if the smell is anything to go by. I hope you won't feel under-housed?'

Richard smiled.

'No, I shall be like the proverbial pea rattling in its pod, until Aunt Carrie comes. When is she coming?'

'Some time next week, I think. She's going to cable. You mustn't let her get you down, you know.'

'Why should she?'

'Oh, I don't know, all those texts. You must restrain her. And now come and meet Edna. She's longing to see you. The kitchen is what used to be the pantry.'

There they found Edna, short and stout and floury-armed. Even if her bearing suggested that she must not be wantonly interrupted, she did seem pleased to see Richard.

'She knows all about you,' said Victor when they were back in the hall. 'She's an old family retainer, and didn't really like being with the people who were here. Another drink? You must be tired from all that sightseeing. No, this way' – for Richard was heading for what was the old drawing-room.

'I don't know what you'll find to do here,' Victor said. 'It's no good asking you to take up farming! We know you turned that down. But you haven't been very well, have you?' he said, giving Richard a look. 'So perhaps you'd like a rest. And, by the way, thinking of things you *could* do – do you remember how keen Aunt Esther was on find-ing things for us to do? – are you still a butterfly-hunter, do you still collect caterpillars?'

'No,' said Richard.

'But you did once, didn't you? I remember hearing how you kept woolly-bears, or something, in a box, and one day they got out and went into Aunt Ada's room and scared her almost to death.'

'It was a privet-hawk moth caterpillar,' Richard said.

'I knew it was some dangerous beast. And you used to look for them in the old Brickfield, didn't you? It was your happy hunting-ground?'

'I suppose you could call it that,' Richard said.

'But you don't collect them now? I'm rather glad, because otherwise I should have some sad news for you. What's the time?' He looked at his wrist-watch. 'It's past seven – I must be off, we keep early hours in the Fens, as I daresay you remember. I meant to leave you to find out for yourself, but I expect you're tired, so if you like I'll run you over and drop you here on my way back.'

Completely mystified, Richard clambered into the car. They hadn't been travelling for more than two minutes, when it stopped. Victor got out and opened the door for Richard.

'I'll give you a hand,' he said, offering it, 'but you must shut your eyes.'

Nothing was easier for Richard than to do what he was told.

'Now you can look.'

Richard looked. 'But I don't see anything unusual,'

he said, trying not to be a wet-blanket. 'There's this grassfield on the right, and the road straight ahead, and a big cornfield on the left – it looks a very good crop—'

'But you don't recognize it?' asked Victor. 'It isn't familiar to you in any way? Look again.'

Richard strained his eyes. 'I must be very stupid.'

'Not stupid at all. But what you're looking at,' said Victor, with the satisfaction of someone springing a surprise, 'is the site of the Brickfield, your old hunting-ground.'

'And it's gone?'

'I'm afraid so,' Victor said, with mock regret. 'I'm afraid so,' he repeated. 'You see, after you left, it wasn't good for anything, except the shooting, and it wasn't much good for that, it was so up and down. Have you ever done any duck-shooting? It's rather exciting, in a way. You have to get up at dawn, and take so many precautions – crawl along, turn up your coat-collar, if you're wearing a white shirt – they're so wary, those birds! It's a young man's game. So after the war – the last war, I mean – we got a couple of bull-dozers and in an astonishingly short time they cleaned it up and laid it flat. You wouldn't know it had ever been there, would you?'

Richard couldn't speak.

'I'm sorry if you're disappointed,' said Victor, noticing his emotion. 'But it really wasn't good for anything, and a bit dangerous, too, with all those pits and holes.' He stole another look at Richard. 'Now it's twelve acres of the best land we have. But no caterpillars, except the odd Death's Head, if we ever grow potatoes on it.'

'I'm glad it's been turned into something useful,' Richard said.

'Well, now I must be off,' said Victor briskly. 'I've shown you all the sights and sites, or nearly. This is The Poplars, this farmhouse on the right, and this is The Hollies, on the left. It used to belong to some odd people called Soames. I believe you knew them, hardly anyone else did.'

'Yes, I knew them,' Richard said.

'There's a nice family living there now,' said Victor, 'young people, very jolly. I'll ask them to come and see you if you like – unless you'd rather not be bothered with neighbours.'

'Well, perhaps for the first day or two—' Richard began.

'I'm not surprised. If I drop you here at the gate, can you make your own way in? And talking of neighbours – if you should want a doctor, which I hope you won't – Killigrew is a very good man – you'll find his number in the telephone-book.'

'The telephone-book?'

Victor laughed. 'Yes, we have one. We hadn't in the days of Dr. Butcher. Well, so long, old boy. Let me know if there is anything you want.'

He drove off. Richard, at the gate, started to wave. It wasn't until the car was out of sight that he remembered he wasn't waving to a horse and trap.

32

Richard sat waiting for the lamps to be lit, as they had been lit in his grandfather's and his uncle's time. But even when he realized that he had only to switch on the electric light, he still sat to drink in the twilight, as it deepened inside the house and outside. He couldn't think of any greater happiness than thus to feel the darkness invade his being, and blot out those areas in his mind which had been blinded by too much illumination in the past.

Perhaps Victor's welcome was the most active cause. That someone – not just someone, but an entire family – was pleased to see him, had no grievances against him, wanted nothing of him, but instead loaded him with kindness, was a revelation to the self that the last months had made him. They were people on whom he had no claims, and they had no reason to think kindly of him, if they thought of him at all, for since Lucy's death he had shunned the district and not kept up with them. Kinship, perhaps they thought, meant nothing to him; he made friends with any newcomer who belonged to his set, and could help him in his career or advance him socially. He was a climber who had forgotten his own origins, who had no feeling for family or place.

Yet apparently they thought none of these things. They had accorded him the welcome given to the Prodigal Son, but without suggesting that he was a prodigal. He might have been conferring a favour on them by returning to their midst and graciously accepting their hospitality.

Had Victor an inkling of his real motive for giving Rookland a wide berth for all these years? Richard thought he might have, otherwise he wouldn't have been at such pains to show him the site of the old Brickfield; but if he had he wouldn't know the fact, he would only know the story put about at the time of the catastrophe, according to which he, Richard, was the victim, almost the hero.

They didn't realize he was their pensioner, of course. What could he do for them in return? Only re-make his will.

That could wait till tomorrow. Tonight he would savour the intense emotions of re-union, re-union with his child-hood before the Fall, his fall, at any rate. He marvelled that this re-union could contain so little pain, and so much joy.

Perhaps it was the changes that had done it. What had been changed was for the better, and what was unchanged was for the better, too. First of all the disappearance of the M, that malign symbol of ugliness that had haunted his childhood. And then, almost equally miraculous, the disappearance of the Brickfield. Like Sodom and Gomorrah it had gone and its place knew it no more. It had been sown – not with salt, but with rich golden grain that was ripening under his eyes, as he was ripening too, he felt, for a spiritual harvest he had never hoped to yield.

But more intimately, if less fundamentally, he had taken comfort from his little tour of the house with Victor – Victor, who had been so touchingly pleased and proud to show it off. In every room there was something new and something old – something changed and something unchanged – in either case, making for reassurance. What remained was what he wanted to remember, and what had been changed was what he wanted to forget.

And the many alterations he discovered for himself, after the god had departed in his car (not in a cloud of dust, as he would have in the old days), all ministered to his comfort. Instead of the bed-time candlesticks that used to stand on the gate-legged table in the hall, the telephone, like a beneficent cobra, reared itself, the telephone which would keep him in touch with Victor, but not, if he could help it, with Dr. Killigrew. Intercommunication had been lacking in the old days. Isolation was the cause of so much that had happened. How easy to take up the telephone; how difficult to leave a note under a stone-heap!

Anxious to recover more vestiges of the past, he sought them out of doors. The numinous silence in the courtyard was still unbroken even if the five straw stacks no longer guarded it. The lawn had kept its shape, though the austere, narrow croquet-hoops had not kept theirs; nor had the cedar which Aunt Ada used to say was rarer than their cedar at Medehamstead; it had shot up, and over-topped the neighbouring lime-tree.

The geraniums in the borders beneath the windows were blackening with the fading light. Now for the west side of the house, behind the thin yew-hedge, which Richard had so far avoided, because, in his regenerate, almost immaculate state, it harboured associations he preferred to forget, for they were part and parcel of the M, of hateful meaning. Those privies, those earthen privies built into the wall, in whose appalling stench he had loved to luxuriate! Not from curiosity, but for the sake of mortification, and perhaps a little for the sake of self-congratulation – that his nature had improved since those days – he must revisit them. But where were they? Gone, like the Brickfield, like the M itself, and only some new masonry in the wall showed where they had once exhaled their nauseous but heady smells.

But the antidote to them – an antidote to which he had always had recourse – that was still there. Enveloping the arch into the kitchen-garden, blown through it and over it and round it, mingled with the hum of bees, were the intoxicating scents of stocks and other flowers, the very perfume of welcome, as breathtaking as before, but without the contrast which used to make it poignant.

'Will you have a bath, Mr. Mardick?' asked Edna. She didn't call him 'sir', but then who did in these days?

'I would like one, Edna, but wouldn't the boiler have to be stoked up?'

'Oh no, it's heated now by electricity – a thermostat, you know.'

So Richard had his ritual bath. The water had no smell, and wasn't rust-coloured, but there were still knots in the door of the airing-cupboard, and Richard began to count them.

Even in a farmhouse in the Fens, you cannot keep the outside world at bay. Letters came – one morning two arrived.

He didn't like the first. It was from his friend Lewis, reproaching him for deserting London. 'I know you weren't well placed in that hotel,' he said, 'but surely it would have been less of an upheaval to have found some nice honest body (I don't use the word in the literal sense) to look after you in your flat, than give it up and store the furniture and cut yourself adrift, as you have done? I can't believe you'll ever settle down to a Georgic existence, however idyllic, and what about us? Have you abandoned us completely? Do we mean nothing to you? I know you are tougher than we thought you were, you seduce young maidens, and so on, like any Minotaur. We were proud of you for that, but there are limits. You say your long-lost relations welcomed you with open arms, but hasn't it occurred to you they might have some ulterior motive for so doing? You're quite well off, or used to be, and perhaps your dear Aunt Carrie is a multi-millionaire! Don't you think they may have an eye to the main chance, inviting you both, in what I won't call your declining years, to live, if not with, at any rate, on them?'

Richard threw the letter away from him in disgust, but it went on rankling in his mind and radiating venom even when it was the other side of the room.

*

The second letter was much more serious, indeed it wiped out the memory of the first. At first he thought he would take Victor into his confidence about it; after all it affected Victor, too: Victor had a right to be consulted. St. Botolph's Lodge was his: he might say, No, and that would be the end of it. Besides, there was Aunt Carrie to consider. How would she react? She was entitled to peace of mind and body, and she would have neither if this proposal was carried out.

For the moment Richard did not feel that he could discuss the question with Victor. It was too intimate: it would be like telling Victor the story of his life, and though Victor would not betray his confidence as Denys had, he was too healthy-minded to understand it. Moreover, Richard could not bear to forfeit his regard, which he would surely do if he told him this story. Never confess! Never confess! He had learned the truth of that by bitter experience.

But in imagination at any rate he could tell Victor, not the real Victor, the prosperous extrovert, the family man, who had increased and multiplied and cultivated his broad acres in the Fens. The Victor he confided in would have some of these qualities, enough to make his judgment sound on what was, after all, a practical issue; but he would ask no awkward questions; he would know how the land lay without being told. But every now and then Aunt Carrie put in her word.

'You see, Victor, this wretched man, Denys Aspin, has done me in one way and another irreparable harm. I needn't tell you how, but he has. I told him something about myself – something most important, and asked him to keep it secret, but he didn't. He gave it away, though I paid him not to, with the most disastrous consequences. You don't want me to tell you the whole thing, do you? I'd much rather not.'

'Of course not, old boy, of course not. Just tell me what you think is right and proper. I shall understand.'

'Well, he went into some café in Soho, a low dive it must have been, and there got beaten up by a young thug, no need to tell you why, but for once it wasn't Denys's fault. The jury sympathized with the thug, as they so often seem to, I don't know what happened to him, or what will happen; but Denys was taken to hospital, I never bothered to find out which hospital. Do you think that was heartless?'

'Of course not. He only got what was coming to him.'

'That's what I thought. Then his wife wrote and said they were hard up – hard up, I ask you, after all the money I had given him.'

'You gave him money?'

'Yes, I had to.'

'So what did you say?'

'I said they were both crooks, and I wouldn't give them another penny.'

'Good for you, old boy.'

'Well, one can't be put upon beyond a certain point, can one? And they are both such liars. That's why I didn't believe Denys's wife, if she is his wife, when she told me, or rather wrote to me, that he had been beaten up. That *was* true – the Press clipping confirmed it. Even liars have to tell the truth sometimes. But in the same letter she told me a great whacking lie. I say, does this bore you, Victor?'

'No, please carry on.'

'She said that they were destitute. Well, they're not. I got a letter from her this morning—'

'Is that what's upset you?'

'Yes. She said that Denys was dying, and the hospital said that they could do no more for him, they wanted his bed and they were going to turn him out.'

'That seems a bit hard.'

'Yes, but is it likely that they would? According to her, they said he had only about a fortnight to live.'

'Hadn't the hospital made any arrangement for him?'

'They said he would go to some home for incurables, full of old people, but Denys said he didn't want to – he wanted to go home – to his home, their flat in Elm Park Gardens. Well, Victor, those flats aren't cheap, so how can his wife be destitute, if she's still living there? Anyhow, she said she wouldn't have him home, because she couldn't bear to watch him suffer, and how would they manage about the dog – she has a revolting corgi called Bungy she's devoted to.'

'Nice sort of wife.'

'Yes, isn't she? He has to have two nurses, because he needs an injection of morphia every three hours, for the pain, you know . . . Yes, Aunt Carrie, he is in great pain, no doubt, but I can't say I feel sorry for him, after what he did.'

'Not sorry for him, Richard?'

'No, I'm not. Would you be, Victor?'

Victor shook his head. 'Well, one point of his going home, apart from the fact that he wanted to, was that *she* could have given him the injections by day – they would have shown her how to, so they need only have had one nurse. But she said she couldn't bear to do that either, and where would the nurse sleep? – they only had two rooms.'

'Haven't they a sofa?'

'Yes, of course. I bet they bought a three-piece suite that cost a fortune. Anyhow, she said they couldn't afford to pay for even one nurse. So can you guess what she proposed?'

'I can't, old boy. A woman like that might propose anything.'

'She proposed that *I* should take him in here. She said she knew that *I* had plenty of room, a friend of mine had told her so and also given her my address.'

'Well, of all the cheek—'

'And as I was so fond of him, she said, I shouldn't mind giving him the injections – it was quite easy, once you learnt the way. Morphia addicts often did it for themselves . . . Yes, Aunt Carrie, I was quite fond of him at one time, but not now, he has treated me too badly . . . Does it matter, now that he's so ill? Yes, Aunt Carrie, it does. He has killed every feeling I ever had for him, except detestation. What do you think, Victor? Would you like me to have him at St. Botolph's? After all, the house is yours.'

'I should have no objection, Richard, I gather it isn't an infectious case. It's up to you whether you want this scoundrel back, and whether you want to turn the place into a hospital – as it was the last time you stayed here.'

'I don't, I don't, and even if I did, there's still Aunt Carrie to think of . . . No, Aunt Carrie' – for she had murmured something indistinctly – 'no, no, no, no.'

'You don't feel any responsibility towards this awful chap?' asked Victor.

'Absolutely *none*. And to tell you the truth – because here we *do* tell the truth – whatever they may tell in other places – I believe that most of the wife's story is a fabrication. It's my belief that they are discharging Denys from the hospital – if they *are* discharging him – because he's *better* – is it likely they would discharge him if he wasn't? – and his wife and he have put their heads together and invented this cock-and-bull story to find him a cheap convalescent home.'

'By jove, I think you're right.'

'So I shall write to that effect to Mrs. Aspin, if she is Mrs. Aspin, and tell her that wherever he gets off he won't get off here.'

'That's the stuff, Richard, just what I should do.'

'Well then, I will . . . No, no, Aunt Carrie. You've probably never come across people of that sort. They're not human beings, they're just beasts. Thank you *so* much, Victor.'

'A pleasure, old boy.'

Richard felt better when he had written the letter. He made it hot and strong: it would scorch the eyeballs of anyone who read it. That will settle them, he thought, and drifted back into his St. Botolph's mood, a delicious dreamy mood of reminiscence, like a nostalgia without the ache. And mingling with it, sweet tinglings of antici-pation, for Aunt Carrie would be coming in three days. Until she came, he would put off going to visit Lucy's grave. Would Lucilla have put flowers on it, fresh flowers? And if she hadn't, should he? No one need see him do it. A conversation – an imaginary conversation, of course – with Aunt Carrie would help him to decide. Meanwhile graves could wait – what else were they for? – and Lucy's could. Of one thing he could be sure – the grave would still be there, unlike the Brickfield and the M and the earthen privies at St. Botolph's. He thought he would like to be buried in the churchyard at Rookland Abbey – he would leave directions in the new will he was making.

33

Two days later he was sitting in the drawing-room, relaxed over his pre-luncheon aperitif, with the window wide open to the glorious sunlight of late June, when he heard indefinable sounds from without – a rhythmic throb in the atmosphere, of which he took no notice. Then a heavy definite sound – the scrunch of wheels on the gravel. It stopped at the front door.

Both by temperament and precept Richard was averse from doing things in a hurry. He rose slowly, and slowly pushed aside the awning that let the air in but not the heat and protected the paint of the front door from those blisters which as a child he dearly loved to squeeze.

Emerging he saw, and didn't need to be told what it was, a large white ambulance. The driver and his assistant were just climbing down, while from the back door descended a hospital nurse. She came up to him.

'Mr. Mardick, I believe?' she said.

'Yes, I am Richard Mardick.'

'I'm afraid we're a little late,' she said. She was pretty and had nice manners. 'We didn't have a very good journey, and once we lost the way – coming from Rookland. That's why we're late.'

'But late for what?' said Richard.

'Oh, late for *you*,' she smiled. 'You got Mrs. Aspin's letter, didn't you? She told me she had written – oh, two days ago, to say how kind it was of you to have Mr. Aspin here – and the time of our arrival. We're nearly half an hour late.'

'I got no letter,' Richard said, as forbiddingly as he could, 'and I know nothing about all this, except that I wrote to Mrs. Aspin, saying I could *not* take in her husband – it was quite impossible.'

The nurse looked bewildered.

'But she told me you had said you would, and she made arrangements with St. Luke's – otherwise we wouldn't have come.'

'You may have come,' said Richard, 'but you can't come *in*, I made that perfectly clear to Mrs. Aspin.'

By now the driver and his mate had joined them.

'Those were our instructions,' said the driver. 'St. Botolph's, Rookland, at twelve noon. Mr. Mardick's house.'

'There must be some misunderstanding,' Richard said, beginning to tremble. 'I'm afraid you must leave at once.'

The three from the ambulance stared at each other, then looked away.

'Mr. Mardick,' said the nurse, 'I don't know how this happened, but Mr. Aspin is a very, very sick man, and he hasn't stood the journey well . . . At one moment—' she broke off.

'I can't help that,' said Richard. 'One thing I'm sure of – he's not staying here.'

'Mr. Mardick,' the nurse said, 'I daren't take the responsibility of trying to find another place for him, in the state he is. He was almost too ill to be moved. No hospital would take him, ours couldn't keep him.'

'But what are hospitals *for*?' stormed Richard, 'unless for people to die in? Have you really turned him out . . . to, to die?'

'Hospitals are for the living,' the nurse said, gravely but not aggressively. 'We only turn people out when we can no longer do anything for them. We have a waiting-list for beds – I can't tell you how long. In Mr. Aspin's case we had no option. I will ring up the hospital if you will allow me, but I know what they will say. If he died, the responsibility would be yours.'

Richard knew that he was beaten.

'Then bring him in,' he said, as loudly and ungraciously as he could, half hoping to be heard by the inmate of the ambulance. 'I'll show you where to put him. But let me tell you this, Nurse, I'm not going to see him.'

He led them into the house and took them to the room prepared for Aunt Carrie, with all its associations of illness. Flowers were there to greet her tomorrow; he took them out. 'Invalids are better without flowers,' he said. He followed Denys's attendants down to the front door and said, 'Let me know when you have fixed him up.'

From the drawing-room he heard the sounds of feet shuffling on the gravel – 'Steady now, don't bump him' – and then treading past him to the hall. Try as he would, he couldn't help listening. Soon the ceiling above him – Aunt Carrie's room – gave out soft thuds, movements suddenly begun and ended as suddenly. Then footsteps came tramping down the stairs and the door opened.

'We've put him in bed,' the nurse said, 'and I've given him a shot. I think he's fairly comfortable. The men are going now. You must be wanting your lunch, Mr. Mardick.'

'I hope you will have it with me,' said Richard stiffly. 'I will see the maid about it.'

He tried to explain to Edna what had happened. She took it much better than he expected. 'What a blessing the room was ready,' was her comment. 'Yes,' said Richard, 'tomorrow I'll change my room to the room that looks towards the Abbey, and Mrs. Eldridge' (he couldn't immediately think of Aunt Carrie's surname) 'can have mine. The nurse will have the little room next to Mr. Aspin's. It may not be for long.'

Now the five bedrooms would be occupied, so he and Aunt Carrie wouldn't be over-housed.

The nurse and he – unwilling host, reluctant guest – sat down to their meal in some constraint. Richard asked her a few questions about Denys, though he couldn't pretend to be interested in her replies. 'He seemed to rally at first,' she said, 'but the injuries were too severe. We have a good many cases of that kind.'

'Of what kind?'

'Of people hurt at cafes' (she called it 'caffs') 'and dances. Gangs come in and break them up. They're mostly men, of course, the gangs are, but the women are often to blame, they egg them on . . . There is something I must ask you, Mr. Mardick.'

'Yes?'

'Mrs. Aspin said that you would be prepared to give her

husband his injections. He has to have them every three hours. We don't *like* doing it.'

'Why not?' asked Richard.

'In case he should become a morphia addict.'

'But you told me he was dying!' Richard said.

'Yes, but you never know, and sometimes they recover. Could you give him the injections in the day-time? I could show you how – it isn't difficult. Of course a nurse should do it, but—'

'No!' cried Richard. 'I've told you, I don't want to set eyes on him.'

'Then,' the nurse said, 'I'm afraid we shall have to find another nurse. I can't look after him at night and by day as well.'

'And who's to pay for all this?' Richard said.

'Mrs. Aspin said that you would.'

Richard rang up Dr. Killigrew, who said that the district nurse, who had a car, would give Denys the injections, at any rate for the time being. 'Perhaps I'd better come and have a look at him myself,' he added.

'I should be most grateful if you would.'

When the doctor's visit was over Richard met him in the hall and took him into the drawing-room. How often had people consulted doctors about him behind closed doors! Now it was the other way round.

'You haven't seen him, I gather,' Dr. Killigrew said. 'Well, you haven't missed much. He's not a pretty picture.'

'Can he speak?'

384

'Yes, a little. But he's had a terrible bashing. I'm glad that sort of thing doesn't happen here.'

'How long do you give him?' Richard asked.

'It's hard to say. At the hospital they said a fortnight, the nurse told me. Might be less, might be more. It's tough on you, I must say, when you came here for a rest.'

'Do you think he may get better?'

'Not a chance.'

That night Richard moved into his old room, Uncle Hal's room, to leave the Lilac Room ready for Aunt Carrie. They would have some time together, he supposed, when the nurse wasn't there; but his rapturous vision of their renewed relationship had quite faded. He was possessed by rancour and resentment, which even her image couldn't banish. He couldn't see her at all in the changed circumstances; she wouldn't belong to the alien atmosphere brought in by Denys.

Before he went to bed he telephoned to Victor who was all sympathy, but couldn't understand how Richard had let himself in for such an imposition. 'You're too kind-hearted, old chap, that's what it is.'

Richard retired early and slept badly. He allowed himself the luxury of breakfast in bed, feeling guilty, seeing that Edna's work was now more than doubled. Would she stay, with a trained nurse in the house?

Shortly before midday he crossed the landing, glanced at Denys's closed door and went downstairs. In the hall he saw an old woman. She had her back to him and was hanging something on a peg.

She turned; it was Aunt Carrie. They embraced.

'My dear,' he said, 'however did you get in without my knowing? I should have been on the doorstep, or out on the road, to welcome you.'

'Oh,' she said, 'dear Richard, I've been here a long time. I took an early train, and then I found a taxi. I didn't want to lose a minute on the way. Kind Victor would have met me had he known, but I didn't want to give him the trouble. How marvellous it is to be back again, how wonderful! Nothing is changed that shouldn't have been changed, don't you feel that?'

'I did, Aunt Carrie, I did, but since yesterday—'

'Oh yes, I know,' Aunt Carrie said. 'I've heard all about it, the nurse has told me, and how sad it is! This poor young man, so dreadfully disfigured, and so ill! But what a blessing that he's here, where at any rate he can be looked after! I haven't seen him yet, he wasn't quite so well this morning, I suppose the journey shook him up, but I shall go and see him later on, and read to him if he would like me to since he's too ill to read himself. Reading aloud is one of the things I can still do, and another is giving injections! Yes, I learned how in Australia. I'm much more practical than I was when you knew me. I like Nurse Haslett, don't you, she's sensible and kind.'

'I haven't seen much of her,' said Richard.

'No? Well, you have so many things to do. But I think she would appreciate it, if you could find the time. She must be rather lonely here, poor soul. It's so isolated.'

'Not so isolated as it used to be,' said Richard. 'There are buses.'

'Yes, of course. How silly of me. I still think of our life here in terms of fifty years ago. Do you remember Frisby, the carrier?'

'Yes.'

'What fun it was to travel in his van. So snug. But we didn't go often – we had horses then. Do you drive, Richard? – a motor-car, I mean?'

Richard said he didn't.

'I can,' Aunt Carrie said. 'I learnt to in Australia. I was never very good, and always rather frightened. But it was one of James's few pleasures, in the last years, I mean, going for drives. It took him out of himself, seeing things go by. I might get a little car here, would you like that? And then Nurse Haslett could use it sometimes. She drives, she tells me.'

'Oh, Aunt Carrie,' Richard said. 'But is it worth it? For yourself, of course, if you want it – and I should only be too glad' – he gave her a self-excusing smile – 'to go with you. But not worth while for the nurse. We don't know how long she will be here, for one thing. The hospital where Denys was didn't think it would be long.'

Aunt Carrie's brows furrowed, and she twitched her sleeves – ruffling them and then smoothing them, it was the gesture he knew her best by, though she used it now more sparingly.

'But we never know, do we? You and I were – well, not given up, but the doctors didn't think we should make old bones. And yet we have, and so may he, your friend.'

'He isn't really my friend,' said Richard. 'He was once, but he isn't now. Sometime I'll tell you about it.'

'How sad, how very sad. The nurse said something to me about it, but I didn't encourage her to talk, and you mustn't tell me, either, unless you really want to. I've lost a good many friends, too, from death and separation, and sometimes, I'm afraid, from neglect.'

'Oh no, Aunt Carrie.'

'Yes, I have. Friendship is a kind of lending of oneself, isn't it, and as time goes on, there's less to lend. Wanting to do something for someone isn't the same as friendship, though it's better than nothing.'

'But you mustn't give Nurse Haslett a motor-car,' said Richard, smiling.

Later on, he saw Nurse Haslett, coming out of Denys's room. He waited till the door was shut, and she was half-way across the landing, and then surprised himself by saying:

'How is he this morning, Nurse?'

'A little brighter, I think,' she said, 'but he's a very sick man, Mr. Mardick.'

Richard said nothing.

'Mrs. Aspin rang up this morning,' the nurse said, 'quite early, about nine o'clock, before you were down.'

'Did she want the charge reversed?' asked Richard.

'Well, yes, she did. I didn't think you'd mind, seeing how ill he is.'

Richard's face darkened.

'In future, Nurse, please don't accept a call of that kind. If she wants to know how he is, she must pay for it.'

The nurse looked stony-faced.

'I shall respect your wishes, of course, Mr. Mardick. But in the circumstances—'

'I'm afraid I'm not a charitable institution,' said Richard, 'though Mrs. Aspin evidently thinks I am. What else had she to say?'

'She asked me if we had got another nurse for him.'

'Another nurse?'

'Yes, Mr. Mardick, he needs two nurses, a night nurse and a day nurse, to give him his injections. He has to have them every two and a half hours.'

'You said every three hours, before.'

'Yes, but now he wants them oftener. It sometimes happens in these cases, when the pain is very persistent.'

'I thought the district nurse was going to give him them.'

'She was, and she came this morning, while you were still in bed. But she says she can't go on doing it. She has a great many cases to attend to, she has no car, and has to cycle to Rookland and back.'

'And who gives him his injections at night? You, I take it?'

'Yes, Mr. Mardick. I've been up, on and off, all night, and I'm dead tired. Unless you can find another nurse, I shall have to give up the case.'

'I see,' said Richard. 'And who is to pay for this other nurse?'

Nurse Haslett was silent. Then she moved further away from Denys's closed door, and said:

'I asked Mrs. Aspin. She said that you would.'

'I like that!' exploded Richard. 'So I'm to pay, am I? What else did Mrs. Aspin say?'

'Well, naturally she wanted to know what the doctor's report was.'

'Has Dr. Killigrew been here?'

'Not yet. I was waiting for you to call him in.'

'Does Mr. Aspin need a doctor as well as two nurses?'

'In the hospital, Mr. Mardick, the doctor saw him twice a day. It is a very serious case, as I'm sure you must appreciate.'

'And who will pay the doctor?' Richard asked. 'Or will Mr. Aspin be a panel patient?'

The nurse hesitated.

'I don't know,' she said. 'It will be for you to arrange with Doctor!'

Richard moved another two steps away from Denys's door.

'Has it ever struck you, Nurse, that all this is a most monstrous imposition? It's a trick, just a trick, that Mr. Aspin and his wife have played on me. She could perfectly well have had him at home, but she said she couldn't bear to watch him suffer. It's a trick, that's what it is, and they're a couple of crooks.'

'I know nothing about that, Mr. Mardick. I only know what Mrs. Aspin told me, that you were a great friend of his, and would do anything for him.'

'Anything!' repeated Richard. 'Anything!' Words failed him, and his indignation was increased by the fact that Nurse Haslett evidently thought that he was heartless.

'I'll ring Dr. Killigrew up now,' he said.

34

How familiar it was, this waiting for the doctor! You couldn't settle down to anything while he was expected. Not that Richard had anything to settle down to except his will. He paced the lawn; he went out on to the road; and back under the arch into the fruit garden, ducking his head, as he had done as a child, to avoid the bees that hummed and clustered there. He could almost hear Aunt Esther's voice saying: 'What shall we find for Richard to *do*?' But there was nothing; not even mischief for his idle hands. In the vegetable-garden he found Edna, picking some Juniton apples which were just coming ripe – the earliest apples of the year. It was the same tree, altered in shape by many prunings, its trunk more gnarled and older-looking, but substantially still the same tree he had known in boyhood.

'Oh, Edna!' he said, 'isn't it a *blow*!'

'A blow?' she repeated, looking up involuntarily into the branches of the apple-tree, as though a thunderbolt might fall from it; '*what* is a blow, Mr. Mardick?'

'Well, all this that has just happened – Mr. Aspin coming here.'

'Oh, poor gentleman,' she said, and could not keep the sympathy out of her voice, or a faint note of reproof.

'And he so ill! And he's a great friend of yours, the nurse told me.'

'He was,' said Richard. Realizing how useless it was to go into all this he changed his tone, and said:

'I was thinking of all the extra work it would make, his being in the house, and the nurse, too.' He waited a moment and added: 'I had no idea that this was going to happen.'

Edna looked surprised.

'But I thought you had asked him to come, sir, being as he was such an old friend.'

I shall never get this straight, thought Richard. They've all got the wrong idea, even Aunt Carrie has.

'It didn't happen quite that way,' he said. 'But what I wanted to tell you, Edna, was that I shouldn't have come here if I'd known that I – that we – were going to be a nuisance. And a nuisance I'm afraid we shall be. It was all quite . . . quite unexpected.'

'Don't you bother about that, Mr. Mardick,' Edna said. 'We should all do what we can for sick people, shouldn't we, especially when they're friends. I don't go much on hospital nurses, I must say – it seems as though they couldn't do a hand's turn for themselves – but Miss Haslett's not so bad.' She lowered her voice, as though she meant the apples not to hear. '*And it may not be for long.*'

Again that fretful drone as of a lost, angry bee! The vegetable garden bordered the road, with only a dyke between.

'What's that?' asked Richard.

Edna laughed. 'It's a car, Mr. Mardick, didn't you know?'

Unconsciously Richard had been waiting for the clip-clop of horse's hooves. 'Perhaps it's the doctor,' he said. 'They always come at lunch-time.' And, with a wave to Edna, he hastened from the garden.

It was the doctor, in a hurry, as doctors of today so often are. How unlike Dr. Butcher, who was always ready to while away half an hour in gossip.

Richard introduced him to the nurse who looked tired and strained and out of humour. She shook hands with Dr. Killigrew but kept her eyes away from Richard. He accompanied them upstairs to the landing, but turned back before the door into Denys's room opened. He didn't want to see the brief sliver of light that had been tainted by contact with Denys.

His fears were groundless, however, or nearly so, for when he went into the garden and looked up at the window of Denys's room (for some reason the window didn't affect him in the same way as the door) he saw a hand drawing aside the curtains. Denys must have been lying in darkness until the doctor's visit. Perhaps his eyes hurt him.

Richard went back into the house, looking for Aunt Carrie. He called her but she didn't answer. She must be in her room, not her old room, which was now Denys's, but the Lilac Room opposite, unpacking her things and arranging them. After all, she had only arrived this morning, and what a lot had happened since then! He had hardly had time to talk to her – not to *her*, not about her concerns, or his concerns. Denys had stolen the whole picture: everything revolved round Denys. For the first time, Richard felt he really hated him. Denys embodied everything that had gone wrong. He had taken Richard's money, and half ruined him; he had robbed him of Lucilla; and now he had robbed him of his sheet-anchor, Aunt Carrie, the only human being left who gave his life a meaning – for he knew instinctively that as long as Denys was in the house, suffering, Aunt Carrie's strongest feelings would go out to him. Where the sharpest point of suffering was, there would Aunt Carrie's sympathies automatically be fixed. How could she help it? It was in her nature.

Denys was the albatross, hung round Richard's neck. And not *my* albatross, he thought. *I* didn't shoot him. That young man in the café should be wearing him, not me. And for a moment his thoughts turned to the unknown youth, who had misinterpreted Denys's habitual lingering gaze, and who had been chosen by Fate to be his, Richard's, avenger.

Richard, performing a ritual act of gratitude for favours from on high, felt almost grateful to the young man, too, and was immediately ashamed, for how could he, a Christian, or what was left of one, harbour such thoughts?

But hadn't he also suffered? He too, was ill though not in a way that caught an onlooker's eye. He looked quite well, and people told him so, until he had one of his bad turns, which, fortunately or not, nearly always happened when he was alone. 'My looks don't pity me' – that was the saying. Only a few people – and Aunt Carrie wasn't one – knew how precarious was his tenure; and they preferred, as much for his sake as for theirs, to ignore it. Who wants to say to anyone, 'How are you, my dear fellow?' – implying that the fellow's state may be very bad indeed. Or would the fellow, to gain sympathy, say to all and sundry, 'You know, I'm nothing like as well as I look'? He knew people who did; but what embarrassment followed, for them – and for him, the sick man, what satisfaction was there in seeing his illness confirmed in other people's faces?

Perhaps Denys was lucky to be so disfigured, so utterly a parody of the human mould, that no one seeing him could ask him how he felt. Richard hadn't seen him, and never would see him. Not because he was like Denys's wife, who couldn't bear to watch him suffer, nor because he flinched from seeing those features, once so dear to him, now mangled out of recognition. No, it was because in Denys was embodied the evil principle that had tracked him down the years, and had at last caught up with him.

Long before Denys was born, he was the villain of the piece.

All this time, Richard was wandering about the garden in front of the house, sometimes skirting the crescent of trees, sometimes by the geranium beds under the windows, but always with an eye on Dr. Killigrew's car, as if it was a horse whose head he ought to hold, in case it bolted. At last the door, half hidden by its striped, flapping sunblind, opened on the doctor, deep in conversation with

Nurse Haslett. Ignoring the nurse, Richard said, 'Can I speak to you a moment?'

Dr. Killigrew glanced at his watch. 'Well, just for a moment,' he said grudgingly, and followed Richard into the drawing-room which had been the scene of so many medical consultations.

'How is he, Dr. Killigrew?' he asked.

'Oh, just the same, there isn't any improvement, there can't be.'

The doctor's manner was less cordial than it had been at their first meeting.

'What do you suggest, then?'

'Suggest? I've nothing to suggest.'

'Couldn't he be moved to a hospital or a nursing-home?'

'Not unless you want to kill him. Besides, no hospital would take him in, after St. Luke's has thrown him out, and I doubt if a nursing-home would, in the state he is.'

Richard was silent, then he quoted, a little self-consciously, the lines:

'Thou shalt not kill, but need not strive
Officiously to keep alive.'

'Is there any point in keeping him alive, Dr. Killigrew?'
The doctor shrugged his shoulders.

'You mustn't say that to me, Mr. Mardick,' he said, 'I'm not a member of the Euthanasia Society, and I have to abide by my Hippocratic Oath. Hypocritic, some people call it, but we doctors have to stick to it. We make a patient's last days as easy for him as we can, of course, especially when he is in as much pain as your friend is.'

'He's not a friend of mine.'

Dr. Killigrew raised his eyebrows.

'Indeed? I understood he was a great friend of yours, a very close friend. I confess I don't quite understand your attitude, Mr. Mardick. I appreciate that it's inconvenient for you having him here, but these things will happen, even in the best-regulated households, and as you invited him to come—'

'I didn't,' Richard said, and wondered if Nurse Haslett was listening through the keyhole.

'Well, all I can say is,' said the doctor, 'that his wife was under the impression that you had. She has not the means to support him herself, and you, I gather' – his active eyebrows sketched a faint inquiry – 'are not too badly off. Even if he isn't a great friend, he must have some claims on you. Even if he was an enemy, he still would have. As a doctor, I have had some experience of pain in patients, and I can assure you, if it's any satisfaction to you to know, that his pain is – to put it mathematically, a hundred per cent. Pain isn't in itself a killer – that is one of our headaches.' The doctor smiled grimly. 'Perhaps headache is not quite the right word in that connection. But I must tell you this, so that you shan't think I am exaggerating. In cases of his sort, the normal procedure is to give an injection of morphia every three hours – we don't like doing it, for fear the patient should recover, and become a morphia-addict.'

'How ridiculous!' exclaimed Richard.

'You say how ridiculous, but it has been known. Well,

for Mr. Aspin, the doctor at St. Luke's said the rate could be increased to once every two and a half hours, if necessary, and even so, Nurse Haslett tells me, he constantly calls out for more. No doubt you've heard him.'

'I haven't,' Richard said.

'Well, the problem for you,' Dr. Killigrew said, his voice and manner showing signs of imminent departure, 'for you,' he repeated, as the friend and Good Samaritan, we should all wish to be – is simply to provide him with these injections. According to the rules, or conventions, of medical practice he should have *three* trained nurses, for they only work eight-hour shifts.'

'Three?' repeated Richard.

'Yes, three,' said the doctor, firmly. 'But I gather from Nurse Haslett – she seems a good soul, but she must be nearly dead with fatigue – you haven't room for three, and even two would be a tight fit—'

'And how long is this to go on for?' Richard interrupted.

'One can't tell – it might be hours, it might be days, it might be weeks. The hospital gave him a fortnight. I should give him longer. You asked me to suggest something and I said I couldn't, but there is one thing—'

'What is that?'

'It isn't professional, and I ought not to propose it, but the circumstances are, as I'm sure you will agree, exceptional. In the war certain troops – commandos, I think, were issued with a shot of morphia which they could give themselves if they were in pain. Your friend is much too ill to give himself one. But *you* could – it isn't difficult, the district nurse would show you how – she's coming this afternoon while Nurse Haslett is in bed. I hoped she could come regularly, but she can't. That way you could dispense with the other nurse, though I still think you need one.'

A dozen thoughts surged through Richard's mind, but didn't reach his face. He said:

'But mightn't it be dangerous?'

'Not if you follow my directions. It could be, if you didn't.'

Richard smiled.

'Whose would be the responsibility – yours or mine?'

Dr. Killigrew replied, 'There could be no question of responsibility, unless you gave him an overdose.'

'We must sit down,' said Richard, drawing a chair up for the doctor, who unwillingly complied. Sitting down too, he said, 'But supposing I had an attack of diminished responsibility?'

Dr. Killigrew laughed.

'That was, Nurse Haslett told me, one of the pleas that the defence put forward. This Alfred Baker – I remember his name because there was more than one picture of him in the Press, with his wife and family grouped about him – said he was suffering from diminished responsibility, something came over him, he saw red, and so he set about your friend, Aspin, whom he suspected, on rather flimsy grounds, I gather, of making improper advances to him. It wasn't his *fault*, he just had to do it. The wretched chap's in jail, I suppose, on a charge of causing grievous bodily harm. But when Aspin dies, as he certainly will, the charge will be manslaughter, or even murder. He'll get off, though, with a nominal sentence, for the jury are always lenient in such cases – although they wouldn't be with you, if you happened to give Aspin more morphia than his system could take.'

'It's very good of you, Dr. Killigrew,' said Richard, rising, 'to have given so much thought to all this. I don't quite know what to do. I'll consult you, if I may—'

The doctor was also on his feet.

'I see it's very inconvenient for you,' he said, rather stiffly, 'but we have to make sacrifices for our friends, rather than sacrifice them.'

'I appreciate that,' said Richard, 'but I simply do not want to see him, either as a ministering angel, or in any other capacity.'

There were sounds in the passage, the door opened and Aunt Carrie stood on the threshold. Her arms were loaded with parcels, some of which, in the surprise of seeing Richard with the doctor, she let fall on the floor.

Both men bent down to pick them up.

'Oh,' she exclaimed, 'I am so sorry—' and she was beating a hasty retreat when Richard called her back.

'No, please don't go away,' he said. 'This concerns you as much as it does me, Aunt Carrie. Victor lent the house to you, not me.'

'It's a question of how many nurses we should have, to give Mr. Aspin his injections.' He introduced her to Dr. Killigrew, whose mien and manner changed at once.

'Why,' he said, 'you must be Victor Cornford's long-lost aunt!'

'And mine, too,' said Richard.

'Yes, and yours too,' said the doctor, as if this was less of a recommendation. 'Victor,' he added, looking away from Richard towards Aunt Carrie – 'Victor told me some time ago you were coming to St. Botolph's, but this unfortunate business of Mr. Aspin put it out of my mind. Too bad – it must be a worry for both of you. I know it is for Mr. Mardick.'

'Oh, I don't think Richard minds,' said Aunt Carrie defensively, 'I certainly don't. I've seen a lot of illness in my life, in a way it's more normal to me than health.'

Feeling he was not coming out of this very well, Richard said, hoping to change the subject:

'What are all those parcels for, Aunt Carrie?'

'Oh, my dear, I'll tell you. But I don't think I ought to take up Dr. Killigrew's time.' She looked at the doctor with that agonized expression of anxiety that Richard remembered seeing on his mother's face when she was afraid she had come between any man and the claims of his career.

'Don't let that worry you, Mrs. Eldridge,' he said, this time without looking at his watch. 'I have heard so much about you. Let me stay for another minute or two.'

'Oh dear, and it's past lunch-time, and you must be famished, Dr. Killigrew, and what will Edna say and poor Nurse Haslett, who has been up all night?'

'You've already had a long day yourself, Aunt Carrie,' Richard said. 'She arrived from London before I was up,' he explained to Dr. Killigrew, hoping he would take the hint.

'Oh, that was nothing. I was so determined to get

here, and in Australia we are early risers. But you asked me, Richard, why I had these parcels. Well, I was in the garden, remembering what it used to feel like to be there – when suddenly our kind neighbour, who lives in the other part of the house – Mr. Stainforth, I think his name is' – she looked at Richard for confirmation, but he couldn't give it – 'came by, and asked me if I would like a lift to Rookland, as he was going there, and I couldn't resist it, I just had to go! And on the way I remembered our poor invalid, and stopped at Filling-hams's, the grocers', to get some things like Brand's Essence, that might tempt his appetite, and next door was the greengrocers', where I got some grapes, and then I thought of other things, and went from shop to shop, and finally to Victor's, where by luck I found him in, and Margaret and quite a number of the family – such an exciting morning – and Mr. Stainforth was kind enough to wait and bring me back. That was all, but now I'm late, and have made you late, too.'

She looked quite conscience-stricken.

'I'm sure the patient will be grateful to you,' Dr. Killigrew said, 'there isn't much he *can* eat, but grapes and Brand's Essence, yes. How kind you were, Mrs. Eldridge, to have thought of it, but Victor told me you had a name for kindness which is still remembered in Rookland, after all these years.'

Again Richard felt himself left out of the doctor's enco-mium, and a feeling stirred in his breast, which wasn't so much resentment against Aunt Carrie, as envy of her superior qualities of heart.

But surely no one could be kind to Denys, if they knew what he was like?

Arranging the parcels in a pattern on the table, he said, turning to Aunt Carrie, 'Shall we ask Nurse Haslett to take charge of these as soon as lunch is over, and before she goes to bed?' He waited for a moment, the time-factor pressing on him, and then blurted out:

'It *is* a bit of a complication about Denys – about Mr. Aspin.' He went on, almost vindictively: 'Dr. Killigrew thinks we ought to have three nurses for him, as by regulation they only work an eight-hour shift. We could scrape by with two, if they didn't mind sharing the same room, which Nurse Haslett, apparently, is prepared to do.'

'There is another alternative,' Dr. Killigrew said, looking away from Richard to Aunt Carrie, 'which I've just thought of but I don't know that I could propose it in your presence.'

'Please say anything you like,' Aunt Carrie said. 'I'm much too old to mind, and as I told you, illness has no horrors for me.'

Dr. Killigrew withdrew into himself, as one does when announcing a decision which may not please one's hearers. 'It's a question of the injections of morphine which Mr. Aspin has to have to keep the pain – well, bearable. In a terminal illness (forgive the technical expression) – it means a patient's last illness' – he glanced at Richard – 'we do all we can to alleviate his sufferings. Mr. Aspin, as I've told Mr. Mardick, has been having injections of morphine every two and a half hours. We do not like morphine injections to be administered by an unskilled person, and as a rule those nearest to the patient – his wife or children, for instance, shrink from giving them – partly because of the pain of the injection, though it's only momentary, and partly from some more deep-seated reason – the tie is too close to allow of the necessary objectivity that any doctor or nurse is obliged to acquire. I know that you, Mr. Mardick,' he turned to Richard, 'take a dim view of Mr. Aspin's wife for not wanting to see him suffer – but this seems to me an excusable weakness, especially in a sensitive person—'

'Mrs. Aspin isn't sensitive,' interrupted Richard. 'Quite the opposite.'

'Well, you may be right. But it *could* argue the presence rather than the absence of affection, don't you think so, Mrs. Eldridge?'

Ruffling her sleeves, unhappy at being appealed to, Aunt Carrie conceded that it could.

'We have to be indulgent to people's feelings and failings in these matters – no two react alike. You, Mr. Mardick, told me yourself that you didn't want to see Mr. Aspin, though I gather you have no special ties with him to make you squeamish.'

'No, I haven't,' said Richard.

'And yet you invited him to come here.'

'I didn't,' said Richard, furiously. 'I told you so before.'

The doctor shrugged his shoulders.

'Well, Nurse Haslett thinks you did and it's difficult to see how he could have come without being asked. But to go back to what I was saying, there is an alternative to the injections,' he cleared his throat, 'and a more effective one: that is, suppositories. You know what they are, I expect?'

Both Richard and Aunt Carrie did know.

'They are decidedly more effective – in fact one suppository, last thing at night, can ensure the patient a good night's rest. But of course one person couldn't give it – there would have to be two.'

Before Richard had time to answer, Aunt Carrie said: 'I'm sure the nurse and I could manage that between us.'

'There would be the question of lifting him, of course. Mr. Aspin must have been a big man once. He's lost a lot of flesh, of course, but he must be quite a weight, even for two women to tackle. I'm not sure you ought to try to, Mrs. Eldridge. You look rather frail. Now if Mr. Mardick could be persuaded . . . Well, that's all I have to say, and I'm keeping you from your lunch. I'll be round tomorrow morning.'

He said his good-byes, but Richard followed him out to the car.

'How long do you give him, Dr. Killigrew?'

'As I said, it might be hours, it might be days, it might be weeks. One cannot tell. Morphine lengthens life, you know, and he must have it, whoever gives it to him. And to be frank with you, I don't think Mrs. Eldridge should help to do it. She must be eighty, if she's a day.'

'I suppose she is,' said Richard.

'And we don't want two invalids on our hands, do we?'

'Certainly not,' said Richard. 'By the way, who is footing your bill for the one we have now? Or is he on the Health Service?'

'I don't think so,' said the doctor. 'I understood that you would pay the expenses of his illness.' He gave Richard a look. 'Perhaps you could persuade Mrs. Eldridge to join in.'

The Aspins had got their story in first, and Richard's now would never be believed, not even by Aunt Carrie.

In the afternoon a visitor arrived. Richard was snoozing in his bedroom, curtains drawn, when Edna knocked and said, 'The policeman to see you, sir.'

The officer was in the hall, which already seemed to belong to him.

'I apologize,' he said, 'for calling without notice, but I understand you have a Mr. Aspin here.'

Richard said he had.

'This Mr. Aspin,' said the policeman, 'has been concerned in an affray, and if he was to die—'

'Well, officer?'

'The man who is alleged to have attacked him might incur a very serious charge. He is being held, of course.'

'And you would like to be kept informed of Mr. Aspin's condition?' Richard asked.

The policeman nodded.

'I gather he is more or less unconscious, but if he should come round, perhaps you would give us a tinkle, because there are some questions we want to ask him. Nothing to do with you, of course. We can be out here in a jiffy. It seems easier than to ask you to put one of us up – not everyone likes a policeman on the premises.'

35

'I'm afraid you must find me changed,' Aunt Carrie said.

Richard and she were sitting in the drawing-room after supper. It was, or seemed to be, the first time they had been alone together since she arrived in the morning. Only a few hours ago, but it might have been as many years. Now they would have an interval to themselves, for the nurse was still asleep and did not come on duty until ten. True to her promise, the district nurse had given Denys his injection at half-past seven. For the time being, Richard's thoughts need not turn to him, but turn they did.

It was the moment he had been waiting for – the moment of emotional re-union with Aunt Carrie. He had expected a great deal from it, he didn't quite know what: a renewal of the feelings of his youth, perhaps. And it was a propitious moment. The long summer twilight had not faded from the sky; the silence was absolute. He tried to yield himself to the magic of the hour and its invitation to détente and rapprochement, but he couldn't feel in tune with himself or even with Aunt Carrie. A struggle was going on in him: he heard her speak, but did not catch the words.

'What did you say, Aunt Carrie?'

'I said I was afraid that you would find me changed.' Almost wishing he hadn't asked her to repeat it, Richard protested automatically, 'You haven't changed, Aunt Carrie. You are just the same.'

'Oh no, my dear, I'm not. At least, I'm not the same as I was when you knew me. I don't know how well you knew me. We only saw each other in snatches, even before my illness, which was mostly nerves. It was a nightmare time when we were here together, for me and I think for you. And yet they were all so kind.'

'They were all so kind,' repeated Richard.

'I often think,' Aunt Carrie said, 'that the self I had then wasn't my real self – it was an image, a golden image that your dear mother and my sister Florrie, and indeed all my family except Ada, who had sharper eyes, set up—'

'And worshipped,' Richard put in. 'I know that I did.'

Aunt Carrie gave him a long look, full of the old distress.

'Yes, I believe you did, I believe you all did, except Ada.'

'And she was jealous of you,' Richard said.

'Oh no, I don't think so, she just didn't want to join the chorus . . . the chorus . . . of . . . of praise. I ought to have enjoyed all that . . . appreciation . . . oughtn't I, and in a way I did, but all the time I had an uneasy feeling that it wasn't me – not the real me, that they held in so much affection, but this image they had made of me – not only of what I was, but of what I should become. Oh, but they had ambitions for me! I had some talents, I suppose; but even if I hadn't broken down, I'm sure I should never have realized them. The fear was always with me that I should be a disappointment.'

'You wouldn't have been,' said Richard. 'They saw you more clearly than you saw yourself.'

'You may be right,' said Aunt Carrie, 'but I didn't think I had it in me – what they thought I had – either morally or intellectually.' She smiled. 'And when I got to Australia, where they didn't know anything about all this, and treated me, very kindly, I must say, but like any other emigrant school-teacher, not like a golden image, or a golden calf! – well, I stopped being one, and slipped back into being something else – something perhaps that God had always meant me to be. I hope I stuck to some ideals, but they were mine, or what the circumstances out there imposed on me, not the ideals of what Austin used to call the Holy Family, do you remember? I became another person, that's why I said I'd changed.'

'And shall you mind changing back again?' said Richard. 'Because you'll have to, here. Your legend hasn't died away, you know. Victor has inherited it, I have inherited it. You can't escape! Even Dr. Killigrew knows about it. You saw with what reverence he treated you. He was quite short with me.'

'I noticed something, but couldn't understand it,' said Aunt Carrie, troubled.

'I was at my worst,' said Richard. 'Quite at my worst. And when you said you'd changed, Aunt Carrie, you really meant to say that *I* had changed.'

Aunt Carrie looked as startled and shocked as if a scorpion had stung her.

'My dear,' she said, with much tremulous ruffling of her sleeves, 'I can assure you I meant nothing of the kind.'

'You did, Aunt Carrie, and it was so like you, and such a sure sign you hadn't changed, to apologize to me, so as to conceal your disappointment from me.'

'You are quite wrong, my dear,' and Aunt Carrie looked almost hunted. 'Such a thought never crossed my mind.'

'Oh, but it must have. I was so disagreeable, and perhaps seemed mean as well. Dr. Killigrew evidently thought I was.'

'I daresay he isn't very perceptive, Richard. Doctors nowadays don't have time to think of much outside the physical aspect of their cases. Years ago, when you and I were ill, doctors were friends of the family and knew all sorts of things about us, besides our clinical symptoms. Dr. Butcher wasn't a specially perceptive man, but I always felt that he knew the whole psychological set-up, as they say now, and I'm sure you felt the same. It was he who advised me to get married.'

'*Advised* you, Aunt Carrie?'

'Yes, he did, although your dear mother, and indeed all the family were against it. First because they thought it would be bad for my health and then – they didn't tell me this but I well knew it – they didn't think James worthy of me. It was Dr. Butcher who persuaded them.'

'I never knew that,' Richard said.

'Oh yes, he was a great benefactor to us all. If he had had his way, you wouldn't have stayed on at St. Botolph's, but your mother was adamant.'

'She thought she knew what was best for everyone.'

'Yes, but how unkind that sounds, and she was the kindest person in the world. Can you think of anyone else who minded so much if one lived or died? I can't.'

'And yet at the end,' said Richard, 'she only minded if *she* lived or died.'

'Yes,' said Aunt Carrie, 'I believe it was so, but we mustn't be judged by our last years, must we? So many things we fought for – personal . . . personal . . . improvements, ways of seeming nicer than we are, have to be abandoned. One's personality is like a leaky roof, one's vigilance flags, one can't keep it in repair.'

'You mean me,' Richard said.

'I don't, I don't, my dear boy. But I wish . . . I wish . . .'

'Yes?' prompted Richard.

'I wish you could feel happier about Mr. Aspin being here.'

Richard looked out on to the darkening lawn.

'Need we talk of him, Aunt Carrie?'

'Of course not, my dear, if you don't want to. But he's a fact, isn't he, a fact that has to be faced?'

'He's a fact that I will never face,' said Richard, fiercely. 'Forgive give me, Carrie, if I drop the "Aunt" for once, but I cannot set eyes on him, and I will not. That man has done me untold harm, untold and untellable. And now he has planted himself here, to die on me. "Planted" is the word, because it was a "plant". I don't know if they have that sort of plant in Australia.'

'Oh yes, Richard, they do.'

'When the hospital was going to throw him out – and I don't blame them – he and his wife – if she is his wife – laid their heads together – or perhaps she did it off her own bat – I don't know whether he can speak or not – and said I had asked him to come here, because I was a great friend of his. The hospital believed it, Nurse Haslett believed it, Dr. Killigrew believed it, and I think that you, Aunt Carrie, believed it.'

'Yes, I suppose I did.'

'Well, it was a lie, an absolute lie, and if there had been nowhere else in the world for him to go to, if he'd had to die, as well as lie, in the street, I wouldn't have asked him to come here. Do you want to know why?'

'Not unless you want to tell me.'

'Dear Aunt Carrie, I don't want to tell you, it would take too long, for one thing, but I'll tell you this – that thanks to him and, in a lesser degree, the series of scoundrels that came after him – his spawn, you might call them, though I doubt if he has ever had a child – I no longer feel, as I used to feel when I was a boy, that happiness is infectious, like some beneficent germ, and I could give it as well as catch it.'

'How sad,' Aunt Carrie said, 'how very sad.'

'Well, it was sad for me,' said Richard. 'But let me say a word more, before we both start laughing, because it *is* funny, isn't it, that one old buffer, whom Fate has treated very well – at least most people would say so, because I've never been without material comforts – should feel that morality has been offended in his person, and therefore we must all, all weep! It doesn't argue much sense of humour, does it, nor much sense of proportion, when you think of deeper and more wide-spread sufferings – your own, Aunt Carrie, for instance – for me to take this tragic line. But before we dissolve in mirth, I must say this – not in self-justification, but simply as a fact – that all this dishonesty I've been living with, has made me suspicious of people, present company excepted! I don't really *like* them, I don't even like myself! and *dislike*, although it is a strong tonic and energizer, isn't so nourishing. And now let's laugh, Aunt Carrie, do let's laugh, or you'll begin to wish you had never come.'

Suiting the action to the word, Richard began to laugh, at first experimentally, and then, as the absurdity of the situation dawned on him, more heartily and finally quite hysterically. The quiet, twilit room resounded with guffaws. When at length Richard noticed that his companion wasn't joining in, he said:

'But you aren't amused, Aunt Carrie. Let's have a drink – I'm sure you need one, after your long day.'

'You have a drink, my dear, by all means,' Aunt Carrie said. 'I don't really want one now, but I might have one later, to keep you company. What was that?'

Richard, who was already standing by the drink-tray, and still laughing, said:

'What was what, Aunt Carrie?'

'I thought I heard a sound.'

'Where did it come from?'

'I think from somewhere in the house.'

Richard went to the door and opened it. There was a sound, like no sound he had ever heard – it might have been a baby crying, but it wasn't.

Shutting the door, and coming back into the room, he said: 'There was something, Aunt Carrie, but it could have been anything – a new-born calf, for instance, crying for its mother. Let's forget about it, and have another laugh, but you must join me, this time.'

It was no effort to Richard to start laughing again; it had been going on inside him, like hiccups. But to his disappointment he didn't get an answering laugh from Aunt Carrie, though he did get a smile.

'I can't laugh to order,' she said, 'and what you told me, Richard, didn't seem a laughing matter. You tried to make light of it, but it seemed to me sad, very sad, that you should have had all these trials and sorrows.'

'Oh they were nothing, as I told you before – mere flea-bites compared with yours.'

'Flea-bites can be very irritating, to say the least. I've heard it said that when someone is really very ill, like your fr . . . like Mr. Aspin, upstairs, it isn't the disease, the terminal disease, as Dr. Killigrew called it, that he minds most: it's the surface irritations that a weakened frame can't stand. A fly walking across one's face, at that stage, might be more unbearable than the real illness.'

'I think you're right,' said Richard, still heaving and rumbling with the laughter he was trying to suppress.

'I'm glad it isn't so with you,' Aunt Carrie said. 'You're not ill, are you, Richard?'

'Well, not so's you'd notice.'

'I'm glad to hear that. You weren't always strong, you know, but perhaps stronger than your darling mother thought you were. And speaking of her— Did you hear that noise again?'

Richard let his laughter escape him. 'I did but I'm sure it's just a new-born lamb.'

414

'Do they have lambs in summer? But what I meant to say was, do you remember how your mother hated those buttresses on the tower of Rookland Abbey?'

'I do, indeed.'

'Did you know they've gone?'

'Yes, and how thankful she would have been.'

'She would, because she couldn't bear to look at anything ugly, and I'm glad, too, for her sake. We were very close to each other, too close, perhaps. But do you think she was right? – right to look the other way, I mean? Those buttresses were a warning – a warning against evil, and you can't escape evil by not looking at it. If the warning has been taken away, it isn't because we no longer need it—'

'No, how right you are.'

'We need it more than ever, and that's why I was almost sorry to see that lovely window – for it is lovely – standing in its place. Ugliness is a symptom you can't afford to disregard – you must know that.'

Richard's unseasonable mirth broke out again.

'I didn't mean to laugh, Aunt Carrie, it's something that keeps bubbling up in me – an automatic reflex, do they call it?'

'Yes, I believe they do. Richard, I told you I'd become religious – not in any important way, not in any conventional way, perhaps not in any *real* way – I wouldn't like to claim that, for myself. I have suffered, as you know, but the suffering was its own reward. I . . . I *consented* to it. And why? Because it wasn't moral, it wasn't something done *against* me, it was what I was *meant for*—'

'Oh, Aunt Carrie!'

'Yes, it was. But you, who have evidently come up against so much dishonesty, and ingratitude, all done *against* you, how can you feel, as I do, that it's a kind of fulfilment? But try to think it is. Try to think that all these things that have so distressed you are really Stations of the Cross, and they are a privilege, and not a punishment!' Aunt Carrie's small, faded hazel eyes opened wide and almost blazed. 'Can you see it in that way, Richard? That you have been especially chosen by God for the honour of these sufferings? Ordinary people' – Aunt Carrie ruffled her sleeves in a gesture that seemed at once to include and dismiss ordinary people – 'cannot suffer in the way that you can. They cannot profit by suffering, they cannot be enhanced by it, they cannot let God's image shine through their tears! It is all purposeless to them, but surely not to you! To them it is no evidence of special favour! To them it is just any pain, like an earache or a headache, to be treated with aspirin, or whatever it may be! They cannot see it, as they should see it, as a peculiar instance of God's favour, of His mercy, I should say, for what can be more merciful than the capacity to be reconciled to one's hardships? – and not only to be reconciled to them, but to welcome them and be glad of them, as a sign of His especial grace? We cannot, of course, take credit for anything we do – "nothing in my hand I bring" – but we can, periodically, share the credit of what is done for us, and yes! of what is done against us! Because such experiences are not under our control, they are what God means for us – they are His arrows, and we are His target, they are messengers

416

from Him, and whatever hits the bullseye, and gives the greatest pain, is the surest proof that we are chosen by Him. Do you remember, Richard, a text that your dear mother was very fond of, and often said to me, to console me, although in those days it didn't console me – I was blinded by the bewilderment of what I thought to be my grief. She may not have had a very deep nature, Richard, or a profound understanding of what goes on inside us, and outside, but she had an instinct for the truth, she knew that it isn't our happiness that counts with God, or is a sign that we are accepted by Him, if I may put it so – it's our unhappiness, for whom the Lord loveth he chasteneth, and scourgeth every son whom he receiveth.'

Aunt Carrie leaned back in her chair with half-closed eyes; even in the fading light the fatigue of her long day showed in her face. Richard got up, and switched the light on.

'Thank you, Aunt Carrie,' he said, 'I wish I could believe what you have just told me, but I can't. To me it seems like blasphemy to say that God should find anything to . . . to please Him in our sufferings. If that were so, the . . . the man upstairs must be one of His favourites. He's being chastened enough in all conscience, at least so we're told. But though I cannot read the mind of God, I should doubt if He really loved Denys Aspin . . . Oh, what *is* that noise, Aunt Carrie? It sounds like a woman wailing for her demon-lover.'

Richard held the door ajar and they peered round it into the dark hall, as if the sound might become visible and concrete, and attack them.

'Could it be Mr. Aspin,' asked Aunt Carrie, 'calling for his injection?'

Richard, who had suspected all along that it was Denys, said: 'Well, let him call.'

This shocked Aunt Carrie, as he hoped it would.

'Oh no, my dear, I think we must do something for him. It's ten o'clock. I'll go and wake Nurse Haslett, and perhaps, between us—'

'Were you thinking of the suppository?' Richard asked.

'Yes, I suppose I was. It isn't anything so terrible, is it? The body—'

'Oh yes, the body,' said Richard vaguely. 'But it isn't a job for a lady, still less for an old lady.'

'Oh, I don't know,' said Aunt Carrie, 'perhaps the older the better. Anyhow, I'll go.'

The thing that Richard minded most was that Denys's wretched body – almost all that was left of him, thank goodness, should come between him and Aunt Carrie. They would never get it straight now; he could never explain to her his grievance against Denys; and she, who had no experience of wilful human injury, only of too much love, would always think him heartless.

How could he find a way out of this horrible dilemma? That she, who had always represented to him what was humanly most valuable, a justification for living, a standard set up, albeit against her will, for the elect to worship, should be cut off from him by this worthless, wicked man, whose only claim on anyone's consideration was that he was ill. Just ill! How many people in the world were ill, why he himself was, without their illness weakening friendship – life's last hope! Idly he said, 'I'll go and call her, dear Aunt Carrie. You stay here, or still better, go to bed. Fold your wings and rest, as even angels must. There's nothing more for you to do, nothing whatever.'

Standing in the darkness of the hall-way he couldn't read her expression as she said, 'Oh, but there is, just this one little thing, to prove to you, to prove to you, dear Richard, that though I'm old I'm still the friend you thought I was! Don't take that happiness from me, please don't! I should have made my sympathy much plainer. What is Mr. Aspin to me? Nothing. What are you? Well, the dearest thing I have. You mustn't see him, Richard, you mustn't see him! It wouldn't be good for you, your instinct is against it, whereas mine! – No, no, no, don't misunderstand me – I only mean that what would appal you would hardly distress me!'

But Richard slipped past her in the darkness, and ran up the curving staircase like a two-year-old. Which door was Nurse Haslett's? The middle one, that used to be Aunt Ada's. He thundered on it, then angry with himself, knocked again twice, hardly more loudly than his heart was knocking. Steady! Steady! But he couldn't pay any attention to it now.

'Who's that?' asked a sleepy voice from within.

'It's Mr. Mardick, Nurse. Mr. Aspin is calling for his injection.'

As though to confirm his words, a moan went up, louder and more eerie than before.

'I'll be there in a minute or two,' Nurse Haslett said. 'They're always in a hurry. It'll do him no harm to wait.'

It seemed to be doing Richard harm, though. He recognized his symptoms all too well, and knew he ought to be lying down. But he couldn't – this time he really couldn't. Instead he turned the landing light on, and took some comfort from it. It lit up the hall below, too, and in a moment he heard a step on the stair: Aunt Carrie coming up.

'Good night, Aunt Carrie. Pleasant dreams!'

'Good night, my dear, and pleasant dreams to you, too. I'm not going to bed for a moment, I want to help Nurse Haslett with her patient.'

'No, Aunt Carrie, you're not! The doctor said you mustn't. I'll do it! He's much too heavy for you to lift!'

'My dear, lifting is just a knack. I often did it for James, when he was ill. It's nothing, really.'

'But I want to do it, Aunt Carrie, I really want to. I *want* to see him!'

'You *want* to see him? Oh no, I can't believe it! God wouldn't expect it of you, Richard. It would be too great a strain. Forgive him in your heart, but don't, don't see him!'

The middle door opened, and Nurse Haslett, partially but protectively dressed, came out on the landing.

'Now what's all this?' she said almost automatically, as if it was her habit to quell riots. 'You'll be disturbing my patient.' Instinctively changing her tone she said: 'Oh, I see. It's Mrs. Eldridge and Mr. Mardick.'

'I was telling my aunt,' Richard explained, 'that I would like to help you with the . . . the . . .'

'Oh, the suppository? I'd forgotten. Yes, Doctor did recommend them, because they give the patient a better night's sleep – and me too,' she added, 'I can doze. It's just a matter of inserting them.'

Another wail came through the door of Denys's room.

'I'll go and get one,' the nurse said. She left them and came back with something in her hand.

'I *can* do it myself,' she said, 'though it's a messy job. But as Mrs. Eldridge was kind enough to say she'd help me—'

'No, *I* will,' Richard said.

For a moment he and Aunt Carrie circled round each other warily, like opponents in a boxing-ring. They were too intent on their unseemly scuffle to realize how absurd it was, but Nurse Haslett did.

'Come on, one of you!' she said, her native coarseness of fibre getting the better of professional discipline. 'We can't wait here all night.'

'No, Aunt Carrie!'

'No, Richard!'

Their cries rang out, charged, it seemed, with hostility to each other, their first and only disagreement. But Richard reached the door first. He had his hand on the knob, he was turning it, when all at once he said, in a quite natural voice, that expressed the deep affection he had always felt for her, 'Oh, Aunt Carrie, I'm done for!' and with that slid to the floor.

Another wail from within.

'He's fainted, Nurse,' Aunt Carrie said. 'Have you anything to bring him to? Brandy, sal volatile?'

The nurse pushed roughly past her, knelt down and put her hand on Richard's wrist and her ear to his heart. So she remained, prolonging for a full minute the most intimate gesture Richard had received for years. Then she rose stiffly to her feet.

'He hasn't fainted, Mrs. Eldridge, he's gone.'

And when Aunt Carrie was too bewildered to take this in, she added, on a much softer note, 'He isn't with us any more, he's left us. These things do happen. I never liked the look of him, from a medical point of view, I mean. You go and lie down, dear, lie down and relax as much as you can. When I've seen to Mr. Aspin, I'll come back and give you something to make you sleep. The doctor's coming in the morning, dear, that's a blessing, isn't it?'